orney

Miles Craven

The Country Attorney

When what is real and unreal seem the same.

JustFiction Edition

Cover image: www.ingimage.com

Publisher:
JustFiction! Edition
is a trademark of
International Book Market Service Ltd., member of OmniScriptum Publishing Group
17 Meldrum Street, Beau Bassin 71504, Mauritius

Printed at: see last page
ISBN: 978-613-9-42451-1

THE COUNTRY ATTORNEY

CONTENTS

ONE

The coach journey from London was arduous. By day three I could bear it no longer and was so incommoded by a fat woman and her dog that I surrendered my warm place and joined the shivering outsides. I was soon regretting my decision, wishing I was down below again, crushed but warm inside the new machine they called *The Leeds Fly*. The wind was sharp, ripping through my clothes like a skilled swordsman. And when it finally abated somewhere in Derbyshire, down came the rain in icy droplets of the cruellest torture. I would have wept had I been alone, but in company I must keep my composure. This I managed thanks to the contents of my pocket pistol.

'By my stars, we should be glad we're on the Great North Road,' said a stifled voice beside me. It belonged to my companion, whose only feature was a bottle nose protruding between his hat and collar. 'If this were the Blackstone Edge we'd be blown across the sky like avenging angels.'

I nodded assent for the sake of it and took another sip, but the man's nose turned in accusation and said, 'You *do* know the road I mean?'

'Yes,' I replied, offering him my flask, 'it's the trans-Pennine route, is it not?'

'Halifax to Rochdale to be precise, there's not a wilder stretch of road in all England.' A gloved hand appeared from inside his cape, lifted the flask to muffler height and, with a practised jerk of the wrist, fed it without spillage to the hidden mouth. Then out came the flask again, catching not only an errant dew-drop but the nose itself, which wagged like a loose door-knob. 'Thankee', the man said, 'that's a fine drop of whatever it's a fine drop of.'

'Brandy,' I said, wiping away the dew-drop with my sleeve before taking another sip. I'd met my first Yorkshireman, and was unimpressed. Richard had warned me what a strange lot they were; a proud and forthright people bluff and flint-hearted, not a bit like the Suffolk stock from which he was bred. But he'd been happy among them all the same; happy, I believe, until the night he drowned. The dearest friend I had ever had was gone, and how I missed him. I felt deprived of the fun we'd have shared had fortune done what it promised to do – re-unite us as

4

neighbours. But I mustn't dwell on what was not to be. I turned my thoughts instead to London, which I'd left on Thursday morning. I had said my farewells the night before, drinking with fellow clerks at my favourite tavern in Holborn, a stone's throw from Furnivals Inn where I'd lived and worked. No matter what Congreve's character had said – *I* was proud to have been an attorney's clerk of the family of the Furnivals. I'd spent the last year of my clerkship in the offices of Messrs Allen and Richardson, London agents for my Shrewsbury employer, who'd deemed it essential I complete my training in the capital, learning at first hand the business of Common Pleas, Kings Bench and Chancery. My training had finished a year ago, and I'd stayed with my employers as Managing Clerk, biding my time till an offer came my way.

And patience paid dividends. Mr Allen heard that Abraham Balme of Horseford in the West Riding of Yorkshire was in need of a junior partner to transact the more burdensome aspects of his business. 'It's just the start you've been looking for,' declared my employer, adjusting his hat, which never seemed to sit properly upon his large round head. 'Old Balme's only in a modest way of business, and isn't the sort to set the legal world ablaze, but he's a sound country practitioner with five-hundred clients.'

As on most things, he was right. And besides, I could ill afford to be choosy, for my inheritance was a slender one and had to be used wisely in pursuit of modest aims. Therefore did I write to Mr Balme offering my money and my services, complemented by a summary of my pedigree and training. Within a week I had a reply, penned in his streaky hand, stating that he was much gratified to hear of my offer, and requested the pleasure of my company three weeks hence to discuss the terms he trusted would suit.

I felt the wind rise again, hearing it boom from the west like a great cannon. To look about me at the landscape was to shiver even more. Night had fallen two hours ago, and all looked cold and pitiless in the moonless dark. Either side of the coach was a gaping chasm of empty blackness, beyond, here and there, the raw glaze of a frozen lake, the jagged outline of rocks and scarps, the occasional raging torrent draped across a hillside like a knotted sheet of silk. We were climbing now, and I saw, above the crags, the brooding moorland, the solitary blighted trees, the ragged outlines of sheep whose voices on the wind were like the calls of lost infants. On we went, the coach rumbling and creaking in monotonous rhythm, its wheels drumming on the frozen ruts. The meaty sweat of the horses steamed in the cold night air, magically summoned, it seemed, by the jangle of the harness and the crack of the driver's whip.

There was incantation too in the driver's language as he spoke to his beasts, admonishing them as a stern father here, coaxing them gently like a lover there, the rest a jabbering singsong of gruff snaps and faint lamentations. Onwards further to the next inn, a last chance to thaw out by the fireside in the stone-flagged parlour, recalled to life with food and hot posset before getting up along for the final ten miles.

Those last miles were the worst of the lot. I was fearful of the future – naturally so – but that wasn't all. So helpless, I felt, at the mercy of every hurt. There was danger lurking that was almost tangible, almost, in its close-breathing presence, human – and male, I couldn't help thinking it was so. And how my throat was cold and tight, my heart rigid in my breast, my hat nearly frozen to my head. I could have wept even harder than before, climbed into the luggage basket and breathed my last. Nothing of the sort had I felt before on going to a strange place: here the very air, so icy off the moors, seemed on the verge of speech. And the words the voice was searching for I'd already guessed – go back, John, go back now while you still can. I sensed the evil behind them – I could fair smell it – and that was part of the attraction. But the other part, the repulsion that evil always brings – or should do – left me in thrall to a lonely terror. I prayed it would pass – surely it would, though what a frightened creature I felt gazing down into the swooning blackness. And yet the edge of the coach was a metaphor for the edge I had come to in life: I had reached my great divide, one that split the old world from the new. I had so much to prove, both to myself and those who'd spawned me. My poor mother, God rest her soul, had always believed in me, seen the promise in my nut-brown eyes, which, as she often reminded me, curved upwards at the corners in a faintly Oriental manner. Mother was the source of my vanity too – 'all those hearts you'll break with your comely visage.' I know you are a devil, she would say, but you have so much angel in your face nobody could ever think ill of you.

Father did, however – he saw our closeness and despised it. Proud Welsh farmer of three-hundred acres, Simon Eagle was a masterful man whose boys must be just like him – cold and hard, and the sooner the better. Two were already so; they worked alongside him day after day, tilling the heavy soil that was damp even in the warmest summer.

It was plain that I, the youngest, was different. There was no room on the farm for book-learned talk, for a youth who wanted only to walk in the countryside not work in it, who showed no interest in the mysteries of husbandry. One day, when I'd come upon him in the barn, I'd asked him outright if he loved me. I was fifteen-years-old. 'What kind of talk is that?' he'd asked bitterly. And the more he'd thought about it, the more my question had irked him. He'd dropped the bleating lamb he was holding, and stepped towards me, his trembling lips ajar. 'What kind of talk is that?' he'd repeated in puzzled fury. He just couldn't get any further – every thread of his soul was tangled in a self-accusing knot. He had a hand to his temple, as if a pain were there. I had made him glimpse what he'd always refused to see – the gaping hole at the heart of himself.

He died a year later, leaving the farm to my brothers, with whom mother lived as lodger. I was to move on, taking with me as slim provision five-hundred pounds to be used as I saw fit. I chose the law, for which my brothers mock me still. Mother, though, was pleased and she believed in my future till the day she died. I was determined in my Yorkshire adventures to prove her right.

The driver, as arranged, left me at Stump Cross, a wind-ravaged spot five miles short of my goal. I stood beside my box, the finger post behind me like an empty gallows, the frost sparkling on the tracks that forked away in four directions, dark and narrow till the murky night swallowed them whole a few yards hence. And again on the breeze that strange force, vocal and repellent in funnelled gusts – go-back, go-back, go-back, like the chuckling echo of a startled grouse. Imagination surely, I told myself, or just a distortion of the wind.

By my Hunter it wanted five and twenty to nine. Mr Balme had said
that his man George would meet me with the gig as close to the appointed
hour as the exigencies of weather and travel would permit. Thus was it
nearing ten when the black outline of a conveyance rocked towards me
from the west. As it drew closer I saw a solitary driver wrapped up close
against the cold. The silent swaying of horse and machine was a ghostly
sight, connected in a fit of fancy with the 'gibbet' at my rear.

'Whoa!' he commanded, as the gig juggled to a halt on the iron ground,
the horse snuffling loudly with hoary breath. 'Master Eagle?' enquired
the driver in a rough deferential tone, lingering comically on the capital
vowel of my name. 'I'm George Lister sir, Mister Balme's man. I expect
I'm late but there's no moon and it's hard going for the horse.' He flexed
his eyebrows as he spoke, making his slouch hat joggle on his interesting
head.

I looked at his square-shaped face, wrapped round with a thick wool
comforter. His features were such that they seemed unfinished, as though
the sculptors who had fashioned him tired early of their work that day and
sent him forth just as he was – more Celtic stone head than real human
being of blood and bone. He had a vaguely wounded expression, as if he

were privy to this outrage fifty years ago. This, of course, I couldn't change, but there being in addition a faintly pleading look, as if he wanted absolution for his lateness, I obliged him by saying kindly, 'It's all right George. I'm grateful all the same.'

He smiled, showing more gum than tooth, and climbed down languorously to collect my box. 'You'll be cold I expect,' he said, when I'd clambered up beside him and he'd jerked the horse into motion.

'Yes,' I replied, with an opportune shiver, 'but I'm over the worst I'm glad to say.'

He worked his whip and stared down at the horse's rump with vague abstraction. The lick of the rod upon the helpless flesh he took for granted, like so much else in life I'd have wagered. 'You're not from these parts,' he said at length.

'Wales,' I replied.

Bewilderment flashed across his face, as if he'd thought for a moment of the whales that lived in the sea. 'Wales,' he said, nodding again at the mare's posterior. 'You don't sound Welsh. They fair sing when they speak.'

'I haven't lived there for some time. I've lived elsewhere – Shrewsbury, London.'

'London!' he groaned, cracking the whip more harshly. 'I've heard you can't trust Londoners. Not that I've known many, mind, and no offence meant – it's just what I've heard.'

'Have we far to go?' I asked, grown weary of his chatter already.

'Happen not,' he answered sullenly. 'I have in mind a short cut. God willing, a good hour ought to bring us right to the door.'

It was just as he'd said – in a little over an hour we came to Horseford, a large village nestled in a sort of bowl. Above was an overhanging wedge of moorland, black against the blacker sky. Candle-light flickered dully from the many cottages dotted thereabouts, a brighter glow among them marking an inn or beer-house – I counted two, neither place glowing with welcome. All was dark in the streets themselves, dark and silent as the churchyard we passed at a gentle trot, turning left down a sloping street to journey's end.

'Whoa!' cried George, reining in with a babble of unearthly noises that I hoped was meant for the horse. The horse – I learned its name at this point – Sally – neighed and shook herself. 'She wants her oats,' said George ruefully. 'She's earned them today, she has that. You must get yourself in and meet the Master. It's late and he don't keep late hours as a rule. They makes him worse tempered than he is in the day, and that's saying something, it is that.' I didn't like the sound of this but tiredness and all the emotion I had felt on the coach numbed me against further trepidation like a dull opiate. My eyes strayed to my portmanteau – 'Don't worry about *that*, sir, ' said George, guessing my meaning, 'I'll fetch it when I've finished with the horse' – and then to the house. Built of the sombre millstone grit so typical of the area, it was a long three-storeyed building that fronted the road. Opposite stood the gates of a large estate – that of Sir Walter Spencer-Stanhope Bart, I guessed, wealthy landowner and once the most eminent barrister on the northern circuit. Most convenient, I mused, knowing that Mr Balme acted as land agent to the illustrious Sir Walter, whose fame was renowned even in the capital.

13

As George led horse and gig into a side enclosure, I ventured round the front of the house and knocked quietly on the studded door with its date – 1684 – inscribed upon the lintel. Answer was a long time coming, but eventually a shuffle and a low muttering could be heard within. Bolts were drawn and a key was turned in the lock. The heavy door creaked open, emitting a long streak of yellow light. 'Mister Balme?' I enquired of the strange old man, framed by the doorway candle-in-hand.

He shook his thin head, disturbing wisps of lank grey hair hanging loose at the sides. The wind caused the candle to hiss and flare, and a winding of wax from the guttering flame suddenly dripped on to his fingers. No pain registered on his careworn face. His sunken eyes, devoid of lustre, appeared to stare through me as he jerked his thumb behind him into the house. 'Follow me,' he wheezed, and led the way on his spindle legs.

I followed his threadbare coat, his ruffled stockings, his shoes downtrodden at the heel. No part of his attire showed any trace of freshness: all, even the scrap of ribbon in his hair, had seen much better days.

At the foot of a broad staircase we turned into a spacious parlour. Here, with his back to a meagre fire, was a short, stocky man in his fifties with a hard, sour-expressioned face. He wore a bag wig, and a handsome suit of black cloth with silver buckles at the knees. As we entered he took his glass from the mantelpiece, forced a smile and toasted me. 'Welcome Mister Eagle!' he said, with a half-hearted bow which I returned with more gusto.

'Your servant, sir.'

Mr Balme grunted acquiescence, gulped his wine and swilled it round on his pallet. There was a belch, followed by a gasp, and then: 'A difficult journey no doubt? You must be fatigued.' He adjusted his cravat with his free hand. 'Come, sit down and make yourself at ease.' I noticed that his tongue was too large for his mouth, and lolled unpleasantly when he spoke. There was no comfort to be had here, not in his face, not in my surroundings. Loneliness wrestled with tiredness, each like a dark flood contending. I felt cold yet smothered, and I glanced about me in desperation. The large fireplace with tarnished brass fender and Dutch tiles drew my eye with its gaping dominance. A fireplace should be the focus for warmth and friendship but not this one – take away the fender and the tiles and it might have been seen in a prison.

Of little improvement was the blackened oak dresser ranged along the opposite wall with its cups and plates of dull China. Nothing save an old spinet in lacquered wood betokened any vestige of joy, and *that* was of a bygone age.

'May I offer you some claret?' he said with begrudged cordiality.

'That would be most welcome,' I replied, seating myself in an armchair of which there were two, both upholstered in faded red velvet.

Mr Balme clicked his fingers and fired a sharp glance at the old man standing in the doorway. 'Tom! Another glass for Mister Eagle.' He had addressed him as he might a dog which he wasn't very fond of, and from which he demanded full loyalty and obedience. 'You've met Tom Gill, my Managing Clerk?' he added, as the frail figure followed the order.

'Yes,' I said, and the old man glanced my way. He acknowledgment me with a pained curl of the lips, which was all he seemed capable of.

'That'll be all, Tom. You can go to bed now,' said Mr Balme when Tom had brought my drink. 'But be up betimes tomorrow, my man. I've conveyances galore for you to copy – and by noon at the latest. Do you hear me? By noon!' He widened his legs before the fire, and stared with narrowed eyes as the aged clerk shuffled out. 'Watch him carefully,' he said, in a lowered tone. 'Rule him with an iron rod, it's the only way.' I glanced once more at the frail body that seemed to stretch time as it made its exit. It seemed likely that even a gentle tap with an iron rod would kill the sad soul outright.

My new partner had surprisingly little to say and having just got into my company seemed heartily anxious to be out of it. 'Well, my boy, I won't dally,' he said, peeping at the eight day clock that was close to midnight. 'I'm like my dear old mother in this respect: I need eight hours undisturbed sleep if I am to get through the day without flagging. Waiting up for you tonight has already deprived me of one of those hours...'

'I'm sorry sir,' I interrupted, 'but I...'

'I was not allocating blame,' he interrupted in turn, 'merely stating a fact.' He threw back the last of his wine and set his glass on the mantelpiece. 'That which has waited until now to be discussed, may wait another few hours – *seven* hours, you understand, not eight,' he emphasised with only half suppressed rancour. 'I refer to the terms and conditions, business and otherwise, governing your stay here. I have everything drawn up ready for your approval. The office is just across the corridor. You may have a good look round in the morning. You will also in the morning meet with my mother, a pleasure for the moment you will have to forego.'

Was he in jest or in earnest? My head was aswim with the muddle of tiredness. 'Whatever you please,' I said, to be saying something.

A false smile cracked open his lips, the large teeth graveyard grey from the claret. 'Good,' he said, 'then I'm away to my bed. I'll bid you goodnight, John Eagle. Ring the bell when you are ready for yours. Sukey will show you to your chamber.' He hadn't offered me any food, which made me glad that I had eaten some stew at the last inn. As he strolled away, rather hurriedly I noticed, I was left nursing my glass, staring at the last of the fire. The house was cold, and after the roar of London maddeningly quite, just the crimping of the cinders and the ticking of the clock. There was something about that clock which made me uneasy. It was not the look of the thing – just simple gilt like the candlesticks either side – but the jolting foretaste of something unpleasant yet to come. Mere foolishness, I told myself, a trickery of focus induced by fatigue. I was certainly tired; the pain behind my eyes was intense. I waited a while in tired stupor, gulped back my wine then rang the bell. What poor, downtrodden creature would emerge next? I wondered, as I stared expectantly at the door.

I heard her feet, feathery soft before I saw her. Wretched she was this Sukey, the Balmes' little tweenie, their Jack-of-all-work dressed in plain grey dress, with white pinafore and matching lace bonnet. She was small and thin but pretty nonetheless, with wondrous bright eyes and good clean teeth. 'Can I help you sir?' Her voice was gentle and obliging. 'Would you like me to show you to your room?'

I looked at her and smiled. She glanced at the dark spangled carpet, flushing pink. Here was a girl not used to kindness. 'Yes,' I returned warmly, 'if it isn't too much trouble.'

'No sir, I'll fetch a candle from the kitchen.' She returned presently and led me out into the hall, where I followed her up the staircase that creaked with our tread. My bedroom was the first at the top of the stairs, and, if my mental plan didn't lie, was situated below the servants' quarters and above the office.

'This is the one, sir,' Sukey said, nudging open the door with her knee
and stepping in on the sloping floor. She used her candle to light another
on the small dresser by the window. I observed my surroundings, bare
but tolerable: dresser, with jug and bowl; small deal table and chair; bed
with drapes and a closet for my clothes. 'You should be comfortable,' she
said, turning down the sheets. 'I made the bed myself this afternoon.' She
looked up at me with those eyes still bright. 'I trust you'll be warm
enough. I could fetch you an extra blanket or...' – or *what?* – there was
an awkward pause, charged with what I dared not think. But surely my
tired intuition had lied.

'How old are you?' I asked hesitantly.

'Fourteen...sir,' she said, adding the deference in afterthought. 'You
don't know how lonely it gets here. Please sir, I don't have nothing
never.'

I glanced at the plain little bed, scarcely large enough for one, thinking
how I longed for sleep. But I knew it, I felt it, how she longed for a
loving embrace, anything to soften her daily hurt. 'Please,' she said again
in a whisper.

What must I do? – it was me, a stranger, whom she had trusted on impulse. I felt such pity, guilt and shame. I fingered her chin tenderly, wiped away an errant tear. There was no wantonness in her look, just a craving for affection. And I saw the child in her that she'd never been, the little holiday of childhood she had been denied. But the woman was there too, I might summon it any time – why not? Was every man not a bull waiting to be roused by the call? A libertine wouldn't hesitate, and a libertine strain I knew I had and was willing to nurture. If she didn't leave soon I would be tempted worse than Christ. I need only take her hand and she would know my thoughts. But my thoughts stayed clean – just – and sleep when it came was instant and alone.

TWO

When I woke at seven Sukey was already at her work. It was her duty on winter mornings to start at six o'clock, making three fires before breakfast, one in the kitchen, one in the lounge and the other in the office. These fires had to be kindled by tinderwood, brought in by George the night before. The wood was supposed to be dry but was often damp, hence Sukey's tears at not being able to light it. Next she had to carry in buckets of coal, before creeping softly into the bedrooms to remove the piss-pots from under the beds. She entered my room as I was sleeping, or rather pretending to be: the awkwardness of the previous night made me unable to face her just yet. I waited till she'd gone, then washed myself and dressed for breakfast.

A single egg, a shrivelled kidney, and a wedge of coarse bread was my lot. I should have counted myself lucky, for Tom Gill, whose food was taken through to him in the office by Sukey, being deemed unworthy to break bread with his employers, got nothing but a small bowl of flummery. No meagre portions, though, for the gentleman-attorney himself, whose blue and white plate showed all that was choice from the big black frying pan used by Fanny the cook.

'I trust you slept well, Mister Eagle,' said Abraham, who sat straight-backed in a coffee-coloured suit at the head of the table, napkin pinned to his chest. He forked in a greedy mouthful of egg and awaited my reply.

'Yes,' I answered, about to add some forced pleasantry about the comforts of my room when my host suddenly rose and welcomed the latecomer. 'Good morning Mother!' he cried, greeting the big-boned, bow-legged woman in her seventies who headed purposefully towards the table. Her drab, homespun gown shielded by a flowery bodice served to accentuate her fat neck. 'Sit yourself down, Mother,' he added, pulling out a chair and lifting the lid on another plate as generously portioned as his own.

'Whaaa!' she exclaimed, sitting down with a great gasp. 'That's my Abe, always a perfect gent.'

'Thank you Mother,' he said with exuberant affection, slavering with his large tongue.

The mother by now had ceased her share of the coddling and was eyeing me sharply across the table. 'And who might he be?' she demanded to know.

'This, Mother, is Mister John Eagle,' the son explained as he poured tea for the three of us. 'The young man we've been expecting – remember? He arrived last night after a long journey from London.'

'Whaaa!' There had come from her again that strange moaning prefix, followed by 'Hear that? He says *remember* but why should I at my age?' She was looking at me – peering at me, I should say – as if I were an object in a glass case.

'Good morning, Missis Balme,' I said with a smile.

The old lady grunted, and raised her hand in a half-hearted greeting. 'So you're to live with us, are you?' she asked presently.

'Yes – yes I think so,' I said, returning to my meagre helping.

The old lady mulled this over in her mind, casting meaningful glances at her son, who tried to pre-empt them with silly grins and winks, and jolly shakes of the head. 'Living with us?' repeated the mother rhetorically. 'I hope he'll behave himself. We have enough trouble with the other one.' She had meant Tom, who seemed the opposite of trouble.

'Mister Eagle and I are going to discuss terms as soon as breakfast is over,' broke in Abraham, slurping tea and chewing at the same time. 'Very generous terms too, I'm sure he'll agree.' He threw me a look to consolidate his point.

'Of course they'll be generous,' echoed the mother, her voice croaking with the fatty food. 'The best he'll get anywhere, I'll warrant. And I hope he'll be truly grateful for what he receives. My Abe's built up this practice single-handedly by the straps of his breeches...'

'All right Mother that'll do,' cut in her son with gentle firmness. 'I'm sure Mister Eagle's intentions are honourable enough.'

'Well you can't be too particular these days,' muttered the other, stirring sugar into her tea. 'There's artful people wherever you go.'

'There's nothing wrong with the world, just the people in it, hey Mother?' joked Mr Balme, sucking on a piece of fat.

'Jest all you please, Abe, but it's true – just you mark my words,' said the mother.

There was a smirk on the son's face as he looked at me. 'Artful people's what keeps you and me in business, is that not so Mister Eagle?'

'For sure,' I replied, "tis the way of the world. Would that it were otherwise.'

'Nonsense!' declared the old attorney, uttering the word partly as a belch. 'Let the world spin on just the way it is, that's what I say. That way, we can all get fat.' He aptly pulled a shred of gristle from his teeth, held it up for inspection and belched again.

When breakfast was over, he rose and beckoned me follow to the office across the hall. Unlike the parlour, this chamber was a comfortable affair with a maroon carpet, and a good fire burning in the grate. In the centre of the room stood a round table covered with a green beige cloth, on which lay various ledgers and day books, quills, wafers and ink, and some furled parchment skins. On the shelves either side of the fireplace were bundles of deeds tied round neatly with red ribbon and labelled

chronologically by year. Bills of costs hung from stray nails. Law books
– *Blackstone's Commentaries* stood out bold – filled the opposite shelves,
and more next the window. On the chimney breast, beside a copy of an
almanac, hung the satirical painting of a large shark open-jawed. Finally,
against the far wall, stood a large oak chest, recipient of all that was old
and miscellaneous on the conveyancing side. This chest, I learned later
from Tom, was a Pandora's Box whose opening was invariably a source
of trouble.

Up two steps and through an arched door was a smaller office more
sparsely furnished. A railed partition divided off a small waiting area for
the public, who entered by the door beyond. In this room laboured Tom
on a high stool before a narrow desk. I could see him now through the
half open door, head bent low over his work, his battered hat hanging on
a peg. No fire, I noticed, burned in *his* grate. It was another cold
morning too, and the poor wretch's breath steamed in the chilly air.

Mr Balme observed my distraction and went to close the door. 'Tom
knows his place,' he said, with a contemptuous sniff. 'It's necessary that
such distinctions are understood by both parties, and always adhered to.'
Lighting a taper at the fire, he kindled the bowl of a clay pipe taken from
his pocket. 'Your place, of course, will be in here with me,' he said,

between puffs of foul-smelling tobacco. 'In fact on many occasions,' he continued breezily, 'you'll have the office to yourself. Today for instance – I have calls to make which will keep me off the premises. Which brings me timely to the terms I've proposed.' He unrolled the large parchment on the table and pinned it down with a pair of ledgers. 'This is how I see matters between us.' He donned his spectacles, and fixed his face in a look of concentration. 'It's all there. I'd advise you to study it carefully,' he said, pointing stiffly with his pipe at the arrangements and stipulations of our partnership agreement. Abraham had already signed; it awaited only my signature.

Anxious to know what my five-hundred pounds had bought, I cast my eye steadily along the lines penned in excellent law hand by Tom. I had purchased a co-partnership for ten years in the first instance. For the first three years Mr Balme was to receive three quarters of the profits, and I the remaining quarter. During the next two years he would take two-thirds and I the one; but for the remaining five years profits were to be divided equally, share and share alike. It was further agreed that all sums of money which were advanced in the management of the business would be paid and allowed in the same proportions as we were respectively entitled to the profits. The remaining clauses related to the division of labour within the practice. It was proposed that I should take upon myself the entire management of the common law business and undertake all journeys relating to the partnership. Predictably – and as yet without rancour on my part – none of the work load clauses related to any stewardships, receipt of rents, management of estates, clerkships or offices of any public nature. Mr Balme, I knew, held several such positions, which were for his benefit alone. I could not begrudge him this, for by the same token any such offices that I myself acquired in the coming months and years would be mine and mine alone. The way with it was clear: I, the younger and, so it was presumed, more eager practitioner, was to take from the shoulders of the older man the tiresome burden of litigation. The more senior attorney was reserving for himself the lion's share of the less demanding work: drawing simple conveyances, money-lending, advising, settling accounts, rent receiving, and letter writing.

'As for your board and lodging,' he said, puffing contentedly. 'Well...shall we say twenty-one pounds a year, payable out of your share of the profits?'

I darted him a glance: I had paid as much in London for a capital chamber in Furnivals Inn. It was hard for me to do it but I must stand firm. Making to stir the fire, he went on, 'That would, of course, include

the washing of your personal linen...and your use of a fine horse.'
Sensing I was still not happy, he clacked his tongue and said gruffly, 'I
would not require payment in advance, you understand. No, it could wait
till the half-yearly accounts are done in six months time. Better still, pay
me monthly starting one month hence – that way you'll get the first month
in gratuity.'

'Very well,' I said, feeling bound to agree.

Mr Balme smiled crookedly, showing those large teeth whose true
colour was yellow now that the grey was gone. 'Excellent. Then give me
your hand upon the deal,' he said, holding out a puffy limb as greasy as
parchment. 'Welcome to the practice, John,' he added as I shook it firmly,
but not so firmly as he shook mine; it was more a squeeze than a shake
and was meant to cause me hurt. It seemed his way – and I'd met it
before in men of a professional nature – to out-shake every other man he
met.

'Thank you – Abraham,' I replied, feeling that *Abe* was too familiar and
the sole preserve of his mother.

He poured us each a small glass of madeira to seal the bargain, tossed his off in one and said, 'Now you must excuse me. I have urgent business to attend this morning. If I could leave you to pour over these...' – he took down from the shelf more ledgers, day-books and accounts, and set them on the table – '...All that you need to know about the daily running of the practice can be found in here. I suggest that you scrutinise it all very closely. Come, there's no time like the present.' He opened the smallest account book and ran his finger down the first page. 'Here is a list of my – *our* clients. You'll see that they are arranged alphabetically, and that I have included their places of abode. I don't propose that we simply divide the clients between ourselves – that would be impracticable. Clients cannot be categorised...'

'You mean as litigants or non-litigants?' I ventured.

'Precisely. It might be a deed of conveyance one week, and an action of trespass the next. Some *are* predictable, you understand – we have a number who are very fond of the courts – but most are not. I suggest therefore that we divide the work simply as it arises, following the lines already agreed. Done?'

'Done,' I said, though apprehensive about the heavy work load surely in store.

'Good,' he said, flicking open the nearest of the day-books. 'I suggest you deal first with any business-in-hand that is pressing.' He turned the pages quickly, pausing at an entry for June 1776, and moving on to the later entries for November and December of the same year, and those for the current time: January 1777. 'We shall have to come to some arrangement about those,' he mused, meaning the actions in connection with the Leeds and Liverpool Navigation Company, to which Abraham acted as Law Clerk and drew a generous fee for his services. I could already guess his meaning: he wanted to surrender the arduous court business that the post additionally involved him in, but not the post itself. 'There are two cases that require your immediate attention, namely old Jackie England's will and Lady Larkin's...well it's Lady Larkin's something or other. Give her your utmost attention, John. She and her husband put a lot of business our way, so we can't afford to offend them.'

'I shall do my best,' I said, shivering of a sudden without any obvious cause. There was no draught in the room but the air seemed thinner, unaccountably so, and I felt again something of that alien chill, noisy, tight and repugnant that I'd felt atop the coach.

'Good. May I suggest, then, that you break yourself in gently by riding out to Jackie England's place? He's sure to be there, for he's permanently bed-ridden. You'll find him a most agreeable man, most welcoming of company.' As for new business,' he continued, straightening his flannel waistcoat with its pattern of blue sprigs, 'I'll leave it to your discretion. We charge three and six for advising clients, but don't let your advice run on beyond the hour. Some of them will talk the cows home if you let them. And make sure you know they can pay. We're not poor men's attorneys, not in this practice any way. If they want to sue *in forma pauperis* tell them to go to Leeds or Bradford to do it.' My nod suggested assent. 'Good. I'll take my leave then,' he said, heading off with that bow-legged stride he'd inherited from his mother. As I heard him cross to the outer office and leave by the door beyond, I glanced at the books he'd left me with. I couldn't concentrate; I needed time to settle in. I was a stranger in a strange land, an *off-comer* as they say, an immigrant among natives, one of whom was just next door.

I crossed to Tom's office, intent on a proper introduction. The chill of the room hit me like a cold breath as his narrow frame registered my presence. I saw his shoulder bones, which protruded like fins, twitch then stiffen. 'Busy?' I enquired in a friendly tone when he failed to look up from his work.

The old man straightened a little, then stared at the panelling above his desk. 'No more than usual,' he said at length. His tone was reserved, I noticed, but more from wariness than meanness of character.

'You are doing copying, I see' – engrossed in engrossment, I wanted to add, but I doubted he'd appreciate the joke.

'Making fair copy, yes,' he said. 'It's what I do, make fair copy. Make fair copy of this, make fair copy of that.'

'And you do it exceedingly well. I can't recollect seeing a neater hand. Such excellent penmanship.'

He thought I was patronising him. 'I ought to do it exceedingly well in my sleep,' he said. 'I've written enough law hand to cover parchment from here to China and back. I'm the grand old man of drawing 'n' engrossment.'

'What is it you are working on?' I asked, ignoring his sarcasm.

There was another pause, a longer one this time before he turned and faced me. I noticed his sallow complexion, the downy hair like cobwebs trailing his lantern jaws. There were deep furrows in his marble brow, and the lines on his face seemed beyond computation. The eyes, as I'd seen them the night before, were watery grey and fixed far back in their sockets, and though alive and blinking this morning, were at the same time dead like the eyes of a fish upon a slab. And while it is true that we all look better by candle-light, here was a man you oughtn't to look at *except* by candle-light. It would not have surprised me to learn he had been interred for several weeks, dug up again and found to be still alive.

'It's a will,' he explained tiredly, 'or rather the codicil to one. Not my will, you understand. There would be little point in me writing one – nothing to leave, nobody to leave it to.'

'Poor Tom All Alone,' I said, not without affection as I proffered my hand. 'I hope we can be friends. Please don't see me as your enemy.'

He stared at me, perhaps *through* me, so intense was his look. 'I'll see you as I see you. Time will tell how that might be. And time will tell whether you have the stomach for life under this roof.'

35

'*You* have it,' I said more sternly.

Tom picked up his quill again, about to resume scribbling. 'I have no choice, not any more. I am what *they* want me to be.'

'You'll also be what *I* want you to be,' I said as firmly as before. 'And right now, I want you to be warmer.' I fetched a scuttleful of coals from Mr Balme's office and headed for the empty grate. 'These are for you,' I said, throwing on half the contents. 'There!' I clapped the coal dust from my hands, feeling pretty pleased with myself. 'That sets the future pattern between us on cold days. When Balme's out, I'll make damn sure you have as good a fire as myself. You'll get more to eat at meal times too, if I can manage it. You'll not go hungry, even if I've to find the money myself. Now, will you put a light to that lot yourself, or shall I ask Sukey?'

The old man's lips parted. He raised his bent forefinger as a prelude to speech. 'I'm not used to kindness. Can't you see...' – he broke off, catching his breath – '...I can't be doing with it. What do you want from me?'

I placed a hand on his shoulder, feeling the shine of the worn fabric and the coolness of the bone beneath. 'I don't want anything, Tom. Nothing at all. I won't tolerate injustice.'

I had turned to leave when I heard him call. 'Mister Eagle!' he said in a contrite tone. I turned on my heels and smiled in anticipation. 'Thank you, sir,' and his eyes narrowed earnestly.

'No Mister Eagles, please,' I rejoined, with mock annoyance, 'and no *sirs*. I'll have no airs and graces between us. You must call me John, and I must call you Tom.'

I saw him smile for the first time, a weird and wonderful smile which, though betraying his heavy teeth loss, blew away one third of his sixty summers. My determination to befriend him had worked; it had chipped away the last plaster of his manly pride.

'By the way,' I asked, 'who's will is it that you're working on so neatly?'

'It belongs to Jackie England. It's almost finished.'

'A coincidence indeed,' I said. 'I aim to go there this day. Perhaps I could take it with me?'

'Perhaps,' he repeated. 'So long as you mind the moors, or rather him that lives up there.'

'Meaning?'

'Meaning you should take good care about the evil ways of one – most of them true I'll wager.'

'And the name of this person?'

'Edward Larkin. They call him – among other things – *Long* Larkin on account of his height. But what you don't know about cannot harm you. I'd try to keep it that way if I were you.'

'And yet you say there are tales about him – what sort of tales?'

'I've heard it said he has dealings with the black arts. The occult. Rumour it may be, but I'd mark his name well. He's a dangerous man, a law unto himself up there at Gravehunger Lodge – the name itself is bad enough.'

The old man's words had intrigued me, as I think he'd meant them to do. I took them with me back to the office where I studied the firm's books for several hours. My task wasn't easy; every hour felt like two, my mind like a lense out of focus. Still I had tried, rewarding my exertions with a light luncheon of cold mutton, boiled potatoes and small beer. The meal was brought by Sukey, whom I told to take the same to Tom. Her reaction took me aback.

'What? Give the same to that old bag o' bones?' My kindness the night before had bred a sauciness for which I'd only myself to blame. I tried to reassert my position: 'Now listen, Sukey, you must do as you're told.'

Her lips set firm in a pucker. 'If you say so – *sir.* But listen, he gets as much as I get, and *he's* old, he don't need much.'

I was stung by this too; I hadn't given a thought for her share of the victuals. She had sat there watching me eat, saying nothing in her hunger. 'Are you hungry too Sukey? I know you must be.' Her answer was her tears, which I knew would come. They came extra fast as she laid her body against me. She was a child sobbing on my breast and I tried to comfort her as such. I kissed her but not, alas, as I should have kissed her – once, softly, on the forehead – but passionately on the mouth. Her breath tasted sweet – too sweet for my own spiritual good. I was in danger of becoming what I'd often abhorred in others: an unscrupulous predator preying on slender years. I wondered also what Tom would think. Had I not sensed him spying through the door?

THREE

My first day in Horseford had been eventful indeed. I'd gone to Jackie England's as planned early in the afternoon but hadn't enjoyed the result. Leaving the village behind, I'd heard for the first time, in its cottages and workshops, the whirr of the spinning wheel and the clack of the loom. For this was textiles country, a new and thriving centre of homespun woollen cloth. My grey mare – called Daisy, a cow's name I'd thought – carried me reluctantly to the moors, whose bracken, furze and ling stretched in undulating folds all the way to Lancashire. No wonder Mr Balme had parted with her so easily; a more enervated creature it would be hard to find outside a field of spent pit-ponies. We had gone but two furlongs when her body sank suddenly to the ground, and no admonishments on my part could raise her till she'd lain there on her haunches for twenty minutes or more. I had unfastened my saddle-bag of papers and was ready to resume on foot when the animal consented to be ridden again, eschewing for the present its supine fancies. The rest of the journey was unhindered. Tom's simple directions – follow the beaten track westwards till you reach the finger post for Halifax – soon brought me within sight of my goal. Crowning the steep slope up ahead was a small farmhouse with the queer title High Treason, its walls stained green by a sombre moss.

I found the old man sitting upright in bed in a shabby room. 'You've brought the copies of my will?' he'd asked, pointing a begrimed finger at my bag of deeds.

'Yes,' I'd said, adding that the originals were held safely in our strong box.

'I dare say they are,' he'd replied, 'but that's not the point. You've come here to see me and you'd better listen hard.'

His tone wasn't friendly, certain words of Mr Balme's – *you'll find him a most agreeable man, most welcoming of company* – sticking fast in my throat. Five years of clerkship, and a year in the office of one of the busiest London practitioners had not given me the confidence I thought it had. What was it about these Yorkshire folk, who were so unpredictably strange? I had more to learn about people than I'd realised, and I had to learn it fast. This sick old man with the corpse-thin hair and grizzled face seemed to know it. He had something to tell me too and I doubted his will was the bottom of it. He was staring fixedly into space, his gaze encompassing a stuffed crow upon the window-sill. I half imagined he had secretly consulted the bird, getting the answer he sought before saying on a softer note, 'When I think of lawyers I think of questions – too many questions for the lawyer's own good.' Needing a drink to fortify himself, he took a gulp from the bottle on the bare wooden floor. The burning strength of the liquid made him bear his rotten teeth. 'The one before you had a very enquiring mind.'

'You mean Mister Balme?' The name was already distasteful. I felt older of a sudden, corrupted and soiled by my new association. How could that be so? And how came it that my face, in the dirt-rimed glass, seemed to show such grim distortion? I looked grey at the cheeks, paled and shrunken at the lips, wry-necked like a hanged man. The hair swept back from my temples and forehead, tamed at the back by an eel-skin queue, looked smooth as base metal – and I *felt* base, as if my heart, weak and false, were on show. I swallowed some phlegm at the sight of myself, craved a looking-glass that would show my youthful beauty, reassure me that it lived yet and would bloom for years to come.

'No, I don't mean him,' the hill farmer answered in a lower key. 'That's right, you keep admiring yourself, young fellow, if that's what you've come to do. *I* was a young man once, but look at me now – old,' he said, protruding his lower lip, 'but I've lived to be so, not like some I could name.'

'Please,' I'd said to prompt him, 'if you've something to say, say it, or I'll best be on my way.'

His breath thinned into rapid bursts and again the drink was needed. 'As you wish, but let that stand as your warning.'

'About *what?*'

'About meddling where you shouldn't!' The effort of shouting had cost him dear and he'd slumped back against the damp plaster. A rank smell of moulder, already pervasive, intensified with the impact. 'No good can come of it, not long life that's for sure.' But then, in the next breath, he told me that I *had* to meddle, it was my duty; it was what lawyers did, and no doubt I'd be back to do more in the next few weeks. It was as if he expected it, and he hoped he'd do his part when the time came. 'You *will* come again, won't you?' Lawyers were like doctors, he'd said, they must be good listeners over several visits. *He'd* been a good listener too, and no, he didn't mean Mr Balme, he meant the man whose name escaped him just now, though I sensed that he was lying.

'Your former attorney was not Mister Balme? I was led to believe the relationship was a longstanding one.'

He shook his head. 'Your Mister Balme is a recent arrangement. It was time for a change,' he'd said, with another bout of breathlessness. 'A man must do what he can to make himself safe. There's someone round here we should all be on our guard against – you more than most, John Eagle. I knew your name, you see, even before today.' And now his finger was at his lips to hush me. 'I want to warn you – about Long Larkin – it makes me shiver just saying that man's name, if man he is. I sometimes think he's not of this earth.'

The name had made me shiver too, not for the first time. 'You know him then?'

'I know *of* him and what he's capable of. Anyone with sense would leave it at that.'

'I can't leave it at that. He's one of our clients – he and his wife.'

'Then you must be careful. To say more is more than my old life's worth – and it's worth a lot even at my age – I don't want to die yet – I've too many wills to write!' He was smiling now, and the sky, as if in sympathy, had parted in a patch of ragged blue. It didn't last, however, for almost immediately the cloud was back. So too was that look upon his face. You'll get no more from me today, it said, just leave me with the deeds and go.

What it all meant I knew not, only that it spelt danger. Back to Horseford I had ridden in the owl light, battling all the way against a stiff wind that whistled across the heather. I'd looked around with wind-blasted eyes, endeavouring through their wateriness to be vigilant – about *who?* – about *what?* I hardly knew. There wasn't much to see. Weavers' cottages broke the darkness at intervals, studding the hillsides luminously in ones and twos, running as a dull jewel across a distant slope. Yes there was life to be had, reassurance surely, but it had no effect on me. An aching solitariness, like the end of the world, wormed its way inside me and wouldn't leave. I'd felt the moors' power, frightened in my heart by the music they played and the noise of their foreign speech. And above the moors themselves, in the very air, something was riding the wind, riding it viciously like an evil rider booted and spurred. It was enough to make the wind itself bleed and stain the heather with its blood. All of

46

this, I realised now, I had felt that night in the machine. The moors, the wind, they were more than just fancy then, more than just fancy now. And just as real was the feeling of entrapment, that here was a place I could never leave.

If only I were a brave man, facing the future without any fear. I had made over the years supernummary efforts to strive for bravery, for the strength to carry on until the end. I'd asked God for that strength now, and, as I'd done often of late, pleaded for a sign that would make me believe. For that was the heart of the matter: I couldn't be sure that I *did* believe. And why should I when I'd had no intimation? – nothing save the certainty of life and the certainty of death to follow. I feared death more than ever as I travelled those moors that day, felt my life ebbing on the Pennine breeze. How long had I left? – thirty years at most? My prospects weren't bright when I coloured them thus.

An hour later Horseford's lights leaked out warm on the darkness, drawing me nearer with their oily glow. My spirits should have lifted at the feel of flatter ground, lifted more when I'd reached the village with its rows of cottages and workshops. Much of my gloom, I reasoned, resulted from the strangeness of my new surroundings. I needed company, the sound of laughter, the gaudy finery of a tavern. Most of all I needed drink. Supper would be served at eight, and as it wanted yet an hour to that time I repaired to the Old King's Arms, desperate for a peace that just wouldn't come.

In the low-beamed room with its blazing fire, I was the subject of much curiosity. I'd sat down on a settle with my ale, having walked a gauntlet of nods from landlord, farmers and tradesmen, who spoke among themselves, to wit, 'That's old lawyer's lad.' 'Aye, Mister Balme's young partner from London.' There was some awkward shuffling, a cough or two, then silence, save the ruttling of their pipes.

The ale tasted prodigiously good, both well hopped and malty. I drunk straight down to the bottom of the pot, and had a mind for more but knew I wasn't welcome. My presence had made them uncomfortable and their eyes didn't scruple to stare. Had it been the ale they were wondering about, I could have eased their minds on that account by confessing how much I'd enjoyed it. I fancied, however, that their brooding held more weight; that I had broken an unwritten rule. Hazarding a guess as to what it was, I strolled to the counter and placed my pot down firmly. I was emboldened by drink, and superiority of position as I looked the burly landlord in the eye. His smooth face with its swarthy skin stared straight back, inviting hostility. I kept him within the compass of my vision as I turned to face the rest of the men. 'You may rest assured, gentlemen, that I am not at all incommoded by your presence, and wish you would do me the honour in feeling likewise with respect to myself. After all, we share a common purpose, do we not? – namely a liking for good ale.' I delved into the purse at my belt and counted out a shilling. 'Now, if you would be so good as to take a further pint at my expense I would deem it a great honour. Perhaps on the next occasion all awkwardness between us may be laid to rest. Your servant, sir,' I said, making a bow to the landlord, who opened his mouth at last.

'A word in your ear before you leave, I know we're all sorry to see you go.' His satirical tone sat well with his small narrow eyes.

'I suppose you're about to warn me as well,' I said jocosely to disarm him. We were standing outside by now, both hunched against the cold.

'Now what should I have to warn you about? You're a lawyer, aren't you? Can't lawyers take care of themselves *even when they're drunk?* But they do have to watch their step, especially when they tread where they shouldn't.' He knocked against me heavily, an ambiguous gesture that might have been accident or design. 'Begging your pardon young sir. The nights are dark up here and our waters run deep.'

I worked hard to maintain my jocular tone. 'Just what are you insinuating? – that I'll go the same way as Richard Hudson?'

'Don't know anyone of that name' – not any more, he might as well have said. 'A friend of yours was he – this Richard Hudson? Tut, tut tut – sounds to me as if you've lost him. Never mind, there are always other friends to be had, but I'd keep yours close if I were you.'

'And my enemies? – you mean I ought to keep them closer still?' I asked of his retreating back, which seemed to be the essence of him, broad, lumpy and animal dumb.

'You don't even know who they are yet,' I heard him mutter and chuckle. 'And when you do you'll wish to God that you didn't.'

The small mercy was, that I'd been put further on my guard – against *what* I was still no wiser. Most of all I felt resentful, toyed with and shamed. I came away nursing my hurts, and in no good mood for supper.

'You did what? You drank at the Old King's Arms?' Mr Balme was looking at me across a forkful of roasted partridge. His bulbous nose was twitching beneath his angry eyes. His mother, who sat close beside him, echoed his sentiment with a full mouth.

'You must keep out of there, do you hear?' she spluttered, laying siege to my own dinner with fragments of meat that landed only inches from the plate. 'A respectable genteel young man oughtn't to be seen even passing such a low den as that.'

'Mother's right – as always,' said Abraham, softening a little as he extracted a slither of bone from his lower gum. He forced a smile with those large yellow teeth. 'If you must take a drink in the village try the Black Bull. It's the only establishment with a modicum of respectability hereabouts.'

I resented their tone and was quick to show it. 'I shall drink where I like,' I said, looking from one to the other. 'You have no business telling me otherwise. And you, Mister Balme,' I added for good measure, 'have no business lying to me about my clients. Jackie England is a recent acquisition I hear. The man was queer to say the least, no wonder you didn't wish to visit him yourself. The same is even truer of the Larkins no doubt!' I was about to mention Daisy, the sorry creature that masqueraded as a mare, but there was no need: my charges had struck home.

'Whaaa!..' was as far as the old woman got; she had nearly choked on a mouthful of cold tongue and had to be attended by her son.

'Now look what you've done!' He was fussing over her as he might an infant in swaddling clothes. 'Her constitution won't take such an upset.' The mother was indeed in some distress, her face apoplectically red. 'Quickly!' exclaimed Mr Balme, loosening the neck of her blouse. 'Call the maid and bid her fetch a dose of Mother's physick.' His glance was full of kindled hate. I knew I'd gone too far, but they *had* provoked me.

'We'll talk later if we must,' he said, waving me away with flustered impatience. 'Just do as I say and get the medicine!'

I did as I was told. I ran out into the hall shouting of Sukey, whom I quickly collided with. 'It's Missis Balme,' I said, 'she's taken ill.'

Her glance said it all as she hurried through the door. She'd guessed I was the cause of the old woman's seizure and she – Sukey – wouldn't get away unscathed. From the hall, I heard her ask Mr Balme whether he desired his mother's pills or a dose of rhubarb.

'The pills, girl, the pills!' came his stinging reply.

'But they're all gone, sir!'

'Then you must run to Doctor Stables for some more! Put your shawl on and go this minute!'

Sukey fled sobbing, near knocking over Tom who'd emerged from the office.

'Hardly what you'd call a civilised evening,' I said, stooping to retrieve what he'd dropped – a rabbit's hind leg. 'I see they're fattening you up for the slaughter again.'

Tom forced a laugh. 'I'm glad you've come to live here,' he said, turning away. 'With you daggers drawn all the time they'll forget about me. By the way....,' he added, about to close the door, 'don't fret yourself on *her* account. She has one of those attacks every other week and never seems the worse for it. The old Amazon's as tough as an ox.'

'Must be all that tongue she eats,' I said, determined not to feel guilty.

Tom laughed, and before disappearing beckoned with his finger that was crooked at the end. 'A word of advice,' he said in a low voice. 'Beware of the girl – Sukey. Don't trust her. She's on *their* side at bottom of her, not ours. And I suggest you stop doing what I saw you doing earlier. Not good for the heart at my age.'

'You *were* watching us!' I said, more shocked than annoyed.

'Aye, and it gave me quite a bulge in my breeches. I did an hour's copying afterwards and I still had it when I'd finished. Quite an achievement for an eel that's lain dormant in the mud these thirty years.'

'But we were *only* kissing,' I said in disbelief.

'I have a vivid imagination,' he said with a wink.

'So have I,' I answered, remembering the sum of my fears that day – fear of the moors, fear of dying, fear of enemies unknown. Most of all there was fear of a name that seemed to stand for it all. The name was

Edward Larkin.

FOUR

The next few days saw their share of drudgery. Ensconced in the office, more often alone than not, I fagged about methodically to master the details of every letter book, day book and account book, every ledger and box of deeds. Hence did I learn the details of all our clients since 1749, memorising the work they had brought to the practice. I learned in addition the sitting times and venues of the principal courts, and the names and abodes of legal personnel who resided locally. By careful scrutiny of all Mr Balme's cases, especially those he had sought Counsel upon, I was able to arrive at a sound appraisal of my partner's knowledge of the law, matching this against my own that I might comprehend more completely the range and nature of his weaknesses. One had revealed itself already, namely the prodigious number of letters shockingly bad wrote.

The administrative system that prevailed at the office I also quickly mastered, familiarising myself with the speed of business, Abraham's system of recording, filing and accounting, and his dealings with the London agents, Messrs Farrer and Davies of Barnards Inn. In addition I checked our stocks of parchment skins and paper, stamps, wafers, and quills, plus the method of ordering and paying via the Stamp Office at York.

The pains I took were purely on my own account. I was realistic enough to expect no gratitude from my partner, who was a very mean fellow in all respects. He had shown his true character the night of his mother's seizure, and had scarce spoken a word to me since. Needless to say that we had not yet *talked,* as he had intimated that evening. Not that he had grounds for this resentment, for as Tom had predicted the woman made an instant recovery the moment her pills had arrived. But that I now found myself irretrievably in their bad books was indisputable, and perhaps this outcome was inevitable. For in truth Mr Balme had not desired a partner, and resented a course of action forced upon him through age and debility. Add to this an intrinsic distrust of strangers, a trait shared to an even fiercer degree by his mother, and it will be understood why my struggle to be accepted at Fink Hill House was hopeless from the start. I was at best an unwelcome guest, and at worst a profligate abandoned intruder. Nay more, for I had heard them defile me in their cups one night, Mrs Balme as the most wicked, artful, ungrateful and deceiving wretch she had ever heard of.

Although it had made me uneasy, I refused to be vexed or fretted by this turn of events, and was determined to bury their memory in the Gulf of Oblivion. I even congratulated myself on having cause to be sanguine. After all, I had a contract binding in law that entitled me to a growing share in the profits of the practice. I would work hard over the coming years, seeking to gain, as soon as possible, a higher footing in the legal world. I would not be denied what my talents might lead me to achieve, or what destiny had in store for me. The worst that could befall me in the meantime – a notice to quit the house and find lodgings in the village – was not a prospect to be dreaded; rather one to be welcomed should it arise. Indeed, I might even pre-empt my marching orders by leaving of my own accord. After all, I already had one offer of an alternative roof, and under normal circumstances would not have hesitated to accept. But I say *normal*, and what transpired between myself and my potential saviour could not, by any stretch of the imagination, be termed so.

The offer had come from the doctor to whose house Sukey had fled on her quest for Mrs Balme's pills. His name was Marshall Stables, an uncommonly fine gent not two years above my own age, to whom I had been attracted when I met him in the street.

Intent on a stroll about the village, I had walked up Fink Hill to an area known colloquially as the Green. Apropos its name, there was much greenery around even in January – pinfold grazing land beside every approach road, a large swathe of grass next the graveyard, green lichen too, not to be outdone, on the numerous gritstone walls. A pleasing prospect but a busy one, for this was the heart of the village where all its roads converged. The church also stood here – a dark hump-backed structure with its name – St Mary the Virgin – on a battered gilded clock; two inns likewise – the shabby-genteel Black Bull, which I hadn't yet visited, and the Old King's Arms of ill repute where, I now noticed in daylight, the stocks sat grimly outside, a warning to passers-by that ale and religion didn't mix, especially on the Sabbath. Here in addition was the site of the market and major festivities, the home of a dozen tradesmen whose shops and houses were huddled together in a broken horseshoe of jerry-built gloom. The doctor's house was here too, forming, along with its surgery, one of a pair of fine capital messuages opposite the church.

It was a cold clear Sunday, and this tall, slender man was taking the air dressed in three-cornered hat, a fine blue coat with gilt buttons, nankeen breeches and buff cashmere waistcoat. Although his visage was stately and reserved, I was drawn irresistibly to his warm grey-blue eyes which betokened, as my own no doubt did, an instant regard. He turned out to be a very affable good-natured man, a very good sort indeed. He was most cordial to me. 'Good morrow to you Mister Eagle!' he declared, espying me as he crossed the street.

I was a surprised at him knowing my name, but lost none of my composure. 'Your servant sir!' I replied, doffing my hat and making him a bow.

He halted to let a carriage pass, then drew near. He made me a bow in turn and spoke elegantly and genteelly. 'Excuse my presumption, but I already know who you are. Your little serving wench described you perfectly. I am Doctor Stables, apothecary and surgeon here. A fine morning is it not?' he said, gesturing to the heavens with his silver-headed cane. 'Thank the Lord that confounded wind has dropped. I was beginning to hear it moan in my sleep.'

When I remarked drolly that I liked the wind, he called me a contrary fellow, and wagered that I'd not feel the same in ten years time when my bones and joints were beset with ache. And on the subject of which, how was Mother Balme keeping? He had asked the question in a faintly mocking way, and with a glint in his worldly eye.

'She is tolerably well I presume. I would no doubt have heard otherwise by now.'

'To be sure,' replied Marshall smiling. 'She would have had the roof down on you with her protracted Whaaas!' We both laughed heartily at this, drawing out the first buds of friendship. 'My house is just there,' he said, pointing again with his cane. 'I was on my way thither. May I tempt you with a glass of something? I make the offer, of course, purely for medicinal purposes, to keep the cold out.'

'Of course,' I said knowingly.

'Come,' he said, taking my arm, 'I'll sing all the heartier in church for having something burning in my breast. It'll make old Gaunt's sermon bearable too. The fool spouts his endless poppycock Sunday after Sunday. It's about time somebody took a pistol and put us all out of our misery.' I liked his droll irreverence. Life in Horseford, I thought, might be tolerable after all.

'Do you live alone?' I asked, as we walked up the short neat path fenced by wrought iron rails.

'No, I have a lodger. But he's harmless enough, keeps himself to himself most times.'

Marshall opened the freshly-painted door and entered a narrow hallway. 'This way,' he said, leading on past two rooms either side of the staircase, which collectively served as waiting room, surgery and dispensary. A disordered fusion of medicinal aromas filled me with dread, a sensation that was not allayed by that glimpse of surgical instruments lying on a table. It was the bone saw that worked on me the keenest; I was sure I felt its teeth rasping at my spine.

We came presently to his back parlour, a cold, shuttered room thinly furnished with sofa and table, dark brown carpet, and shelves filled with medical books. 'My apologies,' he said, seeing me shiver as he drew back the shutters with a great clatter. 'I rarely light a fire in the forenoon, not even in the coldest season. Along with the house, it's a habit I inherited from my late father, and old habits die the hardest.'

'No matter,' I said with a shrug, wondering what it was that made so many Yorkshiremen make sparse with their fires, even in the depths of winter.

'Do be seated,' he said, opening a small cupboard that rattled with bottle and glass. 'I trust that brandy will suit?' I gave him a decided nod. 'It's the finest French,' he added, pouring us each a generous measure. 'I buy it from my supplier in Leeds who sends it highly recommended. Taste it and tell me what you think.'

He handed me the glass but that's as far as I got. I had scarce put the vessel to my lips when it flew across the room, its trajectory favouring the far wall where it shattered in a dozen pieces. I was able to watch its progress in the fraction of a second before the cause of this action, a wild-eyed creature, scarce human in feature, leapt at my face with uncommonly long nails. Not content with scratching me, and tearing the ribbon from my hair, my assailant bared its teeth and sunk them into my neck. It was about to take another bite when Marshall coshed it with the brandy bottle. There was a low guttural moan; the creature's eyes rolled then glazed over as it fell unconscious.

'My dear fellow!' exclaimed Marshall, hurrying to my aid. 'Whatever must you think of me? Here, let me assist you to the sofa.'

'What was it that attacked me?' I stammered, when he'd got me thither and laid me down.

'Shush now, all in good time. Drink this,' he said, giving me another glass of brandy, which this time I *did* get to taste.

'I think you owe me an explanation,' I said, feeling right to be annoyed. *Harmless enough* this lodger certainly wasn't.

'All in good time,' he said again, feeling my brow with his hand, taking my pulse, and weighing up the size of my hurts. 'First you must let me get you something for those cuts.'

'How apt that I'm here, then, and not elsewhere,' I said mockingly. 'But is it not customary for a man to visit his doctor when he is ill, not be given injury when he gets there?' We caught one another's eye and laughed, I in spite of the pain.

'Forsooth I have never known it otherwise – until today,' he replied, still chortling as he turned away. He quitted the room for his dispensary, leaving me to ponder the mystery of the body on the floor – male, I now believed, and naked too, except for a pair of dirty breeches several sizes too small. It seemed incongruous that a creature so wild only moments ago could now lie perfectly still. I'd been about to study it more closely when Marshall returned with a small green gallipot. 'This'll sting,' he said in a fatherly tone, 'but it'll suit the purpose admirably. I'd go so far as to swear by it.'

'What is it?' I hissed, as he applied it to my clawed face, wanting to swear myself in a different sense.

'Yellow Basilicum ointment, the very best,' he said, delicately dabbing my cheeks and neck. 'You'll be sore for a day or two but there's no permanent harm done. Your good looks will stay intact,' he added, tweaking my chin and looking me in the eye uncommonly fondly. As if to discipline himself, he turned away and glanced at the prostrate figure. 'I suppose I ought to do something for him too,' he said resignedly. 'His skull's so thick, I doubt I've done him much harm. All the same, it's my duty to check. I'm really quite fond of the poor wretch.'

'But who is he?' I insisted.

'I suppose I do owe you an explanation,' he said with a sigh. 'Very well. His name's Philip…'

'Philip?' I interrupted. 'That's *most* enlightening!'

'You didn't let me finish,' said Marshall curtly.

He met my eye again, and we both smiled. 'I'm sorry,' I said. 'Do go on.'

He went on to explain how, following discussions with both the parish and the local magistrate, no lesser person than Sir Walter Spencer-Stanhope, it was agreed that Philip – or *Phil,* as he tended to call him – should be boarded with Marshall himself, a medical man experienced in dealing with distempered persons. 'It's a most satisfactory arrangement all round,' Marshall concluded with a smile. 'The parish has a dangerous lunatic taken off its hands, I get a generous stipend for my pains, and the chance to further my experiments, and poor Phil here, affluent as he is, is saved from a fate worse than death – in short, confinement in the madhouse at York.'

'Rather you than me,' I said, feeling my sores throb. 'Do you not fear for your own safety?'

'In truth, I do not. The poor soul seems to like me. He treats me with a motherly gentleness rather as an ape might one of its babes. Strange that he should attack you, though. After all, you're not the first visitor to the house. He usually keeps well away in perfect quiet. He must sense something wicked in you, John, something that agitates his innards.'

A trifle offended, I reminded him that Phil had not been labelled 'dangerous' for nothing, and what had happened to me was reminder of what he was capable of.

'Touche,' said Marshall with a playful bow. 'I was forgetting I was dealing with a legal man. Your sort can spot a flaw in any argument.' He smiled afresh with his neat-cut sensuous mouth. 'Now, let me have another look at those wounds,' he said, sitting down beside me and lifting my chin. He was looking at me again with that disquieting fondness. I sensed a knowing awkwardness in my own eyes, but saw none in his, only that intensive stare, affectionate still but with something else – I durst not think *what* – lurking behind. 'Should life with the Balmes ever become untenable,' he said, 'there would always be room for you here.' Our eyes were linked by a thread neither of us could, nor perhaps wanted to break. I allowed him to stroke my cheek, feeling his slender fingers play about my jaw and slide down to my neck. Part of me was curious, it wanted to experiment. I'd always been the same – I had wanted to *do* as well as dare. In starlit ruins as a boy I had called upon ghosts with names abusive enough to make them blush. I had drunk hard spirits at an early age, put the pipe to my lips and lifted my first petticoat. But my tastes, premature as they were, had all been natural, so when his practised fingers began to stray further I knew it was time to stop.

'No,' I said, staying his hand. 'I can't. I *won't.*'

'Not ever?' he said with heavy breath.

'No, not ever. And I think I should leave now.'

'*Think* or *know?*' he said, drawing away.

'All right then, *know,*' I said adamantly.

'As you wish. The door is in the same place as when you came in.'

We had parted amicably enough, but I was anxious to be rid of the place. It was a poor beginning to the friendship I'd craved. And I had gone away without unburdening myself, as I'd sorely wished to do. Un*button* myself I had almost done, but that was another matter. I had felt instinctively I might trust Marshall, though what must become of us now? What could have possessed me – yes *possessed* was the word – to stray so near the edge? It seemed crassly inadequate to think so, but I hadn't been myself in those few desperate moments. Or had I? Perhaps I wasn't being honest. I had been in the grip of something that I'd struggled to control, something which, truth be known, I more than half wanted. It was there after all, then, that other side of me whose existence I had hitherto denied. First with Richard and now with Marshall Stables. And however much I might gainsay it, claiming doxies fair were my only choice, deep down I would always know that my tastes ran both ways. For such a thought there was only one remedy – work.

* * *

Next morning at breakfast Mr Balme condescended to speak. It wasn't civility exactly, though something that swam in the same sea. 'How's business?' he asked, pausing to lick the porridge from his spoon.

'Yes, how's business?' echoed his mother in a teasing voice.

'It's going as well as could be expected,' I replied flatly. 'I have endeavoured most assiduously to prepare the ground.'

She leaned forward across the table and pointed rudely with her spoon. 'That's all very well, but have yer made any money?'

'Aye, Mother's right – again,' broke in the son. 'Preparation's all well and good, but it's money that we'll be needing sooner or later.'

'And the sooner the better,' snapped Mrs Balme. 'We can't have my Abe making it all, that wouldn't be right. You'd be getting your share of the profits from his share of the work.'

With a false generosity of spirit the son turned to her and said, 'Now, now Mother, we mustn't be too impatient with young John. We should give him time. The remittances will start coming soon enough.'

'Whaaa! Yer too generous by half Abe, that you are. Too generous with him in there...' – meaning Tom – '...and too generous with him in here. And *I'm* too generous with *her*!' she exclaimed, turning on Sukey who had just re-entered the room. 'Get a move on girl! Whatever's got into you this morning, you're moving about like a cart-horse!'

Sukey tried to look sharp, her young face miserable as she gathered the breakfast things. Abraham watched her shuffle out. 'She wants a firecracker up her skirts does that one,' he said, stirring his tea with ambivalent look. Had it meant what I thought it had? – that he, her employer and protector, was the predator she had to fear? Yes, I decided with disgust, for my intuition rarely lied.

I begged their pardon and walked promptly to the office, taking care to call on Tom before beginning my day's work. Porridge being a cheap food, he had dined on a bowlful too. One of the Balmes' cats lay purring across his legs, white flecks on its whiskers proof it had shared his meal. I told him all that had transpired over breakfast, not least that charge against me for laggardness in business.

Tom gave his habitual look – downcast, sour but knowing. 'All gloom as usual. I bet nobody mentioned the piss-pots. Mine was frozen solid when I woke this morning.'

'Mine too,' I said laughing. 'Sukey would have needed a hammer.'

'Theirs must have been the same,' said Tom, lowering the cat to the floor. 'In a happy household – and, believe it or not, the one I grew up in was such – comment would have been made and heartfelt humour felt all around. But not in this house, oh no, not in this one. A deathliness of spirit rules here. Fine place to lay out the dead should ever the plague return.'

It was good to know that Tom was of the same mind, that he was on my side. In his soothing smile and voice, he had a way of making everything feel all right – and I mean *everything*. Never mind that I seemed to have failed with Marshall, I had the feeling that whatever I had done, and whatever I did in the future, Tom would be the balsam I needed; he would make me at peace with myself, be the ointment to my guilty soul. In short, he would be my absolution. I watched him as he sat there, an old man so thin, so frail, rocking absently on his stool. By a trick of the light perhaps, just that and no more I hoped, I saw both through and beyond him, just for an instant. I communed with him in a silent invisible place – an open place, a field or a moor, yes a moor, for I felt the wind in my hair. And on that moor, he was sitting and I was standing, just like we were now. I couldn't understand it, but to feel it was to feel its power. I was trembling with excitement and fear. Tears were in my eyes, whose cause I couldn't fathom; I felt old with forgotten years, old with futures yet to come. And then it was gone: nothing but a sense of coming struggle, and a fight I couldn't win.

I looked Tom in the eye and he seemed to know what I was thinking, as if he had felt it too. *'Did* you feel it Tom?' I asked him.

'And what might that be?' he answered blandly, but with a light of recognition in his sunken eyes.

'I don't know,' I said, feeling a booby. 'I don't know how to express it. Just tiredness I expect, so much newness all around me, so many strange feelings.'

'Preparation is the thing, you've said so yourself. Question is, what are you preparing for?'

'A confrontation of some sort I'm sure. I feel it coming, just like night follows day. How can that be so?'

'Because you feel it, and if you feel it then it must be true – true for you, which is all that matters.'

'It's true for you too I'll warrant. And I think you know who I am to fight.'

He looked away, distracted by the cat which had leapt back into his lap. 'Cats are fickle creatures,' he said abstractedly, as the creature yawned with a snake-like gape. 'They'll attach themselves to anybody. They are the whores of the animal kingdom. Like women, you must never take them to heart. I don't mean Sukey,' he said, when he'd read my thoughts. 'Be warned my young friend,' and he glanced again at the parchment he was working on.

'I don't know what you mean.' He stroked the cat harder, increasing the loudness of its throaty engine. 'I'll say it again – I don't know what you mean.'

'Don't you? Well if it's any consolation neither do I. All I know for sure is the name on this conveyance I'm so carefully drawing. I take more care with his documents than I do with anyone else's. I daren't do otherwise.'

I glanced over his shoulder, as if the parchment were a magnet, such was the strength of its pull. The confirmation I received gave me no pleasure, for I'd already guessed the name. 'Tell me about him,' I said, 'Edward Larkin I mean.'

Deliberately so, I believe, he told me little, and little had I learned in general about this mystery man. But all that was soon to change, and in ways I could never have imagined.

FIVE

January ended with two momentous meetings. I received on the Thursday a letter from Sir Walter Spencer-Stanhope requesting my attendance at Stanhope Hall the following Monday at four of the clock. No explanation was given, nor could I imagine any. By next day's post came an equally mysterious note from Mr Bolland, the attorney at Leeds with whom my friend Richard had enjoyed a junior a partnership prior to his tragic end. I had written to Mr Bolland soon after my arrival, offering my commiserations for the loss of his partner, and explaining that I, as Richard's friend, might be of use in executing matters attendant on his death. The purport of the reply was this, that should I call at the Leeds office the same Monday between ten and eleven in the forenoon, what I might hear couldn't fail to be of interest. An unprompted summons from an illustrious personage, and a guarded message from my dead friend's partner were too intriguing to be missed. I was determined to take both as offered.

The twelve mile journey to Leeds took three hours. A speedier mare than Daisy would have managed it in half that time, but such mares do not slump down at will, refusing to stir lest bribed with sweet-meats and carrots. It wanted ten minutes to eleven as I entered the town from a westerly direction, the road in its singular projection having taken me en-route through the very nave of ancient Kirkstall Abbey. The prospect now was one of ordered streets in the foreground, leading by a gently rising gradient to the older quarter beyond. Here, where the huddled buildings leaned inwards either side of the road, chimney smoke merged in a grey pall above the blackened rooftops.

London's roar night and day had, I believed, fully accustomed me to urban noise. Leeds made me see my mistake. The concerted rumble of gigs and carts, the calls of street-hawkers and the day-to-day throb of business played havoc with my senses in a way the metropolis never had. Here the noises were each so separately painful that I seemed to hear the sound of every horse's hooves, every chairman's whistle, every closing door. Carriage doors snapped shut gently with a soft clip; house doors banged like percussion caps; taking-in doors at tradesmen's premises high on gabled walls juddered like the lids on ill-made coffins. The air itself seemed noisy of its own accord, charged with the energy of accumulated souls, past, present and future – most of all the future. It was another unsettling moment, of which there'd been so many of late, each inexplicably real in my own too fanciful breast. And yet I saw it, I was sure – as sure as I saw anything just now – all the misery that the old town would one day inflict. I saw it before me as a huge tank, a retort of some kind built of black iron that was church, chapel, factory and workshop hammered into one vast dome of trapped suffering. Inside were not human beings as such, but rather their essence in the form of gas or liquid poison. It was the human condition gone festeringly wrong, the human heart – my own in particular? – turned witheringly black.

My heart, like the rest of me, felt heavy in the saddle and nothing in the air gave respite. The smells of the town were as harsh as the sounds, each distinctly offensive – the cloying reek of textiles, leather and forged iron, of smoke and manure and stinking river. With great labour, as if the day were broiling instead of chilled, I spurred myself forward in defiant spirit. My course took me up the principal street, the Headrow, my eyes on the look-out for what they soon espied – the short narrow passage Mr Bolland had mentioned in his note. Entry lay betwixt a tobacconist's shop with its sign of the black boy and the garishly-fronted Horse and Trumpet Inn. Leaving my mare with a stable lad at the latter, I came quickly to a door with a polished brass-plate on the wall: Messrs Bolland and Snell, Attorneys-at-Law said the neatly-cut letters thrown into fleeting darkness by the bulk of a passing cart. With a last glance at my pocket watch, I nudged open the door and introduced myself to the young clerk on a high-stool. He leaned back with his quill in his mouth, looking as a clerk ought to look – young, confident and with prospects, doing only what a clerk should do; not at all like Tom Gill, old and downtrodden, no hope of anything better, doing the work of two clerks, and doubling as butler to boot.

The young man, dressed smartly in a dark suit and white lace cravat, gave his quill an affected chew. Mr Bolland was expecting me, he said in a reedy voice, and was waiting in the parlour adjacent the office. Not so enamoured of his saucy manner, I thanked him curtly and headed for the room beyond. I found Mr Bolland seated in an armchair drinking a dish of tea. A slight and elderly man of sixty, he was dressed in a green silk morning gown and maroon cap, suggesting a late rise from his bed. A deep reverie occupied him, and it was only when I had closed the door and called his name that he came to. I quickly informed him who I was, and that I had come in answer to his letter.

'Mister Eagle!' he said in a velvety voice as he rose to make me a bow. 'Your servant, sir. You must excuse me, I was far away in thought. Thank you for answering my note so promptly. Please be good enough to take a seat while I pour you some tea. You *do* take tea I hope?' His words sounded sticky as he shaped them with his tongue, as if each were a morsel of pudding that had to be chewed as he spoke.

'To be sure,' I said, and as he poured with trembling hand he begged my pardon for the recent illness that had left him listless. 'I hope you are on the mend,' I added, as he handed me my tea.

'Oh yes, ' he said, removing his cap and stooping to poke the fire, 'I'm much better now, thanks to several good doses of rhubarb and ginger.' I watched as he lifted the coals, scattering sparks up the cavernous chimney back. His head, I noticed now, was bald and spread with numerous tiny blemishes – sores, I quickly surmised, as if someone had showered him with darts. 'And how is business out there in Horseford?' he asked, returning to his chair before the fire. 'Mister Balme is treating you well I trust? You must give him my compliments on your return.'

From his matter-of-fact tone I was unable to gauge his true opinion of my partner. I therefore answered in the same vein, politely and non-committal. A considered nod was his response, as though he were weighing *me* up in turn. 'Yes,' he said reflectively as he sat once more in his seat, 'you may well be everything you seem, John Eagle. On the other hand, you may be nothing of the sort. The question for me is this:

can I trust you? I must also ask myself whether I *need* to trust you.' He

tutted, and added rhetorically, 'Oh come now Thomas, you've already

decided, have you not?' I sipped my tea, endeavouring to guess his

meaning. He looked at me and smiled, a very kindly smile for a man

with thin lips. 'I should get to the point, shouldn't I?'

'Yes, I expect so,' I said, speaking plainly because I'd guessed that's

what he'd want. Playing the sycophant, saying it was his privilege to take

as long as he wished would cut no ice with a man who, more likely than

not, was a shrewd gentleman of the law whose playful procrastination

was a calculated ploy.

'Very well, then.' He hemmed loudly and continued, 'One Richard

Hudson lately of this firm was your close friend, was he not? You

needn't answer – he spoke of you so often that your regard for each

another could never be in doubt. 'Tis clear, then, that the intelligence I

have to communicate will indeed be of significance.' He lowered his

voice and jerked a thumb over his shoulder. 'Walls, my dear fellow, have

ears, as we attorneys well know. We also know that we can never be too

careful. The case of young Richard teaches us this like no other I have

known, and,' he added, leaning forward with emphasis, 'I've been in

business an uncommonly long time.'

I sorely wished he *would* get to the point. The room itself, though it may not have ears, was not to my liking. Solid enough it seemed with its vine-tendrilled wallpaper, high ceiling and hard stone floor; expensive and appropriate its furniture of cabinet, table and chairs, the former in polished walnut. But the L-shaped plan failed to reassure me and I was troubled by the thought that someone might be lurking around that blind corner. Mr Bolland noticed my impatience. He gave his head a vigorous scratch and resumed, 'Prevarication has been my weakness, but it's also been my strength. It's won me many a case before the Bench. However, my hesitation today is due neither to habit nor policy, it is due to fear. I can't even find the courage to speak my mind. I need to spit it out and cannot. Rather like the genie in his bottle, I fear that once I've let him out I won't be able to get him back.'

I reminded him that he had gone too far already, that he had brought me here with the express purpose of doing precisely that: spitting it out, releasing the genie for better or for worse.

'Very well then,' he said. 'Here it is at last, for better or for worse as you say. I believe that Richard Hudson, lately of this town, was murdered. Nay, more than that, I have a good idea who killed him.' He scratched his head anew. 'There, 'tis said and done. Make of it what you will.'

The startling news made me spill some tea on my new breeches of fine duck cloth. The pain was intense, enough to make the Pope shout Fuck! at the top of his voice, and yet I felt detached from the hurt, too distracted to care. 'Upon my word, you have waxed very pale sir,' said Mr Bolland, who had watched my reaction carefully, donning spectacles for the purpose. 'Will you join me in something stronger than tea? – a little brandy perhaps, smuggled though it probably is?' He was frowning at the stain on my thigh. 'I feel we are both in need of fortification. After all, the genie now sits before us on the rug, does he not?'

'Brandy would be very welcome,' I said, struck by a sudden recollection. Instinctively I had glanced at the door, half expecting to see Phil bound in. I strove to collect myself, to get to the crux of the matter. A shot of something stiff would set my thoughts racing. I had a lot of questions for Mr Bolland, all of them plainly obvious: how did he know that Richard was murdered? – who did he think had done it, and why? – and, most obvious all, had he not reported this intelligence to a magistrate? His answers formed the following remarkable account.

It transpired that Richard had handled a disputed legacy case involving the daughter of a Leeds costermonger and Edward Larkin Esquire of Gravehunger Lodge. Mr Bolland pointedly asked if I'd heard of the notorious Long Larkin who, correct him if he was wrong, was also one of our clients. He was not mistaken, I told him swiftly, neglecting to add, for my own pride's sake, that the man's name was repeatedly in my ears and had come to exert a strange influence. Mr Bolland seemed to know it and was searching for a sign – a flicker of the eyes perhaps or a secret aversion of the face. Finding nothing of note, he went on to say that the probate case in question was complicated and had resurfaced after some fifteen years. Would that it had stayed hidden, he said, for Richard may still be alive today. That he was not was partly his own doing, for the boy had been a victim of his own good nature. He was determined to represent *all* clients, whatever their station in life, and word getting round that his aim was such, had gained, to the dismay of fellow practitioners, not least that of my own partner, Abraham Balme, a reputation as a poor man's attorney.

On this occasion, however, his behaviour had other motives than mere altruism. The pretty young girl had turned his head with her fulsome smile and beguiling eyes. Poor Richard, smitten at first sight the moment she entered the office, offered to represent her in a tortuous quest to recover what was rightfully hers – a legacy of three-hundred pounds bequeathed in a codicil by her late aunt, who had been Edward Larkin's elder sister. Despite the hostility on Larkin's side (he alone claimed to manage the funds of her estate), Richard had tried for a compromise. He had ridden out to Gravehunger Lodge on two separate occasions, returning the second time heavily bruised at the hands of Larkin's keepers. Undeterred by this assault, he had taken the opinion both of proctors and Counsel on his chances of success by one tack or another this side of the Prerogative Court and, failing that, outside the Court of Chancery, anxious as he was to save his client from ruinous costs. But the case was, as Mr Bolland had already told him, hopeless: Larkin would make good his threat to take the case to equity, where poor folk always came to grief.

Strangely enough, it was not the case in itself that brought Richard his watery end that November night. Something else on those trips to the moorland wilds had taken seed in his mind. Here Mr Bolland was on less firm ground. The terrain had got boggier, as treacherously so as the bogs up there on Larkin's own land, capable, as rumour had it, of swallowing without trace the combined height of man and beast. Mr Bolland had in mind the sweating trade of the Crag Vale Coiners, whose infamous counterfeiting activities had caused a stir even among the criminal fraternity of the capital.

'I say only this in conclusion,' said the eminent attorney, scratching his head in a much more agitated manner, 'young Richard stumbled on some telling connection between the practice of coining and Long Larkin. He may possibly have tried to expose that connection. What the precise nature of the link was I am unable to say, and truly so rather than not at liberty. Richard kept that side of his work very close to his chest, committing nothing to paper save a few scraps that amount to little of consequence.' The evidence was tenuous, he said, but he felt as certain of its reality as of I sitting there before him with tea-stained breeches. And he did know this much too: that being a stickler for justice, Richard had taken out writs of complaint against the two bullies who had beaten him senseless in the grounds of Gravehunger Lodge. During his enquiries about their whereabouts he discovered that both were known coiners, who, along with their so-called monarch, King David, had inexplicably escaped justice for years. 'But that was as far as he got,' he said, ending on a note of grim formality.

I asked about the circumstances of Richard's demise, remarking at the same time what I already knew – that the coroner's verdict was one of death by misadventure.

'It was the only possible verdict in the circumstances,' said Mr Bolland. 'As was his custom, Richard had drunk late at the Swan that night and walked home along the river bank. It had been a dark and moonless evening, and a wet and windy one. He must have lost his footing and slid into the river. The Aire runs fast and deep in that quarter of the town, and a boy much in his cups...' – yes, I reflected relevantly, Richard was always a good bottleman – '...would have had little chance in the black swirling water. 'Tis plain enough why the inquest concluded as it did: the evidence for an alternative verdict was not forthcoming.'

'A pity there were no witnesses,' I said ruefully into my brandy.

'Ah, but there were,' said Mr Bolland, his eyes widening behind the spectacles. '*One* to be precise, but it's only lately that he's made himself known. What he saw, he has felt too frightened to communicate until now, and though he has brought the intelligence to my notice, and better late than never, I am at a loss what to do with it. Telling as the information is, it doesn't amount to clear cut evidence, not in the eyes of the law. But I have to say so now, that I don't think I've the heart for this fight. Both I and Mister Snell are too old and yes, it has to be said also, too frightened.' He sighed into his glass, just as I had done. 'Men do in wartime what they'd like to do in peace, but can't. These are dangerous times, John Eagle, the arm of the law is so much shorter in its reach.'

I saw it all plainly in a barbed instant: the old man was handing the mantel of justice to me, hoping I'd not refuse. The ladder-backed chair I was seated in had arms, and I was glad to grab just one of them while steadying my glass upon the other. Coward though I was in many ways, I was cursed (some would say blessed) with a will to overcome it. This, and a need to see justice done, made my acceptance inevitable. There was added ingredient too, in that I realised now, unequivocally so, that my life in recent weeks had tended towards this moment as surely as Mr Newton's gravity. And what a moment it was, with all its attendant danger! I gulped the last of my brandy, a large mouthful which burnt my pipes though it gave me a rush of courage. Just how much danger was I really in? I was a lawyer after all, and the law was on *my* side. But Richard was a lawyer too, I reflected bleakly, and no law had protected *him.*

Mr Bolland folded his hands in a supplicating manner. 'I know that what I ask is a lot, and I would understand perfectly if you refused. I don't seriously expect you to do anything with the information I have given you. My motive in communicating it was purely as I have stated: as Richard's closest friend I felt it incumbent upon me to impart the truth as I saw it, and for you to do with that truth as you please.'

'And what do you propose to do with it should I do nothing?' I asked sharply.

'Likewise I would do nothing.'

'But why me?' I asked, unable to fathom why such a person as himself, with a legion of contacts in the legal world, some of whom in their time must have set both bench and bar alight, should have turned to one so young and untried. Nor was I a barrister or a magistrate; I was just an attorney of the King's Bench, barely trained in the criminal law, which was deemed not to be my business.

'Those contacts, as you call them,' replied Mr Bolland when I'd voiced this point, 'would not touch the case with a roach pole. They would tell me outright that my evidence was a trifle.' The old attorney stared sadly into the fire. How its flames leapt up forked and lively, showing me the face I'd rather not see, evil and red, just as I'd imagined it. Edward Larkin – *Long* Larkin – his name was on everyone's lips, jolting my heart every time I heard it. But I *had* heard it, many times, and this was the outcome, the begotten outcome – everything had tended towards this point.

'And would they be right?' I asked, 'to call it a trifle?'

He shook his head. 'Not to be trifled *with* perhaps, but that's a different matter.' It was his firm belief that some persons and the places they inhabited were out of bounds when it came to prosecution. They were allowed to be laws unto themselves for such time as the real law deemed fit. Until that changed, all attempts to balance the scales of justice in the usual way seemed doomed to fail, and those who had tried went without justice themselves for their pains. 'Crag Vale and Gravehunger Lodge are two such places,' said Mr Bolland, 'King David and Squire Larkin two such persons. Who knows, they may be one and the same. What the wider purpose of such laxity may be, a man like me can only guess. But mark my words, I have seen it happen before, it is happening now, and it will happen again, in your lifetime if not in mine. If you wish to satisfy your curiosity in the matter – and believe me, John, I push neither one way nor the other – you could start by asking the most prominent man in your neighbourhood. I refer to your partner's patron, Sir Walter Spencer-Stanhope, the finest barrister in the northern shires, and the leading magistrate on top. You are bound to come into contact with him sooner or later. If a man like that doesn't know what's afoot, I doubt anybody else will.'

'Then how opportune that I have been asked to call on him this afternoon,' I replied with an ominous flutter in my chest.

'Upon my soul, there it is then – you have your chance! Speak boldly and to the point when you go thither. He'll think the better of you for it.'

There was a long pause; we were both in need of a settlement. Be done with prevarication, I thought, accept the gauntlet that has been flung down, if only by proxy. As the Larkins' attorney, you are well placed for getting at the truth. You're a naive newcomer in their eyes, they'll hide less from you than most. And you'll always have an ostensible reason for calling at the Lodge – that business of *Lady Larkin's something or other* being a case in point. By keeping your ears open who knows what you might discover?

'All right,' I said suddenly. 'I'll do it.'

Mr Bolland clapped his hands together and laughed. 'I knew you would, my boy, I knew it!' He plied me with more drink, fussing around me in gratitude. He even offered me the nuts he'd started to nibble – more like the beads on an oral rosary than something to be relished or enjoyed. 'Just bide your time,' he said. 'The tide will turn, you'll see. Larkin and his accomplices will get their just deserts.' He appeared relaxed of a sudden, a straighter-backed, more sprightly man for his years. And the cause was plain – he had offloaded his burden on to me. 'Until that time comes – and I must stress again the importance of waiting until it does – striking too early may be fatal – I say again, until that time comes you must busy yourself with amassing evidence, however piecemeal in substance. Don't forget that you have a witness, and, as a kinder twist of fate would have it, he lives local.' Mr Bolland opened a small drawer in his bureau. 'I already have the man's signed deposition, although I fear he knows more than he's committed to paper.' He handed me the single sheet with great care. 'There you have it, the signed testimony of our material witness, one William Winn, known in your part of the world as Little Willie or the Little Baked Man, the latter on account of his skin – very dark and much wrinkled.'

But fate hadn't been too kind. There were problems with this material witness, which Mr Bolland would have me know about at the outset. His character was blemished; he was a drunkard and a curser, a vagrant and associate of low criminal elements; a filthy creature of the gutter who, with like-minded men of his acquaintance, had a taste for unnatural sexual practices.

'It states here,' I said, being as careful with the paper as he had, 'that the informant saw the two blackguards follow Richard from the inn. If, as you say, he hails from Horseford, he was a long way from home that night.'

Mr Bolland grinned impressed. 'You are as sharp as Richard said you were. The clue is in what I have already told you of the man's appetites. It would seem that some illicit connection existed between Winn and one of the two assassins. Drink and excitement – he swears that he knew not what they were about – induced him to tag along on the back of one of their prancers.'

I read on to the bottom of the page, digesting the remainder of the testimony, to wit how the informant had been slumped in a dark corner of the tavern while the two men went about their business. Not half so drunk as they imagined, and fearing they would leave him stranded so far from home, he followed unbeknown in their wake. He thought little of the route they were taking as he followed them down to the river and its dank over-grown path. It was some distance more before he noticed another figure up ahead. The three were to merge in a brief scuffle before one man plunged into the water. Winn hid in thick undergrowth as the first pair returned and passed by his hiding place. There was no doubt at all, he said, that these were the two he had set out with earlier that night. By the time he reached the spot where the third man had gone in there was nothing to see save the murky water. He made his way home as best he could, learning the full truth later that week when, in the bar of the Old King's Arms, news of the young attorney's death had been broken by the landlord – now there surely was a man to watch – reading aloud from the *Leeds Intelligencer.*

And so it was that armed with my own copy of the vagrant's deposition (the attorney had made him sign two), I took my leave of Mr Bolland and rode home. We had parted on friendly terms with mutual pledges to meet again, but I knew on his part the enthusiasm was false and that he secretly hoped to be rid of me. For my own part, committed as I was to keeping my pledge, I couldn't help quaking in my stirrups. The bravado I had shown in Mr Bolland's study had worn off quicker than the drink, leaving just the cold reality of fear. And before me was the image I had glimpsed jagged and red among the coals. If the Devil had a face then surely this was it, yet the names he went by – Lucifer, Old Nick and Beelzebub – came and went from my lips like the snowflakes in the biting wind. The only name that stayed, as if it belonged there like a permanent sore, was Larkin's.

SIX

On arrival back I left my horse with George and went upstairs to change.

I was surprised to find in my washstand an uncommonly large spider with

spiky hairs upon its legs. Spiders, even the small ones, had never been to

my liking, which made my behaviour that afternoon all the more unusual.

I couldn't help myself at the time – the spider of its own accord, it

seemed, was willing me to keep him as a pet. My decision to do so I put

down to loneliness, or even perversity caused by worry and fatigue. Be

that as it may I had done it – caught the creature in a jar, a decision I

would come to regret.

Close on four, with the wind and sleet abated, I entered the gates of

Horseford Hall. A long broad avenue lined with beech trees led through

the grounds, where jays chattered at my intrusion and a stray pheasant,

fugitive no doubt from a recent battue, broke cover in the well-garnered

undergrowth. Further ahead a pair of peacocks was soon in sight,

walking with clumsy grace across the vast expanse of lawn. Their

indifference to my presence was absolute, a supercilious birdly disdain

reserved for unworthy visitors. And the venerable pile itself was by now in view, a large rectangular structure with ashlar facing and tall sash windows on three floors. It was the grandest house I had ever seen, a jewel of tranquillity of exquisite proportions there amidst nature tamed. The London town houses of the wealthy were nothing to this; however fine their construction, however noble their owners, the lurid taint of the city always spoiled their show.

Up a flight of steps, unexpectedly steep, I reached the front door; it was flanked by half-pilasters and topped by a generous fanlight. Before working the knocker I took a deep breath and cleared my throat. 'Sir Walter *is* expecting me,' I explained to the poker-faced, liveried footman who paused condescendingly on hearing my name and profession.

'Then you had better follow me,' he said at length, in affectedly polished tones which betrayed absurdly the flat, rounded vowels he had singularly failed to disguise.

I trailed in his wake through the high vaulted hallway, the clack of my shoes echoing on the black-and-white-chequered floor. From gilt-framed portraits on the panelled walls faces followed with wary eyes till we'd reached the door beyond. The footman held it ajar and we moved on down a dark corridor, at the end of which was another door. Here he halted, hemmed propitiatorily, and knocked just once.

'Come!' I heard from within, and the door opened on a spacious drawing room at the rear of the house. The fading daylight could be seen through a row of elegant casements, each almost level with the floor. Candles were already lit, their flames licking in ragged unison from the golden chandeliers and table candelabras; others lolled lazily from gilded sockets fixed beside the mirrors. Next the fire, in a blue-upholstered armchair, sat the master of the house, an open book resting delicately in the palm of his hand. He sat cross-legged, so stately and serene, the shapely calf of one fine leg bulging through its close-weave hose. His was the image of refined posture, the effortless pose of a man used to sitting for his portrait. I recognised him immediately from his likeness in the hall, realising it was *his* likeness that had watched me closest. The same hooded eyes were evident now, a family trait for sure.

'Mister John Eagle, to see you sir,' the footman announced in a docile tone.

'Ah, Mister Eagle, I'm so glad that you could come.' The Baronet snapped his book shut and rose abruptly to his lean-framed height of six feet. Aged forty or more, he wore his own hair dark but thinning at the temples, fastened at the back with a splay of purple ribbon. His coat was of dove grey, tight-fitting and cut away into curving tails. This he wore with a cream waistcoat, white breeches and stockings. Instead of the cravat he had opted for a stiff stock, which gave his long face, with its delicately pointed nose, something of a pinched look.

'Your servant, sir,' I said, returning his elegant bow as the footman left in deferential silence.

Sir Walter beckoned me nearer, saying with a sweeping confidence, 'Come, make yourself comfortable. Will you take a glass of sherry?'

I thanked him politely, seating myself in a fine soft armchair that looked out on to the copious park. Another peacock strutted proudly and spread its tail, the clink of glasses as Sir Walter busied himself with our drinks merging discordantly with its plaintive call.

'I trust you are settling in at Fink Hill House?' he asked as he headed towards me, the swishing of his garments unduly loud in the gaping expanse of the room.

'Yes – yes I am, thank you.'

He had seen straight through my hesitancy, reading behind it the lack of conviction. He nodded to himself as he settled back into his own comfortable chair. A smile parted his lips, and for a man of his years he had uncommonly fine teeth. 'I expect you are wondering why I asked you here?' Unlike Mr Bolland he was not for prolonging pleasantries.

'It *had* crossed my mind,' I said, catching his eye, whereupon we both smiled. In spite of his huge presence, the unbridgeable gulf in our stations, I sensed that we might be friends. There may not be love at first sight – though poor Richard would have said otherwise – but there is certainly friendship.

'Then let me explain,' Sir Walter said, finishing his sherry and rising for more. 'I've been making enquiries amongst my acquaintance in London. You will understand that I have a *large* acquaintance,' he added, rising with the bottle and topping up my glass. It went without saying that he was very well known and respected among the legal fraternity of the capital. Had Sir Walter chosen to leave his beloved Yorkshire, my old employer had once said, he could have risen with ease all the way to Lord Chief Justice.

'I can tell you that you come highly recommended,' he continued, pointing a friendly finger. 'Your attorneying is second to none. We are short of fine minds out here in the country.'

I thanked him for the compliment, squirming with embarrassed pleasure. 'You must enjoy the compliment,' he replied as he sat down once more. 'I'm not in the habit of bestowing them. You may never have another from me as long as you live.' His tone of fatherly badgering persisted as he went on, 'And yet I have summoned you – no, that's too strong, let's say *called* – you here today because I want to make you an offer. It is an offer I feel sure you will not refuse. In short,' he said, seeing off his second glass and smacking his lips, 'I want you for my agent. What say you to that?' He was staring vacantly into the empty vessel as if he were looking there for answer to his question. 'You'll have an annual salary of one-hundred pounds and, believe me, countless perquisites appertaining to the post.'

The magnitude of his offer amazed me, for he already had an agent in the shape of Mr Balme. Was he looking to make an additional appointment or was he about to do the unthinkable and name me as his replacement? I didn't have to wait long for my answer: 'Balme's getting too old for the post,' Sir Walter explained. 'The work demands a younger man and, I don't mind saying so, a more able one. He never was the right person for the job. Too much of a blusterer in complex situations, the mark of a man who is struggling to comprehend a problem. Attention to detail is often what's needed when dealing with tenants and their rights. Believe me, that man has lost me many an advantage. I'm weary too of all his flattery. No, my mind's made up,' he said, helping himself to more liquor. 'The position is yours – if you'll accept it.' He threw me a glance that brooked no resistance. Nor would I have dreamed of staging any: a position of that nature so early in my career was the stuff of wildest dreams.

'I accept, and with pleasure,' I said, rising to shake his hand.

He responded merely by filling my glass again and bidding me drink up. 'You will be aware, of course, that by accepting you will spawn an enemy in your bosom. Mister Balme will no longer be all kindness and smiles.' He smiled himself with cruel jest. 'That fact will distress you?'

'Hardly,' I replied grinning. 'I've scarce put a foot right since I lighted here. Both he and his mother despise me, though for what, exactly, I am at a loss to fathom.'

'Rest assured, they despise everybody,' said Sir Walter, 'and that includes me. Fools they are too for not realising, for I've known it all along. But come now, what should we expect from an old hag and her poison offspring? I trust that you are man enough to tolerate their displeasure?'

I assured him that I was, relieved all the same when Sir Walter announced that *he* would be the one to break the news. He would do so first thing in the morning when Abraham was due at the Hall to discuss an ejectment case. There would be no going back, he said, and I was to call again in the afternoon to discuss the nature of the post and the duties it entailed.

I was so thankful to the Baronet that I hadn't the nerve to mention that other, more distasteful news from Mr Bolland. Mention it I must but not yet: perhaps tomorrow or the day after that when I'd heard the rough music the Balmes. But even that prospect failed to dim the glories of my glowing sense of worth. Accordingly after dinner did I set to work, studying a manual I had brought from London on the art and practice of the land agent and steward. I supplemented this with detailed notes on how best to execute my new role, so that when I met with Sir Walter next day I would be able to impress him with my knowledge.

I had burnt the candle late, and at ten o'clock I strolled out into the village for a well-earned drink. The world, it seemed, was truly before me and I walked up Fink Hill tall and proud. I was blessed among men and loved myself much. Heads turned to look in admiration and wonder, if not in truth then for sure in my mind's eye. Such a handsome young man, such a fine figure and – haven't you heard? – Sir Walter Spencer-Stanhope has made him his agent! I fancied that even my spider loved me, grateful for the bread I had started to feed him on. Just my imagination surely, that look he appeared to give me, though the brain has a way with the truth sometimes that makes the world look strange. And as I turned the corner by the graveyard even little Horseford looked strange: tilted slightly, more uphill than usual and patched with coiling mist. Nothing normal at all save the glow of the inn lights, the sounds from within coarse and shrill like brass on brass.

I glanced from one murky form to the other: the Black Bull or the Old King's Arms: to which should I now repair? My pledge to Mr Bolland intruded, as I knew it would, and its weight could not be denied. The landlord at the King's was I man I must watch from now on but again that duty could wait. I was here to celebrate and must not court trouble. I chose the Bull without hesitation, finding there in the dim light Marshall Stables sitting alone with pipe and ale. The embarrassment was all on my part, for the doctor rose to greet me and called to the landlord for another pot.

Preliminaries over, he began to speak his mind. 'I want you to put what happened between us firmly in the past,' he said *sotto voce* as he poured me some ale. 'I see at a glance that it's been troubling you. I realise that your tastes don't usually run that way.' He held out his hand for me to shake. 'I feel that we can still be friends. What do you say?'

'I say very well and no hard feelings.' His disarming tone was impossible to refuse and, coming as it did from a medical man, added right and reason to his words.

'Capital John, capital,' and the two of us shook again. 'I've wrestled with this matter many times,' he said, as he puffed on his long clay pipe. 'I've come to the conclusion that there's no right or wrong of it, we are what we are. We have no control over our coming into this world, or whether in our make up we have this or that ingredient. We have different preferences, but *which* we have is not our fault. Short of the need to further the numbers of this God-forsaken multitude, I can see no reason why it should be one rather than the other.'

It was quite an outburst, and it was from the heart as well as the mind. *I* was an educated man, he had said, one above the multitude, who ought to understand. I did understand, I told him, or at least I tried to. What had happened betwixt us had left its mark, but for the sake of friendship it could be lived with. And I mustn't play the hypocrite; I had almost let it happen: indeed, part of me had wanted it to. I needed to face this flaw – nay, as Marshall would have it, this ingredient – in my being. I too was what I was. I must know myself, accept myself and not spurn the friendship that he offered. Befriending him could do me no harm and may even do me some good. My recent good news aside, I needed all the friends I could get. As for knowing myself inside out: it seemed at the moment that I knew myself less than ever. Great changes were afoot, not all of which I cared to own.

'So,' I said, completing the bridging process from my side of the divide, 'how goes it with the sick of this world? How is Phil? You have left him alone I presume. Do you not worry that he might burn down the house?'

'It's as I said before – the boy is calm and trustworthy…' – he glanced at me awkwardly – '…most of the time. I'm glad to see that your cuts have healed.'

'Thanks to you and your Bas...', I said, forgetting the name.

'Basilicum,' he said, setting me right.

'Perhaps next time I meet him he'll be more civil,' I said lightly.

Marshall nodded good humouredly. 'Perhaps.'

Perhaps, I mused, and a fleeting thought crossed my mind – did Marshall keep Phil partly for a certain purpose? Perhaps; perhaps not – either way it was not my business. I asked him again about his work, about his life in Horseford and whether he were happy there.

He said he was happy enough, though at a loss about the true meaning of the word. To be happy, one would have to exist in a state of heightened delirium. Like prolonging one's orgasms the effect on the heart would be intolerable. Better make do with a state of quiet contentment, a benevolent neutrality that made one settle for his lot. Yes, he had thought of moving on but had soon thought better of it. He had been to London many times; he had been to the continent once; but he had seen nothing in either, nor in countless towns up and down the land that induced him to think there was a better life than the one he led there, in small-minded, parochial Horseford. He loved it for its worthlessness in the great scheme of things.

But when I looked into his eyes, as striking as ever, I read behind them a sadness. He seemed to be mourning his own lack of fight, his own weariness of life. How could a man blessed with his advantages be left with such weak ambition? To hear him speak so dourly, to hear of his tiredness of worldly things, was to think prematurely of your own coffin. Refusing to be drawn by darker talk, I drank my beer to the bottom of the pot, poured some more and, seeing the jug near its end, called for another.

'No,' said Marshall, 'fetch us the brandy bottle!' He turned and looked at me firmly. 'We'll push that around instead, and you'll let *me* pay the reckoning.'

'Agreed, but on one condition – that you indulge in no more morbid talk. That you make merry, like a...'

He cut me short, still mournful but with his voice slurred with drink. 'Like a normal man?' Then, like the saviour of the moment, out it broke, a most beautifully rich laugh that made his eyes flash. 'Let us get drunk,' he said. 'Let us live for the night and the Devil take the morrow.'

'My sentiment entirely, but is that wise? – for a doctor, I mean?'

'It's more than wise, my dear fellow, it's damn near essential most of the time.'

'But what if,' I asked suddenly, 'one of your patients called you out? Come quickly doctor!' I mimicked, 'you are needed urgently! Remember Sukey when she fetched you for Mister Balme.'

Marshall leaned back nonchalantly in his chair, which creaked and strained on two legs. 'The fact that I was sober was mere accident. If drunk I had been, then drunk I should have gone to him,' he replied, leaning forward to add, 'and who's to say I wouldn't have done a better job?'

'You mean you might have killed him,' I said, and though the jest formed a smile on my lips, in my heart there was no laughter – just the strangest notion of imminent deed. My body felt hazy too and scarcely my own; I was sitting there, it seemed, with someone sharing my skin. And then a noise intruded, loud beyond its proportions – like a gun retort or the crack of artillery right beside my ear. Reality quickly overlapped and I soon realised my mistake: it was merely the landlord setting the brandy bottle clumsily down on the table.

'Begging your pardon sir,' he said with grudging apology.

'You see what I have to deal with here?' said Marshall, uncorking the stopper and glugging brandy into the glasses. 'I may treat them when they're ill, I may treat them *gratis* if they're poor and ill, administering to all their vile and smelly ailments as it behoves a man of conscience to do, but that's as far as it goes. They are not and never will be my social equals. They are my dirty, unwashed inferiors and neither they nor I must ever forget it.'

I was in the company of no radical, and in a different mood may have challenged his forthright views. I had done so with others in the past, and would do so again. Or would I? I had been honest with myself on one issue that night, so why not another? Was I really that much different from Marshall? Did my help for the poor really extend any further than offering them, free of charge, my professional services? Was it no more, at bottom, than a matter of conscience, a detached desire to see justice done? I realised now, as deep down I had always done, that I hadn't been sincere. Part of me *was* with Marshall: the dirty people of no name must be kept in their place. I was more suited than I had realised to being Sir Walter's man.

Time passed, and the fog of drunkenness thickened, just like the fog outdoors. I could see it through the window swirling of its own agitated volition. Could Marshall not see it too? 'No, what fog?' he answered when I asked. And the room, with its low ceiling, had begun to spin, and three Marshalls sat before me instead of one, when the door opened to reveal new custom. I half heard talk of a carriage that needed its wheel attending, whether a wheelwright could be engaged at this hour. I say *half* heard, for my mind was elsewhere, namely on the dark-haired woman who stood wrapped in furs by the door – a Lady, I guessed, for the landlord had hurried to debase himself, making a show of ridiculous bows and effeminate lifts of his long heavy apron. Of the others in her party – a Ladies Maid, a burly man who was probably her coachman and a black boy in garish livery – he took no notice. His attention, like mine, was centred on her Ladyship, on that voice with its richly feminine key: 'No, it is out of the question, we must not intrude on the Baronet's hospitality,' I heard it reply with surprising abruptness when he mentioned Sir Walter's name, connected as it was with more 'genteel' assistance. She never turned round, not once, but my eyes were drawn irresistibly. Though her back was towards me, this ermined star of mature years had made my loins sore.

Marshall was speaking throughout, his voice whirring about me in a breathy babble. I cared no more for it now than I would the Balmes' cats for I was lost in hopeless distraction. The woman seemed to sense my gaze, and though she never turned to look she stiffened her shoulders in acknowledgment and faintly tossed her head. It was only when she had gone that Marshall's words broke through: 'My dear fellow, you have not been listening to a word I've said.'

'No?'

'No, and I'm afraid you look to be in lust if not in love – an unalloyed beauty is she not?'

'It would seem so, and yet I never saw her face,' I said, half with regret and half with relief.

'Believe me, it would not have disappointed.'

'You know the Lady in question?'

'I know *of* her – and how robust her constitution must be for she has never called upon me for physick. As for calling here at the Black Bull, that will be the first and only time I'll hazard. Lady Larkin is not in the habit of…'

'Lady Larkin?' I interrupted. '*The* Lady Larkin?'

'There is only the one to my knowledge. And not to be meddled with if you know what's good for you.' Apposite his point was the dangerous speed with which they had fixed that carriage wheel – the coaching staff at the inn would have gambled fingers and thumbs so long as her husband was appeased. Long Larkin, warned Marshall, was a not a man to be crossed.

So I keep hearing, I reflected, but what about *Lady* Larkin? Those two words, whichever way round you said them – *Lady Larkin/Larkin Lady* – were oddly at variance – hard against soft, good against evil, beauty versus the beast. How could she marry such a man? – and how was I to match his towering stature? Match it I knew I must, but how, how how? – the word itself was a byword for pain. 'What am I to do?' I said, more to myself than to Marshall. 'You know I really think there might be love at first sight after all.'

'You may say so,' he said, rising with a look of concern. 'I think you need some air.'

'I agree.'

We were both unsteady as we walked out into the cold moonless night. Her Ladyship's carriage was indeed gone, and again I felt that regret mingled with relief.

'What am I to do?' I repeated.

'Like that fog you saw,' said Marshall, already sounding more sober, 'we must lay it at the door of drink.'

The fog had certainly gone, but not my fogginess of mind. 'I doubt I'll forget her in the morning.'

'You are not in London any more,' said Marshall in a schoolmasterly tone. 'If a man falls in the mud here, his dirty breeches are there for everyone to see. A man must heed the warnings.'

'But I want her,' I said, 'I can't help it.'

'My dear fellow, you can't be serious.'

I had slumped against the wall of the graveyard, scraping at the cold damp moss with both hands. 'That's just it, you see, I can't be this, I can't be that – I don't know what I can be any more. I don't know what I was, I don't know what I am now or what I might be in the future. I'm changing – almost as fast as they changed that wheel.' The graveyard itself, or something lurking there was drawing me; I knew I'd have to go inside even at *that* hour. Larkin's name was on my lips once more; it made them sticky like glue. My mouth would barely open; the Larkin glue refused to be expunged. I spoke with difficulty and in much pain: 'That man has got a hold on me.' Marshall nodded, as if he knew just *who*. 'You may not believe me but it's true,' and at that point I vomited upon the cobbles. My throat burned and the taste in my mouth was foul as brimstone.

'Take this,' Marshall said, handing me his pocket handkerchief. 'It's just the drink, I'm sure. Here, let me help you.'

'And I'm sure it's not the drink, but I wish to be alone. Go home Marshall – please,' I said, prizing away his fingers that grabbed my arm too fondly.

'As you wish, John, as you wish,' he said, turning wearily away.

His house was just across the street. I waited till he'd gone inside, till I'd seen his curtains dance with light and shadow, and entered the graveyard alone. I walked till I'd found its heart in the darkest densest quarter. I could smell the dead as I lowered my nose to the dank wet ground. They didn't bury them deep, I reasoned, and if I listened hard I might hear them whispering through the mouldering leaves. I felt welcome there, as I knew I would be. 'It won't be long before you're joining them,' I thought I heard one say, like the deepest, gruffest voice of the dead. And then on top, in a kind of counterpoint, Marshall's living tones as I'd heard them in the Bull: 'As you wish, John, as you wish.'

'Yes,' I answered, 'but what *do* I wish?' A righter of wrongs done to others, I was nevertheless drawn to committing them myself. I was seeing that same self in a new light, a self that could do harm and wrong with no real thought of contrition. It was hard versus soft again, good against evil, beauty and the beast. I saw myself clearly as a man of two halves, a human moiety of black and white, share and share alike. As for the half that seemed to be winning, my actions that night left me in no doubt.

I rested on my haunches, my back against a gravestone marking the spot where one Daniel Vine of that parish had been laid to rest in 1754. It was the year of my sorry birth, the start of my sorry climb to this unChristian juncture. And now the chill of the dead-blessed air roused me almost to nakedness. I wanted to be naked, exposed, pleasured and flogged for my shame. I was sick at heart, disgusted at the creature I was letting myself become. Dear God, how was I reduced to this? What putrefaction of soul has taken its hold on me? Befittingly an angel amongst the graves seemed to point down at me in outrage. The image, fashioned in shining white stone, had a terrible stare that was all punishment. Suddenly, I felt my own sense of outrage – how dare it judge me? – offer me no redemption? I'd not be judged, I'd not be punished, neither by it nor what it represented.

I resolved to piss on its disapproval, watching with fascination as the wetness spread across its sculptured robes. Then, glimpsing the church through the trees, I confronted that greater displeasure, throwing down a challenge to the Lord, daring Him punish me for the sacrilege committed on His consecrated ground. I had no desire to be redeemed, and that voice I had heard was urging me to go further, *much* further in my renouncement of God. Hadn't Marshall said so himself? – *let the Devil take the morrow.* Thus did I do it, the unthinkable: I pleaded with the Devil to enter my heart, to blacken my soul as much as He liked so long as I reaped some reward – so long as I rose in the world fast and sure.

I shook away the droplets and re-buttoned myself, expecting only silence – the sort I'd received from God many a time when I'd pleaded for a sign from above. But this time came that voice again, clear as a bell in my head: Go home now, it said in gruff and manly tones, go home to your creature in the jar.

SEVEN

I slept late next day, and missed my breakfast. Abraham had left early on money-scrivening business, and his mother had breakfasted in her chamber. My late stirring was noticed only by Sukey, who left me in peace as bid when she'd knocked at my door. I had slept badly in my drunken state, troubled all night by my visit to the graveyard. Monstrous visions taunted me from the curtains, frightening me so much that I had risen in a cold sweat to check that the pattern was indeed just flowers and not so many grinning faces. Becalmed at last by the peeping dawn, I had slumbered fitfully for an hour and risen with a weight on my mind. The weight was female, older than me by ten years and much more beautiful. Though I hadn't seen her face I knew it would not disappoint. See it I must very soon, and I had in that piece of business of hers the perfect excuse to call. Which is why I was sweating again, and no less profusely than I'd done in the night. The image of her husband was like a red hot surface I dared not touch. And if that weren't enough, there was also the problem of my spider.

I didn't need reminding what the voice had said: go home to your

creature in the jar. It was only now, when I had risen, that I summoned

the nerve to look at it, as if I'd needed, for my sanity's sake, the cold light

of day. But there he was, more real than ever, and so much larger than

he'd looked before. And more to my horror, if that were possible, was

the substance he was living in – a slimy deposit not unlike human sperm.

The creature itself seemed delighted with the new arrangement, rolling on

its back in the thicker, curd-like part and appearing to sup of the whey.

But was it really exactly as I saw it? – might I not be drunk still with a

gallon of brandy on the brain? No, I decided, he was real enough, real

enough to make me shiver. Just what did it all mean and who, if anyone,

could I tell? I was shamed to speak of him even to Marshall, nay, even to

Tom. I knew too that I must cease to feed him forthwith and hide him

away where he couldn't be seen.

It was near ten when I finally quit my room. I had washed

superficially, making up for my laxity with queued hair, new coat of

black worsted and a pair of white stockings ribbed with red and blue.

First stop was the steamy kitchen at the rear of the house where, from

Fanny the cook, I demanded some bread and a dish of tea. I bid her cut a

second slice for Tom and lather it thick with butter. She did so

reluctantly and threatened to tell the mistress when she came downstairs.

This I'd have none of, saying that if she breathed a word of what I'd made her do – and would make her do every day from now on – I would dream up a charge and have her brought before a magistrate. It was a hollow threat but it worked. Not only did she give me the bread, she threw in an oat cake and another dish of tea for good measure. These I carried through to Tom, who looked as starved as ever on that high-stool, drawing and engrossing his first long deed of the day. He seemed asleep in the sheer routine of his work as I gave him the victuals with a smile.

The old man's mouth opened slowly in surprise; it was like watching a slit visibly widen in a piece of over-ripe fruit. 'Thank you,' he replied, his face reborn in the smile, becoming young again for an instant.

'Now eat, drink and...' – I hurried back to my office and returned with the coals – '...be warm.'

'You're a bobby dazzler,' Tom said, biting the bread though his gums did most of the work.

'I'm your friend Tom,' I said, emptying coals on the paltry fire, which crackled and spat like well-basted meat.

Tom's glow soon began to fade. 'Aye lad, friend to him that needs one,' he said, as the careworn look returned. 'I wonder if it'll always be so.'

There was mystery in his words I was too yet befuddled to decode. 'Yes it will,' I said, with impromptu optimism. 'From now on, my destiny is your destiny. My good fortune will be your good fortune. Should I rise in the world you must attach yourself to my coat tails.'

Tom Gill looked at me long and hard, saying at last, 'And you *will* rise, won't you? Yes,' he said, considering, 'I see that now most plainly...But there are things I might do that could make your rise difficult. You see lad, your coming here has awakened things in me that I thought were dead. For years now I've known the future, mainly because there wasn't any. Things unfolded just how I knew they would. I no longer have that foresight. Rather like the northern weather, I've become unpredictable.'

Here was more mystery, which I was determined to make light of. 'I rather like unpredictable weather. Yesterday cold and clear...' – though not quite, I remembered with unease – what about that fog? – '...today mild and windy, *very* windy.'

'You call this a wind?' cried Tom, in a challenging voice that startled me. '*I* remember the great wind of '39. Now that *was* a wind.' He chortled to himself. 'They say whatever goes up must come down. Well I tell you this: there were things blown upwards in that wind that have not come down to this day, and some blown so far they defy comprehension. Take my mother's undergarments for instance – blown from a washing line in Pudsey all the way across the Pennines to Burnley. They were found by a travelling tinker whose cart overturned when they landed in his face. And that's the gospel truth,' he said, catching my eye as he said so, 'may I be struck down dead right now with this piece of bread in my mouth.'

The riddles in his talk were multiplying, interlarded as they were with levity. But his tone was adamant and I dared not voice an obvious question – how had he known it was *his* mother's clouts that had caused the tinker to crash? I left him to his memories instead and went to do some work.

I got little done, merely a letter to our agents to send Yorkshire *Latitats* in actions for debt, the perusal of a suit in Chancery threatened for this Hilary Term. The case was a complex one that needed Counsel's opinion. Sir Walter would give me what I wanted, I hoped, when we met that afternoon. In the meantime I would advise the client that filing the Bill in the Court of Exchequer would be cheaper than an action in Chancery, but that the cheaper option by far was to file a Bill in neither. Much better that the matter be settled amicably with the other party directly or, failing that, via arbitration of independent gentlemen. A letter to that effect, with instructions to Tom that he send them by the day's post, was as far as I got. Shortly after twelve I fell asleep at my desk, waking on the rudest terms to Balme's angry face.

'So this is how you behave when I'm out,' he fumed, a fleck of hot spittle finding my eye. 'If Sir Walter could see you now – snoozing away your working hours like the sleeping rat that your are – I wonder if he'd be so eager to employ you then? Yes,' he added, nodding with dilated nostrils, 'I know all about your little game, Mister Eagle, how you've charmed your way in to his favour, persuaded him to – God knows, God *only* knows! how you did it – persuaded him to give you my position. A position I was not at all yet ready to relinquish, a position that was to furnish me with a steady income in my retirement. You've robbed me of it with your youthful flattery and fine London talk. Well, you may have taken *him* in, but I know the truth – that he's a bigger fool than I could ever have given him credit for, and you, you – you're a man of base principles, the most underhand, scheming little miscreant I've ever had the misfortune to set eyes on...'

'I won't stay here and be insulted,' I said, rising and brushing past. 'But while we're on the subject,' I added, pausing at the door, 'don't talk to me of base principles. I've read through your books, Abraham, and I know the way you work. I've seen how you mislead clients, entice them down the costliest path. You've never been one for recommending compromise. Quite the contrary – you're the most litigious attorney I've ever come across. And then there's your charge for conveyancing. Three cheers for wasteful duplication! You're nought but an old shark!' and I left him and slammed the door, thinking of that image, so appropriate, on his whitewashed chimney-breast.

I felt uplifted by my diatribe never mind what Balme might do. And what *would* he do? – try to terminate our partnership? No, hate me as he did the old rascal needed me as much as I needed him. We were a crutch to each another, one that bruised the armpit nonetheless. I reminded myself of that promise to bide my time, to build up sufficient clients to branch out on my own. That opportunity would surely come, and if anyone were to end the partnership before its time, that person would be me.

I had crossed the street by now and found myself on noble ground for the second time in two days. The peacocks whined incessantly as I made my way up the avenue where, on either side, trees swayed in the stormy wind. It felt good to be alive, but only in a bitter sense. That graveyard nearby was still a thorn. Death, I reflected, came to every living thing, no matter how alive and seemingly invincible. We were all gone tomorrow, with nothing to be done. Human beings – even Sir Walter – were mayflies on a grander scale. I saw him standing up ahead with two younger figures – his offspring, I supposed – mounted at his side. Imposing as he was in his genteel stature, I knew that he also would end as dust. Horseford Hall too, its stately walls would one day crumble and collapse. There was, I decided, a terrifying pointlessness to life. What did anything matter if such as he, who had reached the zenith of human aspiration, would one day vanish? And if such was our meagre destiny, why bother a single day to strive and endure? Why should I, so young, so ambitious, dream so longingly of worldly success? To be driven by the urge to succeed, to rise in the law until I'd reached the heights scaled by Sir Walter, to enjoy the life that he enjoyed with numerous servants and a fine chaise and pair – what did any of it signify?...

Sir Walter had espied me and waved, bidding farewell to the riders with a slap of their horses' rumps. They rode at a gallop, one male, one female, forking each side of me as they passed, laughing together with an arrogant lilt, the male whipping his beast as he bobbed disdainfully in the saddle. Pride before a fall, I reflected, happy to unhorse him and thrash him with his own whip. As for the girl, who rode an insolent side-saddle, there was striking beauty in her cruel visage. I wondered if our paths might one day cross, and rather hoped they would – only a dribbling fool in his dotage wouldn't want to fuck her at first sight. Yes, that's the spirit, John, enjoy life while you can!

'You must excuse my wayward kin,' declared Sir Walter, stepping forward to greet me. 'They have all the advantages of their position but few of the graces. I fear God has punished me for naming them so flippantly.' He had named them March (him) and October (her) after his favourite months. Each had lived up to their name – 'Frequently stormy,' he explained, not without affection and a good deal more of pride. They were my own favourites too, those months, and he seemed delighted to hear it. 'Come then,' he said, taking my arm, 'let us walk in the grounds and enjoy this fine wind. Not a March or October wind, but one to be relished nonetheless.'

We talked inconsequentially at first – of the landscape, of nature and such like. We came presently to Abraham and how ill he had taken his news. There being little to add, however, other than time heals all wounds, we were soon discussing my duties. I was willing to begin immediately – that ejectment case, for example, Sir Walter had mentioned earlier.

'Good man,' said the Baronet, slapping me heartily on the shoulder. 'Very good man indeed.'

We returned a while to trivialities – the windy weather; Tom's story about his mother's underwear, which made Sir Walter laugh; the numerous statues that littered the grounds. He explained his liking for such adornments, how he valued in particular those which his gardeners had hidden so that Sir Walter, on his perambulations, might come upon them unawares in delighted surprise. 'Here is a case in point,' he said, as we turned a corner into an overgrown section dense with bracken and weeds. 'It never ceases to startle me.' The well-secluded Hercules startled me too, for I didn't see it until I'd cracked my ankle on the plinth and tripped over the figure's spiny club. I was in the wars too over a sleeping nymph, and the smallest grotto of marbled stone. One came upon its low doorway so much unawares there was no time to duck. I had a lump on my head to prove it and was heartily glad to be out on the grass again.

Conversation returned now to weightier things. I was keen to sound Sir Walter out, find out where he stood on the nature of justice, how far the writ of the law should, and did, run. Mr Bolland's words still boiled within me and needed to lose their heat. The only way was to say them out loud. I did exactly that, barely pausing for air as I told him of Richard's death, who was responsible, and why, according to Mr Bolland, nothing was likely to be done.

Sir Walter stared fixedly ahead as I spoke. When I'd finished he pointedly began to talk pleasantries again, drawing my attention to a solitary crow blown perilously across the parkland on the buffeting breeze. I made no answer, and he clearly sensed my impatience. Our tread was slowing now and tacitly we both halted. Sir Walter drew a silver snuff-box from his coat, opened the clasp and applied a generous pinch to each nostril. Returning the box to his pocket, he produced an embroidered handkerchief emblazoned red with his family crest (a gloved hand) and blew his nose ostentatiously loud. The delay in his reply was intolerable.

'These are difficult times,' he said at length. 'They call for extraordinary measures.'

I didn't follow his meaning, and said so. He glanced my way for the first time in minutes, saying after a sigh, 'We are at war now, are we not?'

'Yes,' I replied, with a puzzled shrug.

'This is no ordinary war, John. Its dangerous doctrines are finding root even in remote shires such as this. Why, I can name a dozen influential renegades around Leeds alone. To Liberty in America Triumphant – such is their toast over port at dinner. It is most regrettable and it's got to stop. We need all the help we can get, however unintentional.' He looked at me and smiled wryly. 'I see I am still not making myself clear. Then I shall deal more plainly, and trust we'll see eye to eye.' To emphasise his point, he narrowed his eyes in a searching glance for solidarity. 'As individuals, we better sort of men do as we like. If you said that we get away with murder you'd be nearer the truth than you imagine. Such is the way of the world, the common populace think, if they ever think at all. They would not dare, would not know how to criticise our affairs, which are not for the likes of them. Their hatred is reserved only for one another. But as I said before, these are abnormal times, and people may be manipulated. Consequently we need the help of our friend Edward Larkin.'

'Then it's true – you know all about him after all!'

Sir Walter laughed. 'My dear young sir, do you give us no credit? We have known these past five years. Be sure of it, had it not been for the war we would have crushed him by now. We tolerate him only because it is convenient to do so. 'Tis unfortunate he should have chosen counterfeiting the coin of the realm as his principal vocation, but that cannot be helped...'

'Coining is a treasonable offence,' I interrupted in dismay. 'You allow him to practise it openly?'

'If only things were that simple,' replied Sir Walter, stabbing the earth with his nigger's head cane. 'You are clearly unfamiliar with the vagaries of the coining laws.'

I was more familiar with their working than he imagined, though I listened to what he had to say. He explained how the practice of clipping and counterfeiting gold coin had divided the community. The yellow trade, as it was known locally, enjoyed much support. Many people, particularly weavers and woolcombers hit by the late depression, supplemented their incomes by clipping guineas and moidores. Even the big wool manufacturers and merchants were in on the trade, putting out gold coin to their workers for clipping as they would do wool for working up into cloth. Larkin purchased all the clippings produced, and turned them into coin at Gravehunger Lodge, known colloquially as the 'Horseford Mint.' He would even pay a generous premium to those who would lend him good gold coin for clipping. The coin Larkin produced had an intrinsic bullion value not far short of legitimate coin, and was acceptable locally because of the chronic cash shortage that had dogged the area for many years. The government was to blame for the shortage, and people knew it.

'So you see,' said Sir Walter resignedly, 'to move against Larkin now would upset a delicate equilibrium. And to try, and then fail, would be far more dangerous than not to try at all. As I have said already, there is growing opposition to the government hereabouts. A mishandled coining charge might boost that opposition.' He added that it was difficult enough to force a conviction in better times, for they had failed against Larkin before in a capital coining case, when he was acquitted against the evidence at Lent Assizes 1774. The evidence had looked sound indeed:

the discovery at his home of a hammer, fixed block, rollers and crucibles: equipment suitable for coining, which he could have no occasion for in his usual business. But the jury, as usual, were mostly middling men of property who handled large amounts of gold coin and were familiar with the inadequacies of the Royal Mint.

I could not let the heady mixture I'd heard go without a protest. I still had principles, or at least I thought I had. 'Where, in the meantime, is justice?' I asked.

'Where indeed,' reflected Sir Walter. 'Perhaps in the end it is no more than an ideal. We magistrates must dispense it as we think fit.'

'It all sounds so ordinary,' I said, struggling to speak my mind. 'I thought he was more than that you've made him out to be.'

'Ah,' said Sir Walter,' I suppose you think there should be more. You've no doubt heard the stories people tell about him.' There was distance in his hooded eyes, a hint of admiration in his voice. 'He is certainly a cruel and masterful man – unworldly in some respects – some would say *other*worldly – possessed of occultist powers to steer men's thoughts. All nonsense you understand, this business of the supernatural,' and for the first time in a long time it felt exactly so, a series of trifles of the mind.

'And *Lady* Larkin?'

'Why mention *her* name? You think it pertinent to your case?' It was a sharp retort, its stinging tone uncalled for. I'd read impatience in his voice, frustration too and something more, I didn't know what. 'My apologies, John, you must excuse my manner,' he said presently. He pleaded pressure of work, as I had done of late apropos the balance of my mind. I knew the contagion well, a switching of mood from light to black, though my mind right now was stable. I'd thought to tell him of my own dark forces, not to mention dark *voices* and a certain spider in a small glass jar.

I was glad that I didn't do so, for I'd surely have been ridiculed by this man whose feet were always on the ground, whose head was never in the clouds, though it did have its own – very earthly – secrets. *Earthly,* I say, for a stark sense of realism was in the air, ubiquitous, potent with its own overwhelming mundanity. I felt relieved yet also disappointed. The feeling was, that nothing else ever would or ever had gripped mankind but mere ordinariness in the here and now; reality itself was unsettlingly fixed, nought else but the sky above and the shabby earth below. Only the natural existed; the *super*natural was impossible, a far off dream of acute proportions no man of sense should court. I felt it again, relief mingled with disappointment. Perhaps, like justice, it was no more than an ideal, there to be countenanced as sane men saw fit. But I wanted more to contend with than earthly tasks, earthly mysteries – I wanted to tempt fate. It was as if, deep down, I wanted to be mad, a candidate, like Phil, for York Asylum. Was it this, a fellow sufferer, he had recognised and attacked? Again, as I had done so often lately, I tried to take refuge in my own version of worldly things. Some of them had spice and interest; one of them at least had a selfless motive: 'And what of my friend, murdered probably at Larkin's hands?' I asked of Sir Walter, knowing I must press him more.

He shook his head with affected solemnity. 'Very regrettable, and you have my commiserations. And believe me, John, you will have your revenge too as soon as the emergency is passed. We will tolerate Larkin not a moment longer than is necessary. He *is* a dangerous irritant, and needs to be nipped in the bud. He has murdered your friend, you say, and I must believe you. More worrying for us, he has divided the community in a new way. Normally, we can make do with the usual scapegoats, which the people turn on rather than us.' He laughed bitterly at the *poorer sort of people.* 'If only they'd the sense to realise that those gypsies, blackamoors and Jews spring from the same filthy loins as themselves. But how can we expect them to realise it when they haven't even the sense to blow on their porridge?'

The truth hurts and I felt its power as a sharp pain. I too, when I stripped away my outer skin, felt the same as he did. What lurked at the heart of me, however, was something far worse than instinctively-shared philosophy; it was a frightening emptiness with little care how it was filled. In the name of ambition I might swallow anything: in short, I had my price. Sir Walter was in need of a good man, an able man whom he could trust to run his estate. Reading between the lines, imbibing the subtle scents of his talk, I sensed there would be added riches – perhaps riches I had only dreamed of – if that same good man proved right in every way. I was determined to be that good man, to become, like Sir Walter, not the poorer sort, not even the middling sort – why should I settle for that? – but the better sort of man. I told the Baronet he need look no further for his loyal associate in all respects.

Sir Walter's smile was scarcely perceptible. 'Then take my hand, John Eagle,' he said, proffering his own, 'and come *fully* into the fold.'

He had emphasised the word *fully,* and during our walk back towards the house I understood why. As our talk turned to matters of the law – that Chancery case on which I sought his opinion – he mentioned what he'd heard from Balme that I suffered the poor too gladly. Like love across the social divide, the poor were to be pitied from afar, he said, not from across the desk where time was paid for and not dispensed for free. He trusted I would soon rethink my attitude and take another more befitting my station. The willingness to please still uppermost in my mind, I told him that I *would* rethink it, that I'd been naive in my professional outlook.

'We all have our puppy fat to shed,' he said jovially. 'The sooner we shed it, the better.'

We parted very amicably, he genuinely so because he thought he had found his loyal servant, I still masking my inner turmoil. True, I had found my patron and need only serve him well in order to rise in the world. Try as I might, however, I couldn't go easily into that comfortable fold. The path was strewn with thorns, each a matter of conscience. Not quite an empty vessel after all then; principles I had, however ill-defined. There was also the question of Richard, who ought to have justice *now,* not when some great man thought he should have it. It was the old duality again: cowardice versus bravery, fair play versus selfishness and callous disregard. And one thing more was true: true for me, whether mad or sane: the darkness and the light would battle inside for months to come. As for which might win, not even I would risk a wager.

EIGHT

I commenced my duties for Sir Walter ruthlessly enough, beginning with that ejectment case he had mentioned, which turned out to be an elderly couple for non payment of rent. The ejectment I executed swiftly, writing to state Sir Walter's reasons – that one month's rent arrears was sufficient cause – and giving them notice to quit by the end of the month, with no compensation for improvements they had made to land and farm buildings. Quit they did, and I tried not to be moved by the account I heard of them leaving on foot in heavy rain, carrying their meagre belongings as they walked to Troy Hill Workhouse at the western extremity of the village.

I was equally implacable in the case of Josiah Sutcliffe, a young tenant farmer on Sir Walter's estate who had refused to pay a small yearly rent for use of a spring that arose in a neighbour's land. Sutcliffe, now facing an action at law, lacked neither steel nor intelligence. He argued that the suit should be brought not against the tenant but the landlord to whom he paid his quarterly rent for use of a farm 'with all conveniences there appended.' That the man had a case was as obvious to Sir Walter as it was to me, but without help his resistance was useless. Needless to say I offered him no advice. More than that, I told him no attorney would touch his case, lacing my letter with appropriate quirks to show that the action was undefendable, that additional rent had been paid by the incumbent time immemorial and had reached such a state of unshiftable usage and custom that not even the most eminent Special Pleader could find a way round it. Sutcliffe succumbed and paid what was due.

It soon became clear that Sir Walter's ruthlessness arose from his misguided belief that his tenants were not sufficiently afraid of him. Occasional lapses on rent days stemmed, he believed, along with other misdemeanours, not from hardship but wilful disobedience. That the hurt done was invariably petty did not matter to the Baronet; it was the principle that counted, and any act of firmness on my part helping to rectify the position was generously rewarded over and above my already ample salary. A stiff letter might earn me an extra five shillings, an oral warning the same, while an action for trespass or poaching prosecuted with vigour might bring me as much as a guinea.

There was temptation to work solely for Sir Walter and neglect my other work, which as yet paid little. This I refused do, and for my own sake as much as my clients I accepted the lot of a country practiser. I had much still to learn and variety of business served me best. By careful planning both mainstream and agency business was accommodated. For a while too I managed successfully another incongruity in my work: the juxtaposition of principle and greed. I continued to handle *gratis* the occasional pauper case that came my way. Risking my patron's displeasure I went even further at times, speaking out against injustice on my own doorstep – the reputed mistreatment of bastard children at the workhouse; the miserable plight of child sweeps; the iniquities of slavery – always aware, as I did so, of the hypocrite within me: that he who denounced others with such venom had sold his soul to Sir Walter for so many pieces of silver; a man who, should it come to it, would defend his patron's right to do whatever he liked with bastards, child sweeps and ominously-coloured blacks. I was tangled in a knot of my own making but it couldn't last. Something had to give – and soon.

That my battle between good and evil raged on a wider front became clear two weeks later when I rode out on law business towards the tiny hamlet of Lighthazzles. The moors had been heavily misted, causing me to stray from the beaten track. Hopelessly lost, I dismounted at the door of a small white cottage hoping to ask the way. The old battered door, loose on its fish-strap hinges, was answered by a woman with long black hair and small blue eyes whose pupils narrowed to a pin-prick. Her skin was thick and deeply-wrinkled, like the cracks in hardened clay. Though I'd never seen her before, she seemed to know me and beckoned me in. The pull of her presence was equalled only by its opposite – the power of my own will to stay upon the threshold. I stood awhile, I don't know how long, fixed in the present, remembering the past. It was the moors again, just as they were that first time when I'd crossed them in the coach. Then the force had been invisible – more breath of wind than tangible flesh and blood. Here the power had a visible source – and in daylight not in dark. I was inside before I'd realised, standing on that cold earth floor hardened with bull's blood.

The cottage itself comprised a single room with a ladder to the loft. The furniture was common and crude: two rush-bottomed chairs, a deal table with some dishes and cups, a three-legged stool low upon the floor. In the far corner was an old bedstead, whereupon some sacking and straw served for bedding. The only inviting feature was the inglenook fire glowing brightly in its brazier. As I watched the red-raw twinkling of the coals I was put in mind of brutal torture, of human flesh torn asunder with scorching tongs.

My strange host had read my mind: 'The brazier reminds you of cruelty,' she said, watching me intently with eyes grown dark and heavy, all pupil now in full reversal, two black beads, oily like a crow's, and I thought of the bird stuffed and silent on Jackie England's sill. She drew towards me so that we stood only inches apart. 'Robert Francois Damiens – Oh, how he suffered. They took hours to kill him, twenty years ago in the heart of Paris. The pain, the terror, the burning glow of coals – crowd cheered as the blood spurted, and where is the sufferer now? – in heaven or hell and who is this creature who sleeps on that filthy bed?' She was speaking my thoughts as they came, word for word, her voice a replica of my own. 'Cruelty interests you,' she said, reverting to herself at last. 'It repels but it also attracts. Deep down you have a taste for it – just like the Romans of old.'

It was true, at least in part: the Damiens execution had fascinated me ever since I'd read of it in the *Gentleman's Magazine*. But how could she know such things and what did it all mean? 'Who are you?' I felt drained of strength, rather as a fly must feel when paralysed by a spider's venom. 'Are you really *it* – the spider?' I asked unwittingly aloud.

'You may call me that if you wish. Appearances, as you know, can be deceiving.' She squared up to me, and placed her hands on my shoulders. 'How easily you have succumbed,' she said, with something of a smile. It was only now that I realised her face had changed, the switch occurring with the hazy swiftness of a dream. Her lips were purple, marked with the rippled texture of freshly-dug worms. Beyond them was her mouth, replete with all the blackness of a pit. So much for normality, for the tedious reality of Sir Walter's park that day! Our natural talk was almost forgotten now; in its place, as if forever, a stark and vengeful other. 'Please,' I said. 'Let me go.'

She stroked my cheek, her fingers ingrained with dirt. 'Why go, John Eagle, when your prayer has been answered?'

'*What* prayer?' I said, forcing a false scoff.

Word for word she quoted my plea in the graveyard: 'Enter my heart, blacken my soul as much as you like so long as I reap some reward, so long as I rise in the world fast and sure. You thought nobody had heard,' she said, her lips parted around that dark chasm. 'Oh, but they *did* hear, and the pact was made the moment your words were uttered. The Master has never refused a plea when it has come from the heart.' She had mentioned the *Master*, and she hadn't meant a Master in Chancery, devils though they must have seemed to those whose suits dragged on for years.

I slapped my hands to my face, ran anguished fingers high up my forehead and dislodged my hat. 'But I never meant...'

'Shush, my dear,' said my succubus host, drawing me to her breast which was hard as flint, 'enjoy the fruits he brings.' She sealed the deal with a kiss, withdrawing those wormy lips to ask: 'Have you not felt them already?' There was no need to answer; I knew in an instant to what she referred: my appointment to Sir Walter had been no chance windfall.

'Unfortunately, you are not yet finished,' she said, drawing away in faint pique and bending to poke the fire. Her ragged black dress, bunched in a dovetail at the back, fluttered as she worked. 'The scales have tipped but not wholly so. Not wholly so and not fast enough for he that's sent me hither.'

'*He* being?' but she did not answer me straight.

'There are a few solid ounces of goodness left that are stubborn and refuse to move,' she said, as she straightened up, poker-in-hand. 'To blacken all will require more work, some further sweating till you're fully debased.'

'Like bad coinage,' I said. 'How apt that you should use such a metaphor. Will you not now speak his name?'

'There's no need,' she said, turning towards the door. 'You have heard it often enough – too much, I'm sure you'll say. A man like him never questions the evil he does. You, though, are different.' She opened the door, which moaned on its hinges. A dozen yards from the house the mist had gathered in one great billowing cloud. I fancied among it the shape of a man, tall with much bulk, a sword hanging at his hip. 'You are crossing over from the other side. There is great rejoicing for such as you. Hence the powers that may be your reward.'

Relieved as I was to be free to go, I was to carry away an indescribable burden, a hundred questions with only this one voiced: '*What* powers?' I asked, when I'd read in her eyes, pin-pricked again as they'd been at the start, a firm instruction to leave.

'Powers in proportion to your badness,' she replied, her hunched figure framed by the doorway. 'Never fight evil with goodness or your powers will desert you. Would that he had found you earlier, before the lines were crossed and tangled. I see a great conflict ahead, whose outcome is uncertain.'

I mounted my mare in much confusion, my head aswirl like the mist. There was no need to pinch myself; reality now was as real as the soil beneath my horse's hooves. Daisy whinnied fretfully, and I leaned over to stroke her neck: familiar sound and familiar action jarring against the oddness of the minutes just passed. I forced myself to look down from the saddle. The woman nodded to me just the once – less of a parting gesture than an aide memoir to all that she had said. 'Follow their sound,' she said solemnly, as a pair of magpies rattled their call from out of the mist. 'They will guide you where you wish to go.'

I could scarce remember where I *did* want to go, and as I headed away towards the magpies' chatter my memory continued to fail. But the mist was thinning fast, and as it did so the sound of the birds was no more. I rode at a fair gallop without any noise in my ears. Not even the sound of Daisy's hooves, or the creak of the saddle or the flapping of the bags at my side. There was only silence, that muffled deadness following heavy snow. Gradually the mist spread aside, widening to a clearing bright and blessed by sun. I saw hills of gorse and heather, above them a sky that was clear except for cloud – good old cloud, up there on high where it belonged. Nestled in the valley on my left was a dark-stoned settlement of a dozen houses. Sounds again now as well as vision. Chimneys smoked, and the disordered noises of a workshop reached me on the breeze: Lighthazzles, and I knew of a sudden just where I was headed. Ten o'clock in the forenoon, my pocket-watch said, the very hour I was due at the house of Ely Rhodes, worsted manufacturer of that place; the very hour I had called at the cottage of 'the Lighthazzles witch.'

The business that had brought me those eight miles distant was ordinary enough: a case of bad debt. Descending the steep path that led down to the hamlet, I found Mr Rhodes at home in a commodious cottage aside his workshop. The rhythmic clack of his looms filled my ears as I tethered the mare and knocked upon his stout black door. His young but portly wife, who answered, directed me to a small sitting room-cum-office at the rear of the building. Here, where the weaving sounds were still faintly audible, I found the clothier seated before a writing bureau, his back to a roaring fire. 'Welcome!' he said rising, introducing his wife of half his three score years and bidding her fetch some refreshment.

I seated myself as directed, and made pleasant talk about the noises and smells of textiles, the vagaries of the post which had made his first letter miscarry, and finally the inclemency of the weather. 'Mist? – what mist? The air's been clear upon the moor all morning,' he exclaimed in surprise.

'Perhaps it was just a small patch lurking in a hollow,' I replied, feeling foolish and unable to look him in the eye. Not surprisingly, my appetite for the law was in abeyance and I found it hard to concentrate. Fumbling for my pocket-book to lessen my discomfort, I produced a stub of pencil and suggested a start on his business.

The manufacturer sensed my unease. His big ruddy face, its cheeks and forehead cracked and creased, contorted into puzzled displeasure. No supernatural aid was needed to know just what he was thinking: that so far he was singularly unimpressed with this young attorney of budding reputation. The arrival of his wife with bread and cheese and a jug of ale gave us both a welcome respite. Having fortified myself with a generous pull, I was ready to press on.

'Pray tell me how I may be of assistance,' I began, when his wife had left anew. 'Rest assured that I will endeavour to get something done with all imaginable expedition.'

'Thank you,' he said in a neutral tone as he placed his large hands, corned and callused, on the table. 'You might like to use this,' he added, handing me a small penknife when he saw, with disappointment, that my pencil was blunt. He waited till I'd sharpened the lead before giving me the details of his problem. There was a considerable sum owing to him on mortgage from a person that lived in my locale. When the year's interest that was due had been added to the principal the amount owed stood at £525, and the whole debt should have been discharged on 13th November last. Mr Rhodes' previous attorney, the late Mr Rider of Halifax, had pressed the debtor to no avail shortly before his death, suggesting that a suit at law was now the only remedy.

'That would be a great pity,' I said, as I noted down the particulars. 'I would always recommend that you try to settle the matter in an amicable manner between yourselves. Avoid the law if you possibly can, for you will find her a costly machine.'

'I need no reminding of that fact, Mister Eagle,' said the clothier, sipping his ale. 'But when there's no other way, and the client's possessed of the means.'

'I take it that his circumstances have been enquired into?' I asked as a matter of course.

'He's certainly worth proceeding against,' said Mr Rhodes, with a sour laugh.

'Be that as it may,' I said, 'I think we should try him again, that he may pay what is just and right without a law suit. It behoves me to write to him again in a stern manner...' I considered a space, then resumed, 'What say you to a letter worded thus: that my client has been much too long out of his money, and that he and I are determined to have an end of this matter some way or other, to wit that if the debt is not paid an action will be immediately commenced for recovering it. Threatening him might be just the trick.'

'I fear your letter will fall on deaf ears, sir. This man is no ordinary debtor. He's a man well used to behaving oddly in all manner of things. He's a fellow on which there's no dependency. Would that I'd known more about his character at the start. I wouldn't have treated with him for twopence. No, Mister Eagle, I've resigned myself to litigation. I have the law on my side, and he's the means to pay – costs of the action and all. Come now, you have the stomach for the fight have you not?'

He'd stabbed me sorely with his last point, and I told him so. Then I had this to say: 'Though you have great reason to think me averse to a law suit, as certainly I am, it is on my client's behalf not my own, and should necessity bring us to that course you will find that I will neither want spirit or abilities to do myself justice.' He gave me a curt nod. A fearless man who spoke bluntly, he valued that trait in others. 'Trust my judgment, sir,' I continued more calmly. 'We can but try the gentler approach one last time. It might just be enough to shift him. Come, give me the man's address so that I may try him.'

'His name and abode should not be unfamiliar to you,' he said, replenishing our tankards. 'It is Edward Larkin of Gravehunger Lodge.'

The words blew hard and all my composure vanished in the blast. The assault on my senses from this one man was relentless. Was there to be no end to it? My legs were trembling and I thanked the Lord I was sitting down.

'I see you know the name well,' he said, watching me close. 'Why, you've gone white in the face!'

White I may have been, and who, if they'd known the cause, would have been surprised? For try as I would to avoid it, I was being drawn by another tack towards that fight with Larkin. But why? I reasoned – had not the hag at the cottage warned me not to cross him? I was no longer sure what my own decisions were and which were the work of others. My mind was being tampered with at every turn.

'Pass the business up if you'd prefer,' goaded the clothier. 'You'd not be the first to give Larkin a wide berth. If you're wanting a way out,' he said pointing, 'the door's over there and you're welcome to use it. If I can't get a lawyer to represent me, I'll fight the blackguard myself. *I'm* no coward.'

'And nor am I sir,' I retorted sharply, for he'd hit me once again where it hurt. 'You'll have your lawyer. I do have reasons for disquiet but rest assured they have nothing to do with cowardice.' An excuse had come to mind that served my purpose admirably. 'Your case is an awkward one,' I said. 'To represent one client against the other flies in the face of orthodox practice. Furthermore my partner, Mister Balme, has in the past done much business for the Larkin family. He might not take kindly to my acting on a plaintiff's behalf against one of his most important clients.'

Mr Rhodes moved a hand supplicatingly. 'Please accept my apologies,' he said, smiling pleasantly. 'I've jumped to hasty conclusions. I'd never make an attorney I fear.'

'Perhaps not,' I said, returning his smile, whereupon we both relaxed a little with our ale and collected our thoughts. Mine predictably were painful again; they just wouldn't leave me in peace. I remembered what the witch had said about the lines being tangled, hopelessly so. But what lines did she mean and who was pulling them like strings? I deplored the loss of my own free will, that sense of being a pawn in a chess game. 'I refuse to do it!' I cried, startling my host into spilling his ale.

'Good God man,' he said, patting his thighs with his pocket-handkerchief. 'I wish you'd make your mind up. First you want the case, then you don't.'

'I apologise,' I said flustered, adding in broken bursts, 'You misunderstand me. I was lost in thought. I wasn't thinking of the case. I was thinking of – my spider.'

'Your spider?' said the baffled clothier, looking up at the worm-eaten rafters where cobwebs hung festooned – but nothing with eight legs dangled.

'It's time I left,' I said, already on my feet. 'I should not have come today. I am not myself you see.' I placed a hand to my brow. 'A touch of the ague I fear, and it's making me ramble. Please – I must leave now.'

He rose quickly, spilling more ale and treading on the plate I'd left on the floor. Some soggy food mess had caught in the buckle of his shoe. He worked hard to collect himself as he came towards me with outstretched hand. 'I'm sorry to hear you're unwell. I trust we'll meet again under more auspicious circumstances.'

'I'm sure of it,' I said unconvincingly, a nagging feeling that I might not find auspiciousness for a long time to come.

In my chamber that evening I pondered my future. Light from a full moon flushed silver the surface of the table where I slumped chin down, arms folded, one eye on the jar where my spider broodily rested, his body the size of a pistol ball. No spider was ever so large, if *real* spider he were. *What* are you? I mused, as the creature turned sluggishly in the gluey mess, an arachnidan devil watching *me* as much as I watched *it*. Nothing now was impossible, and had Lucifer himself flown through my casement on a beam of moonlight I would have glanced up in only vague dismay. Could it be that I was losing my mind? Had Phil's attack that day really been something else? – excitement at meeting a kindred spirit – the first he'd seen since leaving the asylum. I tried my best not to think so. I *was* sane, eccentric maybe, but sane. In that year of too many sevens – 1777 – it was the world that was mad, not me. Marshall had said so that very afternoon when I'd called on him burdened to the hilt, with unwonted tears in my eyes.

If only I'd told it all, as I'd fully intended to do, but for shame I held it back, that which worried me most. Hence his judgment based on only half the facts. 'You are over-wrought,' he had said, 'nothing more.' We talked about them each in turn, my deep-set worries fixed in the heart like far from precious stones. First the old life I had left behind with all its jealousy and spite; next the burden of my new one, heavy as it was with Sir Walter's demands and the troubling news of my old friend's death. And all of it lived among the odious Balmes, the heart beating lonely all the while, its duties too much for *shoulders young and tender* – such a look in his eye as he'd said so, and a worry in itself for sure. And for sure I had told him much, but had plenty left yet to tell.

Again I did what I always did – forced myself to think of work. I moved aside my food tray – I'd eaten alone in my chamber yet again – and considered the week ahead. Larkin came to mind immediately, for I knew what had to be done. The letter I had penned threatening him with a law suit would go by tomorrow's post – if I let it. To cap it all there was the question of his wife's *something or other*. Mr Balme had been vague right from the start; something about a deed – he'd been as vague as that – nothing urgent to merit any personal calls. The details could be found in the big old chest, which following Tom's warning I'd been loath to open. But I did want to see her Ladyship, though my loins and not my head were to blame. And now a note had arrived by her own black footman requesting my attendance the following afternoon. I would go of course, I must, and should her husband be there too it would be craven indeed not to meet him face-to-face – on Mr Rhodes' behalf, if not my own. I stared again at my letter, its paper neatly folded and sealed. I might take it with me and deliver it in person, just like a bailiff serving a writ. I might do it or not, the choice was mine. I decided to sleep on it.

As luck would have it I got but little sleep. The decision was made however: I would see Larkin in person or, failing that, leave the letter at the Lodge so he would have it on his return. My shivering ablutions at the wash-stand were quickly done, as was my dressing, and with that fateful letter sequestered in my coat pocket I descended the stairs, intending, with the wind of courage at my back, to breakfast with the Balmes.

They were already seated when I entered the lounge, he in his usual place at the head of the table, she on the corner so their knees were touching. I'd not joined them for over a week now, and their mouths, crammed with black pudding, opened in surprise as I entered. 'A fine morning!' I said, as they vied with each other to have first say. The mother had a lump go down wrong and burst into a fit of coughing that turned her bad old face bright red.

'Now look what you've done!' spluttered Abraham, spraying black pudding, barely chewed, over my side of the table. It was a full three minutes before he'd coddled her back from discomfort, wrapped her hands around her knife and fork and coaxed her to resume eating. This she did only after several Whaaas! and a glance at me that would have stripped the feathers from an owl.

Determined to hide my hatred for the crone, I feigned a smile and asked if she were feeling better. Her reply was nothing more than a grunt, and she left it to her son to enlighten me. 'Mother has been most unwell of late,' he said coldly.

'I have Abe, I have that – not well and poorly besides,' said the mother at last, lapping up his sympathy like an old hearth cat, shaking her fork and adding, as if I wasn't there, 'Not that *he'd* care. Thinks only of himself does that one.'

Abraham shook his head regretfully. 'I'm sorry to say that Mister Eagle has proved himself a very selfish young man. But, if we're to be truthful, Mother, he's but one of a generation of very selfish young men. How different things were in my youthful day.'

Simpering mother stroked simpering son's cheek, saying, 'My darling Abe was perfect right from the cradle. Them were better days all round,' she snarled, as Sukey appeared in clean new apron and bonnet. 'The servants knew their place.'

'Leave the girl alone Mother,' said Abraham gently, and I knew at once from the way he looked at Sukey that he'd started taking her to his bed. I could tell as much too from the shame-faced glance the drudge gave me as she poured me some tea. Her look had said it all – if only you'd taken me to *your* bed, it wouldn't have happened.

'Pray what business are you engaged on today?' asked Abraham sarcastically as the servant bobbed and left, followed all the way by the spiteful gaze of his mother.

'I'm to visit Lady Larkin,' I replied flatly. 'The precise nature of the business remains unknown to me.' Thanks to you, I almost said, for though he may not have known its true purpose he knew well enough the smell of trouble. Attendance at the Lodge disturbed him, perhaps more than ever of late, but he now had me on hand to cushion him against all blows. He wouldn't say so, but he'd hoped I would go all along. And go I must of course. As for that other matter, threatening her husband with an action at law, I would take care to broach it when I found him alone. That way there was a chance, albeit a slim one, that his harpy of a mother might be kept in the dark.

'Lady Larkin you say?' Abraham hemmed uncomfortably, a guilt-edged gesture he couldn't avoid. 'And yet without knowing that precise purpose you still insist on intruding yourself.'

'I am invited as it happens.'

Another forced cough, as if he might choke on any instruction to tread carefully and mind that I come back safe. 'It had quite slipped my mind that I had handed you that work.' I heard the lie but said nothing. 'Take care that you make a good impression. The remittances have been most generous these last few years. Which reminds me of the terms of our partnership – that I should have the lion's share of the conveyancing work. If such is what her Ladyship desires – and pray let's hope so – please be good enough to steer it my way on your return.'

Such would have been my intention, I assured him, without any need for prompting. There was another grunt from the mother, as if to say, 'Whaaa! Don't you believe it Abe,' but the needled talk at last was petering out. Another ordeal by repast had been survived.

Shortly before noon I donned my heavy overcoat against the weather and crossed to the stables. George was hard at work as usual, grooming Balme's fine bay ready for his journey to Leeds on navigation business. The animal appeared huge in the confined space, its breath smoking copiously, mingling with its body steam all the way to the rafters.

'Saddle my mare George,' I said, addressing him through the open door.

He lifted his head sluggishly and glanced my way, the horse snuffling displeasure at removal of the soothing brushes. 'She's already saddled, sir,' he said, nodding at Daisy who stood like a silent shadow to his rear. 'How's she been lately?' he asked, as I led her out into the cobbled yard. 'Has she stopped lying down?'

'Now that I come to think of it – yes – she has.'

'It could be that she's got used to yer,' he said, holding the animal steady as I climbed into the saddle. 'On the other hand it could be them rabbit's droppins I've been putting in her food.' He stroked her haunches affectionately, clucking all the while like a hen. 'They can work wonders for an horse, can rabbit's droppins. Trouble is, they often stops them lying down altogether.' He gave an oafish smile, the dark stain on his few remaining teeth making me wonder if he didn't partake of rabbit's droppings himself from time to time, such were the poor rations the Balmes no doubt fed him. There was the added clue that, apart from the time he'd brought me to the house, I had never seen him seated, never mind lying down. The man was forever on his feet – he slept on his feet for all I knew.

So much for lying down, but what about lying in store? Just what did the future hold, and how would I feel when I went to my bed that night? Indeed, would I make it to my bed at all?

NINE

Apprehensive to say the least, I rode out the village on the north side and made for Gravehunger Lodge. The rough track led past pinfolds and stretches of common land where cattle grazed; past small industrial works either side of the Oil Mill Beck; past woodland and tangled thickets towards the higher ground beyond. Half an hour more and I had passed Bogles Bog, that treacherous tongue of land both Tom and Mr Bolland had warned me about, the narrow road snaking perilously as it climbed. I had already sighted the house through the trees, whose leaves would have hidden it fully in summer time. Its presence had struck me even at a distance, though that was but a fraction of its impact at close quarters. There was something in the sheer blackness of the stone, in the multiple twisted chimneys, and in the random sprawl of the building that made my innards tingle. One could fair hear the house whisper on the breeze. Nothing could have prepared me for this. Powerful forces indeed that could have reached me so physically.

You must be strong, I said, reaching the front door straddled by creepers, aware, as I did so, of being watched. An unruly-looking man, the slit-eyed pugilist sort, was standing beneath a tree with a brindled dog to my rear. One of Larkin's men, I reflected, probably the one who had beaten Richard senseless, possibly the one who had murdered him. Behind me, while I worked the knocker – such irony that its size reminded me of a sanctuary knocker – his feet crunched slowly towards me like stones on broken glass. As the door opened, the footsteps ceased: I was being given time to state my business.

'Yes?' growled the fearsome butler in black, whose face was like a fist flanked by wild grey hair.

'John Eagle, Attorney-at-Law,' I said with proud impertinence. 'I have an appointment with Lady Larkin. Please inform your mistress...' – I emphasised the word *mistress* – '...that I have arrived.'

The servant considered a moment, sniffing contemptuously. 'Come this way,' he said. 'Rawlings there will see to your beast.' I glanced at the man behind me, who made no sign of acknowledgment. His body was swaying slightly in the breeze and, though the chains were absent, I thought of the pirate I had once seen hanging on the Isle of Dogs. Such an end would have suited this man too, a thought which his dog seemed to hear for it soon began to growl.

A mouldering smell greeted me as I entered the hall, a large and airless place as dark and gloomy as a crypt. Nor more cheerful were the standing suits of armour, the firearms fixed to the wall, the stuffed animals that stared with frightened wonder from their dim glass cases on the floor. This, then, was where he – Long Larkin – lived; I was breathing the air he breathed, seeing the things he saw. His belongings for instance lurking in the corner by the door. They looked ordinary enough – a walking stick and a pair of top-boots – but they were *his* walking stick, *his* top-boots, and that made them different: no ordinary man carried the one or wore the other. And never mind the lack of logic: the attraction was instant and mutual: one to the other, animate to inanimate, without no rhyme or reason.

Up the oak staircase now, my eyes on the woodwork with its carved demon faces and once, gaping-mouthed and dominant in the middle of the panelling, the big-faced Green Man with hair as hoary as a comet. Along a short gallery next into a large chamber with heavy curtains and inordinately loud clock.

'Wait here,' croaked my irascible guide, leaving to fetch her Ladyship. He had left me before the great fireplace of sombre marble, over which hung a painting of chilling import. Its subject was the snake-riddled head of a woman severed by a sword. My eyes were fixed still in fascination when a voice broke the enchantment.

'I see Medusa has you in her spell,' it said in tones of rich depth and feminine maturity. Her voice was just as I'd envisaged. Her look too, when I turned abruptly to find a figure of hard, almost cruel beauty in a taffeta gown of fetching blue. Twenty years my senior, she had a full bosom that hooked the admiring eye with a firm strike. Her own eyes were a rare and inordinate green, the mouth heavy-lipped, sensuously wide when she smiled. The power of her presence was as heady as laudanum; I was helpless, lost, capable of little but a feeble bow.

'It was kind of you to come, Mister Eagle,' she said, steering me towards the couch that squatted invitingly though it faced that horror on the wall.

'I am at your service, madam,' I faltered, as she seated herself in an armchair closeby. The rustle of her gown was beguiling; more so those eyes – enough to overwhelm the gazer if he stared too long. And no respite to be had from the luscious mouth with its neat cleft chin below; nor the freckled edges of those milk-white breasts, the blue-stockinged ankles, the feet hidden by delicate shoes with high black heel and rose brocade.

Lady Larkin smiled deliciously. My turmoil was unbearable; it turned me a little sick. 'You are very young,' she said, almost wantonly, adding in dubious qualification, 'to be immersed, I mean, in the fug and fust of the law.'

'One has to make one's way in the world,' I said, still fumbling my introductions.

She nodded once with mock sympathy, for she was amused by my answer. Yet I had no other, nor could I think of a single word, on any subject, to follow it with. I sat in my juvenile silence looking up at that terrifying image of the gorgon, seeing, through my eye corner, Lady Larkin's watchful stare. The clock sounded louder in my ears. Had I been on my feet I would have swooned.

Time passed, I didn't know how or how long in duration.

'Do you – like me?' she said, breaking the intolerable impasse. The question was not as startling as it should have been; the air between us had thickened, like that before a thunderstorm.

'Yes,' I said in a low voice, finally managing to look at her.

'And do you – want me?' she went on, delicately fingering the chair arm.

'Yes,' I answered, unable to believe what I'd heard or said.

She rose with deliberate slowness and held out her hand. Its colour was unusually white – whiter than her breasts, whiter than bone.

'Rest assured, my husband is at York,' she said on seeing me hesitate. 'I don't expect him back till tomorrow evening. Come,' she added, leading me off by the hand. It was as if it were all pre-planned, written, transmuted through the back of her head that night in the Bull. She didn't need to say how she felt it too; it was as much for granted between us as the floor beneath our feet. What it meant, however, I could scarcely imagine.

Her bedchamber lay adjacent. Dominating the room was a huge four-poster bed with drapes; the marriage bed, I reflected, wherein slept Long Larkin, whose wife, following my drink at the fountain of madness, I was about to enjoy. I must call her Phoebe, she said, already undressing. There was no fire in the grate, and I lied to myself that I shivered solely with cold.

'What about your law business?' I asked rather lamely. 'It does exist, does it not?'

'Oh it exists all right,' she replied, 'and so does this.' She beckoned me closer. The pale voluptuous flesh above her stockings aroused me to a throbbing urge. A genteel woman twice my age was excitement for sure, enough to make me spend at the very *thought* of having her.

'There are parts of a woman that never age,' she said, guiding my hand to her quim. In unison with her mouth, its lips parted at the press of my finger. She wanted me naked now, and tore my shirt in her haste. She took me in her mouth next but only for a second. 'Quickly now,' she said, almost a command. 'This way I think,' and she bent over the bed in readiness.

I had guessed she was well versed in the art of pleasuring a man, and I wasn't disappointed. I entered her easily, for she was roomy and slippery warm – 'well greased' as my fellow clerks used to say. I came with a sigh that was grandly understated.

We lay together afterwards, her head on my breast, her fingers toying with my exhausted engine. Her breath was quick with exertion. 'You've no idea how lonely I get,' I heard her say. She had sounded like Sukey that first night, and what I had spared the tweenie I was more than making up for here. With this woman anything was possible, no matter how wild, how debased, how heinous. In perversions more twisted than her chimneys she would join me willingly I was sure. Her unabashed pursuit of sexual pleasure, probably in all its forms, thrilled me to the quick. Her approach was revolutionary, an illicit revelation of unabashed joy. Such a creature I had never encountered; she was, in her self-indulgent lust, more man than woman. And male was how she seemed at heart; she had journeyed to that central fold where the sexes merged as one.

'Do you believe in God?' I asked of a sudden with no clear reason why.

'No,' she said with icy calm. 'I believe in nothing – nothing, that is, but life itself. Today you have been my life. Tomorrow – who knows?' She leaned over and kissed me on the mouth. 'I didn't mean it, my little eaglet...' – she had a pet name for me already – '...There are days when I know not what I say – or what I do.'

Is she mad? I thought.

'No more than you,' she replied at once.

I glanced at her startled. Had *she* read my mind too? – or had it been her all along, drawing me here to this predestined moment? Again the stifling strangeness of things, that feeling of otherness coursing through me like a dark flood. And this time too the oddest, cruellest yearning, a sickness in itself, like grief, but one that the heart craved. The malady was almost visible there in the half-light of a winter afternoon, there in the candlelight that only added to the gloom. I watched the candle-flame lambent upon the dresser, its yellow glow drawing unto itself the damp lurid grey pressing like a face at the leaded pane. But the gloom itself was the pleasure, mingled though it was with the scent of death. The moments were passing and I wanted them to stop: I wanted to stop time. And I wondered at a life spent here in this room where time stood still, the only thought, the only sustenance, a ceaseless alternation of wine and cunt.

'I wash away my cares with wine and fall to cunt again. Some minds are easy to read,' she said, stroking my cheek and then, for good measure, my balls. 'Is there truly nothing left?' she asked in a childish tone. 'Has the tiny workshop finished its creaming for the day?' She had made to check for herself, caressing my knee-caps, her tongue licking my inner thigh till it reached my prick, her eyes up close at the puckered end, the lashes a delight as they flickered faster than a humming bird's wings.

And afterwards, a second time, her laughter deep yet sweet, a captivating laugh that aroused and mothered in one. I felt unfathomably drawn to her, embarked upon a course that couldn't be stopped.

'The moment I saw you I knew you'd become my lover,' she said. 'And you, like any other boy in fine buckled shoes, had no choice but to accept. But we must be discrete – *very* discrete, or I can't answer for the consequences.'

'Tell me about him – your husband,' I said, assuming a note of casual curiosity.

She laughed again, but this time it masked an inner pain. 'Where would I begin? And who would I be talking of? In my husband's mind there are many mansions, each with a different lord. The truth is, I know not the man I have married.' She waxed suddenly stern. 'But I will not say more. It's not my place.'

Disappointed by her taciturnity, I pushed her a little more. 'Are you frightened of him?' I asked delicately, for I felt some pity at her plight.

She answered without emotion. 'I'd be a liar if I said I was not.'

'And yet you would take a risk like this,' I said incredulously, 'here, in his very bed.'

'I am determined to have life. And, as I think you've gathered, my woman's desires are strong. I must take a risk if needs be – nay though I walk through the valley of the shadow of death.'

My hand strayed out and gripped the sheet. How should I defend myself against this man if he came hunting for my blood? I saw him in my mind's eye as a great bear that would crush the life out of me. Should he choose to run me through with his sword, I, who was no swordsman, would be less of a match for him than a Tom cat. He was probably a crack shot too, whereas I, who had fired with youthful friends a pistol or two at rats on the river-bank, would be hard put to hit a water butt at twenty paces.

'Have no fear, little eaglet, you are safe for the present. Rest assured that I shall say nothing. As for Jarett...' – it was the name of her butler – '...he's my man more than my husband's and I pay him generously for his discretion.'

'I'm *not* frightened,' I said, but I was lying and she knew it. I felt weak and unmanly, and wished to God that I was braver.

'But you *are* brave, my eaglet,' said Phoebe, stunning me anew with her intuition. 'There are many types of bravery. It took one sort to come here today, believe me it did.'

'What about the other one? – Rawlings?' I said, close to telling all and why not? How much did she know of Richard's death, the part played by Rawlings, the part played by her own wedded groom? No, for the moment at least, I dared not ask.

'Rawlings saw you too?' Phoebe sighed. 'That's unfortunate. He is unpredictable. To try *him* with money might backfire. Should questions arise, and they might not, I shall say that the reason for you staying so long was the intractable nature of the problem I had set you.'

She had made me feel better, about my cowardice at least. I began to relax a little, but not for long: fear that Larkin might return early struck me like a bolt. 'It's time I was gone,' I said, stooping for my clothes, groaning at the sight of the letter protruding from my coat pocket: should I leave it or take it away?

'Wait!' cried Phoebe, flustered. 'We haven't discussed the case.' She flew out of bed to join me on the cold floorboards. 'Don't go. Not yet.' She threw her arms around my neck, pressing herself against me with her thighs, her breasts, and her quim. It was all I could do to stay upright. And though she kissed me with the salt and sweat of sex on her tongue, the great fear in my heart kept my manhood down. There would be no third helping today – no more at all if I had any sense in my brain.

'About the case,' I reminded her soberly.

'Very well,' she said a little piqued, and went to gather her things.

I was glad to feel my own garments back upon my body, though my hard-worked penis rested uncomfortably against the tight-fitting crotch. And as I dressed, watching Phoebe brush her long dark hair before the dressing-table mirror, I told myself that no woman I had ever met, or was ever likely to meet, had pleasured and pained me as she had done. Such a heady mixture she embodied, that to have it regularly would be treading the road to ruin. Yet I feared I had already taken that road some weeks ago, perhaps the moment I arrived in Horseford; all that Phoebe had done was hurtle me closer to the edge. She rose abruptly now and crossed to the table by the window. Daylight was almost gone and she lighted another candle. Shadows danced on the walls, swimming in shoals across the embossed ceiling. The shadows played on her face too, heightening the mystery of her smile as she carried the candle towards me. 'Come this way,' she said, and I followed her back to the adjoining room. Here, with the candle she had brought, she kindled more either side of the two large mirrors, saying Jarrett would light the chandelier if I wished. There was no need, I replied, and declined also her offer of food. I was determined not to prolong my stay nor, if I could help it, meet with Jarrett again.

'How can I be of assistance?' I began as I always did, feeling the absurdity of formal talk. Would that I could make the law an instrument of idle chatter!

Lady Larkin – she had ceased to be Phoebe for the moment – sensed my discomfort and smiled. I fumbled for my pocket-book, pulling out by mistake at the same time the letter to her husband, which now grew hot in my hand. As I struggled to hide it, first beneath my coat and then inside the pocket-book, I knew she'd grown curious. 'And what have you there that you want to hide?' she asked, seating herself as before.

Medusa's head in all its gore dared me to speak the truth. I was held in limbo, repelled by fear yet drawn by an alien bravery. 'It's a letter,' I began, still transfixed by the painting, adding, as I broke the thread that bound me to the frightful image, 'a letter to your husband. Pray be good enough to give it to him on his return.' I held it out for her to take, letting it drop, half deliberately, to the floor. 'It relates to a business matter, ' I said, watching as she stooped to retrieve it, thinking there was time yet, one last chance, to cheat my destiny.

'Be careful what you do,' she said, delicately probing the seal and the outer edges of the paper. It was as if she sensed the letter's purpose. 'My husband – as I think you know – is a dangerous man.' I nodded, a nervous flutter at the corner of my mouth as she went on, 'Think twice about what you do.'

'It's only a trifle,' I shrugged, but I was lying again and she knew it.

'You have only to say the word and I shall tear it up. Come, why not make an end of it?' She looked at me earnestly. 'Have we not enough to contend with from that quarter?'

'The law is the law. Without its justice we are all lost.'

Lady Larkin sat frowning. 'You are a strange young man, and I think just a little the hypocrite. Only minutes ago you were my little eaglet satisfying yourself with a married woman, now you are the upright eminent attorney speaking high and mightily of justice. The glove doesn't fit the hand, I fear.'

'Private vice and public virtue,' I said satirically. 'It's what makes the world go round so smoothly.'

'I don't want us to fight,' she said softly, though I knew I had angered her.

'Then you will give him the letter?' I said, puzzled by my new-found strength, as if I'd drunk liberally from the brandy bottle.

'Yes,' she said, 'I'll give him the letter, and I must shift as best I can.'

'Yes,' I answered, without thinking.

'And in the meantime,' she said, 'you will undertake some business for me. I trust you will find it defensible.'

'You are faced with an action?' I was struggling to keep my professional detachment.

'I fear it will come to that. You see, Mister Eagle...' – she laughed wickedly – '...how strange to call you so after what we've just done!' She composed herself and resumed, 'But you see – Mister Eagle – I must be honest about my grasping nature, a trait I share with my husband. When I see something I want, I must have it. And I jealously guard what is mine, even things to which I have only dubious claim. I never let go.' She had looked me in the eye with that last remark, and I felt her clutches beneath my skin.

'Do go on,' I said, seeking refuge in the taking of detailed notes.

It transpired that her father died intestate twelve months ago, leaving Phoebe, his eldest daughter, and Caroline his youngest daughter, wife of Charles Wood of Bowling Hall in the parish of Bradford Esquire. Those were his only children, and his wife having died the year previously there was no widow. Phoebe, as her nature dictated, had taken out Letters of Administration to her late father's effects before the vicar of Otley. Mr Wood, however, who in right of his wife was entitled to a distributive share of the late Mr Myers' effects, had desired an inventory and appraisal thereof together with an account of Phoebe's receipts and disbursements as administratrix to her late father. This inventory and appraisal Phoebe had, in part, given but had significantly left out the monies which were in the house at Mr Myers' death, also what debts were owing to the late Mr Myers. Here was the crux of the matter, for Phoebe steadfastly refused to give any account of these extras which, on my insistent enquiry of her, I discovered amounted to over a thousand pounds.

'And will you? – defend me, I mean?' she asked, when I'd considered the facts.

'We shall have a poor case at law, I fear. No doubt Mister Wood, who is an eminent gentleman of reputation in his locality, will shortly be asking his attorney to take out a citation to compel you to exhibit a true and perfect inventory, and pay him what is his due share of the surplusage. There is a statute of, I think, the 22nd or 23rd Charles II that entitles him to do precisely that. We shall be upon the forlorn hope if we try to defend the action.'

Lady Larkin listened carefully, showing no outward concern. 'But will you use all the skills at your disposal to turn the thing my way? Will you play every card in the pack, even the marked ones?

'You are asking me to pervert the course of justice?' I prayed that she hadn't been serious.

'I am,' she said, with devastating surety.

'Then I'm afraid I can't be your man,' I said, slapping shut my book.

She glanced up at me with mocking eyes. 'You forget, my little eaglet, that I have you at a disadvantage.'

I picked up my coat, and clasped it to my chest. 'I don't follow you,' I said.

'That which you have had this afternoon and enjoyed so much I will use against you,' she said, staring coolly ahead.

'You – wouldn't blackmail me,' I said, steadying myself on the chair arm.

'Oh but you are wrong. Do as I wish or I shall tell the world that you had me against my will. But there is no need to go that far – my husband's ears would suffice. He would find you, and kill you.'

I strode blindly about the room in my anguish, knocking my head with random beats against the panelled wall. I watched her from behind, calm and still in the candle-light, waiting for her poison to reach my bloodstream. She knew I was beaten, and by one more wily than me.

'Don't take it too hard, my little eaglet,' she said, now at my side with her fingers in my hair, coiling the ribbon around her thumb. 'I enjoyed every inch of you today, and I will again. You may hate me now but in a night or two, when you lie alone in your chamber, you will think longingly of what we did together. Your prick will stiffen at the thought of me, and you'll wish it was *my* hand that was slowly, delectably, drawing you off. You'll be back for more, believe me you will, or, should it be I who comes to you, you'll not refuse me. You'll take what I offer, as any man would.'

She had the gall to kiss me again, and I hadn't the will to resist. 'Yes,' I sighed, when she'd asked me again if I'd take the case. We both knew it was a *fait accompli.*

'Just tell me this,' I asked bitterly as I paused at the door, 'did you plan it all between you?' I asked bitterly, as I paused at the door. 'Was your husband privy to everything? – and I mean *everything*? After all, aside from your paraphernalia, what's yours is his – husband and wife are alike in the eyes of the law. 'Tis him who is fighting this case, not you, though he fights it *through* you.'

I knew that it wasn't all true – that Phoebe, through the equitable doctrine of the separate use, had for her sole ownership half the property she brought to her marriage, plus any she acquired after. But I had spoken only to wound, and in that I'd succeeded. Her face reddened as she rose, saying fiercely, 'What I have done, I have done alone, for *my* benefit as much as his. My husband is many things, but he is no master of his wife. He knew my strength of character before he married me. I have a certain freedom in my affairs that other women can only dream of. It is I who have snared you, my little eaglet, and Oh how easy it was!'

'Then what a fool I've been,' I said miserably.

'Yes,' she said, 'but don't be vexed.' Her tone softened further as she drew towards me. 'True, I set out to trap you, and you mustn't let me down in what I've asked, but remember this: I never expected you to be beautiful, I never expected such divine coupling. I must see you again, despite the risks. I didn't lie about those either – he *would* kill you. '

I left the house like a beaten dog, ejected cold into the twilight. And beaten, in a sense, I had been, wrong-footed and defeated, with little room to turn. If victory by the wife was so easily won, what hope now at the hands of the husband?

TEN

Two days passed quietly. I spent them at my desk working, choosing cases that were easy, devoid of blight or contention. Lady Larkin's for example – my pocket-book stayed in my coat, vexing me much at the thought of its latest close-written page. The nights were better – just. I spent them with Marshall at the Bull, talking common issues and persiflage that brought me little joy. Life was uncomfortable, very nearly untenable. Something, perhaps everything, had to change. That changes *were* coming became evident that second night as I walked home. From the churchyard there came towards me a strange white light. I saw it very plain and continued so to do as it followed me down Fink Hill, dancing like a moonbeam at my feet, tricking out the cobbles in a jagged line two chains long. It was nothing of real import, just a length of shimmering moonshine, but I took it as an omen nonetheless.

And next day it happened, a worsening storm of accumulated incident. I remember the gloomy tone of the weather that day, the raw dampness of the air, the clouds strung low and heavy with grey. It was Sunday, my invite to 'break the fast of the night with him,' bringing me to Marshall's house at the appointed hour. I was on my guard, and needed to be, the moment I sat down to the plain fare of odds and ends. No sooner had I put the bread to my mouth than Phil attacked me with a toasting fork. That I'd managed to duck meant nothing when he fell upon me armed with a plate of cold mutton. This he screwed to my face, plastering my features with fat and lean before he knocked me to the floor. I endured near a minute of his pummelling till Marshall rendered him senseless with a pan-lid.

'That ought to hold him for a while,' said the doctor out of breath. 'I'll take him upstairs shortly and lock the door.'

'You'll have to get that pumpernickel caged!' I cried, as Marshall steered me to a chair. 'Why do you let him roam free?'

'For the same reason as I mentioned before – you are the only person that triggers this behaviour,' replied Marshall, wiping the blood and grease from my face. 'In fact, I'd come close to recommending his release.'

'No!' I beseeched him. 'Promise me you won't do that. I have enough reasons for not sleeping at night.'

'My dear fellow, you have my word,' he said, laughing as he slapped my shoulder.

I knew his word was good, and aside from Tom he was my one true friend in these parts. Why, then, did I not confide in him to the absolute hilt? Wouldn't the warmth of friendship soothe my pains? Truly it would, if my pains were made of ordinary stuff. Pains like mine were not easily explained, not even to the closest, most learned of friends. Besides, there was the nagging notion that they were not true pains at all, merely figments of an increasingly disordered mind. Perhaps I *was* mad – who but a madman would keep a spider in a jar? – a spider so fat, so odious, that I dared not look any more.

Clearly Phil read the torment in me; it jarred against his own search for sanity there beneath his master's roof. A kindly master, a kindly doctor – I reminded myself of Marshall's vocation, the peculiar interest that had brought Phil into his home. He, more than anybody, would know about madness and its early signs. He was also a man of science, a virtuoso thinker who would have no truck with irrational thought. Those numerous shelves, heavy with volumes in every colour of binding, were proof alone of serious enquiry. But Marshall too was a spiritual man; his attendance at church a sign that he took his devotions seriously. If he believed in the love of God, he must, by the same token, believe in the evil of the Devil, which was evil with a capital D. I ventured to try him cautiously.

'Pray tell me what you think of the power of evil,' I said, as he poured me some hot gin and water and dropped in a lump of sugar.

Placing the glass on the table, he stood considering a while. 'If, by that,' he said at last, 'you mean do I think that evil exists in the world, and is able to get a hold on many men, I would have to say, yes: I think it exists, and I think it very powerful.'

'And do you also believe,' I said, taking heart from his answer, 'that the Devil is the source of such evil, that he's able to reach us through his agents?'

'To be sure, these are weighty questions for a sober Sunday morning,' said Marshall sitting down. 'Would that you had raised them on an evening when we found ourselves in our cups. They would have added spice to our rather dull chatter.'

'Vex me not,' I said, with an injured edge. 'I've had much on my mind of late. But we stray from the issue – pray answer me that point because, weighty or not, I am sorely in need of your opinion.'

'My dear fellow, you *are* out of sorts,' said Marshall, leaning forward earnestly. 'As for your face, you really must let me bathe it. Phil's had quite a meal out of you again.'

'Forget my face,' I said testily.

'Forget your face?' interrupted Marshall, with wounded tenderness. 'I shall never forget it, so long as I live. It's one of the most beautiful faces I have ever set eyes on.' He stayed the air with his hand, adding with a clap, 'There! 'Tis said, once and no more, you have my word.'

I sighed with frustration. So the man loved as well as lusted after me. What new force was this conspiring against our friendship, stifling its growth with the sordid shadow of his longing? One last time I charged him to answer my question.

His reply was that of the cold rationalist, so common these days among his class of men. 'Beware the evil of blind superstition,' he began vehemently. 'There's no case yet of communing with the Devil that can't be laid at its door. Nor am I dependent on mere books for my opinions.' He gestured proudly to his many tomes, perhaps a thousand in all. 'Mark it well, for there was an incident in this very village when I was only a boy that ought to put pay to talk like that for good.'

With dramatic conviction he told me the story of Mary and Joe Lapish, an elderly couple whom a local butcher had accused of bewitching him. He and the mob he had mustered stripped them naked and dragged them to the Oil Mill Beck where, with toes and thumbs bound together, they were repeatedly ducked. Though the couple were half drowned, the mob beat them with sticks until they were dead, completing their sport by putting them to bed together in the hovel they had shared. Marshall, who had gone with his surgeon father to view the poor wretches, had been haunted by their faces ever since. 'I still see them in my dreams,' he said, staring regretfully into space. 'The look of pure terror that even death couldn't wipe away...' – he glanced at me sharply – '...it was mob justice, John, of the worst sort, the same that would surely turn on me should news of my preferences leak out. They are simple people that we live among, people fired by hysteria, by blind hatred of they knew not what. Agents of the Devil indeed! – that old couple were as much in Lucifer's pay as that sausage on your plate or that duck egg on mine!'

191

I nodded acknowledgment, keeping the reverent silence his story deserved. And to myself was kept the home truth Sir Walter had spun about the vile mob needing to be checked. But Marshall had said nothing of his view of religion, revealed or otherwise, or his motives for attending church. What about true goodness via Jehovah? – what about true evil via Satan? Up to a point his theory was sound – the blind ignorance of the *feax populi* had much to answer for. And yet there were things that couldn't be explained by the clever simplicity of science, by what a doubting Thomas of the new age might call the blindness of rationalism. Science, for example, could not explain my spider. Nor, among other things, could it solve the mystery of the Lighthazzles witch. I had seen her, I had felt her powers. Or *had* I? Perhaps it *was* all work and worry; perhaps I *was* over-wrought and the first signs had come that fateful night in the graveyard. What a night that had been, and ought to have *not* been; sufficient unto the day is the evil thereof. I had gone too far in my perverse defiance, gone too far in provoking what I shouldn't. I alone was to blame, I said, and I didn't like it. Seeking distraction, I gulped my gin to the bottom of the glass. When Marshall replenished it, I half hoped his grip would linger. He saw the glint in my eye and read its cause. 'You'll regret it I fear,' he said swiftly.

'We are coming to know each other very well,' I said, glad he had broken the spell.

'Is this a time for confidences?' he asked jovially. 'You forget what I know already of that streak within you. I accept that it's only a streak and that your main taste lies elsewhere. For my sake *that* is a pity, but I know that's the way of it. Agreed?'

'Agreed,' I said as we shook on it, 'but that wasn't the confidence I had in mind. As you rightly say, we have had that one out already. No, I speak of another matter I keep close to my breast. Marshall, I shall ask you plainly – do you think that I am mad? Is there anything in my outward behaviour that has led you to consider me so? For if that be the case, I implore you to tell me.'

'My dear John!' exclaimed the doctor, 'whatever put that notion into your head? A man as worldly as you, who questions life at every turn, *must* be sane.'

'Must he?' I was near to telling him the whole sorry tale, unloosening all the skeletons I had stowed in my cupboard. In the end I told him nothing new; I made do with his belief in my sanity, based though it was on outward appearances only.

Later, when I took my leave, I feigned the cheeriness I knew he preferred. 'Adieu Marshall,' I said. 'It's been another interesting morning.' I cast a glance at the figure still lying on the rug. 'I think you should work on him when he awakes,' I said, giving Phil a gentle kick. 'Try to convince him, in that *bewitching...*' – I chose the word deliberately to irritate him – '...bedside manner of yours, that John Eagle is the sanest man alive, merely the sort who confines his eccentricity to coupling with married women old enough to be his mother.'

Marshall had laughed as a matter of course, but wasn't sure if he should: the poor doctor had sensed a joke that he hadn't understood.

After quitting his house I took a stroll round the village, as I was wont to do on Sunday morning. I headed for Woodside, that straggling southern end of Horseford which bordered the Oil Mill Beck, along whose banks stood corn mills, textile workshops, and tanneries. The sounds and smells of industry were absent on the Sabbath, as were the workers who toiled beneath the low-pitched roofs. All was quiet in the buildings and yards, each a separate complex divided from its neighbour by a stretch of rough ground. And nothing incongruous or thoughtlessly juxtaposed. Be it mill-stone, tenter or sluice-gate, ruinous chimney or broken wall – no discord showed between the ugly mark of man and the settled forms of nature in wood, field and stream.

Picking my way along the banks of the beck, which ran fast over its pebbled bed, I crossed the clapper bridge that led up through a small wood to the mill pond above. Here, when I'd gazed down at the beer-brown waters where a stickleback's breast flashed silver-red, I took in the overhanging willows and oaks, the swan that drifted silently on the far side of the pond, and the aged horse grazing lazily in the pinfold beyond. Presently I sat upon a tree stump, avoiding the moss that would have stained my breeches. I looked at the stream again, following the line of the head-race to the water wheel below. Next, as I traced the routes of the rills or gutters funnelling water to the manufacturies downstream, I caught the flight of a crow as it swept up towards me with the body of a mouse clasped limply in its thick black beak. The bird flew over the pond and landed on the trunk of an uprooted tree, where, disturbed immediately in its meal, it took off again with a loud cawing and waited in the branches above. Twigs cracked noisily underfoot as a man staggered down the hill. Even a child would have seen that he was drunk, his inevitable destination, wilful or otherwise, the pond.

'Stop!' I called, but he paid no heed. He headed on towards the water, his speed increasing with the growing steepness of the slope. Seconds later he was in, emitting a groan that was more relief than alarm. The water had depth to swallow him, and all that remained on the surface was his hat.

As quickly as I could I ran to where I'd seen him go in. All the while I knew not how I would reach him: I couldn't swim and I saw all the signs of a double drowning. Up there aloft still the crow was watching, till suddenly it flew down, dipping low over the water, trying, as it swept the pond, to pick up the man's hat. Coincidental though it was, his head popped up at that very moment, checking the bird mid-flight. The man had surfaced and I had my chance. Fortunately I carried a cane, and by lying on my belly at full stretch I was able to reach him as he thrashed about in the water.

'Here! Take it!' I cried, watching as his nut-brown fingers grabbed first the ferrule then the middle part of the stick. As I began to land him like a huge fish, I saw that his face was as brown as his hands. It was as if his whole body had once been baked.

I beached him as best I could, this man of small stature, thirtyish, hair bristling like an otter's wet coat. On land he became a dead weight, and I was forced to leave him, foetal-like, coughing and spewing on the muddy bank. It was mostly water in his lungs but amidst it was vomit streaked with blood.

'Yer should have let me drown,' he said as he retched. 'I've nowt to live for.'

I bent down to comfort him, grudgingly so when I noticed my stockings soiled by the stinking mud. 'Be thankful for life,' I said, to be saying something, feeling it should have been Marshall, with his repertoire of professional sympathy, that found him instead. The offer of my hip-flask would have proved inappropriate – the man had drunk too liberally already.

'What do they call you?' I asked, as his biliousness subsided with a last guttural heave. 'Are you a local man?'

'Aye, I'm local all right,' said my charge, screwing up his toothless jaws so that his face resembled a squashed orange. 'Do I know thee?' he added, struggling to focus with eyes that were small, round, and deeply set in his rutted brow.

'I doubt that very much. Here, put this on,' I said, covering the shivering oaf with my thick warm coat.

'Much obliged,' he muttered, plunging his hands into the pockets where, to my dismay, he found the hip-flask, unscrewed the cap and downed the contents in one. 'Don't suppose yer've any more?' he said, with a satisfied belch at the end.

'No, damn your eyes, I haven't,' I replied, snatching back the flask. 'And I would have thought you'd had enough already.'

'A man like me can never have enough,' he said, scrambling to his feet and scratching his drenched head. 'A man like me drinks to forget.'

'Forget what?' I asked, following him slowly up the bank, where I stopped and gagged as he squatted to shit. 'Have you no shame?' I asked, pressing a handkerchief to my mouth.

'Not much,' he replied, still straddling the steaming pile as he pulled up his well-patched breeches. 'Little Willie had it kicked out of him at a very young age.'

'So it's you,' I said, retching at the stench of his turds, 'the one they also call the Baked Man.' Here before me was the only witness to Richard's death, the very man I ought to have seen by now should feeble excuses not have intervened.

'Aye, that's what they call me – among other things.' He fell flat on his face at that point, and for helping him to his feet again my reward was a shit-stained hand.

'Wash it over there if it bothers thee,' said Willie, peeved by my scruples. 'It's only a bit of shite.'

'Yes, and it's *your* shite,' I said, 'so kindly keep it to yourself in future.' I returned to the pond, dipped my handkerchief and wiped my besmeared hand. 'Some of us live outside the farmyard,' I said as I rejoined him.

'Some of us can afford to,' he said, squelching at my side as we walked on towards the elfin knoll, a small hillock in the middle of a field where, according to Tom, a stone circle once stood and where now, on moonlit nights, elfish folk danced and played. 'You may offer me money if yer like,' added Willie, turning his empty pockets inside out. 'I've no shame.'

'So I've noticed,' I replied, his shit visible still in the distance and faintly steaming. 'Now you want money you say, but what do I get in return? First you must tell me why you were trying to drown yourself,' I said, as we reached the Knoll with its smooth grassy mound.

'What do yer want to know for?' he asked, scratching first his balls and then his arse.

'I'm curious, that's all,' I said, with enough indifference to appease him.

Little Willie threw himself on the Knoll, kicking his short thin legs in the air like a frisky child. 'It's like I told yer – there's nowt to live for,' he said, and fastened every button on the coat that was much too long for him, sealing himself in from neck to ankle as if that might make him safe.

'And is that the only reason?' I enquired, fishing with my lawyer's line.

The drunkard's face scowled and looked away. 'Aye, there *were* another reason. Somebody told me to do away with myself. He said if *I* didn't do it *he* would. So I got drunk 'n' went to do it. I would have done it 'n' all,' he said, 'if thee hadn't stopped me.'

'I did what I had to do. It's what any man would have done.'

The baked fellow threw me a glance that showed the fear in his eyes. 'Aye, well where does it leave me now, eh? – that's what I want to know. I'm not sure what bothers me the most – the when or the how of it. I've been partial to my prick all my life, I don't want it fed to me at the end of it.'

Did I really wish to hear more? Had I not, in the matter of Richard's death, resolved to follow Sir Walter's advice, convenient as it was to do so? It was not so simple any more; the wound had opened to a gaping hole. I couldn't believe that mere chance had thrown us together that morning; it was as if I'd been meant to save him. To restore him to life only to discard him again would be an unforgivable wrong. A man of bad character he may be, he could still play his part in a just and honourable cause.

'Who wants you dead, Willie?' I asked, sure of the answer I would hear.

'Him that lives at the big Lodge,' he said, staring vacantly at the leaden sky.

'Gravehunger Lodge?' I prompted.

'That's the place, 'n' him that lives there's hungry for *my* grave. He'd no sooner do me in than he would a toad.'

'No one's going to *do you in,* Willie,' I said, 'not if I have anything to do with it.' Shitty-arsed low-life he may be, I reasoned, but he has the right to live.

'What can *you* do?' asked the vagrant sharply. 'Yer might have a decent coat 'n' brandy in yer pocket, but yer nowt at side of him.'

It wasn't what I'd wanted to hear but I still said fervently, 'Trust me, I'm an attorney, there's much I can do. Let's face it – you don't really have any choice. You've said yourself that you're as good as dead.'

Willie's eyes widened as he fingered his leathery face. 'Aye, I am that, 'n' drowning me will be too quick for him.'

'It was quick enough for Richard Hudson,' I said, keeping the pressure on. 'But that depends how long he struggled in the water.'

His dark skin suddenly blanched as he tried to rise. 'Wha...what do *you* know about that?' he said, as I kept him in place with my hand.

I spilled the salient points from his own deposition – how Willie had travelled with the killers to Leeds that fateful night, drunk with them thoroughly at the sign of the Swan, and, when they'd thought him in a stupor, followed them to the river where he'd witnessed the deed.

'I had no part in it!' spluttered Willie, rocking back and forth in agitation. 'I didn't know they were going to kill anyone.' I assured him that neither I, nor Mr Bolland was in any doubt about his innocence. 'So what did yer mention it for?' he asked, still rocking hard. 'Why are yer questioning me?'

I tugged his sleeve and forced him to look at me. 'Just tell me this, Willie, why does Larkin want you dead?'

'Because he knows what I know – that he put them up to it.'

I squeezed his arm a little to make him talk. 'And how do you know he put them up to it?'

'Because Jeremiah...' – the so-called friend who had helped murder Richard – '...let it slip when he were drunk in the King's Arms one night – he drinks there because the landlord's one o' Larkin's men, yer see, he collects gold coin for clipping and takes it...'

'Yes, yes, I know all about our traitorous money-makers,' I said, growing impatient and tightening my hold. He was shrieking with pain but I wouldn't let go. 'Stick to the facts Willie.'

'Well Jeremiah, he got a beating soon after when Rawlings told Larkin I were with them in Leeds that night.' I had got what I needed, and released my grip. 'Some attorney!' cried Willie, rubbing his arm. 'Yer a fucking torturer!'

I apologised mechanically, and stroked my chin in thought. What was to be done next? Willie was vital to bringing Larkin to justice. If, as he insisted, his life was in danger he must be protected forthwith. But where was I to secure him sanctuary? There were few, if any choices: Mr Bolland had washed his hands of the case; Sir Walter would not approve and may well try to thwart my plans. As for the Balmes – no, the options boiled down to one man – Marshall Stables. A conscience that stretched to taking a lunatic into one's house, could surely run to a little board and lodging for a hounded vagrant. There was the added bonus too, I mused mischievously, of Willie's sexual preferences which, were the little man bathed and groomed, Marshall might stoop to enjoy.

'Here,' I said, tossing him a shilling, 'find the nearest public house while I see about your lodgings. I have in mind a good man who might shield you for the present.'

'But it's the Sabbath,' he feigned to protest.

'And has the Sabbath stopped you before?'

'No,' he said grinning with those toothless gums. 'Not even when they shoved me in the stocks.'

There was nothing to be gained by prolonging the discussion. A low dive known as the Wasp being just around the corner, I arranged to rendezvous with him there at two and went in search of Marshall.

To my frustration the good doctor was no longer at home, and, unwilling to risk by persistent knocking another assault from Phil, I returned to Fink Hill House to decide my next move. The sight that greeted me there was extraordinary. At the bottom of the stairs in a twisted heap lay the body of Mrs Balme, while at the stair-head, clasping the balustrade, stood Tom. He was staring down at me with crazed eyes, his whole body a tremble.

'I couldn't take any more,' he said, tugging at his long grey hair, alternately bending and straightening his legs like a child in need of a chamber pot.

It needed no doctor to state the result: Mrs Balme was as dead as Adam's unborn mother.

ELEVEN

She had broken her neck in the fall, and her head was slumped so far back that her face glared from between her shoulder blades. What a hideous sight it was! Her tongue protruded like a slice of ham, while her eyes, wide open in a frozen stare, were the eyes of a fish on a slab. She wore her usual drab gown and flowery apron, the difference being that both, owing to her fall, were yanked up around her waist, her best kept secret exposed, that Mrs Balme, on this occasion at least, wasn't wearing any underclothes. Those two bowed trunks of rippling lard, the vast pumpkin of an arse and balding seventy-year-old cunt were enough to give me nightmares for years to come. I turned away in disgust, following the line of her finger that pointed accusingly at a small portrait of Charles I. The comedy of this chance arrangement jolted me to my senses: *somebody* was guilty of the crime but it wasn't the stuttering little Stuart. The real culprit was at the top of the stairs, pleading for my help.

What was I to do? Ogress though she was, she hadn't deserved to die. But by the same token neither did Tom didn't deserve to hang on her account, as surely he would if the case went to trial. I would not have him indicted for murder, and there was every chance, if no one had witnessed the crime, that he wouldn't be implicated. Therefore did I charge myself to keep a clear head, to act calmly and swiftly in his interest. 'Come down the stairs. Now!' I commanded in a fierce whisper.

He descended obediently, with both hands on the banister rail, each step laboured and pronounced. 'Hurry!' I said, rushing to help him down. 'Quickly now, into the parlour.' I eased the door gently ajar to check the room was empty. 'Where's Balme?' I asked, when I'd got him to a chair.

'Out,' he said, still trembling. 'Went straight on to Bradford from church.'

Excellent, I thought. 'And Sukey? – Fanny? – George?'

The old man shook his head. 'I don't know. I've not seen them since breakfast time. I think George might have driven Abraham in the trap.'

I grabbed him by the shoulders and forced him to look at me. 'So nobody saw what happened?'

'No – no, I don't think so,' said Tom, spittle dribbling down his stubbly chin.

'Are you sure?' I demanded, shaking him hard for good measure.

'As sure as I can be,' he said, his lips still juddering from the violence.

'Oh why did you do it?' I shouted, with brief loss of nerve. 'What possessed you to kill her?' His words of a few weeks ago sounded in my head, namely how, since my arrival, he'd grown as unpredictable as the northern weather. Was it really so that *I* might have driven him to this? I recalled what else he'd said that day, how my own advancement could be hindered by the untoward things he might do. The old fool had been as good as his word, and that augured ill for us both.

Tom looked at me imploringly. 'I'm sorry lad. I didn't plan it – it just happened.' His eyes strayed out into the hall, where the old woman's cats, Romulus and Remus – a different sort of tom – were prowling and meowing round their mistress's corpse. 'I was behind her on the landing,' he went on. 'She was so slow on the stairs with those legs of hers. As she turned the bend in the staircase, I was right behind her. I was overcome with such hate that if I'd had an axe in my hand I'd have cleaved her head in two. But I'd only these, my bare hands...' – he raised the offending limbs palm upwards for my inspection – '...and so I pushed her. I don't think she suffered. She hit the bottom afore I could blink.'

I felt distracted by a sudden curiosity – had there been a last almighty Whaaa! as she hurtled down? 'She didn't even cry out,' said Tom, unwittingly answering my query.

'Come on, old friend,' I said, rousing myself on both our accounts, 'we've got work to do, and we haven't a moment to lose.' I shooed the grieving cats into the office and shut the door on their noise. 'Listen Tom,' I said, on my return. 'We must pretend it happened while you were working. It was I who walked through the door and found her lying there. Will you agree to that story and stick to it?' The old man nodded wearily. 'Come then,' I said, guiding him back to the hall. 'I shall raise the alarm now as if I've just come in.'

Leaving him at the foot of the stairs, I hurried to the kitchen bellowing the servants' names. I found Fanny busy making bread, and Sukey seated on the settle by the fire. 'Come quickly!' I exclaimed, adding in the same panicked tone, 'It's Missis Balme! She's fallen down the stairs!'

'Oh my Lord, no!' cried Fanny, dropping the mixing bowl with a great crash, and pressing her doughy hands to her face. Sukey sprang up in anguish, and clasped the cook's arm.

The three of us rushed to the hall, where Tom was on his knees by the body. 'It's no use,' he said, with a brilliant display of concern, 'she's done for. I think her neck's broken.'

The fat cook covered her face with her apron, sobbing, while Sukey cowered in the corner. Neither girl being used to death, they had smashed like glass in its presence. 'Pull yourselves together,' I said, confident they suspected nothing. 'Sukey, you must run to Doctor Stables immediately and tell him what's happened. Fanny, I suggest you fetch strong liquor to fortify us with.' Both girls obeying like well-trained dogs, I winked at Tom the moment their backs were turned. 'Home and dry,' I whispered, as Sukey rushed out the door.

She returned with Marshall just ten minutes later, having met with him on the Green. His examination of the patient was brief, for he could tell at a glance that she was dead. 'Slipped on the stairs, I presume,' he said, shaking his head regretfully. 'Such a steep staircase for an elderly woman.' Dear Marshall had played into our hands, diagnosing without prompting, and with all the authority of his profession, not merely the cause of death but the circumstances. 'We must do what is proper and carry her to the lounge,' he said, bending down to manoeuvre the corpse. 'If you, John, could take her arms, I think I can manage the legs.'

With some difficulty, for she was heavy as the ox whose tongue she had once enjoyed, we succeeded in laying her on the couch. Marshall placed coins over those accusing eyes, and when Fanny had fetched a blanket to cover her with, there was nothing else to be done till Abraham returned.

'What a shock it will be for him,' Marshall said, as the girls left to resume their duties. He would need some comforting, he believed, especially this evening, and as I saw Sukey's backside disappear through the door I guessed she'd be the one to oblige when she climbed into his well-strung bed.

'Abraham was very close to his mother,' I now heard Marshall say.

'Yes, *very* close,' I said, maintaining my solemn tone. He knew I'd had little regard for the woman but had marked me down as a man of principle who would behave with appropriate decorum.

'Nevertheless,' said Marshall with a sigh, 'these things do happen. Missis Balme was not a young woman.' He turned to us with his honest, open face. 'We must be thankful she didn't suffer.'

I cast a furtive glance at Tom. 'Yes, we must,' I said.

'If you'll excuse me, Doctor,' said Tom, turning to leave. 'This has been such a shock I really must go and lie down.' What a marvellous hidden talent for acting the old man had! It was all I could do not to applaud him.

'Yes, of course Tom,' said Marshall, and offered to mix something to help him sleep.

'No Doctor, that's quite all right,' said Tom, hand pathetically to brow – and again to excellent effect. 'I'd like to be alone with my thoughts.'

'Tom Gill is such a dear old soul,' said Marshall, as the killer shuffled out. 'I doubt if he'd harm a fly.' Perhaps not a fly, I thought, but Mrs Balme was a different matter.

Now that I knew we were safe, I was preoccupied with Little Willie again. 'Marshall, it may be disrespectful to change the subject, but my needs are pressing. I have a favour to ask.'

The doctor looked at me perplexed. 'My dear fellow, of course. You have only to ask.'

I thanked him for his kindness and sat down. The room was familiar, as it ought to be, yet how different from that first night, an hour before twelve, when I had sat in the same faded chair. The same dour surroundings too, that old spinet the only relief from the pent-up Yorkshire gloom. In two months I had come so far – yet how much farther still to go? The corpse – florin-eyed where it lay despite that covering of blanket – half appeared to be reckoning the miles.

'Well then,' I began, when Marshall had joined me in a neighbouring chair, "tis like this: I want you to take someone into your home, to provide a safe haven till a certain danger is passed.' I enlightened him only so far as was necessary, informing him who his new charge would be, with only a vague account of why he needed protection. I was unable, I said, to provide any detailed information at present but beseeched him to do as I asked.

'And you say there is nowhere else you might place him? – you have considered the appropriate institutions, I take it? – the Poor House at Troy for example?'

'Not safe enough,' I insisted. 'It's imperative that his whereabouts are kept secret. No institution could guarantee that.'

Marshall reflected a while, and not without the odd grimace. 'Mister Winn *is* a very uncouth little man, not to mention a smelly one.'

'Dirt washes off,' I countered quickly. 'You could bath him.'

'That would be a task for Phil,' replied Marshall with a wry smile. 'I should tell him it was his penance for attacking you...Very well,' he said, after more consideration. 'So long as it's not a permanent arrangement, and your cause is a good one. I see it must be or you would not have asked.'

'Thank you, Marsh,' I said, fondly shortening his name for the first time and setting a precedent between us. 'I'm forever in your debt. But heavens above I quite forgot the time. If you'll excuse me.' I checked my Hunter against the eight-day clock on the mantle, where Balme himself had once stood. His image that night was only half clear, hazy as it was with the unknown shadows of the future. And when I thought of that future and Abraham's part in it why, I wondered, did my heart feel brimful of hate? 'Now if you'll excuse me,' I said to forget it, 'I really must to be going. Willie will be waiting for me. May I bring him straight to the house?'

Marshall's brow knit in irritation; he would have preferred a few days grace. 'My dear fellow, if it were not for your charm,' he said, relenting.

I thanked him again, collected a clean coat from upstairs and hurried out. I ought to have ridden, but being such a poor saddler of a horse I wouldn't have saved much time. So I went on foot, arriving at the Wasp half an hour late. There was no sign of Willie in the dingy one-roomed interior, where a crook-backed fiddler played a mournful air.

'He hasn't been here,' growled the landlady, drawing ale for two besotted wretches sharing a half-lit pipe. 'Haven't seen him since last week.' I was perplexed by her reply, and asked if she were sure. 'How many more times? If I tells yer he hasn't been here, he hasn't been here.' There was a jagged scar on her face, token, I guessed, of some vicious tavern brawl. She was not a person to be argued with, so I thanked her curtly and left.

Hoping to find Willie nearby, I traced my steps back along the stream to the mill pond, wooded slope and elfin knoll. My searches were useless however: the little man was nowhere to be seen. I was puzzled as to his whereabouts but not unduly so. His nerve had failed him, I concluded, and he had gone to ground, slinked off to some hideout till evening when he'd no doubt resurface in one of his haunts – back there, perhaps, at the Wasp, or that far-flung dive they called the Cony Warren, low enough in the earth down its well-worn steps to be termed a cellar. I resolved to search again after nightfall.

I arrived back at the house to find three horsemen drawn up at the door. There was trouble even at a distance in the way they edged right up to the lintel itself, allowing their horses to butt their heads against the wood. Both my hands were deep in my pockets, closing hard on what they found there – nothing but a length of sealing wax and a ball of string. The grip of one hand was hard however, enough to soften the wax when I recognised Rawlings from Gravehunger Lodge. And now the wax near melted in my hand, for could it be that the giant to his left, shifting impatiently in the saddle, was none other than Larkin himself? Curse my

217

intuition that never let me down! – curse the dreams of day and night that matched themselves to reality! And as I neared and saw his long red hair and close-cropped beard I knew for sure it was he. It had come to this at last, as I knew it would. And it was so real, so frighteningly normal and real; all traces of that strange otherness falling away like so much empty air. What a fool I'd been to think otherwise: it was life and blood and earthly struggle: nothing more; nothing less. Or so I hoped.

The horses barred my path as I approached. 'Are you Eagle?' Larkin asked, fair snarling my name as his horse snuffled loudly. His voice was gruff and resonant, deeply sourced from his copious belly. And so familiar – how could that be so? It wasn't just the night in the graveyard; I felt I had known it all my life.

'Yes, I'm *Mister* Eagle,' I replied, emphasising the prefix. The two who straddled him picked up on my defiance and looked to their master to act.

'Then, sir, you are the author of this.' Larkin leaned towards me in the saddle with my letter in his hand. He crumpled it to a ball before I could see and threw it at my feet. I was determined to appear unmoved, and somehow, with unwonted courage, I managed to return his stare.

'That signifies nothing,' I said, but though my gaze was trained on his thick square jaw, it was unable, as if gravity intervened and kept it down, to meet those yellow-brown eyes with the lashless reddened rims. To turn away from them was inevitable, a defeat in itself, yet my insolence had vexed him enough to cause him to dismount. Well over six feet tall he stood, weighing all of twenty stone. Booted and spurred, clad in a long buff coat, his sword dangling at his side, he seemed of another place or time; a war lord of the Middle Ages or a ruthless mercenary from foreign parts.

'And *nothing* is what I'll pay, neither to you or your client,' he said, eyeing me *de haut en bas.*. 'I'm not a man to be crossed, so think twice. You'll feel my bite right till the very end,' he added, through appropriately clenched teeth. His speech betrayed hints of refinement, of distant good breeding before the badness in the apple took hold and made him what he'd patently become – the antithesis of civilisation and culture. He got what he wanted by brute force, and he settled his own scores. Of the latter there must have been many, for he seemed inordinately susceptible to slights. If he but knew how I had slighted him already! as thoughts of his Lady came to mind. And perversely, suicidally – and with much hypocrisy given what I'd done for Tom – I wanted to go further – accuse him of murder direct.

'And the law will take its course,' was all I said instead. Yet my words, inexplicably, had burst forth without quaver. I saw in his eyes the mark of surprise, heard in his laugh a faint edge of unease. He knew well, though, the power of silence, and faced me out with a long pause. His aides glowered supportively, Rawlings narrowing his pirate's eyes, and the other, who I now realised must be Willie's Jeremiah, leaning back in the saddle to aim his foul spit. I might have called him a filthy swine but used the vagrant as a weapon instead. And never mind his henchmen as I asked the question of Larkin himself: 'Know you Little Willie? Of course you do, but where is he? – have you killed him too?' Though I'd nothing material to accuse him with, my searching eyes accompanied the question.

The smirks receded from the faces of the hirelings. Larkin's reaction was more complex; he blinked his rheumy eyes and leaned his head to one side. 'What mean you by that?' he said thickly. I saw his hand stray towards his sword hilt and find comfort there in a soft grip. Surely even *he* wouldn't risk cutting me down in broad daylight. Probably not, but it was all I could do to keep my composure. You must be strong, I urged myself, live to fight another day.

There was another intimidating silence, but with a difference: Larkin used it to think things over, to conclude that he too, in order to plan his next step, wished to retreat from the fray. 'You've thrown down the gauntlet, *boy*,' he said, turning on his heels and remounting his fine dark roan. 'From this moment on, you and I are enemies. And remember this!...' he shouted, turning his animal fast and expertly, 'you cannot win against me. I shall destroy you!'

My throat was dry and my brow tingled with sweat as I watched them ride away. How I'd held my ground I would never know. The burden lay so heavy that I sat down on the doorstep dejected. Across the road, beyond the gates of Horseford Hall, I saw the high trees stirring in a freshening breeze. I pictured the Hall itself and Sir Walter elegant within. 'Young fool,' he would no doubt say, 'do you not know which side your bread is buttered? Cross the Rubicon at your peril,' he would add, 'but do not, in these dangerous times, expect the law to rush to your defence.' And crossed it I had, I reasoned, but only with a single tremulous toe. By letting matters drop, there was still time to step back completely. Let conscience be your guide, I said, but conscience – curse it! – told me to press on. And as if to tease me, the door behind fell open with my weight, pitching me backwards into the hall.

'Nay lad, what do yer think yer playing at?' I turned to see a pair of buckled shoes, followed by stockings, breeches and waistcoat. Craning my neck still further I saw Tom's face staring with a devilish grin. 'I thought you'd fallen down the stairs,' he said, with all the irony in the world.

TWELVE

That night I searched for Little Willie. I found him not at the promising
Cony Warren, nor did my enquiries there yield much fruit. As I entered
that dark hole where drinkers huddled with their dogs round the smoky
fire, I was greeted with hostility from man and beast, and was fortunate to
leave unmolested. My questions yielded farts, grunts and abuse, but the
one civil answer I did receive – from a cripple so deformed he looked to
have two heads – told me what I wished to know: that Willie hadn't been
there since Saturday last. Visits to his other haunts proved as fruitless, as
did my walks round the village though I tried not to fear the worst. It was
only a matter of time, I said, before he turned up.

I returned home exhausted at eleven o'clock. As I crossed the hall I
noticed the parlour door open and a figure crouching on the floor. I
quickly realised it was Abraham kneeling in prayer beside a coffin, whose
head and foot were lit by candles. The undertaker had called in my
absence, I concluded, edging in quietly to pay my respects. My tread
disturbed a floorboard and the son glanced round in agony. His face was

rimed with so many tears it looked to have been pickled. The grown man had become a child again.

'It's Mother,' he sobbed. 'Mother's gone...'

'I'm sorry Abraham, truly I am.' The attorney didn't seem to hear me; he was a prisoner of his own grief, blind and alone in his cell. I was but a shadow to him, this man who was a victim himself now, a sufferer deserving of pity. 'My apologies for disturbing you,' I said, retreating with a heavy heart.

Tom was waiting in the hall. Unable to leave the area for long, he was like a ghost condemned to haunt the scene of his wickedness. 'Do you think he suspects?' he asked in a frightened whisper. 'He's been down on his knees afore that coffin over an hour. He keeps whispering to her. What do you think he's saying?'

'He suspects nothing. The poor bastard's grieving that's all,' I said, and brushed past him up the stairs.

In my cold chamber I lay down on the bed to think. The storm of that momentous day had abated at last, leaving me to count the cost. Had its

wind, so violent at times, blown me any good? In aiding and abetting
Tom I had not behaved well; the act made me miserable to think of. And
yet how easy its accomplishment had been – and how tempting the next.
One evil deed begot another, making it difficult, if not impossible, to
return to a righteous path. I felt compelled to be bad, the desire to be so
unfathomably linked to sex. Lady Larkin came to mind, her naked body
and distinctive smell; the ripe womanly laugh that held in its ringing
tones the very essence of her moist and ageless cunt. I remembered her
breasts, their firmness and their heaviness; two delicious globes lined
with a stockwork of faint blue veins. How right she had been in saying I
would want her again. It wasn't just the tumbling we had shared, hungry,
gluttonous and wildly pleasurable; it was the strength imparted to my
fighting resolve. And the person I was fighting was her husband. His
face and hers had merged together in my mind's eye, the outcome oddly
appealing. Though her own hand would have felt much softer, I decided
to frig myself. Despite the cold I finished in a few seconds, lying there
sighing at the mess I'd made.

Naturally or otherwise my thoughts turned to the spider and what – if I
didn't know better – the creature appeared to live upon there in its half-
pint jar. I thought to take a peep, if only in the hope that the hideous
thing had grown small. It wasn't to be, I discovered with a shudder, and

nothing but the dread of releasing it kept me from dropping the jar. For by now its body was the size of an oak apple, and its legs were thorny and long. The gluey deposit was half way up the glass and would surely have been higher had the spider not fed upon it. This defied logic, but what else *could* it be eating? And now my shaking of the vessel so upset the creature's delicate balancing on the sticky surface that its whole body went under. My own body jerked in a terrified spasm and I all but threw the jar on to the sill. I had no sooner done so when a knock sounded at the door. Sukey, in her agitated state, hadn't waited for me to answer. She was there in the doorway facing where I stood by the window, blocking more, a lot more, than the darkness beyond. And I was barely buttoned, I now realised, there in my red breeches with the tell-tale stains.

'I hope I'm not disturbing you,' she said, clutching herself for comfort.

'Not at all,' I lied, and motioned her to sit on the bed. She was too preoccupied, I hoped, to notice anything amiss.

'Oh sir, what's to become of us?' she asked, wringing her hands as she spoke. 'I'm nowt but a bag of nerves, 'n' Fanny's the same – George too I shouldn't wonder.' It wasn't just the mistress's death, she said, they were worried about the master and how queer he looked. 'What's to become of us?' she repeated, bursting into tears as she toyed with the counterpane.

Her womanly ministrations, such as they were, had clearly had no effect. But despite Tom's warning of her artful nature, I had a genuine regard for the girl and it pained me to see her distressed. 'You'll feel better in a day or two,' I said, taking her small hand in mine and feeling its roughened palm. 'Just you wait and see.'

My kindness went unheeded; I had, by straying unwittingly from the window, exposed my dark secret. Sukey had spotted the jar and was now regarding it with baffled wonder. 'What – is it?' she asked, taking both candles and edging towards the sill.

'I don't know,' I said, which happened to be the truth.

Her expression switched to a silent scream before she suddenly screamed for real. It was the kind of bilious scream, so loud and hysterical, one needed to strike her to stop. But she was out the door by now, screaming along the corridor, down the stairs and out into the street where, even from the rear of the house, I could hear her shrill notes half way down the hill.

So my secret is out, I told myself, as the spider lunged clumsily against the glass. What's to become of us? I asked, to quote Sukey's own tearful phrase. The simple solution was to jettison what I did not need in any sense of the word. I knew it was the way – the only way – but the gap between saying and doing was wide – and growing wider every day. The spider had a hold on me impossible to explain, least of all to myself. I could no more cast it out than I could my own soul. All I could do from now on was hide it more carefully, choosing, after careful consideration, the narrow space behind the heavy wardrobe. To see it again would necessitate strenuous effort that even I, never mind Sukey, would find it a struggle to summon. As for the previous scare, the tweenie must be placated and I had my excuse to hand. I would cite her distress apropos Mrs Balme and plead all ignorance in the affair: 'Creature in the jar? – what creature in the jar? My poor Sukey, you must have imagined it.'

They buried Mrs Balme three days later on a cold wet Tuesday morning. A hearse with four plumed horses conveyed her coffin to the church, where a small crowd had gathered to pay their respects. Abraham having no living relatives, the mourners were, with the exception of his immediate household, a mixture of neighbours and long-standing clients of the practice. Some were both, and a few, such as Sir Walter and his

Lady were very eminent people indeed. What a hypocrite I felt as I sat in the dusty pew beside Tom, listening to the Reverend Gaunt, who was old and due to retire, drone on interminably about the life and death of Maude Matilda (it was the first time I'd heard mention of her Christian names) Balme. 'Death came upon her,' he intoned nasally, 'at an hour when she little thought upon it, and very sudden.' The irony of the phrase pricked me exceedingly; I wanted to cry out in mingled laughter and pain. And next, when 'It pleased Almighty God of his goodness to take her unto himself out of this sinful world, which she went out of as easy as it was possible for anyone,' I wanted to shout, 'Yes, she had a good push down the bedroom stairs!' I glanced sideways at the solemn face of Tom, saw how he rested his hat, with its crepe hat-band, reverently in his lap, along with his black mourning gloves and black silk scarf. And you, I thought, did the pushing, my friend – how can you sit there so perfectly sorrowful and devout? You have missed your vocation, Tom – you ought to have been an undertaker's mute.

'Don't stare at me,' he whispered out the corner of his mouth. 'I'm trying to keep a straight face.'

'You're doing exceptionally well,' I replied, as the aged minister reached his peroration. 'I hope she is now eternally happy in everlasting glory,' he wailed with uplifted arms, and I heard in my head Mrs Balme's voice as she entered the pearly gates. To the angels who called her name she cried, 'Whaaa! Oh Whaaa! – *I* might be here but my darling Abe isn't!' But there was comfort for the son grieving below in the Reverend's final words, 'Oh Lord God Almighty send help from Thy Holy Place to her dear son Abraham to withstand so great a shock, and to live and die so easily as she did.'

'Mmmm,' grunted Tom strangely, as something turned over in his mind. It had turned over in mine too, though what it was exactly my mind had yet to shape.

Later, as we stood shivering at the graveside in that biting easterly wind, I felt a rush of pity for my bereaved partner in his mud-splattered suit of mourning. His cloak had blown open in the breeze, and his face, as it looked down into that oblong chasm, was raw with grief. Odious bitch though she was, and gone not to paradise but the other place for all I knew, her son had truly loved her. I knew this and respected it, making my horror as genuine as his love when Tom whispered in my ear, 'We should do *him* in next. It wouldn't be difficult in his state, and I think we'd get away with it.'

I knew at once that the old man was serious, that the demon I'd helped unleash in him was an evil one indeed. That he had good cause to hate the Balmes went without saying; his desire for revenge was understandable. So too, when one considered the facts, was that push on the staircase. Though he'd done a terrible wrong, it *was* possible to condone it. But a moment of rashness was one thing; cold-bloodied murder was another. To make him understand I was not his man, I drew nearer to Abraham at the graveside and, as he watched the soil fall from the preacher's hand on to his mother's coffin, I made a show of wrapping his cloak about his body and offering words of comfort. The smirk on Tom's face as I glanced fleetingly back told me he wasn't convinced.

Nor had I heard the last. Over the funeral dinner that followed he repeated his suggestion, adding that, if we planned the deed carefully, the coroner's verdict would be that Abraham killed himself whilst the balance of his mind was disturbed.

'And where would that leave us?' I asked, as he helped himself to more boiled beef and greens. Foodwise, I concluded, Tom's life had become an orgy after Mrs Balme's death.

'That's for you to work out,' he said, enjoying a mouthful of roasted potato. I asked him what he meant, and he said I knew very well. 'You're a cleverer lawyer than I could ever have been. Get your mind to work,' he said, chewing hard. 'Where there's a will there's a way. Or in this case, where there's a way, there's a will – a will to suit *us*.' He looked at me with an odd twinkle in his eye. 'You do get my meaning I hope. I'm talking about *wills.*'

At what I thought he was suggesting – that prior to murdering him we induce Abraham to make us the sole beneficiaries of his will – I could scarce get my breath. I glanced round the table at the faces of the other diners: twenty persons of genteel respectability, each one, as they talked and ate, taking it for granted that Tom and I, trusted members of the Balme household, shared with them a common purpose of decency and duty, namely to mourn the loss of Maude Matilda Balme and offer comfort to her grieving son now picking absently at his food. The heat of the room became suddenly oppressive, the voices louder, nothing but mourning wear rustling black and blurred before my eyes. Marsh was seated downtable and caught my eye. Sensing his concern as I rose, I pleaded dumbshow my urgent need for air. Sukey, who had been officiating at table, came with me to the door, her face glistening with a young girl's sweat.

'Convey my apologies to our guests,' I said. 'Tell them I wish to walk and clear my head.' The girl was so credulous. She wiped her face on her apron and nodded convinced. How easily too she'd accepted my opinion on the spider – an hallucination, I'd said, caused by your state of mind – shall I ask Doctor Stables to confirm?

'Oh no sir, there's no need for that,' she'd said, all trust and naïve dismay. 'What a fool he'd think me if he heard.'

Yes, but what would he think of me, I wondered, should he ever look behind my wardrobe?

* * *

Tom's words plagued me the rest of the day, and when Abraham approached me that evening he must have seen the worry on my face. 'If you could spare me a few minutes, John,' he said, in the friendly tone he had reserved for me since Mrs Balme's death, 'I'd be very grateful. It concerns my mother's will,' he continued, closing the parlour door behind us.

A reading of the will before expectant guests had proved unnecessary. Abraham had acted as his mother's attorney, and was in addition the testator's sole executor and heir at law. He was merely wishing, for the sake of propriety, to have me verify that the document was sound. It *was*, though its contents surprised me: Mrs Balme had been a richer woman than I'd imagined. Her personal estate alone, comprising cash at the house, monies in the Leeds bank and various sums lent on mortgage and bond amounted to over six-hundred pounds, while the two cottages and fine capital messuage near Wakefield had a combined value of near a thousand.

'All would seem to be in order,' I said with assumed casualness, sliding the document back across the table. The attorney seemed needlessly grateful, as if I'd helped him solve an intractable problem. I realised instantly that in matters great and small he *more* than needed my help: he couldn't do without it. The strength I had heard him praying for had deserted him as soon as his mother was interred.

My judgement was vindicated over the coming weeks when Abraham turned malleable in my hands. No longer did he talk roughly with me, nor with Tom either for that matter. Never again did he strut about the room on those bow legs inherited from his mother. His appetite dwindled to that of a faddy infant, and soon he was eating less than the miserly pair had once fed Tom. And as Tom now fattened and appeared to grow taller, Abraham grew thinner and shrunken, as though one were feeding on the other. The attorney's complexion grew pale and wan; he developed a pronounced stoop and a slouched way of walking. He took less care over his dress and toilet, shuffling round the house in dressing-gown and slippers, spending long hours in the lounge with pipe and sherry till he fell into a heavy snooze. Sometimes he would come into the office and sit awhile at his desk, staring into space or invisibly doodling with a dry quill. Sometimes too, having looked over my shoulder to watch me at work, he would appear to puzzle at the complexity, shake his head in dejection and drift back slowly to his seat. In body and spirit, life was deserting him; either that, or *he* had given up on life.

When it came to business he confined himself to the simplest tasks, a bit of drawing and engrossing here, some copying there. No more use to the practice was he than an articled clerk in his first months of training. His pride and joy of recent years – the position as Law Clerk to the Navigation Company – he no longer cared for; he had neither the mind nor the energy for its demands, and it was I who kept him up to date, taking over the various causes the company was defending, placing the necessary advertisements, and doing all that was required on the conveyancing side. The ease with which I persuaded him to part with a share of his salary plus all attendant fees emboldened me to suggest that he write to the Company pleading ill health and recommending me as his immediate successor. In short, I had become master of the house and practice in all but name.

But that question of name was all important, for without it I stood to gain only trifles. Wait – had I really said *trifles*? If a fortune-teller had told me that, within a year of the expiration of my clerkship, I would have secured not only a quarter share in a good country practice, but also two lucrative appointments normally reserved for the most eminent and mature practitioner, I would have told her to think again. Such good fortune, I would have said, could not be mine in twenty years, never mind in one. That fortune *had* shone on me was surprising enough; much more so was my lack of joy. I felt not a morsel of contentment with my new-found lot. Satisfaction would only come, I told myself, when I had everything – everything that was Abraham's lock stock and barrel. Thanks to Tom, those seeds of avarice that must have lain dormant for years had sprouted shoots. They would not be denied their growth, and, nurtured as they were by his helping hand, had now the option of foul means as well as fair.

Tom, whose door was ajar, was watching me from his high stool. A foxy smile lighted his face and the old man seemed happy. He nodded once, sharply and definitively, as if to say, 'All will be well. Trust your old Tom.' And as I watched him resume his scribbling, whistling some odd little tune as he worked that goose-quill so deftly, I reflected that nothing in the world now seemed to trouble him, that having scaled the initial and, to his mind, insurmountable heights, he could go on to conquer the world even at his time of life. Dream though it was that he lived, and delusion he was living under, I took heart nonetheless from this would-be Alexander in his dotage, knowing that he, aged and frail as he was, would be right behind me through thick and thin. A cynic would say there was obvious cause for his behaviour: that his murder of Mrs Balme, and my complicity, had bound him to my side inextricably. But there was more to it than that; his attitude had been there from the start. His was my mother's role of blind, unquestioning loyalty. Even when ignorant of the true nature of a problem, its degree of seriousness and danger, he'd still be sure he could help. That too was a delusion, but a comforting one all the same.

It comforted me now as I flung open my books; it allowed me to dream that all *would* be well; that even if the worst should happen Old Mother Tom would protect me, all would come out in Sukey's Monday wash. I glanced up again and found him watching me still. It was I who nodded this time, *sharply and definitively*. The message behind it was vague even to me but it served the purpose. He believed he'd got what he wanted – confirmation that I'd always take his part, that come what may we would face the future together. Tom Goose-Quill, Tom All-Alone, Old Mother Tom – my names for him were all on my tongue as I looked up one more time. With head bent low over his desk, he had returned earnestly to his copying, fashioning with inky scratches letters perfect as his contentment.

I may be a better lawyer, I thought, unfurling a large skin of parchment on which I'd drawn up a deed, but I'll never have as fine a law hand or make such perfect copies...or make such *perfect* copies...where there's a *will*, there's a way. I cursed the fine mind I'd been blessed with. Its machinery wanted no supervision; it need only get wind of a problem and off it would go, spinning a solution. Tom to draft a will for Abraham, you say, leaving every thing to us? Tom to forge his signature, as he is well capable of doing? And we, who have become his bosom friends, shall be his witnesses, executors and administrators? Then we kill him and enjoy the golden egg? All well and good, I said, but it may not be fool-proof: the time must be right and so must the method. Yet merely saying so would turn things faster still; even when asleep the machinery would run; it wouldn't stop till the plan was perfect. Conscience, as I'd hoped it would, tried to intervene but the business it chose was soiled.

Lady Larkin's more than most. The action I'd predicted had come to pass. Mr Wood's attorney had taken out a citation to compel her to deal plainly about her late father's effects. That her chances of victory were excellent, however, if I took the dishonourable path was not in doubt. She need only swear an affidavit that her father left no monies in the house, act prudently in disposing of the twelve-hundred pounds she had found there, and, as she had every reason to do, keep her silence. Moreover, as the debts owing to her father had turned out to be trifles, and were marginally outweighed by his own debts to his creditors, she could have no qualms about giving a true account of her receipts and disbursements as administratrix. For my part, I could rest assured that there was little chance of this business bringing me into discredit either in the courts where I practised or in the eyes of my clients and neighbours. Any damage done was solely to my own sense honour, to that view of myself as an incorruptible practiser of the law. Yet if I were honest, I had ceased to live up to that image the moment I left London; indeed, my life of late had made a mockery of it. How could a man who was planning murder speak of honour? The truth was that part of me *did* speak of it and meant it. I still abhorred injustice, still had sympathy for the poor and oppressed. And what else but a love of justice made me pursue Long Larkin? – pursue him not only in the matter of his debt but for the murder of my friend? So spoke that man again who'd condemn murder in another and condone it in himself!

But we were what we were, I reasoned, and there was far more grey than black or white. So too with the law and politics, with the country and the world at large. Sir Walter understood how it was; he took it for granted that things were rarely straightforward, that such was the way of the world. The waters of the law, though their spring was pure in origin, had soon been blackened by the human stain. The Baronet had tried to tell me as much in his park that day. I had been naive, blind to the realities of life. Now, seeing the essence of his argument so plainly, and seeing it at work in myself, I saw its truth in a wider sense. All humanity was flawed, therefore all institutions created by it were flawed also. None of us could change our allotted portions of good and bad. We must follow one or the other as circumstance, mood, and, if one believed in such things, greater forces directed. Perhaps we all had our good and bad angels.

A better angel of mine, and one to value, had helped me to fight my own cowardice. Fight it hard, as I'd done with Larkin, and the evil inside me began to recede. Of this I was sure – in so far as I was sure of anything. I picked up my quill accordingly; I dipped it in the ink dark as liver blood. Do it, I said, addressing my own hand that hesitated. It's only a small thing in truth, not Richard whose killers walked free; not Little Willie, of whom nothing yet had been heard. It's just a debt, a sum owed on personal bond. The hand moved, a little sticky on the paper but it moved. It wrote to my agents in London enclosing an affidavit of debt and requesting they send a writ of *Latitat* for Ely Rhodes against Edward Larkin Esquire. The warrant issued thereon I *would* have executed by a bailiff, whom I *would* instruct to arrest Larkin should he refuse to pay what was owed, provide good security for the debt, or meet the cost of bail.

I leaned back in my chair and tried to stomach the outcome. The prospect was bleak: even if the bailiff took care to meet with Larkin alone, perhaps on the road, the defendant was such a dangerous and desperate fellow that the officer's safety couldn't be guaranteed. And Larkin, in refusing to let me lay hold of him, would be spitting defiance in my face, daring me to go further, confident that every attempt I made to invoke the law against him would end in his triumph and my humiliation.

As the local magistrate, Sir Walter was my main, perhaps my only hope, and should the outcome turn out as I'd predicted, I resolved to try him one last time.

THIRTEEN

March was here at last, and with it came wind, rooks and talk of mad hares. I felt the wind keenly in that early spring, wild and sharp as it blew off the moors; I heard the rooks atop the oaks in the churchyard; I tasted the hares (mad or otherwise) coursed by Tom, who took Abraham with him dog-like at his side. How the mighty do fall; how the tables do turn! The master attorney was Tom's to command; he who was once the abused was now the abuser. But only so far – like me, though without the guilt, Tom had a pretence to keep up, and not only in public. Even about the house we must be careful; merely to talk roughly to Abraham would raise the servants' suspicions. Tom and I must reach our goal gradually, with no outward show of leaps and bounds. We must be vigilant even in our sleep so as not to drop our guard. Any mistakes must be quickly rectified. Fortunately as lawyers we were both well versed in contingency.

The time of year found me busy with Assizes work, the first I had handled directly.

The work included more ejectment cases, a land valuation dispute concerning the Canal Navigation, and an action of Replevin transferred from a minor court. All of it was tedious rather than complex, and necessitated my absence at York for over a week. I couldn't afford to be away, for it left vital business unattended. To have a boy come clerk with us would have solved matters, but we couldn't engage one yet – not till we were safe and settled.

Lady Day found me holding a Court Leet for Sir Walter's manor of Stanhope, collecting his tenants' rents, hearing their complaints, charging them to make repairs to cottages and farms, threatening eviction over broken leases. I threatened even in doubtful cases, remembering my employer's precept that the landlord was always right. Poor James Robinson, whose barn was fallen down on account of age and not through any default of his own, ought, as tenant at will, and without a lease, to have had redress via Sir Walter. Obliged though the Baronet was to repair it, his answer was predictable: 'He must repair it himself, or quit the farm forthwith.' Such was what I told the tenant, never mind his wife and eight children who, like so many more of late, must go into the poor house. I heard later, however, with secret relief that a neighbour had kept a roof over the family's head by supporting the expense of repairs.

'Excellent, you have put the frighteners on them all, I do declare!' said Sir Walter, when I called upon him to pay him his rents and wish him happy in his favourite month. 'Here is five pounds for your loyalty. 'Tis time I trusted you more.' Thus was it so, and the same month found me handling my patron's finances, lending his money on mortgage and bond, making purchases and sales on his behalf. Most notably I treated with one James Lomax of Barnsley Esquire about letting a considerable colliery of thirty acres of coals in the Stanhope estate. This I was able to arrange on very generous terms to Sir Walter, namely that he would receive a good part of the profits, yet not be at any risk or expense in the getting of the coals, nor be under any obligation to keep the roads in good repair or make any satisfaction for damages done to the tenants. The Baronet was exceedingly grateful and made me another present of ten pounds, plus a barrel of oysters.

And yet a March which had served me well gave way to a troublesome April. The debt suit against Larkin had stuck fast. I had prepared my client for a long fight through the courts, where Larkin would seek to delay matters every step of the way. I expected him too, the moment he was arrested, to procure bail and try to put the plaintiff off that way, letting him see that to force a trial would be throwing good money after bad. That he should dig his heels, however, at the very outset, saying thus far and no farther, was an outcome I had not envisaged. Repeated attempts by the bailiff to have the defendant served with the warrant ended in failure, either by Larkin keeping out of the way, or having his bullies threaten to break the officer's head. It was as though he were goading me, calling my bluff at every throw. Such was his arrogance, this man of base principles, that he believed he was above the law. I decided I must do as I'd planned, keep faith with my resolve and go again to Sir Walter. My recent efforts on his behalf would surely count in the reckoning.

I was shown through to the Baronet in his drawing room at the rear of the Hall. He was dressed in readiness for a journey, and could spare me but a few minutes. At my mention of Larkin I saw his countenance change from kindly welcome to scowl. 'I am very busy,' he said impatiently, donning his gold-laced hat. 'Perhaps some other time.'

'Hear me out, Sir Walter,' I pleaded, as he headed for the door. 'I know not which way to turn. That man flouts the law with impunity. He makes a mockery of my attempts to arrest him. The bailiff's hands are tied.'

Sir Walter, with a hand on the door-knob, prevaricated. 'Those King's Bench clerks make the writs out with such short returns these days. They are so well off for business they do as they like. It may be unfashionable to say so, but I prefer the Common Pleas.'

'It has little to do with the writs *or* the respective merits of the two courts,' I said. 'The problem is Larkin. He won't bow to the law.'

My employer turned on his heels and faced me sternly. 'You disappoint me, John,' he said, pointing with a gloved finger. 'I had you marked down for a shrewd young man. Did I not tell you to bide your time?'

'Yes, you did,' I answered heatedly, 'but there is such a thing as honour, not to mention reputation. I have a client to whom Larkin owes a considerable sum.'

'Oh John...' – the Baronet drew near and clasped my sleeve – '...I have a fondness for you but you have much to learn. Drop this suit, I beg of you. Leave Larkin and his money alone.'

'But the money is not his,' I insisted. 'It belongs to my client, who has charged me to recover it. I must do my duty by him.'

'Then you must do it alone,' said Sir Walter, waxing cold again. 'I'll not move against Larkin for debt, he is too useful to be pursued for trifles. You must have greater cause than that.'

'What about murder? Is that not cause enough?'

The Baronet took a pinch of snuff from a delicate silver box. 'You are referring again to your late friend, I presume?' he said, sniffing affectedly and snapping shut the lid. 'The attorney who was drowned in the Aire?'

'Aye, and deliberately so.'

'Though you have no proof,' Sir Walter said, in the accusatory tone of a barrister.

'And what if I had? – would Larkin find in you a powerful adversary?'

'You question my abilities?' the Baronet asked in furious amazement.

I was quick to assure him on that point, but I did wonder about his view of the law.

The great man crossed the room and leaned his hand against the casement. Staring out at the broad expanse of parkland, he asked disappointed, 'Did I not make myself plain that day?' He told me again about the talk coming out of the Americas – seditious talk of freedom and secession, all preached daily from their traitorous pulpits. 'How dare they demand a republic? How dare they call themselves *the best people?*' he railed, turning to face me. 'To think those vile ungrateful wretches are of British stock!'

I felt compelled to nod agreement, sensing that this loyal king's-man and patriot was giving me another chance to nail my colours to the mast. His tone softened when he saw me agree. 'And to cap it all John,' he said, bidding me take his hand, 'we have traitors in our midst. One fine swine in Yorkshire – a nobleman too would you believe? – has built a Liberty Arch in his grounds commemorating their damned Declaration of Independence. What say you to that?'

'Despicable,' I said, comforted by his scented fragrance and the fatherly squeeze of his hand.

'So you *do* understand how we need all the help we can get?'

I allowed him to lecture me again on Larkin's essential utility, how he was a hero to many – a 'King David' – and a villain only to some. To put a halter round his neck now would create more problems than it solved. Sir Walter's powerful charm seemed to mix with the perfumes of his body, working up a heady potion that lulled and appeased. Part of me wanted it to be so, and though there were flaws in the arguments I had heard, I was unwilling to voice them too passionately. Modulating my tone to that of the doubting confederate, I merely asked whether the benefits of Larkin's tyranny, so manifest among the low and ignorant mob, transferred to men of middling means. How did they – the merchants, farmers and clergy hereabouts – feel about his unchecked rule?

'I doubt if any one of them has lost a minute's sleep,' replied Sir Walter languidly. 'They care for nothing so long as their property is safe, so long as they remain free to pursue wealth in the manner they desire. And I can say to them, most categorically, that they are safe in the one and free in the other.' He added that Larkin himself would remain so too as long as he kept within bounds. 'The man is clever enough to know his limitations. He knows how far he can go. No harm must come to any of the *best people* – and I use that term in its one true sense. I realise the same can't be said for some of those he employs.'

'But Richard was one too – those *best people* as you term them. He was an Attorney-at-law, like me. In killing him, Larkin did what you said he must never do – he went too far.'

Sir Walter frowned and withdrew his hand. At length he said, 'Then for argument's sake let's suppose that Larkin *was* implicated in your friend's death. The question is, how much? It may be that he didn't intend the murder. Perhaps it was his men that went too far.'

'Most unlikely,' I said. 'Larkin wanted Richard out of the way – for good.'

Up came his finger again to check and admonish. 'My dear John, there is still that matter of proof. You haven't a shred of it.' The truth hurt a little here: I had indeed only a shred – the deposition of a sodomite vagrant whose person wasn't even to be found. I had hoped to supplement my case with Jackie England's testimony, but that too had proved forlorn. The old farmer had known that I'd be back – indeed his words that afternoon – *you'll get no more from me today* – had constituted half an invite. What I had learned, however, was tantalisingly small. The mystery attorney who preceded Mr Balme had turned out to be Richard, but tell me any more he would not. Bedridden he was, and that's how he hoped to stay, dying in his bed unmolested.

'Not a shred I say,' repeated Sir Walter, still refusing to bend. That he felt some pressure nonetheless was evident in his manner. His hooded eyes looked guiltily averted, focused for the sake of it on a fine japanned cabinet with its image of the sun resplendent. 'Get *more* that a shred and we shall see.'

'See *what?*' I ventured, striving to pin him down but to no avail. Enough was enough, said his languorous wave. I had made him late, he added, and it didn't do to keep a beautiful woman waiting. Who was she? I wondered, for I doubted he had meant his wife. It was the way he'd pronounced *beautiful,* and beauty alone might explain the frippery of his dress.

'In the meantime,' he said, 'I'd be grateful if you'd stop pursuing Larkin for debt. If you're worried about losing face, I could – how shall I put it? – square matters. I might say it was I who asked you to let things rest. As for your client, you must shift there as best you can. Tell him his suit must surely fail. Probably in his heart he knows it to be so.'

'Very well – I agree.' I knew in my own heart that Larkin wouldn't be fooled but the plan saved face of sorts. More importantly, it bought me some time.

'Good, then I'll bid you adieu,' said Sir Walter, striding towards the door. 'The servants will show you out.'

* * *

That same evening as I worked at my desk Tom announced I had a visitor. 'It's her – Lady Larkin,' he whispered, adding that she waited in the outer office. Unwilling to risk the servants, and having learned that Tom was discrete, she had entered that way on purpose.

'Then you had better show her through,' I said, emerging from my desk with racing heart.

'Come this way, your Ladyship,' I heard him say, my mind teeming with fears and passions I'd tried to forget. Indeed, since that day at the Lodge I had seen her but once, briefly, to take the affidavit, and though we'd corresponded by letter it was solely on matters of business. I knew not what to expect, bracing myself at the rustle of garments, the clack of heels on the wooden floor. Suddenly she was there in the doorway, a haughty goddess of fierce beauty, signals of exquisite womanhood alive like breath on the musty air. I watched her negotiate the step, couldn't keep my eyes from staring. She wore a pink sackback dress that showed the frills of her shift at the neck. On her head was a muslin cap, and her hands were tucked inside a giant Swan's down muff.

'Leave us Tom,' I said faintly, my tongue lame at the sight of her.

'And close the door if you please,' she said curtly, as if she knew his habit of peeping.

'To what do I owe this honour?' I asked, when she'd pulled a hand from her muff and allowed me to kiss it.

She drew back with a playful laugh. 'Here am I in your humble office and you're as stiff and starchy as my corset,' she said, seating herself delicately on the edge of a chair. 'Come – why do you *think* I'm here? – to see my little eaglet of course.' She rose again and embraced me, tickling my face with that enormous muff till she'd made me sneeze. Next she scattered some papers on my desk, picked up a Precedent-Book and dropped it purposely hard. 'It makes you grow old and wrinkly just looking at it all,' she said yawning. 'How do you tolerate such tedium?'

'One has to make a living,' I said with a shrug.

'I expect you're right,' she said, removing her muff completely and glancing about the office. 'Thank you, by the way, for handling my little case. It proceeds very well I trust?'

'Well enough,' I said guardedly. 'Have no fear, madam, you'll get what you think you deserve.'

The sarcasm of my tone was lost on her as she ran her fingers over my papers again. 'Call me Phoebe, won't you?' she said, her eyes smouldering with a fierce animal magnetism.

'Very well – *Phoebe,*' I said quietly, fearful of what she might suggest. 'But what are you doing here? It's not safe.'

'Fear not, I came alone in the gig which I've left discretely at the rear. I'm as safe here as...' She had paused mid-sentence, attracted by one of the documents. 'That looks familiar,' she said, straightening out the parchment and squinting at the law hand.

'Yes, it's your Marriage Settlement. I had one or two points to look up,' I said with a casual air, keeping to myself what I'd really been doing: scrutinising her husband's papers for incriminating evidence.

'Do you know what it feels like to love and hate someone?' she asked of a sudden, more in accusation than enquiry. 'I could die for him and I could also kill him – that is the extent of my love and hate.' She picked up the Marriage Deed and flapped it fiercely like a fan. Fans, it is said, have their own secret code and I wondered at the message I was meant to read. 'At this moment I would like to kill him, to despoil all that he holds dear – if such he holds anything. This document, for instance...' – she crossed to the table in the centre of the room – '...I want to despoil it in a way that comes natural to me,' she added, spreading it out on the green-beige cloth and securing it with a pair of books.

'I don't understand.'

'Oh but I think you do.' Her mouth was close to mine as she said so, and soon she had kissed me there. Her breath tasted thin and sharp, not wholly sweet. 'The language we speak is a simple one. Age-old and simple. I doubt even if we like each other. I live, as you know, for my appetites.' She had leaned against the table in her clumsy skirts and hoops, smiling coquettishly, shaking her head with erotic abandon.

'Come – you must help me,' she said, tugging and twisting her complicated attire, guiding my hand here, there, and everywhere till passage to her sex was found. Suddenly I was curious – how came that smear on my fingertips? It wasn't just her own dear womanly juices; the smell was half male and pungently sour. Someone had been there before me, and I quickly guessed who – what doubt could there be? Surprisingly I felt no jealousy, no sense of repulsion, only the pleasure, the heightened pleasure of a shared finish. Discomfort, though, had got the better of me and I ended the bout with aching knees. Pulling up my breeches, I noticed that the Marriage Deed bore the signs of our passion – one large blob there, and a smaller on the green-beige cloth – my own sperm, I reflected, mingled with that of Larkin. I felt some comfort in this merging of secretions, this vague attempt at becoming one flesh. Perhaps in another life we would have been so for real, maybe even brothers. That thought too was not without appeal.

I looked at Phoebe, alone with her own dark thoughts. She was half sitting, half lying with her legs apart, playfully smearing those neat-written lines of compendious phrase. I thought of the spider and what it would make of the loving sap – mine and Larkin's combined. I laughed a little – I couldn't help it – nervous excitement I supposed. And when the last lump broke and trickled down the parchment like quicksilver, Phoebe laughed too with the saucy timbre of a ripe young girl.

'You'd better get dressed,' I said, feeling the strain of our encounter.

The strain I had felt hitherto, however, paled to nothing in the next few minutes. No sooner had Phoebe dressed when in sprung Tom nonplussed on the threshold. 'It's her husband!' he gasped in an undertone, hands pressed hard to his temples. 'He's about to break the partition down.'

I glanced so quickly at Phoebe that I cricked my neck. 'Jesus Maria – he knows where you are!'

'No he cannot! He's at Pontefract!'

'Well he's not at Pontefract, he's here,' I groaned. 'Quickly! Out into the hall!'

We rushed to the door and found it locked. It was I who had locked it earlier so we wouldn't be disturbed by Sukey, and I had foolishly placed the key in the table drawer. There was no time to retrieve it. 'Done for,' I murmured, as Larkin's footfall sounded in the next room. 'Prepare to meet your...' My eyes had lighted on the chest which sat against the far wall. As I bounded towards it, Tom sensed my intention and went to stall our murderous guest. In frantic whispers I made Phoebe understand what I wanted. To the tune of threats beyond – 'Out of my way old man!' and 'Move aside or I'll dash your brains out!' – I helped her into the chest and, having pressed down hard on the last of her garments, Swan's down muff and all, I closed the lid and secured the lock. The chest had become my seat. I was sitting upon it breathless when Larkin burst in.

FOURTEEN

'Skulking in your office, I see, you gutless little hobbledehoy,' he fumed, tapping his cane against the palm of his hand. 'What pettifoggery are you busy with today? Whose side are you a thorn in? It had better not be mine, for if ever I feel you there again, pricking, I'll tear you out and toss you on the fire.'

I had risen from the chest but my breath was still short. I was sweating too: that vituperative outburst, I'd decided, was the overture to violence, and though he carried no sword at his hip this time, he would have no trouble dispatching me with his cane or even his bare fists. But when, in the next breath, he told me he was withdrawing his business from the practice forthwith and would do his utmost to blacken my name amongst his illustrious associates, I realised he had not come about his wife at all. The relief on my face confused him.

'I've wasted enough of my time already,' he said, glancing about with intense distaste, the fire-light flickering across his bearded face, his long hair shimmering in glaring reds and browns. 'You will gather all the copies of my papers together so I may take them away. I want nothing of mine in this firm's hands, not even a receipt for horse manure. Gather them together now!' he ordered, as his gaze strayed to the desk. His feet soon followed and he'd picked up a deed from among the mass of papers. 'I see you have pried into my circumstances this very day,' he said, rifling through the rest. 'Why, every one of these documents relates to me! Do I interest you *so* much?' He was heading for the table now, with his Marriage Deed upon the green-beige cloth. As he stood there nodding with a knowing look, he traced with his finger a still damp smear. 'What thin sealing wax you use,' he said, smelling the result and smiling ironically.

Shame-faced and clumsily I began to collect his deeds, knowing full well the remainder lay buried in the chest. 'That can't be everything,' he thundered, when I presented him with the meagre pile. 'Your partner used to keep some in there.' He pointed at the chest with his cane. He lumbered towards it, spurs jangling.

'Did he?' My voice had buckled as I'd guessed it would.

He brought his face up close to mine; I smelt the spirits on his breath. 'Open it.'

'I can't,' I said, though the key was in my pocket. 'It's locked. Abraham keeps the key on his person.'

'Then I shall break it open.' He searched the room for the right tool till his fierce impatience got the better of him. 'Confound it! I'll take it as it is,' he said, giving the chest a vicious kick.

'What? But you can't!'

'Can't is a word I never use – I can and I will.'

'But there's not just your deeds in there – we have other clients to think of!'

'Come to my house and collect them then. I can promise you a warm welcome.'

'But it's not the done thing,' I continued to protest lamely. 'It's not – proper. You have many debts unpaid, not just to Mister Rhodes, but to the practice for law work done on your account by Mister Balme. I should remind you that it is the custom and method of an attorney's business to detain deeds till bills are discharged...'

He looked at me as though I were a fly on the window. 'You think I give a fuck for your custom and method?' His huge hand grabbed my cravat. I saw the whites of his knuckles as he fixed them beneath my chin. 'I do things *my* way, Eagle, *my* way – understand?'

'How will you carry it?' I asked feebly when he'd pushed me aside. 'I'm sure you won't be able to manage, even if I helped you.'

'But you *will* help me, won't you? – and so will my men,' he said, knocking on the window.

'You'll never get it on horseback,' I said, with a last desperate throw.

'That's right,' he said smugly, 'but we've got the cart. Haven't we boys?' There was furtive laughter at Tom's expense before the two of them appeared in the doorway. 'I want *that* on the cart – now,' said Larkin, pointing to the chest. 'You'll have to make some space.' At the prospect of such a heavy load, Rawlings' hooded eyes narrowed. Jeremiah stood stroking his small bristly chin, a large blue vein on his stocky neck quivering like a worm under sand. 'Young Eagle here'll give you a hand, and so will I,' said Larkin, strutting towards the chest and crouching down. 'C'mon, you bastards – gather round,' he added, struggling for a hold. Rawlings took up position at the other end; I and Jeremiah took the middle.

'What yer got in here?' he hissed, 'a dead body?'

No, a live one, I thought, as we toted the chest over the threshold, bumping and jarring against the door-frame, which Larkin cursed as if it were a fellow devil. For a moment I thought I heard moaning, but it was only Rawlings whose shin-bone had knocked against the door.

'Through here,' said Larkin, hobbling backwards through the outer office at the head of the load. Tom accompanied us all the way, his face blanched, his hands clasped together as if in prayer. 'Just look at him,' snarled Larkin. 'You'd think I were Colonel Blood stealing the crown jewels.'

We emerged into the darkness of the driveway, where a cart half loaded with provisions stood against the wall, tethered to a sullen horse. A fine chestnut mare belonging to Larkin stood tied to a stake nearby and snuffled at our approach.

'Hold still my beauty,' Larkin gasped, as we set down the chest beside the cart. Rawlings sprung up to clear a space among the lengths of cloth, boxes of fruit and casks of wine – gifts, I presumed, from *grateful* clients. When it was done, the four of us lifted the chest up on to the boards where Larkin's men secured it as best they could. Their best was hardly enough, for the chest, protruding at an angle, resembled a coffin on its way to a cheap funeral. Poor Phoebe! – whose gig, I now noticed, peeped elegantly round a corner of the gable. Mercifully they saw it not, or if they did, marked it down as Abraham's. Of Phoebe's discomfort I thought much – and more so the explaining she'd have to do at journey's end. She would have no choice but to implicate me, unleash the vengeance I had only postponed.

To stay alive two clear options presented themselves. I could flee Yorkshire tonight or use the pistols Abraham kept in his bedside drawer. Armed with those I might shoot Larkin as he walked through the door or, better still, shoot him out there in the yard as he sat upon his horse. Surely he was mortal, surely he was killable! I need only be brave and keep my nerve...*Only!* I might just as well have said that to climb through a key-hole I need only shrink myself to fit. The blood in my face, Tom told me later, had drained away and Larkin must have seen.

'By the way,' he'd said, climbing into the saddle, 'I have some intelligence which might interest you.'

'Oh yes?' I'd replied, with poor attempt at defiance.

'Yes,' he'd said, patting the flat side of his horse's head. 'If you was to make your way down to Marsden's tannery and follow the beck downstream, say, half a mile?...' – he sought confirmation from the other two, who gave it with mock earnestness – '...you might find something to your advantage.' He glanced again at the others, and all three shared a filthy chuckle. 'Leave it till morning if you like,' Larkin went on, pointing out the gathering mist as he edged the beast forward with a dig of his spurs. 'The little surprise ought still to be there, hey boys?'

'It'll be there all right,' said Jeremiah, taking the reins from Rawlings and nudging the cart on with a click of his tongue.

As it rumbled away with its startling cargo, a troubled Tom joined me in the drive, his breath wheezy and slow. 'What a pickle you've got yourself into,' he said, watching them disappear into the mist. 'I thought you were a dead 'un.'

'Don't worry, I will be. I can't see any way out.' I raked my lower lip with my teeth, digging them in till it hurt. 'I either run or I stay and fight. There'll be no compromise with his sort. Not when he's opened that chest.'

'Where would you run to?'

'London. It's like a giant forest in stone. There's nowhere like it for disappearing without a trace. Oh God,' I said, pressing my hands to my cheeks. 'I stand to lose everything – everything I've striven for here – plus all I would have gained by our little plan. I'd be right back where I started, scratching about in friends' offices for bits of work. I can't do it, Tom, I can't.'

'But as you've said yourself, lad, what's the alternative? You can't stay here and fight.'

'Why not?' I demanded to know.

'Because he'd kill you, and then where would you be?'

'*Dead*,' I replied, with hard-fought sarcasm. 'Look Tom, I know he's a better fighter than me, that goes without saying. But remember David and Goliath. Callow youth armed only with a sling triumphed over armoured giant. He was brave and he kept his nerve.'

Tom was silent for a space. 'And are you brave? – able to keep your nerve?'

'Yes – no – Oh, I don't know! But I've got those pistols in Abraham's chamber. When he comes I could ambush him and shoot him. I'd claim it was self defence. You'd back me up of course.' My look triggered a nod. 'That's settled then,' I said, trying to steel myself. 'I'll stay and fight. There's every chance I'll survive.'

'No there isn't,' said Tom flatly. 'Go to London. The Fly leaves from Briggate tonight. You could be at the Swan with Two Necks in Lads Lane by Saturday. Take what money we have in the house, and I'll send you more as soon as you're settled. At least that way you'll live.' I could have kicked his spindly legs till they snapped but I knew he was right – better to be *certain* of survival than to gamble. After all, there was no guarantee that Larkin would act as I'd imagined. He might bide his time for days, or even weeks, waylaying me finally at a time of his choosing and running me through with his sword, his very *long* sword.

'Do you think,' I asked Tom, clutching at one last straw, 'there is any chance of Phoebe getting out of the chest unnoticed? Perhaps Larkin won't open it tonight, perhaps one of the servants will hear her knocking and let her out unbeknown to her husband.'

'I think,' Tom said, heading back inside with his eye on Phoebe's conveyance, 'there's less chance of that happening than somebody driving a horse and carriage up a rat's arse.' And with that comforting remark the old clerk left me to ruminate on the future, *my* eye too on that gig which had brought such trouble my way.

I forced myself to think, pacing up and down to aid the process. To catch the Fly tonight I must pack some things and leave within the hour. To miss it would not be fatal however; I could start my journey by horse and make good distance by morning. A coach from Sheffield the following afternoon would serve me just as well. Rest assured, I told myself, you *do* have the means of escape. What I couldn't fathom, though, was my increasing reluctance to take it. Born no longer of false bravado, my reluctance this time felt steadfast and sound. How it came or why I knew not. Something new had revealed itself nonetheless, something within the air of Horseford itself, a force that would keep me there – at least for now – come what may. The strength it gave me was a comfort; the comfort in turn brought me strength. No man ever needed it more. I looked again at the gig, and knew I must get rid of it. I would do so, I decided, under cover of darkness – the same darkness that would hide me as I went in search of my *surprise*.

FIFTEEN

I drove the gig through deserted streets and left it down a track in
Woodside. A short walk through neighbouring fields brought me to the
tannery gates. It was a moonless night, and with the mist lying thick over
the fields I struggled to see further than my own feet. I had brought no
lantern, though its light would have served me poorly. I found the beck
more by sound than sight, treading the bank carefully as I made my way
downstream. I knew not what I was looking for. Perhaps they had jested
at my expense, sent me wilfully on a goose chase. Thinking it may be so
and about to turn back, I heard something rustle in the undergrowth.
When I stopped and listened the sound stopped too. Then it resumed,
drew closer and stopped again. If this were a trap I had no
weapon…another rustle, a beating of wings and a shrill piping noise –
only a bird! My relief nearly knocked me in the water.

As I struggled on along the winding bank, I became convinced I had
wasted my time. Distance was hard to compute, and I seemed to have
travelled for miles. There was nothing for it but to turn heel and travel
that distance in reverse. I was about to do so when I saw a shape propped

against a tree up ahead. Drawing nearer, I took it for a bundle of rags but a few steps more told me different. Lying there with its back against the trunk, as if just resting, was a body staring open-eyed. It was Little Willie's, though the face was bloody and the hair clotted thick. I sunk to my knees and vomited into the stream. It was the mouth that did it, nought but a dark bloody hole. And when the spewing was over and the dizziness passed, I forced myself to look some more. He wore nothing but a pair of ragged breeches, and his upper torso was gory from neck to navel. Between his thighs the ground also was drenched in blood, and treacly clots smeared the tree bark next his mouth. I knew little of such matters but guessed he was newly killed. As to *what* had killed him there was some doubt – a firearm perhaps, more likely a sharp weapon – but none as to *who*. And Willie was clutching a note, I now observed, whose message was meant to taunt me. *Avenge me if you dare* it said, in letters of smudged blood. They had murdered Willie to silence him, murdered him without a second thought, but what galled me even more was their arrogance, their sense of immunity from prosecution. And I knew now what the shared joke had signified: all three men were fresh from the kill.

I sat down beside the corpse to think, shuffling away moments later on account of the smell. I thought of the butchers shop in the village; I thought of the shambles at York: blood, more blood and the stink of blood – earthy, salty and unique. 'What am I to do?' I asked of his mutilated body, shamefully wondering what had become of that good coat I'd lent him. And wondering – with compassion – about other things too. I was drawn to that mouth again, the excess of blood, the peculiar thickness and darkness of its colour, the way that, except for the tongue whose tip protruded thin and square, all other features hid within the blackened hole. How strange that beyond that hideous inlet some unnatural life existed still. His life-blood had drained but the ghost of life lingered like a sigh on the air.

I knelt beside him and delicately opened the mouth. What transpired next is beyond description. The tongue, or so I'd thought, had dropped down shiny on the soil. It was followed by another, and another, and another – not tongues at all but so many pieces of broken blade. There were four in total on the ground, plus another two on Willie's tongue – his real tongue this time, though one scarcely recognisable as such. How many pieces of blade the wretch had been made to swallow before he died I could only guess, but that this had been the manner of his death there was no doubt. 'You tortured the poor bastard! Who are you? *What* are you?' My blood was up for the first real time in my life. The anger was real and mature, not the boyish petulance I was used to. Smiting my fist against the tree, I saw nothing but a bloody show-down – a showdown that was now inevitable and one I was destined to have. When Larkin came for me tonight or the next day – and I firmly believed that he would – I aimed to fight with all my fury. I was willing to kill or be killed.

I remember little of the journey back, only that I stumbled blindly through the mist, my mind as tangled as the thickets on either side of the bank. The long walk lessened some of my courage but none of my resolve, and when I reached the house I headed straight for Abraham's chamber and took pistols, powder and shot from his drawer. Meeting the puzzled attorney on the landing, I offered no excuse for entering his room; nor did I try to hide the weapons. My presumption did me good: I felt strong in the presence of his weakness, emboldened to carry on. I *was* brave, I told myself, braver than I'd ever been. I meant it, I was sober when I said so and I tested my resolve in my own chamber. I did what in itself took courage, I shouldered aside the wardrobe to inspect my spider. I *am* brave, I said again, and I'll be braver, just you wait and see my gooey friend. And it wasn't my imagination; not the distortion of drink that gave my eyes what they saw – the creature *had* grown smaller; its body *had* shrunk back from oak apple size to pistol ball again. And was this it, the elusive truth all along? – did the spider wax lean and fat according to my strength of mind? Be a coward without conscience and his body grew large; be brave and caring and the thing shrivelled small. That being so, I resolved to reduce it for good.

Be that as it may, I couldn't do so without the comfort of drink, and to the parlour I went next for brandy. Armed thus with two bottles and the pistols, I repaired to the office and locked myself in. That room was now my castle-keep where I'd fight the invader to the end. I wouldn't surrender, I said, not ever. I took a pull from the bottle, busied myself with a fire, took another swig then cleaned and charged the guns. Next I sat in my chair, put my feet up on the desk and prepared for a long sleepless wait. If Larkin came in the night I would be ready; likewise in the morning, and if he hadn't come by noon I would ride out to Gravehunger Lodge and fight him there.

As the night wore on I kept my vigil, ignoring Sukey and Tom who enquired about my well-being. So worried was Tom that he'd been to fetch Marshall, but even he I wouldn't see. 'Yes, believe me, I'm well!' I shouted through the door, 'well in body *and* mind!' And with all that brandy as my friend I was soon feeling better still. I saw myself battle-hardened by life, able to endure its horrors, survive its dangers. I reminisced about recent events, boasted to myself how I'd faced the gore of dead Willie, survived the Lighthazzles witch, done mean things on behalf of Sir Walter, and, though I knew I was bending the truth, stood my ground against Larkin. I rocked back and forth in my chair, awash with drunken pride and addled self love. 'You could do anything, *be* anything,' I said, as I finished my first bottle. 'Here's to you, John Eagle,' I added, uncorking the second and gulping that too. If my stomach was cancered by cowardice still, I felt it not; so steeled was I by drink I could have faced slow surgery with a care-free mind.

By two-o'clock, however, I had passed the joyful stage and was giving way to sickness. Every fixture in the room was spinning in triplicate, the rounder pieces whizzing like cannon balls. The shark on the chimney-breast rose and snapped its jaws, while in the gap where the chest had stood the object loomed up anew to resume its former place, the lid flapping open to tease me with its contents. Feeling the vomit rising – it was all liquid for I'd taken no food – I hurried to the fireplace and spewed a barrage that was almost pure brandy. Like devils unleashed, flames leapt hissing up the chimney.

Soon after, I fell asleep and dreamed of the chest. I saw it fly across the sky with Larkin and his men astride it. They were waving their hats in the air, shouting and singing. A woman's arm trailed naked through a crack, followed by blood which oozed out slowly then fell like rain. It covered the palms of my hands; I tasted it, felt it trickle warm down my throat. After the blood came juices of putrefaction, three shades of green, all of them bright and stinking. Splashes of brain I brushed from my shoulders. I wiped a length of intestine from my breast, kicked from the soles of my shoes lungs, liver and heart. All of it – the arm, the blood, the organs – belonged to Phoebe; I knew this because her voice was present throughout, and I smelt her scent all around me. Then, as her smell receded and her innards faded away, both chest and riders landed at my side. Larkin alighted with a smile of indifference, saying theatrically as he held up his hand, 'Behold the cunt of a traitor!' He motioned me to hold out my own hand, greasing its palm with a slither of flesh and hair. He laughed when I screamed, laughed so much that his heart popped out on the blood-red earth. The heart was studded with segments of blade – a pair, like small wings on a plump bird. Larkin was now Willie in his stead, that gaping hole a black magnet drawing me in. I saw the hole widen to the size of a cave, heard, as I stood in the entrance, a stupendous intake of breath. It was a mouth, and by the queer logic of the dream's definition I knew the mouth was Willie's. Determined to carry on, I crossed the pitted threshold of his gums and the solitary teeth grown large. Voices from the throat below began to taunt me. 'We have him,' they said, and behind me the jaws slammed shut. I was left alone in the darkness, my feet sinking in the bloody quagmire of his tongue.

I came awake with a gasp, beating my fist upon the desk. It was daylight, and Tom stood beside me clasping the spare key. His face was even paler than usual, and his eyes were glazed with fear. 'I heard *such* noises,' he said. 'I thought he'd come to murder you.'

'What's the hour?' I asked, raising my stiffened neck. The pain to my head was unbearable, for I knew I'd been devilish drunk.

'Gone half past ten o'clock,' he said, with a glance at the clock on the wall.

'Sleep has not refreshed me,' I said, my stomach lurching at the sight of the two bottles, one spent, the other half gone – the onion shape a nausea in itself.

'You moved things on very briskly,' said Tom, sharing the sorry sight.

There was no use in lying. 'Dutch courage. I couldn't have stayed without it. And now...' – I glanced up at him imploringly – '...I don't mind saying so, I'm frightened to death.'

'You should have done what I said and fled,' said Tom, as he opened the heavy drapes. 'I thought that's what we'd agreed.'

'Something turned up,' I said, struggling to rise, exhaling heavily to keep the sick at bay. I told him about Willie's tortured body, how his murder compelled me to stay.

'But Larkin didn't come, did he?' said Tom impatiently, 'and believe me it's a blessing he didn't. He'd have killed you as sure as I'm standing here. But there's still time for you to get away,' he added hurriedly. 'George will be back any minute. You could take the fastest horse, he'd have it out back with saddle, reins and bridle. What say you to that?'

'I say that I could no more get on a horse than climb up that chimney there. In fact I can hardly rise from this chair.' Frightened though I was, my *mal de cognac* was more severe. To be killed by Larkin would be almost a release. 'What will be, will be,' I said, and motioned him to go. He left in a huff but returned again soon after. George was with him this time, and both men were curiously agitated. 'What now?' I said, with my head slumped down on the desk.

'Upon my soul, you'll never guess what's happened!' exclaimed Tom, rushing up close. 'You're safe, John! Safe as houses!'

279

'How do you mean? – *safe*,' I said, pawing him away in annoyance. I looked to George for explanation as he stood in the doorway. He looked more dog than man, shuffling there in confusion. Am I to be kicked or stroked? he seemed to be thinking.

'Leave us George,' said Tom excitedly. 'But thank you! – thank you for the wonderful news!'

As George shrugged and retreated, I grabbed Tom by the lapel and demanded an explanation. But the old man wouldn't be cajoled; he leapt up with surprising alacrity, clapped his hands with glee and helped himself to brandy. 'Excellent,' he said, smacking his lips after a good long pull. 'The old bugger always did keep a good drop.' The drink went swiftly to his head; he began playing with me in the manner of an eminent Counsellor, gesturing with the bottle as he said accusingly, 'So, thinking the game was up, you thought to flee Horseford and make a new life for yourself in London. But then, finding the stomach to fight, you decided to stay so that you might surprise the defendant and kill him. To that end, you kept a long candle-lit vigil, plying yourself with this good French brandy...' – he took another swig – '... to steady your nerves. You got exceedingly drunk for your pains and woke in great torment. How little did you know it was all in vain. You might just as well have slept peacefully in your own chamber…'

'For God's sake Tom, get to the point!' I interrupted, too weak to get up and shake him. 'Please tell me what you're trying to say!'

'Very well,' he said, grown suddenly serious. 'This is what George has just told me, and he had it from Crispus Claggett…' – the Larkinite landlord at the Old King's Arms – '…it's nothing much to any of them of course – how could it be? – but to you it's a different matter.'

The news he imparted was shockingly bad. Not only did it get me out of my chair, it made me pace round the table slowly, a human horse attached to a gin. As well as joy I felt great pain. I was safe all right, but at a price. All but I – and perhaps Tom if his good angels allowed – would share Larkin's sentiment that it was no great loss, just a chestful of old papers, most of them copies. 'Good riddance! – serves the little pettifogger right!' Larkin would say. 'I took it only to annoy him, and now I've annoyed him more by losing it.' Little did he know what else he had lost when they strayed from the track in the mist! True, he would learn soon enough that he *had* lost her, but he would never learn *how* – that she had slipped from the cart and sunk to the bottom of the bog.

How long had she taken to die? I wondered fretfully. She would have felt the turmoil as the cart overturned, perhaps the sucking of the glutinous mud as it took her under. Darkness superseded by darkness, but possibly a change of smell, certainly a loss of air as she – slowly? – suffocated. I fought for breath myself as I lived her fate – enough to send her mad before she died. Marsh would know best. I must ask his opinion, praying he would say that she – a *hypothetical* she – wouldn't have suffered long.

'Try not to dwell on it,' Tom said coldly, 'think only that you are rid of *him* – that's if you've a mind to be rid of him and don't go antagonising him any more. Forget your pride, forget your honour – what have *those* ever counted for? – think only of your place here and what we stand to gain.' Although I had lived with the old man's callous streak some weeks now, this reminder still shocked me.

'What about Willie?' I asked determinedly.

'What about him?'

Phoebe was mad with breathlessness; I was mad with frustration:
'Larkin murdered him!'

Tom turned his hands palm upwards in a gesture of indifference. 'He
was only a vagrant,' he said. 'It wasn't much to kill *him*.'

'More than that then,' I said vehemently, 'he killed my friend, had him
drowned in the river. And now he's drowned his own wife in Bogles
Bog!'

'You can hardly accuse him of that. Listen lad,' he said, placing a hand
on my shoulder, 'you've got to decide where you stand. You're all at sea
in some things, have been since I first set eyes on thee. I don't mind
telling you too, I've never come across a bigger hypocrite in all my born
days – it's as if there's one set of rules for others and one for you. At
bottom, I see no difference between you and me – or Larkin either for
that matter – we're all out for what we can get.' He laughed heartily, like
a toothless old mummy. 'There's no such thing as a good man, so live and
let live I say. Let Larkin pursue wealth in *his* way, and we'll pursue it in
ours. I thought we'd lost our chance last night, I really did. But Lady
Larkin Luck has offered us another. Don't let her die in vain. Let her
death be the making of us.'

As Tom left to fetch breakfast, I sat and reflected on all he'd said. He had told me before that I was light come into his life. I had given him strength to rise up against his enslavers, even the power to kill them. I knew that he believed this, and more: that fate or luck – it was all the same in the end – had brought us together. Yet there existed still this difference between us – that his fate fitted him like a glove that he was happy with, whereas mine seemed always to be twin-forked. I seemed the victim of an agonising dualism, doing good one day and evil the next, sometimes doing both the same day, or even the same hour. And I knew that what Tom termed hypocrisy, and I termed helplessness, would continue. Thus would I bring Larkin to justice for his crimes as surely as I'd kill Abraham.

SIXTEEN

Even with the facts of Willie's death laid before him, Sir Walter didn't think there was a charge to answer. 'You must allow me to consider the evidence at my leisure,' he said, when I called on him next morning. 'One mustn't be hasty in these matters. I shall go with the parish constables to the scene and draw my own conclusions.' I didn't hold much hope of a thorough investigation, and as the days went by I came close to consulting another magistrate.

On the Friday, however, one week after my visit, Sir Walter called at the house in person. It was the first time he had done so, and it was clear from the gravity of his visage that this was no social call. Though he wished to be rid of the usual preliminaries of etiquette, Fanny and Sukey were in uproar just the same, rushing everywhere in their efforts to please. Abraham, reduced in his premature dotage to sitting by the fire with a blanket over his knees, could only smile wanly at his former patron as he passed the parlour door.

'Your partner is not the man he was,' said Sir Walter, as he turned away with knitted brow.

'I'm afraid he has never recovered from his mother's death,' I replied dolefully. 'It was such a shock to him. Strange, though, how his illness has brought us closer of late.' I had said so in the hope that he would remember my words in the weeks to come.

'Quite,' he replied, with an understanding nod. 'John, I don't mean to be rude,' he added urgently, 'but is there somewhere private for us to talk?'

'Of course,' I said, and led the way into the office.

When we were seated, the Baronet plied himself generously with snuff, blew his nose and said, 'It's difficult to know where to begin, and even more difficult to tell the whole story.' His eyes shifted restlessly as he went on, 'Larkin is finished, you'll be pleased to know. A warrant has been issued for his arrest, and a detachment of troops left for Gravehunger Lodge early this morning. You have my assurance that he'll be languishing in York Castle before the week is out. 'Tis all done to your satisfaction,' he said, brushing imaginary dust from his pure white breeches.

Delighted as I was, and I told him so, there was more to this than met the eye. I saw it in his manner, the effort he was making to compose himself, the startling sadness of his empty gaze. 'And what of his Lady? – Phoebe,' I asked, with unbridled compulsion.

The effect on the Baronet was amazing; he flung his eyes at me as a hound might do, alert to the sound of a vital word. 'What about her? Do you have news?'

The dropping of his guard had been complete, so resonant with emotion I was hard pressed to keep my own. 'News of what pray?' I answered, with just enough innocence to fool him.

'You haven't heard?' He drooped his head in his hands then rose abruptly.

I forced a bemused smile, hoping it would do the trick. 'Heard what?' I said, in the same naïve tone.

'That she's gone, and I fear the worst,' he said, reaching my desk in two strides and clasping its bevelled edge. 'She's dead, John, I know she is,' he continued, unable to face me in his grief. 'He's killed her and disposed of the body, killed her because...' To spell it out would have been a formality. I had already guessed his meaning – that the two had been lovers – and was now guessing more – that Phoebe's call that evening had been no chance visit. Nor now, when I thought about it, did her visit to the Bull those several weeks ago seem so inexplicably strange. I was Lady Larkin's *other* lover, not her only one. And on the night in question I was second choice, not first – a lustful afterthought who happened to live near. That loving spoonful inside her had not been her husband's from the night before, but Sir Walter's from that very afternoon. The discovery had startled me – wounded me too not a little – but disguise was of the essence still. My face throbbed with the awkward look it no doubt wore. Such a look, however, might easily pass for grave.

'You must excuse my behaviour,' Sir Walter now said, composing himself as he turned to face me. My look, as I'd hoped, had fooled him. His mind seemed fixed and far away, regretting that rare show of weakness. 'I trust that as a gentleman you will keep what you have heard this morning to yourself,' he said, striving for his usual tone.

I gave him the necessary assurance; he could trust me, I said, I would always be at his service. These words too would serve me well, and when he shook my hand in gratitude I read in his eyes the promise of reward.

Later, when I had shown him out, I sat down to reflect on what he'd said. He had spoken in spite of himself, and I saw in his hurried departure the fear of telling more. But *what* exactly? Could it be that all his fine talk of divide and rule had been a sham? – that his real motive for leaving Larkin unmolested was that his Lady had requested it? The womanly charms of that Madam Wanton were powerful; I had felt them myself had I not? Even Sir Walter, happily married it was said, had succumbed; his hardened gentlemanly bearing was touched to the very quick. More than that he had loved the woman, hence his grief at her loss, killed, he believed, by Larkin who, having learned of her treacherous liaisons, had unleashed his murderous jealousy. 'Promise me you'll leave him alone,' she may have coaxed in the bedchamber, the Baronet's body tingling with all that pleasure bestowed. His degree of willingness was immaterial; what mattered was that he'd agreed. I knew it was so, and I lost some respect for the great man. Like me, he was *just* a man, and in some ways a lesser one...

Tom had disturbed my reverie. 'All's well that ends well,' he said, rubbing his hands together as he shuffled in. He was excited, and I realised he'd been listening at the door. 'You've got the luck of the Devil, lad.'

'That statement is truer than you think, Tom,' I replied ruefully, though my meaning was lost on him. He'd no idea what I'd gone through, what demons greater and lesser I was forced to house – and was housing still.

'What does it take to please you?' he asked, throwing up his arms in astonishment. I was reminded of the old lawyer himself in Hogarth's *Marriage a la mode*. 'You have a death on your hands which no one will ever connect you with, most of all the husband; you have a lethal enemy out of the way; a wealthy patron who holds you in high regard; a thriving practice that you'll soon – and I mean *soon* – be the master of. Need I go on?' He looked at me almost tearfully. 'What more do you want? Tell me, because I'm sure *I* don't know.'

With a deep sigh I rose and walked to the window. The sun shone bright for the first time in months, bathing the Hall gates in shimmering gold. 'I don't know either, Tom,' I replied dejectedly, as I watched the shadow of a passing rider. Afterwards there passed the different shadow of a one horse chaise, its jagged shape black and distinct. The gold of future riches and the valley of the shadow of death (Phoebe's words here)

– darkness and light vying for the care of my soul, as always. 'Perhaps I want a better heart. Perhaps I want to get to Heaven.' I looked at Tom's shrivelled frame, bearing in mind how the rasping grinding nature that animated it had been re-kindled by me, that *his* heart was set solely on worldly things. How strange it should be so when his days were manifestly numbered. 'Don't you ever think about Him – God I mean? At your time of life you ought to be making your peace with the Lord, not going hell for leather to anger him.'

The skin on the old clerk's face tightened as he grinned. 'It's too late for me,' he said resignedly. 'He knows I'm a wrong 'un. You forget, though, that there are two Lords. I'm happy to take my chances with the other. Who knows? – it might not be such a bad place down there after all. You could think about joining me when your time comes. Did I not say you had the Devil's own luck?'

Such mischief, which I had come to expect of him, usually cheered me. But not today: I needed to be alone; I needed a dialogue with myself in the open air. I left him without word, walking briskly through the sun-lit streets. Soon I was skirting the village pond and entering a meadow all yellow – so *Godly* yellow, no other word would do – with buttercups. I knew what troubled me, filled my heart with guilt and shame. My victory over Larkin had been a Pyrrhic one marred by Phoebe's death – a death that was partly my own doing. I thought of her lying there at the bottom of the bog, inside her my sperm – Sir Walter's too! – the most telling token of intimacy, fruit of the most lifesome of acts. It wasn't that I'd loved her – I knew for sure that I had not – rather that we'd shared such lust, such bare-faced essence of life. And now her body would live no more, would soon be clay for ever, as much bog as bog. She had been so real, so womanly real. I could smell her still – feel the dimples of her white, fleshy arms. If the likes of her could die – and so absurdly, so ignominiously – what did any earthly deed signify? It was as if, in the abject waste of her life, I saw every life that had ever existed, or ever would exist, for what it was – nothing.

Tom would agree for sure: live a good life, live a bad one, 'tis all the same in the end. He had jested about journeying to Hell rather than to Heaven, but I doubted he believed in either; life was governed by fortune, and when we were dead, we were dead. I could only guess at his younger life before the Balmes bottled his spirit, corked it tight for years on end. What *was* clear was that he'd now freed himself from the usual shackles of conscience. With my help he had opened his own personal chest, his own Pandora's Box, and had no fear of reprisals. Ready to seek good or evil (mostly evil) as the fancy took him, he wanted me to do the same.

Yet what if Phoebe's death had been a judgement upon her life? What if its manner held a clue to the shape of things to come? Phoebe *had* been a bad woman, not as bad as her husband (whose own life would end deservedly on the gallows) but bad enough to merit punishment at Bogles Bog. There was the case too of Mrs Balme, killed without dignity on her own stairs. Her son likewise may well be facing judgement in his swift decline – a decline made final at our hands. That being so, I wondered what fate had in store for Tom and me, though perhaps he was right all along: it was all down to luck: history abounded with bad men who'd died in their beds.

I returned home none the wiser, a victim yet of contrary winds. I yearned for solace, and in the quiet of my chamber, watched, I felt, by the spider even through solid wood, I did what I hadn't done for years: got down on my knees and prayed, feeling bold to say, 'Dear Lord in all your infinite wisdom look down on me, a poor miserable sinner. Come into my heart, I beg of you! Find a place there and stay. Show me the path of righteousness, give me the strength to follow it and the courage to fight wrongs – as I used to believe I did! I ask nothing else, save this. I want neither riches nor power, just your love, your sweet bountiful love...'

I had broken off abruptly. I'd meant it with all my heart – an antidote to my plea in the graveyard that night – but I couldn't go on. The spider was listening, a presence in the room as great as mine – perhaps the other half of me – my own self split like curd and whey. I had to look, gauge the power of my spiritual labours honestly voiced. I heaved aside the wardrobe and held up the jar to the light. The spider's body had visibly stiffened, grown blacker too but the size was much reduced. The prayer had done it, and now the creature was fighting back. Its body was swelling afresh; its legs were pushing at the jar, and I could have sworn I saw the eyes blink and the mouth open wide. In its own warped language the thing was speaking to me, conscience to conscience, enemy to enemy – or even friend to friend. All I knew was that I dared not listen.

I hurried to the window and drew up sharp at the sill. It liked the sill, but not what I had in mind. The creature hissed and spat, fair stamped its barbed feet in the murky glue. The jar was in my hand still: I wanted to smash it on the cobbles below. Why not do it? I asked, as I lifted the casement. There came in answer a buzzing noise that made the jar vibrate. George, emerging from the stable with a freshly-groomed horse, scratched his head in bewilderment. I threw him an excuse about a trapped bee and slammed down the window.

The creature had quietened by now, sensing the danger was passed. I doubt I would have killed it anyway – my hands, my head, my heart – none of them seemed able. The bond had grown too strong, like that between monster and creator. Deep down I felt it was so, that I had made it what it was – something that fed upon me day after day in perverse Eucharist, a thing transmogrified beyond mere spider – a grotesque extension of myself. But the prayer I had uttered so fervently had been genuine, and the change in the spider was real – it *had* grown smaller. There was hope, I decided – I *was* redeemable. But like St Gregory's plea for goodness it wasn't to happen yet. My mind was still at sea, overwhelmed by the burden of duty, actuated by careless compulsion whose source was as puzzling as life.

SEVENTEEN

Heading towards the Green in the afternoon I was gnawed at by loneliness, by a lack of love that saddened to the point of fear. I felt beyond the human race, an outcast who had gone into the wilderness and couldn't get back. Others were abroad but I wasn't one of them; I was one of the damned, exiled from society everywhere on earth. I saw contentment all around me, people who never questioned what they felt – the old carter, his face all sleepy with sunshine; the butcher's boy proud and bloody-aproned in the shop doorway; the idlers smoking their pipes by the graveyard wall; the courting couple sharing a kiss as they passed me by. The last sight made me even more bereft. They were only poor but they were happy in their love; it was enough for them – *more* than enough. I felt beyond the reach of a love like that, yet I craved it desperately. The only love I'd known was mother-love; from this other, richer sort, I felt excluded. If somewhere there was a girl for me I couldn't believe I would ever meet her. There were village girls a plenty, but love one of *them* I could not. It wasn't that I felt superior; a girl higher born would have had the same effect. Phoebe was higher born and...

There she was again – she wouldn't set me free. I felt dizzy with the thought of her as I rested my head against the graveyard wall. Beyond it was the graveyard itself – I owed it so much, none of it worthy in the eyes of the Lord. And now, as if in answer – or even reward – I heard music; a heavenly piece in that style of Corelli I loved so much. It was only in my head but I heard it plain. The violins sounded as they always did, plaintive yet vivacious, a brooding sense of mortality wedded to the joys of life. And as I heard those spirited strains, that celebration of the mutability of things, the sunshine of Horseford perceptibly changed, became the sweet, translucent light of the Venice I had pictured in my dreams. But the change had made me weep, feel a sadness for the countless poor who'd never hear a single note of such beautiful music; music written for men like Sir Walter – and for women like Phoebe. There she was again – she wouldn't let me go...

I had reached Marshall's door and hesitated. I hadn't seen him for some time and felt ashamed. It wasn't that I'd tried to avoid him; there had been no room in my life for society of any sort. But let truth speak out a little plainer: the longer I went without seeing him, the harder it was to resume contact. The malady was such that if many more weeks had passed without my conquering it, I may never have seen him again. Glad to have at least triumphed over *that,* I rapped on the door and awaited his answer, thinking, as I did so, that I needed him more than ever.

His new housekeeper answered, a middle-aged hawk of a woman with hooked nose and darting eyes. 'Doctor Stables is busy with his patients,' she said in a rasping voice. 'He's got poor Mister Hustwit with him just now. Is it urgent?'

'I'm not ill if that's what you mean. Just tell him that John Eagle is here to see him.'

'Oh, I know who you are,' she said satirically, as though Marsh had told her all about me and she'd drawn her own conclusions.

I gave her a look fit to skin her. 'Then what are you waiting for? Go and tell him I'm here.'

'I can but ask him,' she said yielding, and knocked softly at the surgery door. Peeved though I was by her manner, I was beginning to realise I had called inopportunely. I was forgetting that Marsh was a busy doctor, whose free time was a lot more limited than mine. Unlike me, he couldn't simply walk away from his work. Standing there in the hall I could hear his patients coughing, one of whom at least sounded close to death. And if that wasn't enough to discomfit me, I was soon given a glimpse of *poor* Mr Hustwit's condition. This grey-faced man of sixty was lying on his back on the big scrubbed table, his mouth biting on a stick to stifle his cries while Marsh, bending over him with knife and needle, endeavoured to stem the heavy bleeding to his chest and side. Beside him was a surgical saw, red and matted at the teeth, two amputated fingers in a small crucible, and a deep bowl filled with blood. There was more blood upon Marsh's apron, which shone like a puddle in sunlight. The witch had read me well that day, for here again was Robert Damiens strapped to the wheel all broken, bloody and torn. And Marsh, like Damiens' executioner, glanced up from his work with eyes all cruelly afire. He took a moment to recognise me, so fixed was he on his grisly task. 'John!' he exclaimed, more shocked than I that we should meet amid the carnage of his craft; it was a sort of nudity that made him look abashed. Still there was fondness in his voice as he went on, 'You have me at a disadvantage, I fear. Up to my arms in...' – he wiped the sweat from his face and shrugged – '...well, you can see for yourself.'

I caught the housekeeper's eye, which said, 'Well? – what did I tell you?'

'I've called at the wrong time,' I said hurriedly. 'I apologise. Perhaps I'll call again this evening.'

'Yes do!' I heard him shout, though I was already in the hall where, at the top of the stairs, I saw Phil looking down at me with an old lute slung over his shoulder. Strange how, amidst all the comings and goings of a busy practice, he had sensed that I was there. I ventured a wave, and he returned the gesture with a strum on his instrument. There was no sound because there were no strings, and he laughed when he saw my surprise. But my hope that he'd finally accepted me was suddenly dashed. His countenance altered swiftly to hate, and he began to descend the stairs with the lute raised aloft. Had not the housekeeper shooed him away he would for sure have smashed me on the head. I was a devil still in the lunatic's eyes, and would ever remain so.

Needing no reminder of my tortured state, I repaired to the tavern for a pot of ale. My choice, perversely, was the Old King's Arms, whose landlord languished in gaol along with the rest of Larkin's gang. Only Larkin himself remained at large – no thanks to me, these people were thinking. Though nothing was said, I was made to feel uncomfortable. Too conscious of their betters to insult me, the men yielded space at the counter, and the landlord – a temporary replacement, I cared not how –

gave me what I asked. To them all I was a falcon among pigeons; they wouldn't be themselves till I'd flown. They spoke in whispers, the only noise between times the crackle of the fire and the ticking of the clock. But if they thought they could force me out they were grossly mistaken: I refused to leave till I'd had my fill.

Seating myself by the fire, I drank first one quart and then another, ordering within the hour a bottle of the best rum. Near on half-past two I emerged into the street with the remnants of the bottle in my coat pocket. Unmistakably drunk I staggered up the main street, peering through windows with an empty stare. Even the children knew, and pointed me out to their mothers. One small child, seeing me stumble, poked me with a toy windmill. It caught the ribbon in my hair, and that's where it stayed, tangled and stuck. 'Leave him alone, he's very sick!' shouted the mother as she pulled the boy away.

'Yes I'm sick!' I yelled, struggling to my feet with the bottle in my hand. 'Oh so *very* sick...'

I knew not where I was headed. Nowhere that I cared to own. I stumbled on past cottages and workshops, drinking and singing till I came to the beck. Here, overcome by a burning thirst, I lay down on my stomach and drank the cool water, scooping up handfuls to douse my face. I didn't stay long: I was frightened by my own reflection, a shimmering horror that jerked me upright faster than a call of Fire. I pressed on, my destination no longer in doubt – never in doubt at all, I was forced to admit at last.

Bogles Bog on a spring day seemed tranquil enough, the treacherous ground hidden mostly by grasses and reeds. But a patch here and there of black impenetrable mud showed the folly of calling this a friendly place. A narrow track perilously close to the eastern edge was the only passage for man or beast. I surveyed the length of this winding path – it ran beside the bog for over a mile – and wondered where it was she had gone in. There were no clues it seemed until, nearing the end and with Gravehunger Lodge in view, I came upon a stretch badly scored by wheels. This, I convinced myself, was the spot. Down there, below the viscous mass, she lay, though at what depth I knew not. Tom had said the bog was bottomless, repeating the rashness of ignorant country folk. It was enough to know that the bog was deep, as unlikely to yield up its secrets as the sea.

I endeavoured to compose myself, shake off the madness of the ale and the rum. A drunken man may be honest with himself, but he'll rarely be pleased with the result. I delved deep, as deep as the bog, to discover whether my grief was genuine or just an affectation. Though I may not have loved Phoebe, and in most ways was glad to be rid of her, there was no gainsaying our intimacy. Take the passion away, however, and little remained – nothing save the image of a beautiful woman of rare and merciless powers – nothing, I concluded, to feel bereft of. It was a pity she was dead, but what, to me, had she really been? She was someone I briefly had known: a mere acquaintance. The cause of my trouble, then, was just as I'd thought – the antithesis between life and death. I wasn't grieving for Phoebe at all; I was feeling resentful of my own transient life.

I was ready to leave with my penance done when I felt a presence behind me. It was Larkin himself only feet away, a pistol in his hand. He was dirty and roughly clad, his beard grown longer in a ragged mass. His lash-less eyes were inflamed, and a deep gash scarred his cheek-bone. When he drew closer I saw that he limped. His boot was ripped at the ankle; there was blood there partly congealed, a fresh supply slowly oozing.

'Well, well, what have we here?' The effort of speaking had pained him; his free hand reached instinctively for his side. He was wounded there too, and the redness shone dully. 'Finally got the law on to me, didn't you?' he wheezed. 'Well I'm not done yet.' He pointed accusingly, blood dripping from the rings on his fingers. 'There's time to do you...' – the pain silenced him again – '...I'd like to kill you with my bare hands, but you can see how things are.' No sword this time, but his thumb moved on the hammer; I heard a protracted click. Sober now, I began to shake, felt the piss cold against my thighs. He saw my weakness, and the effort of laughing angered him more. 'A cur like you doesn't deserve to die quick.'

'You mean to kill me slowly, like Little Willie?' Hopeless as it seemed, I was trying to stall him.

'He got what he deserved.'

'And did Richard Hudson get what *he* deserved?' I asked, wanting the truth even at the end.

'He had a long nose, just like you,' said Larkin, steadying his piece. But his eyes, already glazed, began to roll and show the whites. The lids too had started to flutter, till his mind switched focus once again. As if from fog into clearer air, he appeared to see me for the first time. 'What are you doing here? – I mean *here*,' he asked confused. He crouched on one knee, his face quarried by pain. 'For pity's sake!' he yelled at the heavens. 'You old fucker up there, why did you take her from me?'

'Take who?' I asked, pretending not to know, grateful for another second of life, curious all the same as to *what* he was alluding – could it really be that he knew she was down there?

'*Who? – he asks me who?'* he replied, seeming to debate with himself. His eye-lids were fluttering again; the pistol grew heavier in his hand. Seizing my chance I edged away, but the crack of a stick roused him. 'Oh no you don't!'

I'd landed on my back, pinned there by his body weight. 'No more time,' he said, prizing my lips open with the barrel of his gun. My control had failed me again; I felt an alien weight in my breeches. Larkin smelled it and laughed bloody-mouthed. 'Your sort always shit themselves,' he said, and spat me a faceful of his blood. 'You thought to lay me low – *you* – *little you* – don't you know that I've manipulated you all along – led you every step of the way?'

'The witch, the spider – all the rest of it – so it *was* you – how?'

He never answered, and the look on his face was all pain and confusion. Was he to blame or not? – I needed to know. I felt frustrated at the point of death. And it *was* death surely, I did verily believe it was so. I saw myself post mortem, brains splashed across the grass, no face left to speak of. As for my body, I concluded with irony, it was likely to end up in the bog.

His finger moved on the trigger. This was it, and the resignation I felt bred a moment of clarity that saved my life. Trapped behind my head all the while was the child's windmill that had chanced to work loose. Calmly and swiftly I gripped the sails, and, with a single deft movement, drew out the makeshift dagger and drove it upwards into Larkin's eye. The murderer roared in agony, his hand grabbing blindly till it closed round the stick embedded in his eye. He held it there, yelling thunder, perhaps as Harold had done on the field of Hastings. And all the while his good eye searched out mine with wounded curiosity, seeking an answer, and just a little compassion. His other wounds conspired now, along with his lost blood, to upset his balance. I rose and pushed him, with both hands, straight into the bog. It was only when the mire had taken him under, leaving the mud sucking and popping on the intumescent surface, that I realised he may not have been dead.

My body ached as from a great physical exertion; I was shaking with the enormity of it all. Though no one deserved death more, it was no small thing to have witnessed his end, to have struggled together so violently, so intimately that I smelt and tasted his blood – blood that was as much his living being as I'd thought his seed that day. And I remembered what else I'd thought, how the merging of our juices, the forging of a manly bond hinted at a single flesh: *in another life we would have been so, would have been friends, maybe even brothers.* Fanciful thinking perhaps, but I thought it all the same.

Till practical things won through. All other traces of him – his boot, which had come off in the struggle, his pistol, which my mouth could still taste – must follow him into the bog; follow him to the bottom where he – not I – would rest beside Phoebe. Soon his disappearance would be legendary, the fires of legend fanned by knowledge that he'd escaped the militia's clutches even though he carried its wounds. The wounds would heal; they would not be fatal. Such men could never be killed for they were never mortal to begin with. Unlike his associates who would be tried and hanged, Long Larkin, alias King David, had never been of this world; he had simply vanished on the moorland air. Only *I* would know the truth, for I shared it not even with Tom, that he was as human as every last one of us; that he had died a miserable death, a death which, through its involvement of a toy windmill, was even more absurd, even more ignominious than his wife's.

EIGHTEEN

Summer faded early that year, bringing afore August was out the unique smell of autumn. Decay, sadness and abandonment; the light gilded and serene, as peaceful and placid as eternal sleep. And in the chilly air, often obscured by mist, such contrariness; thoughts bitter-sweet as apples sent for cider. Tom and I drank last year's cider, made by Fanny for Abraham, who was too ill to drink but bid us enjoy it and be merry. Whether illness was the cause, playing tricks on his fevered brain, I know not, but his character was markedly changed. Towards his staff he grew kinder by the day, and to myself especially so. He liked nothing better than for me to sit beside him on an evening and read some passages from Scripture, or, better still, a chapter from Mr Fielding or that wily Scot, Smollett. It was hard to hate him any more; harder still to plot his murder. But for Tom there must be no going back; the deed as we had planned it must be done. And talking of deeds, he reminded me how well he had copied the master's hand; how for my part I had worked on Abraham, induced him, between doses of liquid laudanum, to sign away his real and personal wealth to me, his most obedient servant and partner, John Eagle; and how together we were named sole executors and administrators of a will proved and registered at York.

That was three months ago – long ago enough to make us above suspicion. It was time for the plan to mature, to reap what we had sown. And Tom, who would benefit from our gentlemen's agreement, demanded his share now while he still had time to enjoy it. He *would* enjoy it too, I reasoned, watching him gulp some cider and wipe his mouth on his frayed cuff. More than material benefit, however, I believed he sought revenge on Abraham and would be greatly satisfied by his death. 'And *you* must do the killing lad, for I haven't the strength,' he said, as we sat together in his draughty office.

'I doubt if Abe's neck will take much squeezing,' I said, startled by what I'd just done – referred to him by that term of endearment.

'All the same,' said Tom, replenishing his pot from the jug, 'whatever method we choose – and I don't think strangling's a good one because it'll leave marks – I'd rather you did it. With a feeble body like mine, there's always the chance he'd struggle and call for help...Aye,' he said, nodding to assure himself, 'it's better that you do it.'

'Better for *whom?* I'm the one that has to live with it afterwards – his knowing eyes, his struggling limbs – he's *bound* to struggle unless its done while he's sleeping.'

'Awake or sleeping, you're the one to do it. Get it over with, that's what *I* say.'

'You know Tom,' I said dourly, 'as he grows kinder, you grow bad in the same degree.'

The elderly clerk appeared to relish this, and smiled between sips. 'What a rum world it is,' he said, and ran his eyes suddenly up the chimney breast. My eyes followed, and I asked him what he saw. 'Listen,' he said, a hand to his ear. 'Many a time when I've heard that barking blown down by the wind, I've come near to believing there's a dog living in the chimney. It would have to be a small dog, of course, but... '– he cocked his head on one side, like a blackbird listening for worms – '...There it is again. Do yer not hear it?'

I confessed that I did not, and he chortled hoarsely. 'Go on, say it – you think I'm mad.'

I sighed as I refilled my pot. 'Perhaps we're both mad, Tom, mad and bad. You and I are bad apples, and I wish it were otherwise.'

'A bad apple stays bad – badder and badder till it rots. It's Tom Gill's rule, and there's no exception.'

'What about Ab...' – I almost said *Abe* again – '...Abraham?'

'He doesn't count,' he said, sniffing his drink laboriously, as if he'd found again, after many years absence, his sense of smell. 'His head's gone soft as a baby's. He's about as much use as a beakless woodpecker. I'm talking about men who are able in mind.' He turned and pointed with his bent finger, the one that found some adjacent object – in this case his hat hanging on its peg – but was really pointing at me. It was a queer, unsettling experience – worse than been winked at by a one-eyed man. 'And before you say what I think you're going to say – that we're *not* able in mind – I say that we are, and what I said before was just in jest – I'm as sane as the next man, and so are you.' He leaned towards me, spilling cider. 'A man doesn't have to be mad to kill, nor must he have a motive.'

'Mad we are not, then, just bad?' I said, becoming in my cups convinced by his logic, which sounded plausible.

Tom nodded as though we'd solved all the problems of the world. 'I'd say that's about the measure of it. So let's drink and be damned,' he said, reaching down for the jug, which was empty. I offered to fetch another but he wanted a promise first. 'Say that you'll kill him,' he said, with his hand on my arm. 'Say that you'll do it tonight – say it.' His beseeching look fitted not the wicked request; he might have been asking me to put in a good word for him somewhere; to treat him more kindly in future; make an honest woman of his daughter. Instead I was to make an old man happy by committing murder.

I didn't have the heart to refuse him. More than that, there was such seductive magnetism in his old watery eyes that refusal was impossible. 'Very well,' I said tiredly, 'I'll do it.'

'Tonight?' he urged eagerly.

'Tonight – when he's sleeping,' I said, finalising the method in my mind. 'I'll use a cushion to smother him. It's sure to be quick, and I won't need to look at his face.'

Tom approved of the plan and thanked me heartily. Again his gratitude was incongruous: he might have been thanking me for those other things – the good word I had put in, the extra kindness bestowed, the troth pledged to his daughter. 'And have no fear, lad,' he said, holding out his hand for me to shake, 'I shall be at your side to guide you. I'll be just as guilty in this as you were in the other.'

'That's very reassuring to know,' I said, my vision clouded by unwelcome imagery – all of Mrs Balme in death.

'Good, now fetch that other jug,' he said, missing the sarcasm.

* * *

Seven o'clock that warm evening found me brooding in my chamber, looking out with arms resting on the sill at the finest sunset I had ever seen. Great rafts of burning flame hung motionless above the moors, turning the heather to darkest blue and the buildings orange and red. Bells for Evensong rang clear and melodiously, the church itself hidden by the graveyard trees. In the yard below, two of our horses waited patiently for George who, with Sukey and Fanny, was gathering apples in the orchard beyond. The arms and necks of the girls were delightfully bare in the bronzing light. Ionian seas came to mind, olive groves and Sukey there upon a ladder, a Dorian Greek beauty wiping the sweat from her teenage brow. Even Fanny, peasant-faced Fanny with the vile tongue, had at that distance a certain appeal, a plump and succulent Earth Mother fruited with the fruits of autumn.

Beauty – and always there beside it, the beast. I wasn't meaning George, bovine and rigid as he shook the laden tree in his shirt-sleeves, his shirt-back rippling with sweat. *This* beast was inside the house, stalking the light as it stalked its own prey, something to be killed and devoured. The spider, *my* spider, which contrary to expectation hadn't died with Larkin; smaller now, granted, but no less volatile or filled with ire; fighting harder to make its point; determined to have life as a judgement, not death – and why not, given what I had in mind? Perhaps *it* was really *me*: my heart and soul in a glass decanter; my heart and soul that it fed upon, for no other food would do. There it now was on the window-sill, where it liked exceedingly to be. How it ran pell-mell towards the side of the jar, splashed playfully there for a few seconds, then settled in the middle with its legs splayed out as though afloat. 'What a pond-skater you are!' I whispered, holding it to the light once more.

The darkness and the light – I, like the creature, might live in both, and just as happily it seemed. In neither shade was it easy to go back. *In blood too deep* said Macbeth, and I'd started to see why. I was so close to committing murder: *this close,* I said, narrowing my fingers to parchment-width. And if murder were a craft, I'd learned its steps easily – that day for instance I had kept clear of Abraham, lest by seeing him my courage should fail. I had gone out for a long stroll in the afternoon, keeping to the office with the door locked, staying in my chamber for hours at a time. How ironic that I – the executioner – should feel like the condemned man in his last hours. Would that I'd been Larkin instead, a murderer without a conscience for whom the humdrum mundanity of life – and despite everything there was sure to have been a lot – would have gone on undisturbed. More than anything else, it was these ordinary things in a killer's life, the things that made him normal like everybody else, that seemed so extraordinary. Those same tasks done without thinking, day in-day out, even in the same hour that murder was committed – my eating and drinking for example, the walking and talking, even that trip to the necessary house – took on a new significance. I became conscious of each simple act in each of its stages, however brief. It was as if, in every one, I saw the simple truth that life should be lived for its own sake – that it was, in short, the only thing that mattered.

And what then now of murder most foul? To say it was I in that room waiting to kill my partner was only part of the truth. It was as if it were not me at all but a fair copy of myself watched by the real me from afar. I told myself there was bound to be this essential strangeness about the thing; that once it was done my old self would return. In saying so a blackness like the sea pressed against my eyes. I felt it come and I felt it go – back into the woodwork whence it came. And as soon as it went the birdsong billowed louder in richly-textured sound; I heard the clip of hooves on the cobbles, the shrill voice of Sukey in the yard. It was happening again, aspects of the ordinary and familiar crashing in waves against a queer old rock inside me. They didn't mix well at all, the waves and the rock, yet both were real in their own way: I felt that blackness as surely as I heard that birdsong, heard horse and Sukey combined. It was time to stay and it was time to go. I was prisoner again and hangman too. The prisoner resisted while the hangman pulled. The pull, as I knew it would be, was too strong.

I walked out on the landing as the light began to fade. Tom was waiting at the top of the stairs with an expectant look. 'Is it time?' he whispered eagerly, with a dull flash of gum. A thrill of expectation swam in his eyes. There were threads either side of the iris, veins like the veins on leaves but not leaves shrivelled and brown. These leaves were fresh and green like the leaves on a tree reborn. 'He's sleeping on the bed,' he hissed behind me as I stepped light-footed to Abraham's chamber. 'I put my head round the door not two minutes since.'

It was just as he'd said: when I'd nudged the door ajar the attorney was lying on his bed sleeping tight, his mouth open and exhaling with a faint click, his mottled hands clasping the edge of the brown velvet coverlet. His puffy face lay slumped across his shoulder, so that his eyes, had they been open, would have rested on his mother's miniature which sat upon the bedside table. Tom's eyes followed mine, and I heard him grunt disparagingly. 'Send him to her now,' he said. 'Don't dally, lad. It has to be done.'

I turned to find his wrinkled face regarding me kindly. How could a fond and homely expression mix with incitement to murder? The true nature of the heart was often hidden, and nothing deceived so well as the human face. What writhing mass of worms was masked by Tom's misleading visage? And what, too, of my own heart? Did I not hold in my hands a cushion ready for my partner's smothering? Had I not deliberately selected that one for its softness and ease of manoeuvre?

I trod cautiously towards the bed, holding the cushion out before me as though it were an offering to a king. The fabric, I now noticed, was embroidered with an image of St Francis surrounded by adoring creatures, and I was aware again of a strange juxtaposition. An object of simple beauty, crafted for worldly comfort, was to be used for the ugliest of acts. Why, unthinkingly it seemed, had I chosen *that* cushion? It was yet another reminder of the sanctity of life. I had reached the last stage of my journey, but there at the finish was a roadside shrine asking me to think again. See him not, it said, as he was once – a nasty, vindictive hypocrite – but as he is now – a victim to be pitied and loved. Beside me, though, was Tom, a countervailing force as steadfast as ever. 'Smother him,' he said, as I caught his eye. 'It'll all be over in a second.'

I brought the cushion nearer, the disturbance to the air fanning a familiar smell. It was Abraham's smell and it belonged to him; it wasn't mine to take away, though Tom was saying otherwise. 'How we hated him,' he said, clenching his fists. 'What misery he caused to me *and* you. Go on, John, kill him.'

As a child I had often done wrong, chosen the forbidden for forbidden's sake. And now the child was become the man; nothing, it seemed, had changed. I felt a faint quiver of resistance, heard a muffled grunt. I pressed harder, then harder still, the tension through my fingers like a fish on the line. Killing him was indeed all so easy, as easy as choking a rabbit with one hand. But then the man became the child again and remembered how it used to be – no sense of joy when the wrong was done, only deep remorse. Suddenly sensing the obvious – that my sorrow this time would be unbearable – I drew away the cushion and cast it aside. It wasn't too late: Abraham's eyes stayed closed, but only in sleep.

But Tom's old face had puckered with a fierce disappointment. 'Why have you stopped?!' he cried, and made to retrieve the cushion.

'No!' I shouted. 'It's over Tom and thank God. It should never have come to this.'

The old clerk sank to his knees, one hand starfished across the whole of his face. 'All those years,' he sobbed, clawing at the carpet with his long fingernails. 'All those wasted years.' He looked up of a sudden with reddened eyes. 'You've no idea how I suffered.' He pointed hatefully at the sleeping invalid. 'Don't be fooled by that sweet face lying there. Judge him by what he was, not by what he is now.'

I made to comfort him but he waved me away in his tears. 'Traitor,' he muttered, curling himself into a misshapen ball. He kept on beating and scratching at the floor till his body was spent. As he lay there quivering in exhausted stupor I bent to comfort him again. 'You and me are finished,' he managed to say, but I told him I didn't believe it.

'Come on old fellow,' I said, and having satisfied myself that Abraham was indeed unharmed, I succeeded in conveying Tom to his chamber. I'd no sooner laid him in his bed than he fell asleep.

NINETEEN

Tom Gill and his sworn enemy, Abraham Balme, slept for two days and two nights, from Sunday evening till late afternoon on the Tuesday. They awoke only seconds apart and, to mine and Sukey's amazement (I had been sitting with Tom and she with Abraham), called for each other the moment they did so. Tom, who showed no recollection of what had taken place, asked if I would accompany him to the master's room.

Their encounter was extraordinary. Sitting up in bed supported by pillows and cushions (including that which I'd tried to kill him with), Abraham, with outstretched arms, welcomed his old clerk and begged his forgiveness. 'Come, Tom, and embrace me,' he said, half commanding, half pleading, and when Tom had obliged, clasped him round the neck, saying, 'Forgive me, old friend, forgive me.'

'I forgive you, master, God knows I do,' responded Tom, who was so far stretched across the bed that he looked to be climbing into it. For each of them a storm had passed, and out of the damage they had been reborn – if not wholly so, at least in part. Both said they had felt the change working as they slept, Abraham mentioning the dream he'd had concerning two angels who, standing at his bedside with a tray of offerings, stooped low and planted upon his face the sweetest kiss. Tom blinked not an eyelid as he listened, adding weight to my conviction that he remembered nothing of what had lately transpired.

'And you, John Eagle,' cried Abraham, with one hand straying my way, 'come likewise and give me your forgiveness. Say that we can be happy partners after all.'

I did as he had asked, and it seemed for a moment that I too had rid myself of a dark oppression. I felt a lightness in my heart, an inner glow, but it wasn't enough: the change had worked only at the surface. Something black lurked still in the lower reaches of my being; I felt it there as a dull ache, like food undigested. Redemption was at hand, close enough to be touched, but I lacked the will to grasp it. Perhaps I wasn't humble enough, not quite ashamed of the life I had led hitherto. Desperate for counsel, I turned once more to Marsh.

I found him at home and this time free of duties. He was at my service, he said, and shepherded me in with such urgency I might have been Mr Hustwit come to have his fingers cut off. But to the back parlour he steered me, sitting me down in my usual armchair surrounded by his numerous books. There followed next the brandy, and that was followed by Phil, who landed at my feet with an acrobatic leap. This time it was all so different. The lunatic sat quietly on the carpet cross-legged, looking up at me with eyes that shared my sadness. He appeared to recognise a friend now, with much of the badness gone, cut out, for all he knew, by the skilled hand of his master. Marsh poured the brandy, nodding and smiling at the outcome. 'Well, well well,' he declared, 'how the tables are turned.'

'You could put that another way,' I managed to jest, 'how the tables are *not* turned – not turned over in the room I mean. It's the very first time he has not attacked me – perhaps he is still thinking about it?'

'No, it would seem that he trusts you at last,' said Marsh, handing me a glass and another for Phil, whom he said deserved it for his civil behaviour. 'To what do we owe this change I wonder – do you have something more to confess?'

'Certainly *more,*' I said, as the drink took immediate effect. 'To tell it all, however, is a different matter.'

As before, it was easy to get so far. I started this time with my early life, the cruelties of childhood, the wild pranks I'd indulged in as an articled clerk. I then turned to Horseford, the ruthless way I'd dealt with Sir Walter's tenants, even my affair with Phoebe. I let him know too about the Lighthazzles witch, the strange lights that had followed me home, and the stranger voices in my head. Finally I told about the Balmes, first the mother and then the son. And in for a penny, in for a pound I *almost* told about the spider and deaths at Bogles Bog.

Marsh sat quietly throughout, his glass in his hand as it rested on his knee. Although he winced at some of the details, whistling surprise here and then, he never once cast opprobrium. I read in his eyes only friendship, sympathy and support. When I had finished he sat silently for a space, then rose and glanced down at his lodger. 'Well Phil, that was quite an out-pouring, was it not?' The lunatic grinned as he fiddled with the buckles on his shoes. Sensing my gaze as he did so, he looked up grinning at me too, as if all three of us had shared a private joke. It occurred to me for the first time that Phil's face, looking beyond its ceaseless twitching, was a very handsome one marred only by an excess of teeth.

'No one could deny that you've done wrong – even done evil,' Marsh began hesitantly, as he poured himself more brandy. He stepped towards me, swinging the black mallet bottle by its neck. 'But neither could they deny that you have suffered for what you have done – you *do* have a conscience,' he said, topping up my glass with a generous measure. He placed a hand on my shoulder, and smiled. 'John, I have often felt that you were in torment.' Phil nodded in agreement. 'I knew there was a darker side,' he continued, smiling at the interruption as he retook his seat, 'though you think it darker than it actually is. Believe me when I say, you are not a Herod or a Nero. You are not John the Cruel, or John the Terrible. There is much kindness in you and gentleness – rare traits these days, and I should know more than most. I see nothing but brutality everywhere I go.'

'I don't feel kind *or* gentle,' I said sulkily, though I felt reassured by Marsh's answer that he saw no real wrong in me. Even the crimes I had not confessed appeared in a better light now, some of which, when all was said and done, were not heinous crimes at all but amalgam of accident (Phoebe) and self-defence (Larkin). And what of Larkin himself who had haunted me from the start? His power in general had been real; his power over me most probably illusionary. For the man was dead, with no marked change to my haunted state.

'You are fishing for compliments, I believe,' said Marsh teasingly, as he straightened his ruffled stocking. 'Do you really want me to chronicle your good points? Very well,' he said, taking my silence for a 'yes.' 'I would remind you of the concern for your fellow men demonstrated through your legal work – the defence of that poor, abused climbing boy and the runaway blackamoor – and the care you showed for that vagrant Willie, whom nobody in the village, myself included, gave a fig for. Not least I would mention the friendship you have given me these last months, a friendship more valuable, I think, for the way you conquered the distaste that certain of my preferences engendered. You were man enough for that – man enough also, I feel, to admit the feminine side of you.'

He had glanced away at that last remark, hoping I'd not take offence. My smile put him right as he turned to weightier things – the lights, the witch and the voices. 'Those matters are not so easily explained,' he said with a sigh. 'That you saw what you saw and heard what you heard, I don't doubt for a moment. All the same...'

'I only *thought* I saw what I saw, only *thought* I heard what I heard – is that it?' I interrupted disappointedly.

Marsh shrugged, and took another pull on his brandy. 'I still say that you were tired, over-worked and over-burdened – too much weight for your young shoulders to bear. It's my considered opinion that you've come damnably close to a full mental breakdown. 'And then again...' – he held up a hand to let him finish – '...And then again there are more things in heaven and earth,' he said uncomfortably. 'I have a natural aversion to popular superstition – as you well know – but I do keep an open mind. It behoves a man in my profession so to do.'

'You *half* believe me, then, and no more?' He assured me again that he believed me whole-heartedly but there may be another explanation. 'Aye, that I'm mad,' I said gloomily.

'My dear fellow, you are as sane as anyone in this room,' he replied, checking himself at the sight of Phil. I had already begun to laugh, and when the infection spread to Marsh and then to Phil himself, all three of us were soon in pain from our delightful malady. Only Phil, poor Phil, had no idea of the cause.

'May I make a suggestion?' Marsh said, when the laughter was done. 'You have no doubt heard we have a new incumbent at our church, a certain Reverend Grimdike?'

'Yes, Sir Walter...' – the living was in the Baronet's gift – '... happened to mention it in passing.'

'Well believe me, John, he's nowhere near as grim as his name suggests. In fact, he's a very droll and most agreeable fellow. Easy of approach, and easy of manner, a man of capital conversation. He's pious, of course, as you might expect, but very learned in all things, a real Mister Worldly-Wiseman in the best possible sense. Not the normal sort of cleric you get round here.'

'It would take little to improve on his predecessor,' I said, recollecting that droning voice the day of Mrs Balme's funeral.

'If you think the Reverend Gaunt had poor form, you ought to have seen the one before him. Reverend Killingbeck was his name. The fellow was incumbent here for over thirty years, twenty-five of which he spent lying on his back after a fall from the bell tower, which he'd climbed to chase away jackdaws. He conducted all his services, and preached all his sermons in the horizontal position. Quite extraordinary, to walk into a church and see the clergyman lying there on a couch, wanting only a laurel-wreath to make an emperor of him. But as I say – this man is different, he's very special, and I like him much.'

'You think I ought to speak with him?' I asked, guessing his meaning. 'You think I ought to *go to God?'*

'I know you've had little time for such things in the past,' said Marsh, 'but this man has much to say that is of merit. He makes you think again about the whole sorry tale of Father, Son and Holy Ghost. I tell you frankly, John, that I'm on the verge of being baptised anew.'

'You are wrong to think me averse to such notions,' I said, adding how, in the past, I'd never criticised the faithful for what they believed, simply didn't have faith myself, though I'd often envied the comfort it brought. Ever since childhood churches had repelled me; in their habitual odour of decay, their unrelenting austerity of dusty drapes and dark wooden pews, the funeral tablets and the Cross, I saw only pain and death. I saw it too in the words of the liturgy, the sermons and the singing of the hymns. Such feelings would never go away, but for now I needed that solace only the church could bring. Whether it could also provide answers would now remain to be seen. 'I can't give you any promises,' I said pointedly. 'That doubting Thomas inside me is a very dogged fellow.'

'But you'll at least give Grimdike a hearing?' Marsh asked, pleased enough all the same. 'You'll call on him soon?'

'Yes, I give you my word. In fact, if the old goat's in, I'll call on him this very night.'

'Excellent,' Marsh said smiling, and Phil smiled too, holding up his empty glass. 'I think you'll find him more of a young goat than an old one,' he added, passing round the bottle one last time. 'The man is only twenty-eight, or so he says.'

* * *

Or so he says! The Reverend Baron Grimdike was the oldest twenty-eight that ever did live, and had he not been a man of the cloth, who was not supposed to lie, nobody would have believed he was a year under fifty. His beard was already grey and, though he wore his own hair, that was grey too and he had precious little of it to wear. If there was a key to his youth, it was in his eyes, which were large and blue, sparkling with warm tenderness and abundant humour. They were the first thing I noticed about him, and they made me instantly at ease.

I had come upon his huge figure locked out on the doorstep of his own rectory, lantern-in-hand, about to knock for his housekeeper. Having introduced myself, I was asked if I'd care to join him in a glass of port wine in his study. Curiously, on my accepting, he insisted on sealing the agreement with a handshake, as though we had just struck a deal that would make us both rich. He showed me next, as he made to knock again, an early sign of his clumsiness. Stepping backwards, while beseeching God to make his deaf housekeeper hear him, he caught his heel on the scraper, tripped, and fell heavily on his belly. 'Confound that blackguardly implement!' he railed, disturbing a cloud of dust as he flapped around on the floor, flailing the night air with great arcs of yellow light. With my assistance he made it to his feet again, panting out plumes of rapid breath. 'It's God's way of punishing me for my sins,' he said, betraying his flat Yorkshire tone. 'I just wish he'd vary the punishment, that's all. Why can't he pelt me with a few apples now and again, or make me slip on a dog's turd? Variety, as you've no doubt heard, is the spice of life.'

'Perhaps the easiest thing would be to stop sinning,' I said, as his housekeeper admitted us at last. She closed the door behind us so suddenly that the force blew out the candles in the hall. Thankfully we could still see by the Reverend's bright lantern.

He threw me a look of contempt (but only a mock one) as I followed him into his study, a large untidy room dominated by a heavy oak desk.

'Would you have me live like a monk?' he asked. 'Even if you did, friend, I'd still get up to no good – aye, even in my cell! Doesn't the Devil find mischief for idle hands to do?' he said, rubbing the crotch of his baggy black breeches and tapping his nose with his finger. 'At least I'm honest about my idle hands, not like that sanctimonious old hypocrite Wesley, who preached here last December. What do you think *his* idle hands are up to when he's travelling about the country on that horse of his, with a Bible balanced on its neck?' In the blatant cheek of his humour alone, he was indeed a very remarkable man. Though I'd known him but a few minutes, I could have followed this latter day goliard to the ends of the earth – or from Leeds to Bradford at least.

'Here,' said the Reverend, handing me a small glass of port which he'd poured from a bottle on the table. 'Not enough to slake yer thirst on but enough to warm the cockles of the heart, wherever *they* are.'

We sat down in the two armchairs either side of the fire, the Reverend groaning a sigh as he threw a leg over the chair arm, and sipped his port with unabashed enjoyment. I watched his full lips shiny with the liquid, saw a droplet glisten like a ruby in his stiff grey beard. His mind was elsewhere, and when an owl hooted in the rectory garden it summoned him back from the land of his thoughts. 'So, young man...' – he had called me *young,* though I was only a few years his junior – '...what is it that I can do for you?'

I was hesitant, embarrassed. 'Now that I'm here, I'm not so sure – I'm not even sure that I was ever sure.'

The Reverend Grimdike sniffed loudly and averted his face; he appeared to be listening for the owl again. 'Something tells me we're in for a long night,' he said, turning his bright eyes upon me and smiling. 'No matter. I have a funeral sermon to write but it can wait till the morrow.'

I thanked him for his kindness, then said pensively, 'I don't know where to begin.'

'It cannot be easy when you're not sure why you are here,' he said, reaching his pipe from a nearby shelf. Taking tobacco from a pouch in his coat pocket, he lit his pipe at the fire with a taper and was soon puffing contentedly. There was silence between us for over a minute; no sound at all save the crimping of the coals on the fire. At length he said, 'Why not start by asking me if I believe in God? Such a question always gets the apple-cart tipped.'

'I took your belief for granted,' I said, disquieted by his remark.

He gestured with his pipe. 'Never take anything for granted. Things are rarely as they seem, nor are they usually simple – least not in my book.'

'But you must believe in Him – you're a clergyman. Why else would you have taken Holy vows?'

'Why else indeed,' he replied ambivalently, and puffed on awhile. 'But don't think I haven't denied Him, because I have,' he added suddenly, with eyes a flashing. 'Aye, enough times to damn me forever if He were wrathfully inclined, and we have one book out of two to suggest He's precisely that.' Then he smiled wryly. 'But who in his right mind would accept the word of a gang of old Jews?'

When I asked him why, if he were such a sceptic, he carried on in his role, he answered assuredly, 'Because, more like Peter, I always come round to trusting again. There is always something to make me rethink my doubting. I'm not talking about the famous miracles – folk rising from the dead, blood changing to wine before my eyes and so on – not miracles in the usual sense, but miracles of a sort nonetheless. I'm talking about the everyday miracles of life that we take for granted – the shape of a tree, the song of a bird, the flow of a brook through a meadow awash with flowers. They are just as profound in their way. And I say this too: there is such a duality in things, an opposite for whatever we care to consider, tangible or otherwise. Most of all, my friend, there is evil to match good ounce for ounce – enough, more often than not, to upset the balance frighteningly in its favour.' He saw how my brow had darkened at his talk of duality. 'But it is you, not me, we are here to speak about – so speak on, the night, like me, is young.'

'I can't tell you everything,' I began cautiously. 'You're a stranger to me.'

'And you to me,' he retorted swiftly, 'but there's nothing about myself I wouldn't share with you this instant with a good heart. I am what I was, and I am what I am, take it or leave it.'

'Perhaps you've nothing to hide,' I said mechanically.

The Reverend laughed, and blew out a blast of smoke. 'You think I have no vices? You think I've never done wrong? Let me tell you, friend, I've had all the vices under the sun at one time or other, and I've done enough wrong to curl your hair. People *can* change – even wicked, troublesome men. Like Saint Francis...' – I jolted at the recollection of Abraham's cushion – '...I'm living proof of that phenomenon.' He leaned forward in his chair to encourage me. 'You can tell me all, and I mean *all*. I promise you I'll not be shocked.'

Telling him was easier than I'd thought, easier than it had been with Marsh. I told it all this time, right down to the last sordid detail. Out it all poured, on and on for half an hour or more, a long jet of poison that I almost saw before me on the green patterned carpet, a hissing pool of putrefaction between the Reverend's feet and mine. Try as he would to disguise it, I could see the clergyman *was* affected by what he'd heard, some of which caused him to fidget and scratch his bristles. And when he rose to weigh better the magnitude of what I'd said, he dropped his pipe unheeded on the hearth, smashing it in a dozen pieces. I could see him struggling to collect himself, give me the reassurance that I craved. Sweat showed on his neck and forehead, the latter which he dabbed with his white pocket-handkerchief. 'Yes,' he said, breathing as though the room had grown suddenly hot, 'there were one or two bits in there that got under the collar. I'm all right now,' and he retook his seat by the fire, glanced briefly in astonishment at his shattered pipe, and forced a smile. 'Out of all you've told me,' he said, still breathing hard, "tis the spider that's affected me the most. The thought of that creature feeding on your soul all these months, getting fatter and fatter, is just too foul to contemplate. What possessed you to...' – he wiped his brow again – '...well yes, I know only too well what possessed you...'

'I know what you think – that the Devil Himself has been at work.' Marsh's words, I realised now, had only deflected this home truth.

'Yes I do,' he said bluntly. 'Not when you were young – childhood pranks are commonplace, and I've come across far worse examples that the ones you mentioned. Most of us are cruel and heartless till we learn to be otherwise. Until recent months – until, as you rightly say, you arrived in this village – you had turned out decent enough. What has happened to you of late is something far more sinister. There's no question about it, absolutely none – Old Nick is behind it all. The vision of the witch, the strange lights following you home, this hideous spider – they are all part of the plan to ensnare you, to make you one of His. That you stopped short of murder is a sure sign of God fighting tooth and nail on your behalf. So too is your supposed change of heart, but that too I'm afraid is insufficient.'

'But the creature *does* grow smaller every time – I've seen it with my own eyes.'

'And its fighting spirit? – has it lost much of that?'

'No,' I was forced to admit, 'if anything it has grown stronger. Sparing Abraham that night had it kicking against the glass.'

'Which only goes to show that little has changed. Mark my words your enemy is still at hand. You must kill the creature, it's the only way.'

'Killing it won't be easy,' I said. 'You know it's strange when I think of it, but I've grown rather attached to it over the months. It's been my little friend up there in my lonely room.'

'Yes, you *will* have grown attached,' the Reverend said bitterly. 'The Devil has seen to that. But you must harden your heart against the creature, and squash it with your shoe. And it would be wise, when you've done that, to throw *it,* and all the contents of the jar on to the fire and let the flames do their natural cleansing. Pray to the Lord while you do it, ask Him to come back into your heart, and tell Him that you seek His forgiveness. Believe me, my friend, it's the only way. I shall pray for you too. Between us, we ought to set things right again.'

'And you really think, when the job is done, that I'll be free?'

'I'm certain. In fact, I'm so certain that I'd wager ten guineas on it. If I had ten guineas, that is,' he added with a wink. 'You must understand that I'm only a poor Christian priest.'

I didn't have his certainty, and I'm not sure he had it himself deep down. I had one more question to ask: 'Why me?' I wanted to know, 'and *how?'*

'That I cannot answer,' said the kindly rector frowning. 'You were in a new part of the country, vulnerable perhaps. Something may have blown down your throat as you sat atop the coach that night.'

'Yes, yes I felt it for sure, I've always said I did!'

'But alas we cannot be certain in the end. I ask only that you do as I say. Will you do that little thing I've suggested? – will you kill the beast?'

I sighed and gave him my word. 'I'll do it tomorrow.'

'Do it tonight,' he urged. 'Tomorrow may be too late. Go home now and tread on it hard.' And as the owl hooted twice more in quick succession I pledged my word a second time: the creature would be dead within the hour. 'Listen for the clock striking ten,' I told him as I rose, 'and know by then it will be done.'

'Thy will be done, on earth as it is in heaven,' mumbled the Reverend, as I walked to the door.

TWENTY

So it was, that later that night, in the quiet of my chamber, I tipped the spider out of its jar and killed it. Killing it was easier than I'd thought and I didn't hesitate. I saw it there on the floor, waiting, and I tried not to catch its eye – it had one, I was sure. I used my foot to block the view, and then I used it to kill. Its bloated body burst like an over-ripe plum, squirting forth a profusion of dark malodorous blood, threaded with mustard-yellow. Scooping what was left on to a small shovel, and pouring on top the murky contents of the jar, I carried the burden downstairs and threw it on the parlour fire, reciting, as I did so, what I could remember of the twenty-third psalm. The spider's remains, which had landed on the coals, crackled and spat then burst into flame. The frogspawn mass that had fed it lasted a while longer, bubbling and sizzling on the fire-back. Soon it was just the smell that remained, a smell of singed hair, sulphur and excrement that made the air thick and hard to breathe.

I backed away with my hand to my mouth, hearing as I did so the resonant sounding of the chimes. The mantelpiece clock, ordinary enough in its faded gilt, but I now knew why, all those months ago, my attention was arrested by it sight. It was if my gaze back then had tended inexorably towards this moment. The church clock tolling in the distance was adding its own confirmation: it was ten o'clock, and I knew the Reverend would be listening hard. I'd killed the beast as instructed, but had no change to report. Not yet, though change extraordinary was coming.

First a deep wound to my face. Foolish I had been to throw the jar on to the fire too, for the glass had exploded and slashed my cheek. How the blood did spurt from the gash; neither hand nor kerchief could staunch the flow. And next from above came Sukey's screams, the pounding of her feet on the stairs. We collided in the hall, where I'd hurried to meet her, my blood on her face as I held her close. She couldn't speak for weeping, just stammered and pointed aloft. I knew full well who was up there: Abraham – *Abe,* as I now was wont to call him. The master attorney had developed a will to live of late; his wasting sickness had appeared to recede. But alas no more; everything for him was over.

I found him slumped on his pillows with eyes and mouth wide open, his face blanched like stone. And he was *stone* dead, his brow already chilling, colder than the broth that oozed from the corners of his mouth.

He had died while Sukey was feeding him, a fact confirmed when she followed through the door. 'He were doing so well,' she cried, wet with tears that had merged with my blood. 'Enjoying that parsnip soup Fanny had made when all of a sudden...' – she wiped her face on her apron – '...when all of a sudden he heard the clock telling him the hour. It seemed to affect him all bad, like. His face flushed scarlet. He couldn't get his breath. Then he said – then he said...'

'What did he say? Tell me, Sukey!'

The tweenie worked hard to collect herself, but couldn't quite say the rest. I had to sit her on a chair by the window, rub her hands in mine as if they were chilled. But her hands were warm, warm and sticky with sweat. At last she resumed, catching my eye to say, 'It didn't make sense but I heard it plain. He said – Eight Legs is no more. Eight Legs is dead.'

I stepped back in a faint swoon, steadying myself on one of the bed posts. Sukey was watching in an agony of bewilderment. 'Who's Eight Legs?' she wanted to know. 'Who did he mean?'

'I don't know,' I muttered anxiously. 'He was obviously in a fevered state.'

'But that's just it,' she persisted. 'He weren't feverish. He were as clear-headed as you or me.'

I certainly didn't feel clear-headed, and I needed time to think. 'We'll never know what he meant, Sukey,' I said. 'He's gone, and I'm truly sorry.'

'No you're not,' she said, springing up fiercely. 'You hated him. You only pretended to like him so yer could get his money. Don't think I don't know what yer've been up to.'

I laughed to hide my nervousness. 'I don't know what you're talking about. Abe and I had our differences, but we resolved them. We became the best of friends.'

'Liar!' she said, and stood before me defiantly, arms akimbo. 'I ought to shout it from the roof-tops what you've done, you 'n' that scheming bag o' bones.'

I could have done with him now – where was he? Wake up Tom if you're sleeping, I said, I need your plausible mask. But Tom didn't come and I was on my own. A bullying tone was my last refuge: 'You can shout what you like,' I said. 'Nobody would believe you. You're nothing but a twopenny drudge.' She backed away, shrinking from me as I edged towards her. It was all that blood gushing from my wound; I'd wiped it, I'd smudged it: my whole face must have looked blood-red. 'You forget that I'm sole master now. I could terminate your service this minute. Don't think I wouldn't do it.' Her little storm of bravery had passed. She was sobbing again in atonement, wanting to appease. 'Go fetch Doctor Stables,' I said simply. 'Tell him your master has passed away this night. And remember what I said – you have a new master now.'

She bobbed obediently, gathered up her skirts and hurried out the room. As I watched her leave I did so with a heavy heart. The sentiment was genuine; for merely speaking roughly to her I was filled with shame. The will to protect her, take care of her, was far stronger than the will to do harm. Was this it, then, first sign of the change the clergyman had predicted? If so, only time would tell just how marked that change would be. One thing for certain, the spider was dead. So too, I reflected, was Abe.

We buried him in the same grave as his mother on a mild blowy morning in October. I saw to it that the funeral was a lavish affair,

346

attended by all the worthies for whom he had toiled over the years. The church was thronged full as it would hold with the cream of local society: magnates of the prosperous woollen manufactory, landed gentlemen, retired army and naval officers, eminent practitioners of law and physick, shopkeepers and tradesmen galore. Above them all, in his elevated pew, sat Sir Walter Spencer-Stanhope, come with wife and pampered offspring to pay his last regards. He was there under sufferance, I could see it in his face. His mind was elsewhere; there was a wistful longing in his eyes and I knew for whom he longed. Not his Lady, comely enough with her white-powdered cheeks and smooth-as-porcelain brow. Not his daughter with the beautifully cruel visage – not unlike another he had once known, and that, I think, had been half the appeal. I would have liked to put him right, tell him of her death and where she could be found. Some day, perhaps, but not yet; perhaps not ever – there was risk of incurring his wrath; greater risk still of losing favour.

For sure he had promised much should I only continue to please. He owed me, though he hadn't said so, a debt of gratitude for the trust I'd repaid over Phoebe. He knew what we'd shared that day, his weakened manliness burning between us in a naked flame of bared emotion. And I'd sensed ever since a growing dependency, as if he trusted my powers more than his own. His prodigiously fine mind was hampered increasingly by his crucial failings of character. He shrank from lowly people as he would from a pestilence; his own tenants for example whom he couldn't abide; he even refused audience to his own parish constables. And I'd marked him now as a lazy man who needed an agent in every sense. He ought to have left alone, retreated from the world he had come to despise. But the one thing he didn't hate was fame. Like a Yorkshire version of the Fielding brothers he craved their reputation as masters of the magistracy: he would have himself as the greatest thief-taker, the greatest law-enforcer, the man who'd laid a dozen Larkins by the heels. Magistrate he was and magistrate he'd remain, but not without my help. He had created, he said, a position as Justice's Clerk at an annual salary of two-hundred pounds – twice the rate I earned as clerk to the Leeds and Liverpool Canal Company.

He wouldn't say outright, but I had an inkling how I'd earn this princely sum. The hearing of cases, the judgements and referrals would be his still – in short he would have the easy business and not the hard. It was Balme and Eagle all over again, but the stakes were so much higher, the work of much more note. The Baronet valued my doggedness for the truth, my search to understand the criminal mind. Crime and its detection would be my remit now. I was to act as his eyes and ears; be what his own eyes and ears refused to be but couldn't and wouldn't deny. I would work behind the scenes on his behalf, receiving praise only from himself. All *public* praise would be his own.

And should the work be done to his satisfaction what of those other rewards merely hinted at? I was beneath him for sure, but he'd hold out a hand to haul me up – me and no other, just once in his lifetime, said that look, that dropping of the eyes, that aversion of the face that left me studying its own pondering profile. Was it really there or had I imagined it? – a hint as faint as the smile on his daughter's perfect lips. October was here like the month; there she was in the pew beside him. Was it really possible that she might be my prize? I had seen her only once before, that windy day in Sir Walter's park. I remembered what I'd felt, how our paths might one day cross – for better, I now hoped, as I looked at her anew, the ache of a different day, several months later, come to mind. Loveless, lonely and defeated I'd felt, no hope ever of a woman's love. Till today.

But for now there was a funeral to be had, a funeral with its own remarkable result. I was sitting with Tom, Marsh, and our three servants in the pew nearest the pulpit, listening to the Reverend Grimdike, in clean bright surplice, descant affectionately, even glowingly, about an Abraham Balme he had never met. But he did it admirably, without a trace of sham or veneer. Grimdike, I reflected, was a rare man, remarkable in the extreme, a man who, along with Marsh, had probably saved my life. I had one life-saver beside me, and the other out there in front. I felt secure and happy in the angle between the two.

'The attorney is dead,' I heard the Reverend say, and I wanted to shout in answer, 'Long live the attorney! Long live John Eagle!' For I had done my bit of weeping days ago and could sit through the service with my heart stitched tight – as tight as the stitches Marsh had sown into my cheek, his work neater than a nimble-fingered seamstress. My scar became me, he had said, as the angry crimson began to fade; my beauty was enhanced not spoiled. A moot point no doubt, but just like Abe's death, what was done, was done.

And best forgotten. Not that it bothered Tom very much – he still remembered nothing about Abe; nothing either of his mother, who he now believed had fallen of her own accord. And who, when all was said and done, could say it wasn't true for I'd only Tom's word at the time to say that he'd pushed her. Seeing him there beside me with his hands on his knees – those knees no thicker than crab tree sticks – he was as he had been when I first set eyes on him, a gentle old man, guileless and true. To look at him now, it was hard to believe it had ever happened, all that mischief stretching like a jagged line over several months. Perhaps it hadn't. No one else was privy to our schemes; we had always plotted alone: no witnesses, no evidence – was that significant in itself or merely in the nature of things?

There were questions I couldn't answer, and to dwell on them profited me not. That Abe should die the moment the spider met the flames was a riddle fit to kill; hardly less so was his baffling announcement that Eight Legs was dead. Could the attorney really have known about the spider, and what it signified? And what *did* it signify? I must confess that I was little the wiser, and for my sanity's sake cared not to look for answers. For my sanity's sake too, and Tom's likewise, the past must be buried. Our ordeal was over and we both must begin anew. Abraham was dead, and though we were there to mourn him, we were there also to think of our future, to give thanks for what we had gained.

We had much to be thankful for, and I for one *was* thankful. I'd been led away from temptation, delivered from evil, even rewarded for my pains. I was a man of substance of a sudden, a master attorney at the age of twenty-three with his pockets full of guineas. It was a prize I had not expected, thus belying the old proverb that all things come to he who waits. I had not waited, I had not expected, I had not coveted: drawing

351

back from the brink of murder had drawn me back from it all. I had even written to my proctor at York informing him of my grave doubts about Abe's soundness of mind when he wrote his will, instructing him, on Mr Balme's behalf, to disregard it and send me the two copies held in the Prerogative Court. These, together with a third copy kept in my desk drawer, I later threw on the fire. Wishing no longer to be part of the fraud, I happily watched them burn. Little did I know that Abraham had written a new will citing me as his main heir, with a share in the practice for Tom.

Messrs Bolland and Snell of Leeds had acted as executors and administrators of the new will, and it was Mr Bolland who had called on me two days ago to break the news. 'You are a very fortunate young man,' the attorney had said, as we sat together in the parlour enjoying fresh tea and muffins. 'Who would have thought, when you came to my office that grey winter's day, that the yarn would unravel like this.'

'Who indeed,' I replied, offering him the plate from which he took his second muffin.

Deliberately so, we spoke only briefly of Richard's death. There was pain and guilt on both sides, with more common cause than he knew. Mr

Bolland, who admitted some cowardice in the matter, little knew how my triumph that day owed more to fortune than bravery. Relieved to change the subject, he asked me how I saw the future, whether I intended making my mark as Horseford's leading attorney or selling up and moving on. Back to London perhaps, where wealth and talent were sure to make me shine arrestingly.

I told him I had every intention of staying put, that Fink Hill House was my home, and that I looked forward to a more peaceful year than the one I had just lived through. 'I feel as if I have been walking the whole time through a dark vale,' I said, glancing at the fire with memories far from sweet – was it truly all gone, I wondered, every last hair and thread? 'Now, by comparison, I wish to sit awhile in a pleasant glade.'

The old lawyer nodded. 'The life of a country practiser is often just that,' he said, tucking into his muffin, whose taste, I think, satisfied him more than our talk. 'To meet such danger and misery, you have been unlucky,' he added, spitting out a spray of crumbs. 'And yet not I say, for see how things have turned out. You have at your age what came to me at fifty. Wealth hasn't come too late, and that, dear boy, is luck, never mind what you may have been through to get it. What say you Tom Gill?'

Tom had just re-joined us. The smile he'd worn was the same as he

wore now when our eyes suddenly locked: dark, obscure and enigmatic.

FINIS

GAMBLING FORTUNES

Brian Coats

For Consuelo

Contents

Author's note

This is a true story, but some scenes and characters have been created or modified for the purpose of dramatisation. The timeline has been slightly altered.

The sums of money wagered were truly eye-watering, so it is useful to understand the value of currency in the 1920s (when most of the gambling takes place). One pound at that time was equivalent to roughly fifty pounds today, and there were approximately 100 French francs to the pound in 1920. Therefore, a million francs – a common bet amongst the players in this book – is equivalent to 500,000 pounds today. One pound was worth close to five US dollars at the time.

Prologue

AS LUCK WOULD HAVE IT

Our lot in life is really a matter of an amazing series of coincidences, but how we make best use of the hand we are dealt is not so haphazard. We have no influence over where we are born, nor our social standing and wealth. A select few emerge with the proverbial silver spoon clutched firmly in their tiny hand; many more are thrust into a life of abject poverty and hunger, with little hope of advancing.

The mere fact of our existence is a minor miracle. Our parents must have met, bonded at a specific moment – literally to the nanosecond – for any particular person to exist. If you extrapolate back a few generations, these chances become truly minuscule, much smaller than those of winning the lottery several times in a month.

Some capitalise on their good fortune and others squander it. The less prosperous must exert themselves to a far greater extent: laziness is not an option if they want to succeed. The smart ones find their talents and use them to come out on top.

These are two such men, separated by language, culture, wealth and social standing, but united in lives of mixed fortunes by a game of luck. Or is it?

BRIAN COATS

Chapter 1

1932 FRANCE

In their luxurious hotel suite in Paris, Didier and Marie Toulemonde both awoke at the same moment. It was 4:57 a.m.

"Did you hear that, Didier?" said the wife.

"Yes, *ma cherie*," was the reply. "And I am pretty sure that it was a gunshot, possibly from a revolver. I remember that sound only too well from the war. I think it came from next door. I'd better contact reception."

He rang the front desk and pretty soon Pierre, the night porter, was outside the neighbouring suite, knocking on the door. There was no reply, so he sent the couple who had trailed along behind him back to their room and then used his passkey to gain entry. He stole quietly through the suite's foyer to the living room, where he noticed that the bedroom door was ajar and the light was on. Upon entering, it did not take him long to find the body of a man lying on the floor by the desk, and a quick check yielded no pulse, no sign of life. An ominous small dark hole in the right temple, and a revolver positioned beside the body, seemed to suggest the cause of death, but that would be for the police to decide.

Pierre felt uneasy in the presence of the lifeless corpse, so rather than telephone from the suite, he returned to the lobby and called for an ambulance. At that time of morning, it took no time to arrive, and the police were alerted as well. After it was confirmed that the man was dead, the police quickly concluded that he had almost certainly taken his own life. His passport revealed that he was a foreigner.

Even with what appeared to be an open-and-shut case, there are procedures to follow, so they interviewed Pierre, who could only tell them that the man was a hard-core gambler, always generous with his winnings, and that he thought that his favourite haunt in the city was the Cercle Haussmann, a nearby casino.

The following day, the detective in charge of the case visited the casino, where the regulars were able to elaborate a little further. "He used to play all over France, but mainly in Deauville, Cannes, Monte Carlo, and occasionally Paris," said Monsieur Beaumont, a sometime patron of the Haussmann for more than a dozen years. "He was part of a group that did the rounds of the different gambling establishments as the seasons progressed. They'd wager huge amounts and competed against anyone who had the resources to survive in their exalted company."

The detective intervened. "Did he borrow his money or was he independently wealthy?"

One of Beaumont's colleagues, a Monsieur Blanc replied, "He and his main rival had massive fortunes at their disposal, but I had heard that things were getting tight. I guess one of them finally came out ahead."

"Would anyone have held a grudge against him?" The detective knew he was fishing with this question, but thought he might learn something.

There was a collective shaking of heads. Monsieur Beaumont appeared to be the group spokesman. "You hear rumours, but nothing concrete. Nobody that I ever met had a bad word to say about him, so if you think that somebody killed him, then I'm afraid you're barking up the wrong tree. It does seem a rather pointless waste of a life, but when you gamble recklessly for that much money, what can you expect? It is honestly surprising that suicide is not more common, given the amounts that some of them lose."

The police concluded their investigation and closed the case. His remains were sent back to his home country and he was buried not far from his birthplace.

Some days later, a group of players were gathered in the same casino and the discussion soon turned to the suicide and the two great competitors Coats and Zographos.

Their most verbose member, Denis, felt he knew it all: "Of course, you know why they clashed so much?"

From across the table a cantankerous voice muttered, "No, but I am sure you are about to inform us" He looked smugly around the assembly, hoping for a laugh.

Denis was undeterred. "They were so different: the Scotsman was courageous, rash, and flamboyant, but generous to the point of extravagance, whereas the Greek was sharp as a tack, shrewd and numerate. He was also very careful and an absolute model of courtesy."

Most of the people present were nodding in agreement as he said this, so he added, "Temperamentally like chalk and cheese, there was a mutual respect there, which grew as they learned more about each other. It is a strange world that throws two such men together."

What this articulate individual had stated was very true, for it is hard to imagine two more singular routes to the gambling dens of France.

Chapter 2

1894 GREECE

The three cups moved with giddying speed, describing figures of eight, circles, ellipses and even the occasional straight line. Keeping track of the one with the rubber ball under it became ever more difficult, and eventually the watcher lost focus for a moment and his chances of winning disappeared with that lapse of concentration.

Nicolas Zographos, known affectionately as Nico, was the seven-year-old boy manipulating them. He had persuaded his friend Dimitri to compete with him at the Shell Game, even though Nico was renowned for his skill at both handling the cups and following the ball. Dimitri reckoned that being a year older gave him an edge, but it seldom translated into victory, so the fact that they were betting on the outcome meant that he was constantly in debt to his rival. Happily, the stakes were only pasteli, sesame seed candy bars made with honey and nuts and a real favourite for both the boys.

Nico brought the cups to a standstill and looked up at his pal. "So, where d'you think the ball is?"

Dimitri pointed at the right-hand cup and when it was lifted to reveal nothing underneath, he groaned. "You move too fast for me. I can never keep up."

"Well, now it's your turn. And stop complaining - we both have the same chance of winning."

The cups duly changed hands and Dimitri placed the ball

under the middle one and started to shift them around in a seemingly bewildering series of moves, at least the equal of what Nico had done, maybe even faster and more intricate. Nico watched intently, like a tiger stalking an antelope, his eyes never wavering from the speeding hands: he seemed completely oblivious to all around him. As soon as the cups were still, he immediately pounced on the middle one and, sure enough, when it was raised, there was a ball sitting under it.

"I don't know how you do that. You've won five in a row and I've got no more candy, so we'll have to stop."

"Classes are about to start up again, so we need to call it a day anyway. Thanks for the candy. It's definitely my favourite and tastes even better when it's free!"

The truth was that Nico wasn't exactly sure why he was so good at the game. He found it very easy to concentrate, and his memory was viewed as being so advanced for his age that his teachers were wont to use the word "prodigy" when discussing his performance in disciplines that required good recall.

He also found his gift to be useful in fending off bullies. He was very small for his age and was constantly picked on. He could not defend himself physically due to sheer lack of size and strength, but he discovered that his tormentors were fascinated by his feats of memory and would leave him be if he performed what they thought of as something bordering on magic. He would recite pi to fifty decimal places, read and remember poems almost instantly, and he knew the name of everyone at the school, pupils and teachers alike. These tricks kept the wolves at bay.

Alongside a downcast Dimitri, Nico returned to class with his pockets bulging and a broad grin on his face.

Later that same day he walked home from school, carrying his books and an empty tea towel, which had earlier contained his lunch of bread and olives. He whistled nonchalantly as he went, practising his newfound musical skill, but his mind was far from concentrated on the tune that emanated from his lips.

Earlier that day, well before his Shell Game triumph, he had literally run into his brother Konstantin in the playground. Kostas, as his sibling was usually called, had been extremely annoyed as he had grazed his knee in the encounter, but while Nico was trying to placate him, it became apparent that his poor humour was nothing to do with their clash. Rather, it was due to a class assignment involving the times tables, which Kostas was struggling to learn. Nico readily agreed to help him, as he wanted to get into his good books and he liked anything to do with numbers.

Kostas showed him the exercise and Nico listened as he stumbled through the whole thing, several times. As multiplication was a new concept to Nico, he was initially slow on the uptake, but despite his brother's impatience, he soon grasped the idea and began to test him.

"What is six times seven?" asked Nico.

"Forty-four."

"No, you twit. It's forty-two! Try this – eight times nine."

"Seventy-two."

"Good. Now recite the four times table."

They continued in the same way for the best part of an hour, both arriving late for their next classes and incurring the wrath of their teachers in the process.

Nico was now running over all these numbers in his head as he approached the family home. He was determined to show both his parents, but particularly his father, how clever he was. Then perhaps there would be time for a game of cards later that evening.

The walk from school to home was not a long one. It usually took only ten minutes and the route took him through wide, tree-lined boulevards, past majestic buildings and, if he glanced upwards, he could view the imposing outline of the Acropolis, which towered over the entire suburb. Their apartment in Panepistimiou Street was modern and spacious, though his nine brothers and sisters filled it to overflowing.

When he got home, he found his mother in the kitchen. Feeding her flock was a full-time job for Anastasia and, despite having many hands to help, she seemed to spend most of her time in the unenviable task of sating the collective appetites of her ten offspring.

She was a striking figure, far removed from the first flush of youth, but nonetheless a handsome, rather heavy-set woman, with bushy eyebrows and a warm smile which lit up her face. Despite the drudgery of housework and cooking, she maintained a cheerful demeanour and obviously adored her children.

"Nico, my treasure," she beamed, "you're just the person I was looking for. Please go to the store and get me the items on this list." She handed him a piece of paper with a dozen assorted ingredients.

He looked at the list for a few seconds and handed it back to her. "Got it, Mama. I'll be back in twenty minutes."

"You'll never remember all that. Take the list with you and stop showing off."

"I promise I have it all. What about some money to pay for it?"

"Tell Mrs Karagiannis to put it on our tab. If she asks when we will settle up, tell her I'll be over before the end of the week. She trusts us."

"Okay, Mama. See you." He grabbed two shopping bags and raced through the main door off down the street.

He arrived at the store, which was as chaotic as ever. Products were piled up all over the place, shelves heaving with fruits, vegetables, cans and sacks, and hidden amongst it all was the magnificently rotund yet imposing figure of the owner behind the counter.

"Hello, Mrs K," said Nico as he entered the premises. "How's tricks?"

"You cheeky little monkey. I hope you're not looking for free samples today – I've no time for your nonsense."

"No, ma'am! My mama's sent me with a list of groceries and I need to collect 'em and get back as quick as possible."

"Okay. So, what d'you need?"

"A box of eggs, five aubergines, ten figs, a bag of salt, a *livre* of olives, a large loaf of bread, a bunch of roikio, five peppers – the red ones that we usually buy – two *okas* of potatoes, a *mina* of feta and also a *livre* of that delicious kefalotyri cheese. Oh, and finally an *oka* of yogurt."

"I'm very surprised you can keep that list in your young head, but I'll be even more impressed if you manage to carry it all. How're you going to get it home?"

"I have two large bags and I'm very strong!"

"Just as well. Let me get it together – and please don't go touching anything while my back's turned or there'll be hell to pay!" She busied herself with collecting the numerous items and Nico stood to one side, reciting the seven times table under his breath. He had to get it all right for when he presented his new talent to his father later on.

"So, tell me, Nico, how're you going to pay for all this?" She had collected all the items together and put them in the two bags in such a way that each one weighed about the same.

"Mama says to put it on our tab, if you wouldn't mind."

"She does appreciate that she already owes me for over two weeks' worth of supplies?"

"Oh . . . no, I didn't know. But she promises she'll be over before the end of the week to pay."

"Okay, but you tell her no more credit till she produces the money. Make sure she understands that."

"Don't worry, I will." And Nico heaved the bags onto his shoulders and hobbled out of the shop.

Once back home, he helped his mother empty the bags and put away those items that weren't needed immediately. "Mrs K says there's no more credit unless we pay off what we owe."

Anastasia looked up at him in surprise. "I thought we'd paid our account with her last week. I guess I must've forgotten. I'll see her first thing tomorrow." She continued to potter and muttered to nobody in particular, "I really hate taking advantage of her, but a line of credit is very useful."

Nico ignored her. "When is Papa getting home? I have something I want to show him."

"He'll be home at the usual time this evening. What d'you want him to see?"

"It's not a thing, but rather something new I've learnt. I think he'll be impressed."

She smiled. "I'll let him know, but right now you have homework to do and you should help everyone get the house tidied up."

So he went through to study, see his siblings and await supper. This would not be forthcoming until his father had returned from the university.

Iaonnis Zographos was a distinguished man: an academic and a member of parliament. As professor of political economy at the National and Kapodistrian University of Athens – better and more succinctly known as the University of Athens – he had the job of teaching the best and brightest amongst the Greek elite. And as his field of expertise was all about how history, structure and institutions shape economic outcomes, it was inevitable that his scholars should include many future politicians and even potential prime ministers. He had therefore developed a rather intimidating manner, which allowed him to deal with the arrogance and presumptuousness of such students. Although not particularly tall, he had dark quizzical eyes and his gaze always seemed to be questioning the point of view of whomever he spoke to. He was expert at detecting insincerity, a positive boon for a man who dealt with so many prospective holders of public office. He was a hard taskmaster, but acknowledged talent and rewarded it. He was therefore considered an excellent, if somewhat exacting, teacher.

Although he applied many of these traits to domestic life, which made him a rather fierce parent sometimes, he adored his family and was delighted to have so many children around him. His one regret was that with so many, it was hard to give sufficient time and attention to any one individual; but he did his best and was particularly caring when it came to his second son, Nico. He saw much of himself in the boy, but acknowledged that his son's ability with numbers far outstripped his own at a similar age, even though he was no slouch.

He arrived home as dusk was descending on the city and was mobbed by his brood, all with stories to tell or questions to ask. He quietly hugged them and went through to the kitchen to see if he could help Anastasia.

"Anything I can do?" he asked.

"Not at the moment. I have it all under control, but you could stay and chat. How was the university today?"

"Fine, but one thing I find slightly wearing – and I've said this to you before – is that there's always at least one student who is trying to be too clever by half." Iaonnis sighed. "They think that a little economic theory suddenly makes them experts. It's hard to deal with the arrogance of some of them, but at least they seem to think that age gives me perspective, so I do get a modicum of respect from most of them."

"Talking of too clever by half . . ." replied Ana. "I can't get over Nico. I gave him a shopping list earlier and he seemed to absorb it in a matter of seconds. Off he went to the shop and came back half an hour later with everything I had asked for. I have enough trouble remembering all the children's names, so I guess he gets it from you." She returned to chopping vegetables and fell silent, but stopped as she recalled her conversation with Nico. "Oh, and he wants to show you something, a new skill he has picked up at school. Perhaps you could find a moment after supper."

"I'm sure I can find five minutes for him. There's no doubt he's bright, particularly with numbers. If he keeps developing as quickly as he has, my hope is that we'll be able to send him to Germany to study engineering. As you know, my time there was incredibly useful and I'm sure it would benefit him just as much. Anyway, we'll see what his latest revelation is after we have eaten."

The free-for-all that was supper came and went and, once all the dishes were cleared away, Nico approached his father to see if he could demonstrate his newfound skill. Unfortunately, all the others were listening, and as he tried to recite the multiplication tables, it was hard to make himself heard above the jeering and catcalling. Iaonnis eventually called for silence and was rewarded with a perfect recitation of the nine times table. At this point he stopped the boy and asked, "When did you learn all this, Nico?"

"Kostas needed help with his times tables, and I thought it would be a great chance for me to get ahead at school. So, I guess the answer is that I learnt them today."

"Well, you are to be congratulated. It was a fine piece of work."

"Could we play cards now as a reward?"

Iaonnis chuckled. "What do you want to play? How about Bohemian Schneider? Or would you prefer Memory Match?"

"I like Memory Match – I think I can beat you! We can play it with those cards you brought back from Germany."

"Sure. I'll get them out and then you can shuffle and deal. You remember how to lay 'em out?"

"Yes, Papa."

So, Iaonnis brought out the cards and marvelled at how well his son handled them, particularly with his relatively small hands. But what really impressed him was the way Nico could recall the position of every card once it had been turned over and revealed. He never forgot any of them and was a clear winner in all three games they played.

"Time for bed," said his father, once they had finished the third game. "Well played – you certainly have an excellent memory. I'm going to get you a set of cards so you can practise this on your own. I'm sure that if you spend enough time at it you'll be able to hone your skill to the point where it will be really useful to you as you get older."

He had no idea how right he was.

Chapter 3

1900 SCOTLAND

Jack Coats lay in bed and tried to get to sleep, but he was too excited. He and his older brother Tom had been staying with their grandparents for the last two weeks and although he enjoyed these visits, he always looked forward to getting back home, where he could at least spend a few moments with his father. He had overheard a conversation earlier in the day and understood that a return home was imminent. This possibility was what was keeping him awake.

Deanston House, where the boys were staying, was a huge imposing mansion with a five-storey tower in the centre and so many rooms that Jack literally could not count them all. He quite regularly got lost and had to seek out a familiar part of the house in order to find his way back to his room. The grounds were just as impressive, a beautiful part of Scotland just outside Doune, eight miles north-west of Stirling, with plenty of places to play and copious wild animals – a veritable paradise for two young boys with boundless energy.

Tom and Jack shared one of the numerous bedrooms, and Miss Donaldson, their governess, was in the next-door room. She had a habit of checking on them to make sure they were not chatting – or worse, fighting – after they had been told to go to sleep. She opened the door and peered in.

"Jack, I can see that you're still awake. Your attempts to pretend you are sleeping do not convince me. I shall leave now and will be back in ten minutes, by which time I expect you to be away with the fairies. If not, there will be consequences, mark my word. No excuses."

"Sorry, Miss Donaldson."

"Goodnight."

Jack was now so tense that sleep became even less likely, but Miss Donaldson never did return and he eventually drifted off.

♦

The next morning, with breakfast out of the way, the governess took the boys up to the room reserved for teaching and sat them down to a series of lessons on mathematics, history, writing and elementary French, which Jack really loved. The day went by quickly: lunch came and went and in the late afternoon she read them a story – Walter Scott was a great favourite – and then they were made to read something of their own choice, which in Jack's case meant *Treasure Island*. He was rushing to finish so he could go and find out if his father might appear and take them back to Skelmorlie Castle, the family home.

Downstairs, Jack's grandmother, Lady Margaret Muir, sipped her tea and looked out of the library window. The loss of her fourth daughter Agnes, the boys' mother, all of six years ago, still burned in her heart. The fact that she had nine other children did not lessen the pain she felt, and the unfortunate nature of Agnes's demise only intensified her feelings of grief. If she had not had that terrible fall during the pregnancy, things might have turned out very differently. The care that Agnes and her husband Willie had taken to ensure that the birth went well after that had been exemplary, but things had never seemed entirely normal and even though the child, Jack, was delivered hale and hearty, his mother had not fared as well. She had struggled on for the next year, and the couple finally decided to escape the rigours of the Scottish winter and go to the south of France to see if the sea air and a warmer climate would allow her to recover her former vitality. This seemed to have some effect for a short time, but she then began to do downhill fast and had succumbed by early spring.

The only joy Lady Margaret got out of this tragedy was that she got to see a lot of her departed daughter's two children. She was a young fifty-nine years old and still had the vitality needed to keep up with them. Her husband, Sir John had neither the time nor the patience, what with his various obligations to the church, the regiment and the local village and county, so she found that she could be alone with them when she wanted; and the presence of their governess meant that if they became tiresome, she could simply hand them back to her for a while.

It was unclear from the demeanour of the boys what effect their mother's sudden departure had had. Tom was only three when it happened and Jack was still in nappies. They both seemed cheerful and playful enough on the surface, but they sometimes cried for no apparent reason, and neither was particularly affectionate with her or indeed anyone else.

She reasoned to herself that despite their lack of maternal love, they at least lived a life of luxury, their father being one for the richest men in Scotland. The fact that he hardly ever saw them was a worry, but his passions for art and his work kept him away from them most of the time. But it was a joy that they could stay with the Muirs, and that filled part of the void left by the absence of Agnes, both for the boys and her.

What she only half-appreciated was that Willie had an almost irrational antipathy to his younger son, as he blamed Jack, directly or indirectly, for the death of his beloved wife. He would never admit such a feeling to anyone, least of all himself, but Margaret had caught the way he looked at the boy, and there was disguised animosity behind his eyes. He was a reserved man at the best of times, but with both his children, and especially the younger one, his demeanour was especially cold and impatient, bordering on hostile. She knew Jack craved his father's love, which was why he was hopeful that they could all return to the family home, where he would have a chance to be with his father. There was nothing more in this world that Jack desired than a nod of approval or a sign of affection. These were extremely rare.

Her thoughts were interrupted by the appearance of said younger boy, who had finished with Robert Louis Stevenson and was looking for fun.

"Hello, Granny. Do you know where Father is?" He was fishing to find out if what he had heard was true.

"As far as I know he has been in Paisley and Glasgow recently, though I know he went to France last week. Why do you ask?"

"Just curious. I haven't seen him for ages."

He looked pensive for a moment, but then his expression brightened, as if he had suddenly dragged up some gem from the depth of his consciousness. "Would you like to have a game of cards?"

"I didn't know you were a card player. What has brought this on?" She knew that Willie frowned upon all card games, so she was mildly surprised at this request.

"I was taught to play Snap and Beggar-my-neighbour by Miss Donaldson and she has just started me on Whist and Rummy, but please don't tell father as he doesn't approve. I have played sometimes with Tom, though he's not that fond of card games and has got very wrapped up in his book, so I hoped you'd play."

So Miss Donaldson was a bit of a dark horse, teaching the boy these card games despite his father's disapproval. Well done her! Lady Muir could only imagine what would happen if she were discovered.

She banished the thought and asked, "What's he reading?"

"*The Sign of the Four*. He is obsessed with Sherlock Holmes – this is the third one he's read in the last month."

"Well, I understand that they *are* very exciting. And it's good that he reads – you should follow his example!"

"I do, Granny. Miss Donaldson makes us sit down with a book every afternoon and I am in the middle of *Treasure Island*."

"Ah, excellent. Are you enjoying it?"

"Absolutely. I think Jim Hawkins is terribly brave standing up to the pirates. Captain Flint is evil and Long John Silver is really sneaky. The story is very exciting."

"If it's that good, why don't you continue to read?"

"Because right now I'd rather play cards with you." He looked pleadingly at her. "Father never lets me play so I don't often get the opportunity with Miss Donaldson either. This may be my last chance before he gets back. If we can play for an hour, I promise I will read another chapter."

"All right, you little rascal. Always negotiating, aren't you. So . . . what would you like to play?"

"I'm too old for games like Snap." He paused and looked up at her with puppy dog eyes, an expression he knew she couldn't resist. "Could we play whist? Or, even better, rummy? I was just beginning to get the hang of it and I wanted to have a shot to see if I can beat you."

"I think whist'd be better for you, but if you really want to play rummy, then I think you are old enough – let's do that. First one to pass 200 points will be the winner."

"We should keep a count using matches, Granny. I'll get them from the mantelpiece. We'll play in the gaming room, right?"

"Yes. I'll follow you there. You're much too quick for me."

Jack dashed across the hall, past the great sweep of the bifurcated staircase, to the gaming room with its various card tables and other accoutrements of the favourite pastimes of the Muirs. Sure enough, just in front of the elegant Adam fireplace, he found two boxes of Bryant & May matches and he had already spread them out on one of the tables by the time his grandmother followed him in. Cards were produced and play commenced.

Pretty soon Jack had a pile of matches in front of him, whilst Lady Margaret had almost none. He seemed to have a knack of winning despite sometimes making rash picks from the discard pile. She couldn't help herself from commenting on this.

"I'm just incredibly lucky, Granny," Jack replied. "I sometimes wonder if my mummy is watching over me from up in the sky and giving me a bit of help when she sees that I need it. I hope so!"

"Don't you wish she was here with you now?" Lady Margaret's tone was casual, but her curiosity was palpable.

"Sometimes, but I don't remember her, and although Miss Donaldson can be quite fierce, she does look after us well."

His grandmother was hoping he might elaborate, but she was out of luck, as Jack fell silent and started to deal again; fairly soon he had declared himself the winner.

"Please put the matches back in their boxes and place them back by the fireplace, Jack."

"Of course, Granny. I wish they were pennies, then I would be rich!"

Lady Margaret always felt uncomfortable talking to the children about money, but recognised she couldn't leave this remark hanging. "You will have riches in your own time, so you don't need to be thinking about playing cards for money. But well played: you deserved to win."

"Thank you very much, Granny. And to show you what a good boy I am, I will now keep my promise and go and read my book."

"That seems like an excellent plan. You can tell me what it is all about once you've finished it."

"Will do." And with that he ran out towards the playroom, but suddenly stopped and turned to face Lady Muir. "Please don't tell my father we were playing cards, Granny. He would be furious if he found out."

"Don't you worry Jack. It'll be our little secret, just between the two of us."

♦

McLeod, the butler, pulled himself up to his full height of six feet two inches and addressed the Muirs' domestic staff. They had all collected at his behest in the servants' hall and were seated round the large dining table that ran almost the entire length of the room.

"Sir John has informed me that he and Lady Muir will be away in London for the next two weeks. This does not mean that there will be any slacking amongst the staff, but obviously there will be no need for certain personal services. They will be taking their valet and maid, as well as the cook, but the two Coats boys, Mister Tom and Master Jack, will continue to be here, as will their governess Miss Donaldson, so the cooking will be done by Flora and we will be required to attend to them. It also goes without saying that the house must remain impeccably clean and tidy, and neither I nor Mrs Cruikshanks will tolerate any tomfoolery."

"Fat chance of that," said Duncan, the footman, under his breath. He was a young man of twenty-two with chiselled features, slicked back hair and what can best be described as a cheeky grin.

"What was that?" McLeod glared angrily from the far end of the table.

"Nothing," mumbled Duncan.

"Very well. Now off you all go, back to your work. Mrs Cruikshanks, can I please have a word?"

The staff quickly dispersed to the four corners of the house to get the remaining tasks of the day completed.

"What can I help you with?" the housekeeper asked.

"The boys are going to have the run of the house and Miss Donaldson will have a hard time keeping them under control, even though they are usually boisterous rather than unruly. Could you be a second pair of eyes and let me know if things get out of hand? Mercifully it is summer and they should be able to get out for lengthy stretches, which will allow them to blow off steam. The rest of the time they should be taking classes."

"Surely, Mr McLeod. I'll watch to make sure they don't misbehave and I'll let Miss Donaldson know if they get up to mischief. You can rest easy."

"Thank you very much." MacLeod smiled thinly and dismissed the housekeeper by turning and retreating to his lair by the pantry.

♦

Not a day after this little exchange, Jack crept down to the basement to seek out Duncan. Unable to locate the footman, he hid near the back door to watch all the toing and froing amongst the staff. Pretty soon there was a knock at the door and Duncan materialised to answer it. Jack melted back into his nook and listened intently.

"Christ, I thought you weren't coming, Jimmy." Duncan grabbed the visitor by the lapels and dragged him into the hallway. "I've been tryin' to work and listen for the door at the same time. What kept you?"

Jimmy was a devious individual with dark, hooded eyes and he never looked at anyone directly. It gave him a distinctly shifty appearance. "It may surprise you, but you're not the only person who lays bets in this area. I had to go to Bridge of Allan and Dunblane before coming here to Deanston. There seem to be more and more punters there, with all the rich folk who have settled in the area. I've been very busy."

"D'you have my money?"

"Sure. This is what you won from last week's wager."

Jack heard the clink of coins as the bookie passed Duncan his winnings. It sounded like an awful lot.

"Thanks. Now I wanna place a couple of bets this week. The *Sporting Times* gave a list of runners at Epsom and Sandown this weekend and I'm playing for several of the household this time. The list is on this paper and the money'll come from my winnings. You can count it out."

"Let's have a look." He took the list and scrutinised it for a minute. Then he looked up at Duncan.

"Gimme the money and if you let me have five minutes, I can get you the odds on each one and separate out the bets, with receipts. Is there somewhere I can sit and write?"

"Sure. Come in here." He indicated a small laundry area where there was a bench and table. The bookie went in and shut the door.

Jack emerged from his hiding place, much to the surprise of Duncan, who gave a start. "Jings, Master Jack, you scared me to death. What're you doing down here?"

"I was bored, so I thought I'd come down and see what was going on. Why did that man give you all that money?'

"With all due respect, that is no affair of yours."

"Tell me or I'll speak to McLeod and you'll be in trouble."

"You're a scallywag sometimes." Duncan paused to check that there was nobody within earshot. He lowered his voice. "Some of us like to bet money on which horse will win a certain race at different racecourses around the country. Your grandfather gets the *Sporting Times* every day, so we can look up information about the racing after he's finished with the paper. On most days he isn't even here, so we get the paper early on, all to ourselves. Jimmy takes our bets and pays us if we win. He comes here once a week from Stirling."

"Can I join in? I've only ever bet matches before on card games, but always wondered what it would be like with real money. I have some pocket money and while I'm staying with my grandparents, there's nothing to spend it on. They say I should save it, but I can't see the fun in that."

"Much as I'd like to help you, we'd get in terrible trouble if anyone found out. You're still a little young for this sort of thing, and I'll tell you this: we probably win less often than we lose. A payday like today happens very seldom. It would be unfair for me to take your money."

"But I want to."

"Tell you what . . . If you can sneak a look at the papers and begin to learn about racing, then I could consider it, but without some idea of what is going on, it would just be unfair to have you involved. It takes time and effort. You could even ask your grandfather; after all, he reads about it every day. Until then, I'm sorry."

Jack was about to argue, but Miss Donaldson appeared, demanding to know what he was doing in the servants' quarters. She whisked him off upstairs for a bath and something to eat. But the seed had been planted and his curiosity was piqued. He'd have to find a subtle way to quiz his grandpa when he next had a chance.

Chapter 4

1905–07 GREECE & GERMANY

"The mathematics prize goes to Nicolas Zographos."

Polite applause from the other parents and a standing ovation from Nico's parents followed the announcement. The school prize-giving had dragged on for an age, but it had all been worth it for this one moment. Nico got up from his seat and ascended the stairs to the stage to receive his prize, a copy of the new book by Poincaré, *Science and Hypothesis*, which was in French. He was not sure when or how he was going to read it, as his school French was fairly basic, but it was a great honour, nonetheless.

"Well, Nico, now that you've graduated from school, have you given any further thought to my idea of studying in Germany?"

They had returned home and Nico was sitting at the dining room table with his father, who was obviously keen to get him thinking about his future. "With your gift for numbers, an institute like the Technical University of Munich would be the ideal place to get a good engineering qualification. It'd give you a great chance of securing a decent job."

"Come on, Papa, I'm just out of school. Do I have to start thinking about it now?" The truth was that Nico was not attracted to a career as an engineer, which he'd heard was a profession that was highly regulated – not the sort of thing that he would enjoy. He liked the discipline of the numbers, but not of the establishment.

Iaonnis tutted. "It's best dealt with soon, as we have to confirm you want a place and we'll need to start paying for it. This sort of chance doesn't come for free! I've already applied for you to go there and your school results will mean they'll accept you, but we need to let them know very soon."

Nico wanted to please his father and he knew that this would make him very happy. If he didn't do it, he wasn't quite sure whether further education in Athens would give him the same earnings potential, and in the end that was extremely important. And engineering as a discipline covered a wide range of industries, so he could well find a job that used his knowledge without necessarily tying him to the worst aspects of the profession. Not everyone would have such a great opportunity and it seemed churlish to refuse.

"All right. I've actually been thinking about it for a time and was really procrastinating for no particular reason, apart from being nervous about living abroad and having to learn another language. I'm really very grateful for the opportunity. It is time to take the decision; I shall start in September."

"Marvellous. I'll let them know. I'm sure you won't regret it."

Nico could see a small tear form in the corner of his father's eye just before he got up and embraced his son.

♦

Nico walked across the quad from the mechanical engineering facility to the maths building for his class on integral calculus. He was in a good mood, partly because his studies were going well and partly because it was a beautiful spring day and the blossoms were out. They had seen the last of the winter snow; the days were getting longer, which meant less studying by dim gaslight, and the prospect of finishing his exams was now looming large. Then he could go home for the summer.

Coming to Germany had been a struggle. The people were very different from his fellow countrymen in Greece – so correct and disciplined. The same could be said for the language. It had a different alphabet and a totally different language structure (why did they put their verbs at the end of sentences?). And there had been a decided lack of help in trying to overcome these obstacles. Even though he had studied hard in preparation for his adventure, nothing could have prepared him for the realities of studying and living in such a place, even if Munich was moderately civilised and the people polite, though rather cold.

He had been lonely at the start, but that had helped him concentrate on his studies. He was also socially inept, particularly when required to speak German, and had taken up smoking as it gave him something to do whilst formulating sentences. He also thought it lent him an air of sophistication. As time went on, his language skills improved and he began to make friends; his initial qualms about his move to Munich gradually melted away.

But all of that was beside the point, as he was wrestling with the next class on integration and its application in engineering. He was also intrigued by its uses in the laws of probability, which was an area he had never really thought about, but which appealed to him intellectually: although he did not appreciate it at the time, this would become very useful to him in later life.

He ran into Johannes, a fellow student from Frankfurt who was in the same dormitory as him and attended many of his classes. He looked anything but cheery and Nico asked him why.

"I've been talking to my professor about my future once I graduate and I confess that it all sounds a bit daunting."

"Why?"

"Well, you know we've been taught a whole screed of procedures that have been introduced to discipline the engineering profession?"

"Absolutely, but that's nothing new."

"Okay, but it seems to be getting worse. Now there are what they call 'duties of care' – I guess you'd call them norms of etiquette – which also have to be followed, and they just seem to make our chosen profession a nightmare."

"Who the hell told you all this?" Nico's expression was one of incredulity. "It honestly *can't* be that bad, otherwise why would anyone become an engineer?"

"The professor hinted at it, but once I started to talk to the others, it took on a far more sinister tone. The politicians want to limit our power in things like building and engine development. The motor car's just one example, but there are others. The pace of technological change is now so fast that they are getting nervous and want to regain control. It'll make our jobs nigh-on impossible. It's too depressing."

"Cheer up, Johan," Nico said. "You're just being a worrywart. Engineering in its broadest sense is needed in all sorts of areas; I'll bet you we'll be able to find one that's not so bound by rules. You're talking to too many pessimists – it just can't be that awful."

"Maybe you're right, but only partly." Johannes thought for a moment. "One thing's for sure – come what may there will be restrictions, which'll make any job both arduous and finicky."

"Good grief, you definitely need cheering up! Right now I've got to get to class, but we can get together later on. How about a game of cards with Wilhelm, a bottle of Schnapps and a good chat this evening? That'll lift your spirits."

"Okay. That's actually not a bad idea. It's been a time since we played Skat. We can all meet at the *weinstube*. What time?"

"Let's go for nine. Okay?"

"Good – see you then."

Nico patted his friend on the back in what he hoped was a reassuring way and moved on to tackle his maths class.

◆

The weeks flew by and the exams approached. Any discussions Nico had about the protocols demanded in his chosen career had been pretty glum. None of the other students were optimistic about it getting any easier and some were considering using their talents elsewhere; teaching and research were popular alternatives. His enquiries about Greek systems did not fill him with joy either. The same anxiety about the role of engineers in the deployment of new technology was causing the same strictures to be put in place in Athens, if his contacts were to be believed.

But all this paled into insignificance with the arrival of a letter from home. It was unusual for his father to write to him, though his mother would religiously send him all the family news in a weekly message, written every Sunday evening. As he opened it, he assumed that his father had found some time to let him know how things were: it never occurred to him that it might be bad news. But once he started reading the letter, written in his father's formal tones, a terrible sinking feeling overcame him as the full horror of what had happened became apparent.

Dear Nico

I know I seldom correspond with you and as you can probably imagine the reason for this letter is not good news: it is very difficult to write and it pains me to do so. What has happened will affect us all, but especially you, deeply and almost immediately.

The long and the short of it is that we are bankrupt. We had two assets, which had given us a steady income, and the growth of the capital had left us with a comfortable nest egg. I was unconcerned about either of them, but we were hit twice, almost simultaneously, by sheer bad luck.

The first investment, which I was reliably informed was rock solid, turned out to be anything but. Without going into too much detail, it was based on the way currency is minted in Greece, as part of the Latin Monetary Union. When Greece was unexpectedly expelled from the LMU, my debts were effectively exposed and the stock vanished overnight.

This would not have been so devastating if my other asset, a share in a coalmine in Germany, had not gone sour. I had been an investor in the mine from as far back as when I studied in Heidelberg and had added gradually to my holding. A decision to close the mine coincided with the LMU catastrophe and I suddenly had nothing.

I feel very guilty that I am putting you all through this. I suppose I should have been more careful with my investments, but either way it means we are now dependent on whatever your mother and I can earn, and that is never going to be enough for any extras. One of these, of course, is the cost of your tuition fees in Munich, without even mentioning your board and lodging.

Suffice it to say that we cannot pay the final instalment of your tuition or, more importantly, your living expenses, so I'm afraid that you are going to have to return to Athens almost immediately. What really pains me is that it also precludes you being able to graduate.

You have no idea how sorry I am that this has happened. I would love to say that it is totally beyond my control, but that is not the case.

The situation is terrible, but without trying to sugar the pill too much, it may have some positives. I know from your letters that you were not one hundred per cent convinced that engineering was the profession for you, and this may give you an opportunity to explore other options. It will also be lovely that we can all be together again.

I realise that I have let all of you down, but please take comfort in the fact that I still love you very much and will do anything I can to help you through this.

Your loving Papa

Nico was shattered. Without his degree, he could perhaps use his knowledge to get work, but never of the calibre that he wanted or felt he deserved. All his worries about the restrictions on the engineering community evaporated as he contemplated a future back in Greece doing menial work of little value or significance.

His father wanted him home immediately, but he reckoned he still had until the end of the month. Not that there was much he could do in Germany, but he did not want to go home, as that would really signify the end of his studies. It would also mean that he'd have to face his father and he wasn't sure that he would be able to restrain himself, such was his anger and frustration. He wanted to kill the old man: how could he have been so careless and irresponsible? And how on earth could he even suggest that this had anything to do with luck? Nico knew from all the mathematics he had studied, that probability was dictated by actions and that luck was merely statistics. His dad had invested unwisely and his family would pay the price. It was as simple and catastrophic as that. As long as Nico remained in Munich, he could postpone that meeting, try and calm his rage and pretend that life was normal, even though it was far from it.

At the end of the week when he received the fateful letter, his landlord confirmed that he would indeed have to be out within thirty days, as the next month's payment had not been forthcoming. The only good news this brought was that he had a little longer than he had thought before he needed to head for home. But instead of using this time productively, he spent his days lying on his bed, allowing dark thoughts to engulf him. He stopped attending classes, as he could see little point in it. His tutors asked about him for the first few days and then gave up. His friends found him withdrawn and uncommunicative and he gradually stopped seeing them altogether. He sat in his room and brooded on his situation, his anger at his father slowly turning into a fury with the world in general, and frustration with how it had treated him in particular. The more time he spent in isolation, the worse his depression became and, as his mood darkened, negative emotions overwhelmed him to the point where his thoughts turned to suicide. But, of course, being the methodical person that he was, his resolution to end it all involved a detailed analysis of his options rather than a headlong rush to self-destruction.

He couldn't easily or cheaply find a gun and he felt uneasy about poison, as his knowledge was limited and procurement complicated. Hanging seemed technically challenging and he might end up choking to death slowly and painfully if he did it wrong. Jumping off a tall building was appealing, but in the end he decided on jumping off a bridge into a freezing cold river, which would either kill him from the fall; or he could drown, as he wasn't a very good swimmer; or he would die of hypothermia, which he understood was quick and not unpleasant. With so many possible fatal outcomes, he reasoned that this seemed the most certain option. When studying stress engineering, his class had visited the Luitpold Bridge and his recollection of it suggested that it would be a likely candidate, particularly as it wasn't far away.

Having made his decision, he sat down to write a note for his family, as he felt that he should at least attempt to explain his reasons for taking his own life. It also allowed him to rationalise his decision for his own benefit. After starting and tearing up the first eight attempts, all of which were too long and inarticulate, he settled on something short and sweet.

Please show this to my family and anyone else who is interested.

Now that my university career is over, I have no desire to spend the rest of my life seeking unfulfilling jobs, unworthy of my talents. Without my degree, that is what awaits me, because that is the way of the world.

I therefore prefer to end it now. This is my own decision and I have been neither coerced nor persuaded into it. It is a shame, but is for the best.

Nicolas Zographos

He propped the note up on his mantelpiece and set out bright and early on a Tuesday morning in April. Unusually for that time of year, it was very cold.

He was not thinking rationally as he trundled along Prinzregentenstrasse towards the Isar River and his date with the Grim Reaper. He had not put on enough clothing and by the time he was halfway there, he thought he might die of cold without even reaching his goal. The walk to the bridge took about half an hour, and as his advance towards death progressed, some semblance of sanity began to prevail, so that by the time he reached his destination, he was less decided on self-destruction. Once he was standing on the bridge looking down at the river, the relative lack of height discouraged him further, as he could imagine that rather than taking his life, the fall might not kill him outright, which would mean a long and horrible drowning, or worse, a painful and debilitating injury.

Despite this, he climbed onto the parapet and stood with his toes over the rushing torrent, his mind once again in turmoil. Should he jump? How would it affect his father? What lay beyond the moment of final extinction? He was not a religious man, but his thoughts turned to eternity and his fear of death began to wrestle with his despair. He became unaware of his surroundings as these thoughts raced through his head: he bent down and sat on the edge, ready to lean forward and let go. But he just couldn't make that final move and remained where he was. It was almost as if he wanted someone to stop him.

His hesitation was his salvation. He had been paralysed in the same position for several minutes when he became aware of someone behind him and off to the left. He turned to look and was confronted by a policeman, not much older than him. The uniformed official was still several paces away and did not attempt to move any closer.

"Hello. My name is Heinrich. What's your name?" The voice was calm and reassuring and Nico felt some of his anxiety melt away as he replied. "I'm Nico," he said.

"Nice to meet you, Nico. It looks to me as if you're in a rather dangerous position and could easily fall into the river. Even if that is your intention, would you not at least like to talk about what brought you here? I've plenty of time to listen and maybe I can help."

"No. My mind's made up." But the way he said it suggested that was not the case at all. It was as if he were daring the policeman to challenge him. Heinrich was not stupid and caught the uncertainty.

"Well, even if that is the case, before you do it, could you explain why, so I can relay your story to your friends and relatives, who I'm sure will miss you and want to try to understand. That'll help spare them from some of the grief they'll feel at your passing. I believe that's the minimum we can do."

Nico was dismissive of this suggestion. His tone was contemptuous. "I left them a note, and they won't care anyway."

"You'd be surprised. I lost an older sister who committed suicide a couple of years ago, and the fact that we never found out what drove her to such extremes has always played on my mind." It was a lie, but Heinrich knew that it was important to establish a common bond with this obviously desperate individual, and this seemed as good a way as any.

Nico fell silent and Heinrich could tell that his words had hit home. He decided to press his advantage. "So, tell me what brought you here. Surely that can't hurt."

This was the trigger for the normally unemotional Greek to pour out his heart. He started with his upbringing at home and went on to his move to Germany and his hopes for the future, now dashed by the devastating news from his father.

Heinrich listened carefully and then said, "But you must see that this is just a short-term setback; you're obviously a highly intelligent man and there's no reason why you shouldn't have considerable success in some other way of life. It seems a shame to take such a drastic and permanent measure."

The conversation continued, and Nico's resolve weakened as they spoke. He began to realise that he was extremely cold and uncomfortable, so he got down from his precarious perch on the edge of the bridge and allowed the policeman to accompany him back to his lodgings. As they walked, his normally logical reasoning returned, and by the time they got to his rooms he had decided to at least go home to Athens, talk to his father and family and then decide on how to face the future.

He took his suicide note down from above the fireplace and lit a fire with it. He then huddled down in front of it and let the warmth permeate his body. He was already feeling better and more positive, and although he did not have the first notion as to what he would do when he got back to Greece, he at least wanted to approach his future as positively as he could. He reflected on what Victor Hugo had said, 'Even the darkest night will end and the sun will rise.'

After a rather fitful night's sleep, he packed his bags, said goodbye to his friends and was on the train, his final destination being Athens.

Chapter 5

1907–12 SCOTLAND, ENGLAND & FRANCE

Willie Coats had just opened the mail when he summoned his two sons to the library at Skelmorlie. They were both home from school for the summer and although he seldom saw them, he did sometimes make an effort to find things they could do together. Just such an opportunity had arisen.

"I have in my hand an invitation for us all to attend the inauguration of the new racecourse at Ayr. As you know, the Western Meeting is held there each year in September, so they view this as a perfect moment to show off their new installations. It's taken them two years to complete the move from the previous location on the other side of town. The new grounds are out in the countryside and, I am told, compare favourably to the track at Epsom, where they hold the Derby. We shall see. The grandstand is far bigger than its predecessor and, more to the point for us, there appears to be more space for entertaining guests indoors, which I consider vital as I am too old to be standing around in the wind and rain outside."

Jack was really excited at the prospect of going racing, but suppressed his emotion for fear that his father might find out about his earlier flirtation with racecourse betting. He asked, "Will any of the rest of the family be going?"

"I'd imagine that most of them have been invited and will probably attend. Several of them should be on the train when we travel down there. It's in three weeks' time, just before you go back to school."

And with that, he dismissed his sons and went back to an art catalogue he had been scrutinising before the mail arrived.

◆

So it was that Jack, his brother Tom and father Willie found themselves in one of the racecourse's brand new hospitality areas in early September 1907. They were seated at one of the longer tables, where waiters served them with champagne, smoked salmon, oysters and other delicacies. As Jack had just celebrated his fifteenth birthday, he was not allowed alcohol, but he managed a clandestine sip from his brother's glass; and although he found oysters almost inedible, mostly because of the texture, there were plenty of other goodies to be had.

"I never thought the speeches were going to end," said Willie. "Those politicians just love the sound of their own voices and when they're given an opportunity like today, they just don't know when to shut up. We have to stand outside to listen to them and they don't seem to appreciate that most of us just want to watch the horses, have something to eat and get a bit of shelter. I felt quite sorry for all the women who were struggling to secure their hats in the wind."

It had been a long trip down from Skelmorlie. They had caught the train in Wemyss Bay for Paisley, where several members of the family had joined them when they changed trains, and then on to Ayr. With Jack's ten aunts and uncles and countless cousins, there was never any lack of family when there were get-togethers, though his father seemed to shun these with greater frequency as he grew older, becoming progressively more reclusive after his wife's death and his subsequent exit from the family business to concentrate full time on his art collection. Jack enjoyed seeing everyone, but opportunities to do so were infrequent. In this instance, his father's cousin Sir James had been invited as he was one of the most important figures in Ayrshire, and the presence of several other family members meant that even Willie felt he couldn't say no.

"Well, I'd like to go down to the paddock to look at the horses running in the Gold Cup." This was Uncle George, who loved animals and was as vibrant as Jack's father was dull. "Are you coming with me, young Jack?"

"Rather. D'you mind if I go, Father?"

"No. Make sure he behaves himself George."

"Will do."

George strode out of the door, down the stairs and out into the brisk Scottish afternoon. The coastal breeze was always present, even this far inland, and Jack drew his tailcoat around him and shivered.

George turned and looked at him. "Don't worry – once we get near the horses it'll be warmer. Have you ever got close to a racehorse before?"

"No. I've ridden horses out hunting, but not these thoroughbreds."

"They're genuinely exciting to be near and if we go down to the track after leaving the paddock, to watch the race up close, you'll be amazed at the sheer power they project. Their speed is impressive and the noise is so intense that it's almost frightening. You'll love it."

They got to the paddock and the horses were parading in an oval, with the jockeys in their different colours.

"You have horses, don't you, Uncle George? Have you never wanted to own racehorses?"

"Oh yes, I have lots, but I really like hunting, and the effort required to train and exercise these beauties is not something that appeals to me. We must have you over to Glentanar and you can spend time with the hounds and learn more about tracking foxes and deerstalking. It is a great outdoor life and mightily stimulating."

"I'd love to, but I'm off back to Eton next week, so it'll have to be after I get back in December."

George nodded. "Actually I knew that. Your cousin Tom is about to start there this year. He couldn't be here today as he and your Aunt Margaret have already gone south to get him kitted up with all that ridiculous paraphernalia that you Etonians have to wear."

"Yes, the clothing is a bit of a bore. But I play a lot of sports, so I get out of it quite often – most afternoons, in fact."

"Ah yes, your pa told me you are quite the sportsman."

"Well, I play the Field Game during the Michaelmas half and rugby in the Lent half. Summer is my favourite, as I get to play cricket; I am in the under-sixteen team this year and may well be in the second eleven before I leave. There's even a slim chance I could reach the first eleven, with an opportunity to play at Lords against Harrow."

"Good for you."

"Thanks. I also really enjoy the Hunt and I imagine that Tom would be up for that. They have a huge pack of beagles and the whole thing is very professionally managed. I'll ask him if he's interested and get him the necessary introductions."

"I'm glad you brought that up – it brings me very neatly onto one of the reasons why I wanted to catch you. It was to ask you if you'd be able to keep an eye on Tom for the first few weeks of school at least. I know he's not in your house, but if you can check up on him occasionally that would be marvellous. We don't want to be overprotective as parents, but just knowing he has someone is a great comfort to us."

"Of course, I'd be delighted to help. I'll try to contact him as soon as I get back there."

"That would be wonderful. I know there are lots of opportunities for hobbies and what they call extra-curricular activities there, and I want to make sure he makes full use of them."

"Don't worry, I'll nudge him in the right direction. Is there anything particular that interests him besides hunting?"

"He loves classical music: it's his real passion. I don't know if you can help with that?" George raised his eyebrows and looked inquiringly at Jack.

"Not my field of expertise, I must admit. I prefer the modern stuff – I really like Harry Lauder. However, I do know that there is a Classical Music Society at school and I'll find out what I can to help him."

"Excellent. Now, let's see which horses are likely to win. Are you going to have a flutter?"

"I've never tried betting before, though I obviously understand the basics, such as racing form and weight handicaps. I haven't studied any of the runners for this meeting, so I have no idea which horses will be the likely winners, but I'd be willing to just try my luck on the basis of a name." Jack was reluctant to admit his earlier interest in the sport when visiting his maternal grandparents, for fear of running afoul of his father.

"Well, I may be able to go one better than that. As you know, this is the first year that they'll run the Gold Cup on this ground. What you probably don't know is that the race has been reduced from a mile and three furlongs to only six furlongs." He winked at Jack and flashed a conspiratorial grin. "Now, here's the clever bit. The rumours are that this reduction to less than half the distance was heavily promoted and influenced by the Duke of Montrose, who has a horse called Raeberry running in the race. This nag is supposedly much better over short distances, to the point of being practically unbeatable. The duke has had a winner before: Dazzle was his and won it three years running from 1889 to '91, so he knows what he's doing."

George put his arm around Jack's shoulders and squeezed. "What I am getting at is, if you can make a bet with inside knowledge then that's a lot safer than doing it just haphazardly. I'm going to put some money on Raeberry; I'd advise you to do the same."

"Okay, Uncle George, I'll bow to your superior knowledge and take the same wager. Where do we go?"

"I seldom bet, but if we go to one of the on-course bookies, we should be fine. I can see one over there." He squinted to make out the name in the distance. "I think they're called W & D Brown. Come with me."

George shepherded Jack towards the bookmaker. They had soon negotiated the odds and their stakes and handed over the money.

"Let's go down to the finish and we can watch the race from there," said George. "It'll be over in a flash. A horse can run six furlongs in just over a minute, so we won't be left hanging around."

Once they got down to the fence that separated the racetrack from the spectators, they couldn't find a space at the front and Jack had to crane his neck to even get a glimpse of the course. George noticed his frustration and leant over.

"Climb on my shoulders and then you'll be able to see everything!"

Jack looked uncomfortable and slightly nervous. "Oh Uncle George, I couldn't do that. I'm really heavy and it would be embarrassing."

"Nonsense – nobody will notice and we're nowhere near any of the old fuddy-duddies from the family who might care. I'll just bend down and hoist you up. Easy as pie."

Sure enough, he got Jack up almost effortlessly and once he was clear of the crowd he could see the runners all milling around three quarters of a mile away. All seemed to be pretty chaotic, but eventually the horses appeared to be lined up, so the starter dropped the flag and they galloped towards the two of them. Jack felt oddly comfortable with his uncle and a tingle of excitement coursed through his body as he watched his prospective winner hurtle down the course. It was unlike any sensation he could remember: he was nervous but exhilarated at the same time. He felt the blood pumping in his ears and everything seemed to happen in slow motion. This was fantastic!

Then it was over and he couldn't work out who had won. The mass of horses and riders had thundered past them in a flurry of turf and mud, so that it was hard to distinguish the colours. He turned to his uncle.

"Who won?"

"The bloody Duke of Montrose must have miscalculated. Raeberry came in second, which does us no good at all. I was so sure it'd dominate the race that we both backed it for the win, not a place. We lost, old son."

"So, which horse did win?"

"The winner's name was Charis. 'Fraid it's a complete unknown to me. Bad luck, but there'll always be another day."

They made their way back to the members' enclosure and the warmth and hospitality of the family's table. When they got there, Jack wanted to tell his father what they had done, but he was in deep conversation with someone who seemed familiar although Jack could not place him. As he came closer he could overhear them discussing art, so he knew not to interrupt. He had the impression that the unknown man must be a dealer he had seen at Skelmorlie.

He was disappointed not to be able to share his experience with Willie, but he was used to being shunned. It was fairly clear to Jack that his father preferred his older brother Tom – and he understood that this happened with a lot of parents, who tended to favour the oldest child, particularly if it was male. His brother said it was because his father blamed him for the death of his mother. Everyone told Jack that she was very frail after she had

had the accident whilst pregnant, and the birth had been complicated, which hadn't helped, but he could hardly be blamed for that, could he? Regardless, what was in little doubt was that he had a great deal of trouble pleasing his old man, and Jack had the distinct impression that his dad avoided him as much as he could.

As his father was occupied, Jack turned his attention to his various relations around the table. In particular, he started to listen to what his Uncle George and cousin James were discussing, something to do with the family company. He couldn't catch it all, but understood that there were some tensions between the Coatses and their relatively new partners, the Clarks. There was a lull in the conversation and James noticed that he was listening.

"Are you interested in hearing about the company, Jack? It is now one of the biggest in the world."

"Not really. Father never talks about it."

Sir James turned to him and smiled knowingly. "Your pa is not the most forthcoming individual, is he? Even so I'm mildly surprised that he hasn't told you more about what we do; you really know almost nothing about it?"

"Zero, apart from the fact that they make sewing thread."

" As I imagine that you and your brother Tom will want to join us some day, would you be interested in hearing more?"

"I'm sure I'll be more interested when that time comes, but I still have to finish school first."

"Absolutely!" George interjected. "Jack has very kindly offered to look after my boy Tom when he starts next half, so we can't have him abandoning school in favour of the company." He roared with laughter and slapped Jack on the back. "There will be plenty of time for you to get acquainted with our little business at a later stage, though you should perhaps try to get to Paisley and visit our two huge production mills at Ferguslie and Seedhill. They are a sight to see."

"That would be neat if it could be arranged." Jack looked less than enthused, but felt he had to show willing, particularly with Uncle George.

"I'll have a word with Willie," said James. "I am sure we can organise something." He took out a wallet from his inside pocket and made a note on a piece of paper. "Just leave it with me."

They eventually got the train home and even then, when there was time to talk, Jack's father showed little interest in his afternoon's adventures apart from a frown at Jack's mention of the betting with Uncle George. Once back at Skelmorlie, they all went their separate ways in the huge mansion and Jack fell asleep that night elated by the joy he had found with his meagre wager.

But what really fascinated him was what it must feel like to actually win.

◆

The thrill that Jack had felt that afternoon stayed with him long after he returned to school, though his enthusiasm for the family company less so. There was no way of going to a racecourse during the school term, so his interest in betting on racing soon waned, but he was a bright young man and saw that there were other avenues down which he could go to explore his newly acquired interest. One in particular, cards, was what attracted him most and he sought out the group most likely to satisfy his interest – the bridge club.

Upon joining the club at the beginning of the next term, it became immediately obvious that his experience playing whist with his grandmother would stand him in good stead. A bit of reading and a good deal of practice quickly made him one of the better players in the group, though he could not rival the more experienced enthusiasts, who read and studied the game constantly. This approach did not interest him, as he viewed this rather stuffy game as a stepping-stone to more hard-core gambling, and the swots – as he called these fanatics – were not the people he was after. Rather, he was constantly on the lookout for people who expressed even a mild curiosity in other games, particularly poker and vingt-et-un.

He started to ask around and one afternoon his curiosity was rewarded at a session of duplicate bridge arranged by the club. He had been placed with a rather tedious partner who, although not a swot, was very focused on the finer points of the game and would do a post-mortem after every hand. Jack was bored rigid by these – the only aspect of this particular variation of bridge that attracted him was that he got to meet several boys from outside his immediate group, and it was during a break that he fell into conversation with one of them, an opponent from the table they had just played.

"Can't say I find this particular card game much fun." Jack was almost talking to himself. "I'd prefer something more edgy, like poker."

His rival turned to face him and his expression brightened. "Really?" He paused and then continued, "If that's the case then I think I may have something that's right up your street. We have a group of about six of us who play a couple of times a week. Not usually poker, but certainly vingt-et-un and lately we have taken to playing chemin-de-fer and baccarat."

"Really?" Jack had read about these last two, but never played them. "Would there be any chance you could introduce me? I am Coats Minor – my friends call me Jack."

"I am Denny, but my Christian name is James. I know your older brother, who's a prefect in my house. And yes, I can get you into the games." He paused and looked around before lowering his voice and adding, "But I warn you – what we play is strictly against school rules and there'll be hell to pay if we get caught."

Jack grinned. "Doesn't worry me in the slightest. What is life without the occasional risk? With my luck, I'm unlikely to ever get caught, and please be assured that I won't breathe a word about it, not even to my brother."

"Good. That's really important."

At that moment a voice rang out across the room asking everyone to move to their next table to resume playing. Denny grabbed Jack's arm and whispered, "Meet me at the gate to Cannon Yard next Thursday afternoon after games. I will take you over to where we play and you can meet the fellows."

"Thanks." They separated and went off to their respective games, but Jack was already anticipating the encounter later in the week.

♦

He duly met with Denny and was introduced to the other players who, much to his delight, were willing to play for decent sums of money, courtesy of generous allowances from their parents. He soon became a fixture at their weekly get-togethers. It was all quite good-natured and nobody seemed to win a great deal more than anyone else, but it meant that Jack could familiarise himself with the rules and conventions of various casino games.

He also played baccarat for the first time.

This proved to be a life-altering moment. He quickly became obsessed with it in all its different guises and he pushed the rest of them to play it exclusively rather than their usual mix of gambling games. He couldn't quite explain what it was about baccarat that gave him such pleasure, but he became so enthusiastic about it that he began to research how and where he could play beyond the school. He soon discovered that although it was largely played in private houses by the very wealthy in Britain, the place where the hard-core players with serious money went was to the casinos of France, where it had just been legalised. His French lessons suddenly became more interesting and important.

His fascination also drove him to want to improve his play and he suspected that the methodology of the best bridge players, involving a lot of practice and copious reading, would lend itself to perfecting his technique, so he started to raid the school library in an attempt to make himself an expert. It turned out that literature on the subject was scarce and exceptionally dry, so he quickly became bored with the theory and concluded that it was a game of luck rather than skill. He yearned to play more.

By the time he left school in 1910, ready for university, he was impatient to tackle the gambling establishments of France. That was where he would become an expert; not through all the principles set out in endless rather dull and theoretical books, but because he would play a lot for a lot of money. His inherent luck would make him successful.

But before he tackled the seasoned players in France, he felt he needed to get some experience away from the rather cloistered atmosphere of school. He kept in touch with his colleagues from the gambling circle at Eton and almost immediately started to travel to house parties arranged by their parents and friends, where significant money would be sloshing around once the less adventurous souls had taken to their beds. He soon ran into others outside the immediate group and came across several who had spent time in France. Their stories of exploits at the tables there only served to whet his appetite further.

Now free of the shackles of single-sex education, he also began to enjoy the company and adulation of several young ladies who came to these parties just to watch the gambling and, more importantly, the gamblers. He had matured into a good looking young man and had grown a rather fine moustache, which, along with his obvious wealth, made him an irresistible prospect for a lot of them; he soon found he had no shortage of admirers and a reputation as a bit of a rogue. His exploits with one such girl, involving a chase through the shrubs and a discarded nightdress, had him banned from a large country estate, where the duke, father of the friend who had invited Jack, would "not stand for such tomfoolery".

Satisfied that he was sufficiently prepared for a sortie abroad, Jack set about persuading his father that a time in France would be beneficial, allowing him both to perfect his language skills and let him see a bit of the world, before going off to a seat of higher learning to study mathematics, his chosen field. Willie agreed, only too glad to have the boy occupied and out of his way, and Jack set off with a tidy sum in his pocket and a grim determination to bring the local casinos to their knees.

His plan did not go quite as he had anticipated, but he had some good days and gradually gained a reputation as a moderately skilled and highly audacious player, even at the tender age of eighteen. His good looks and easy-going nature meant that he was soon being fawned over by all the most desirable young women who frequented the casinos and gambling clubs. This only enhanced his reputation further, and he began to understand that it would help intimidate his opponents and improve his chances of winning. It was also great fun.

He played every game available in the various clubs and casinos he visited, mainly to get to know the places and people, but homed in on chemin-de-fer and baccarat as the two games where serious money was in play. He had never experienced anything like the feeling he had when he won a large and chancy wager. His heart pounded and he felt an almost superhuman adrenaline rush each time he collected the plaques in front of him. There was nothing else like this in the world – the effects of alcohol were as nothing in comparison, and even sex was less satisfying. He also craved the adoration he received from the onlookers, and the attention of every girl in the place was an added bonus. They not only loved him when he won, but were fascinated by his nonchalance when losing.

He concentrated on the area around Paris and on one exceptional night managed to win 5 million francs. He was on his way into the casino in Enghien-les-Bains a few evenings later when a "pretty young thing" stopped him. She was drop-dead gorgeous and he had noticed her before.

"Monsieur Coats. Do you have a moment for me?"

Jack gave her his most charming smile and said, "Who would not have all the time in the world for a creature as lovely as you?

What can I do for you?"

"I saw you at the tables the other night when you won all that money. I wonder – are you going to win another 5 million tonight?"

He laughed and took her in his arms. She did not resist. "My dear," he said, "I have no idea if I will be able to do it again, but if I do, let's make a small pact. You wait for me here and I'll give you half."

With this he kissed her affectionately on the mouth and left her there, flushed and stunned into silence.

Sure enough, several hours later he repeated the gambling feat and as soon as he had accumulated his winnings, he rose from the table and went straight back to the girl, who had remained where she was, ever hopeful.

"I'm glad you waited and I think you will be too. You were obviously a kind of human talisman for me. I have indeed won another 5 mill and a promise is a promise. Here's your half." He handed her twenty-five plaques of 100,000 francs, gave her another kiss and, laughing loudly, turned to re-enter the high rollers' area. She stood there in absolute astonishment, as did several onlookers. He then proceeded to lose the remaining two and a half million, and somewhat more.

The very next week he was visiting another casino and as he came to the back entrance past the swimming pool, an elegant young lady approached him.

"Monsieur Coats, I have been longing to meet you. Would you allow me to accompany you to the tables this evening? I am renowned for being a sort of lucky charm."

Jack was slightly taken aback by this brazen approach, but took it in his stride. "You certainly look charming to me mademoiselle, but much as I would love to take you with me, you will not be allowed into the high stakes area, being of the fairer sex. I am more sorry than I can say."

His new found friend looked disconsolate, so he continued, "You seem disappointed, but you look like a sporting girl, so I am prepared to give you the opportunity to win money without risking anything more than your modesty. I will give you 100,000 francs to disrobe, climb up to the top diving board and jump stark naked into the pool. I will hold your dress while you do."

She looked him directly in the eye, stripped off her dress and underwear, walked brazenly around the pool to the diving board and climbed to the top. After plunging into the pool, she emerged like a siren, walked over to him and held out her hand. He laughed, applauded (along with several onlookers), handed her clothes to her and took out his wallet.

These and other incidents reinforced his reputation for carefree, scandalous behaviour. He felt he absolutely *had* to continue with this lifestyle as long as he could and, given his potential wealth, he didn't see why that shouldn't be a long time.

But all good things must come to an end, and the money he had taken to France eventually ran out. Although he could get credit to continue gambling, that source of finance was also finite and he found himself owing money to several people. With nowhere to turn but his father, Jack returned to Scotland to face the wrath of Willie Coats, who was indeed furious but was loath to ban him from gambling completely, for fear of driving the behaviour underground. Instead, he decided to give Jack one last chance prior to entering higher education, and he sent his son off on a cruise around the Mediterranean, where he could still have some fun but without gambling.

Jack took this enforced exile in his stride. On the first night of the cruise, after dinner at the captain's table he fell into conversation with two brothers, David and Frank Kennedy, who had inherited a fortune from their landowner father. After a couple of large cognacs, they were discussing their mutual love of Paris when the talk turned to casinos. Jack saw an opportunity.

"Do you enjoy a game of cards?"

The brothers nodded in unison. "Rather," the older one said.

"Always up for a game of bridge or rummy, but we prefer casino games such as vingt-et-un."

"Ever played baccarat?" Jack tried not to sound too eager.

This time it was the younger sibling who chipped in. "We've played it a couple of times at house parties outside London. I actually found it quite stimulating, though I confess that there was never much money involved. If I remember rightly, we just played for Cadbury's chocolates the second time. Our host seemed to have an endless supply of them!"

"Would you like a game? I am a great fan and if you are interested, I would love to see if we could interest a few others." Jack peered around the rest of the occupants of the bar.

The brothers looked at each other and nodded. "We'd love to," David said.

"Let's see if we can drum up a few more." Jack stood up and spoke in a tone that carried across the whole bar area. "Would anyone else like to join us in a game of chance? We are thinking of playing baccarat and would ideally like a few more people to join us. It makes it a good deal more fun."

After a flurry of hushed conversation, a number of hands were raised. Another twenty minutes of chaos ensued, after which people were dispatched to find cards, tables were moved around and people sat where Jack indicated. He had decided to take charge and everyone was quite happy for him to do so.

Lastly, the question of how they would bet was raised and after much discussion, a house maximum of fifty pounds was arrived at, sterling being the currency of the vast majority of the participants. Agreement was reached with regard to credit and, as most of those present were obviously wealthy, everyone was assumed to be good for any debts.

Jack couldn't believe his luck. He had boarded the boat with no hope of gambling and within twenty-four hours he was once again in his element.

Unfortunately, things did not go well for him. Although the cruise lasted only a week, by the time the boat docked, he owed so much to the other passengers that they wouldn't let him off until they had been paid. His father was apoplectic and sent him off to study without further ado.

Jack was disappointed to be torn away from the tables, but accepted his fate with equanimity. He was now to study mathematics and he decided to take every opportunity to improve his knowledge of probability – and, in particular, how it would affect outcomes in various card games, especially baccarat. His time at university would not be waste.

Chapter 6

1913 GREECE & FRANCE

Five years had gone by since Nico had returned to Athens, a time spent largely in a desperate search for a decent job. Without his engineering degree he could find nothing that satisfied his intellect or his wallet, and he was barely scraping by economically, particularly as a part of what he earned went to support his parents. His father, now seventy, had retired from teaching and his mother, having raised ten children, was never going to be able to contribute significantly to the family's prosperity.

He finally landed a job as a pageboy for the Emporikon Hotel, less than half a mile from his parents' house, where he still lived, even at the ripe old age of twenty-seven. It didn't pay much, but he found an ingenious way of supplementing his meagre income and helping his parents, though he dared not tell them his dark secret.

He had happened upon this opportunity by sheer chance when sent to take a message to a hotel guest. This gentleman, who was visiting Athens from the north, had asked him if he would like to earn a little extra cash.

"That would be most welcome, sir," was Nico's reply, scrupulously polite as always. "What would you like me to do?"

"I need to find this address." The man handed Nico back the scrap of paper on which the message had been written. A quick glance told him that it was nearby.

"It's only a few streets away, an easy walk," said Nico. "I can explain how to get there or, if convenient, I can take you there."

"That'd be perfect, but I need to be there at nine o'clock this evening. Can you do it then?"

Nico knew he would be long finished with his shift by then, but the inducement of a generous tip made his decision an easy one. "I'll be here in the lobby at twenty to nine sharp. That will give us plenty of time to be there by nine."

At the appointed hour Nico was waiting by the reception desk when the guest appeared. They set off towards the address and, as they walked, the visitor began to quiz Nico about his background. When he had told his story, his companion fell silent for a moment and then asked, "Would you be interested in a job working for me? I find you a very pleasant young man and I took the liberty of investigating your background this afternoon, so I know a bit about you. I need someone bright and numerate to look after my household. I am a bachelor, so my home life is not complicated, but my business takes up all my time and I lose track of social obligations, bill paying, ordering food and so on. Would something like that interest you?"

Nico was unsure how to reply. An offer like this out of the blue seemed odd and he felt slightly uncomfortable with both the proposition itself and the manner in which it had been delivered. At the same time, he didn't want to turn it down immediately without hearing more about what it entailed and, even more importantly, how much it paid. He decided to stall. "Could I have a think about it and then talk with you some more? I can think of many questions I would need answered – like, would I live in? What would my hours be? How much would I earn? – but there must be many more that I haven't even considered."

"Of course!" They had reached their destination, which appeared to be a private house. "I will be here for a couple of hours and if you want to come and collect me later, we could talk some more then."

"Would you mind if I just wait for you? I can think about your proposition in the meantime."

"If that's what you would like to do, then I will see if they can find you a place to sit at the house here. I'll be playing cards and I never stay more than two to three hours when I come to these get-togethers. I am sure we can find you somewhere comfortable and perhaps even a drink."

"Thanks, but I never imbibe. A quiet corner would be all that I need."

A place was found for Nico, but rather than a secluded spot, he was in the main room where he could not help but watch the action. The game was poker and although he had never played, his experience with other card games meant that he soon picked up on the run of play and became so interested that he forgot the job offer completely. By the time they had been there for a couple of hours, he reckoned he could probably hold his own if he ever got the chance to sit at the table with them.

He also recognised one of the other players, who had been at school with him. Although he was much older than Nico, he knew him quite well as he was in the same class as Nico's older brother Kostas. This man, whose name was Christos Angelos, was so enthralled with the cards that he failed to register Nico's presence and the opportunity to reconnect did not present itself before they left.

On the way home, Nico quizzed his companion about the position he was offered, but when it became clear that it would entail living in, and that he would have to leave Athens, he politely declined. His suspicions as to the man's real intentions made his decision an easy one. His companion seemed disappointed, but said he understood and still gave Nico a handsome tip.

The next day, Nico set out to track down Christos and, after spending several days working his way through his network of school friends, he eventually unearthed him in one of the richer neighbourhoods. He had become quite wealthy, firstly working for, and then investing in, one of the Greek shipping companies that had exploited the post-Boer War boom, when the Greeks could command inflated prices, as all the British fleet had been requisitioned for troops and supplies.

Nico visited Christos and after the customary chit-chat, he discovered that several ship-owners' sons, along with Christos and other hangers-on, had taken to having a game of cards in the evenings and that significant sums of money changed hands; one of these was the game that Nico had witnessed. A bit of cajoling persuaded Christos to let him join in.

Given his natural gift with numbers, he quickly became a skilled competitor. He was aware that most people play by instinct and exhibit a number of extraordinarily damaging and illogical behaviours. His view of most card games was that you could use probability to predict the likely outcome of any situation and when he put this philosophy into practice, he found he was generally, but not always, more successful than his friends and opponents. As his experience and skill grew, he became more cavalier in his betting and gradually accumulated a tidy nest egg.

His game of choice was poker, not because he liked it or felt he had an edge when he competed, but rather because it was what everyone else played.

The attraction of the group was that there was plenty of money in circulation, his opponents were affable and relaxed, and they introduced him to baccarat, a game Nico came to enjoy towards the end of an evening. After a time, he also began to excel at it.

Months afterwards, one of these sessions had been going on for several hours and a break had been called for coffee and a smoke. The conversation turned to gambling and, in particular, what was happening in France.

"I hear baccarat has been legalised in France and that they have opened a new luxury casino in Deauville, not far from Paris," commented Spiro, who always seemed to be *au fait* with the latest trends. "You should go there, Nico. You seem to have a natural gift for card games, so you might find it both instructive and lucrative."

It had never occurred to Nico that he could afford to go, or that it would be worth his while, but the general chorus of approval from the rest of the group gave him pause, and he started to look at the possibility seriously. If he used his savings, a trip through Monaco and on to Deauville was within his means, and his confidence in his ability to gamble successfully had grown to the point where he felt he might even make it self-financing. He could win enough in either place and thereby return to Athens with his funds intact.

He decided to give it a try, but getting this past his parents and his employers proved somewhat harder than he hoped. His father forbade him and his employers said that if he left his job it would not be there for him when he returned. But having made his mind up, he decided to defy the collective veto, so he packed his bags under cover of darkness and stole out of the front door while the household was asleep.

The journey was long and tiring, with many changes of trains, but he eventually reached Monaco and found a cheap hotel where he could lay his head and catch up on several sleepless nights.

The following afternoon he awoke refreshed after twelve wonderful uninterrupted hours of sleep. He devoured several croissants, washing them down with coffee, and made his way to the casino, dressed in his finest attire and ready for action. The doorman was rather sniffy about letting him in. Although he was dressed in a fairly appropriate manner, his diminutive stature and olive complexion gave the impression that he was a racing jockey on his day off, rather than a high-roller on a night out. Despite this, he finally entered the hallowed halls.

It just took his breath away. The vaulted ceilings, intricately designed, were truly stunning. The baroque decorations, marble columns, plush furnishings and opulent draperies were so beautiful that it was difficult to know where to look. Even the colour scheme screamed opulence, with deep blues in sharp contrast to shining golds, creating a dazzling combination. He felt overwhelmed, but then he figured that this was all part of the intention.

In preparation for his trip, he had spent several months practising not only his French, but also that nation's casino game, Trente et Quarante, which he had practised but never played. This did not worry him, however, as the game appeared to be straightforward.

A row of cards is dealt until the total of that row exceeds thirty, depending on the value of the cards in that row. All court cards count ten, aces one and other cards their face value. Then a second row is dealt in the same way. The first row is called "Noir" (black) and the second one is "Rouge" (red). The row with the total nearest to thirty is the winning row. There are only four bets: "Noir" (the top row wins), "Rouge" (the bottom row wins), "Couleur" (the first card dealt of the winning row is the same colour as that row) and "Inverse" (the first card is the opposite colour to that row).

It was therefore logical that he should make his way to the Trente et Quarante room to try his luck – or, as he would say, skill – at this particular game. He found a table, but stood and watched the play progress for a long time, trying to get a feel for the way the cards were falling. Having never played the game for money, he was at a distinct disadvantage and he wanted to see if he could level the playing field for himself as much as possible.

He watched as the same ritual played out time and time again. The dealer shuffled six packs of cards and asked one of the players to cut them. The resulting stack was then placed in a card shoe and the game commenced. With each round – or "coup", as Nico learned they were called – the assorted participants placed their bets and after the deal had concluded the result was declared, the losing chips raked to one side, the winning chips paid and the used playing cards discarded. This was repeated until the card shoe was almost exhausted and then the whole process would restart.

Nico studied the procedure, but also the people. There were the very conservative types who nervously bet the minimum and were gradually eliminated, the flamboyant gamblers who either won big or lost quickly, and then there were two or three who actually seemed to be using systems, though he couldn't quite see how any of them worked or gave them an edge.

Satisfied that he had absorbed enough of the atmosphere, he grabbed a recently vacated chair, lit a cigarette and sat down to play. He had understood that the minimum bet was twenty francs and the maximum an alarming 12,000 which, considering his total bankroll of 5,000, was well beyond his reach. He changed 2,000 francs for a hundred twenty-franc chips and set about winning his fortune.

Things did not go his way. After four hours, betting between twenty and a hundred francs a time, he had smoked way too much and lost all the money he had allocated for that session, plus the same amount again, another 2,000 francs. Despite his frustration he decided to call it a day and keep the remaining 1,000 for another opportunity.

He did, however, take away something very useful from the session. He could recall all the cards dealt, even when each shoe had been depleted. This was extremely gratifying, as he had worried that his ability would not hold up in the heady atmosphere of the casino. He was convinced it would be hugely valuable especially when playing baccarat.

He wandered around the building watching all the activity, marvelling at the décor of the rooms and the elegance of the millionaires and their companions, who all seemed to play with nonchalant ease and little care. His observation of the players only helped to confirm his belief that very few, if any of them, possessed the basic skills one needs to compete with the casino, which had the odds stacked significantly in its favour.

Frustrated by his notable lack of success and without the capital to keep playing for any length of time, he decided to head north to Deauville in the morning. He laid his head on the pillow and passed a restless night repeating the many plays he had made and puzzling at the total failure of his technique.

The trip to Deauville was uneventful, apart from a night in Paris, where his lack of funds did not allow him the freedom to do and see whatever he wanted. He wandered the streets in the evening, taking in the sheer scale of the Eiffel Tower, the beauty of the Seine and its multiple bridges and other architectural wonders, in many ways rivalling the splendour of his native Athens. The thing that impressed him most was the mass of cars that crowded the boulevards of the city. Both their number and speed were things he was not entirely prepared for and he was nearly run over on more than one occasion. However, he dared not enter any of the casinos, as his finances would not stand the strain and he wanted to keep what he had for Deauville.

The next morning, he took the Deauville express, which left Paris-Saint-Lazare station at 8:30 a.m. and disgorged its passengers in Trouville-Deauville a brisk three hours later, in plenty of time for lunch. He took a leisurely stroll around Trouville-sur-Mer, a village of 6,000 souls, where life was all about the beachfront, the promenade and spa treatments for the tired Parisians who yearned for rest and relaxation away from the big city. He passed by the casino, but did not even give it a second look.

For his objective was the newly built and much sought-after Deauville Casino, just half an hour's walk across the Touques River. As he strode over, his heart beating ever faster as he approached, he was struck by the marked contrast with Trouville, in particular the sheer elegance of Deauville when compared to its neighbour to the east. The streets were wider, the villas more prosperous and the number of boutiques selling expensive trinkets was a testament to the wealth of their average visitor. He found his hotel, a modest pension away from all the action, deposited his suitcase and lay down on his bed to plan.

He looked at his watch. It was just after three in the afternoon, so there was no point in going to the casino, as everyone would be at the hippodrome watching the horse racing. He would have liked to see it, just to get a feel for the wealthy visitors, but that could wait. He would rest and decide whether and where to bet this evening. He wanted to give baccarat a try and felt he could, by judicious betting, make his money last.

He bathed and dressed in a leisurely fashion and set out towards the casino. He walked down to the beach and along the promenade to get a look at it from that side. He was surprised to find a huge park with endless walkways and beautiful flowers that extended from the striped awnings at the front of the building almost to the beach. It was a delightful setting and there were several elegant couples strolling amongst the blooms, the women with parasols and the men elegantly outfitted, ready for a night's gaming. Others were seated at tables sheltered from the now setting sun and sipping a cocktail. To the left lay the imposing Normandy Hotel with its half-timber Tudor façade and its innumerable windows decorated with geraniums. He could see why it was reputed to be the most beautiful hotel in the world. The combined setting took his breath away, to the point where he was a bundle of nervous excitement. He couldn't put off the moment any longer: he needed to go inside.

He walked round to the entrance at the back of the casino which, with its immensely tall arched windows and numerous columns, giving a distinct impression of the White House in Washington. He passed through the swing doors, barely receiving a glance from the doorman, up the short flight of stairs on the right and into the cavernous square hall, full of chairs, an extensive dance floor and an orchestra playing the latest ragtime tunes. The sparkling opulence of the interior rivalled that of Monte Carlo, but with a less classical touch.

The first game to tempt the visitors to part with their money was on display in this area: the boule tables were set out in a row to one side. This, however, was not where Nico was headed. Apart from his dislike of any game which does not involve playing cards, he was well aware of the casino's edge in this mug's game, which was over eleven per cent.

He glanced to the right, where a theatre was laid out in all its splendour, but continued to the corridor leading to the gambling rooms and the restaurant. He made his way to the end and was astounded by the scale of the restaurant, which he had been told could seat 800 people. One end resembled a farmhouse, the idea presumably being to counteract the excess of the rest of the building with something more homely. Retracing his steps, he found the entrance to the area where proper gambling took place, the baccarat, chemin-de-fer and vingt-et-un tables.

"Good evening, sir." An immaculately uniformed fellow stopped him and looked him over. "As I'm sure you are aware, you will be required to fill in this form." He handed Nico a piece of paper and a pen, which he took to one side and rapidly filled in. When he handed it back, the doorman demanded his passport and a small sum of money. "We hang onto everyone's passport while they are in the playing area, and the cover charge allows you access to the gambling tables." It was just as well he had spent a few days in France already and had been brushing up on his rather rudimentary French, but even so, he had to ask the man to repeat this to be sure he had understood. After this negotiation had concluded, he was in and ready for action.

Ignoring what he considered the inferior games, he made his way to a chemin-de-fer table, where the card shoe was being passed round, as each of the players took turns at being the banker. He was not particularly fond of this version of baccarat, but his objective for the evening did not end here and he wanted to pass the time and get a feel for the room. After watching play for half an hour, he began to get a sense of who played well (not many!) and who were fools and therefore easily separated from their money.

He was hoping that a chair would open up at the table, when the man standing next to him addressed him in German. "Excuse me, sir, but can you explain this game to me? How do you win?"

Nico looked to his right and took in a rotund gentleman with a bright red face and a huge moustache. His colour was such that he looked as if he might burst at any moment. Nico smiled pleasantly and replied, "Have you never played?"

"Never, but I'd like to learn."

"Well, without being too technical, the object of the game is to get a combination of two or three cards with a total value as close to nine as possible. All court cards count zero and if your total score is over nine, then you only count the last digit. In other words, if you have a five and a nine, your total is four, not fourteen."

"Very good, I can see that. So, I understand that each player receives two cards initially. When do they draw a third card?"

"That is when the total score in their hand is less than four. If it is more than six, then the player cannot draw. In the middle, the rules vary according to which variety of baccarat they are playing and where. The rules are quite rigid, which is why many people like to play; there is little room for judgement and therefore for error. Some would say it is all luck, but that is not my view."

The German appeared to be about to ask another question but at that very moment one of the gamblers arose from his chair, vacating his spot at the table. Nico bowed slightly to his newest acquaintance, murmured, "Excuse me," and moved quickly to grab the opening and sit down.

Several hands went by and he won a little, so when the card shoe reached him, he was marginally ahead for the evening. He did not feel comfortable holding the shoe, or with the amount being asked of the banker – in this case him – so he said, *"La banque passe,"* and the play moved to the next player. Given that all his fellow gamblers were wealthy, he grasped that he would have to chose his moment if he wanted to stay in the game and not exhaust his 1,000 francs. He continued to study the others, who appeared to be an established group, and he bet modestly.

When the card shoe next reached him, he felt more relaxed about both his finances and his appraisal of his companions. He laid out a wager of 500 francs, nearly half of his money. There was an immediate cry of *"Banco"* from a large Frenchman with an enormous moustache and an even larger cigar. Nico had noted that he had been winning consistently and obviously fancied his chances. All the other players watched as the four cards were dealt. Nico looked at his hand: he had a jack and a five. Not good.

The Frenchman asked for a card. That meant that at best he had a five, but probably less. His draw was a king. Nico indicated he would not draw, and turned his cards over. His adversary did the same. He had a four. Nico had won.

But now the bank was 1,000 francs and although nobody shouted "*Banco*," the collected players around the table put out enough chips to cover that amount. The cards were dealt and the player who had put in the most money turned over his cards. He had eight. Nico had not looked at his cards but was already sure that this was the end of half of his remaining capital. He revealed his hand – a five and a four, the perfect nine. He had won again.

Then he won a third hand.

His fourth turn as banker now had a maximum of 4,000 francs. This was where chemin-de-fer started to get serious and even the cold and emotionless Nico could feel his palms sweating, not so much at the prospect of losing, but more at the chance of getting back to almost even for the trip. Remarkably he was lucky once again, despite losing. There were so few takers for such a large amount that when he lost, it was a great relief that his pay-out was less than 500 – he could pocket 3,500 francs and walk away. With a sigh of relief he bid the players at the table "*Bon nuit*," and rose from his seat.

There were two reasons for his departure. One was that he wanted to quit whilst ahead, but the other was that he could see the heavy hitters taking their seats at table number four.

Table four was very special. It was separated from the rest of the casino by a barrier with a heavy brass rail running round the top of it and was located in a separate room. Above it hung a sign informing the entire casino that the game was baccarat and the minimum bet allowed for those who dared to take a seat there was 500 Louis, the equivalent of about 8,000 francs. Nico gulped when he saw this, as it was considerably more than the entire capital he had brought with him on his trip to France.

The other thing that made number four so unique was that you had to pay money just to watch the action. Nico had not come so far to baulk at this charge, so he took out the required amount, handed it to the cashier at the door, stepped into the room and found himself a place behind the brass rail where he could take in all the action. He had not been smoking during his successful game, so he now allowed himself the luxury of lighting up. He exhaled the smoke and waited.

The men and women who began to seat themselves at this table dripped wealth. The jewellery was fabulous and obviously expensive, the cufflinks, cigar cases and even the clothing of the group quietly screamed affluence, and the fact that anyone there would think nothing of losing the equivalent of several years' earnings for most mortals spoke volumes about their net worth.

Nico was riveted. He stood at the barrier, having to strain a little to see over it, and watched the game get under way. As things progressed, he began to understand something that he probably should have fathomed long before, but was only obvious once he was physically in the casino. Although the sums of money being wagered were astronomical, the players themselves were no better (and in many cases a good deal worse) than any others he had seen. If he could find enough money and spend enough time practising and perfecting his technique, he could take them on and probably beat them more often than not. Most played with little care or method, and those who did take a more professional attitude to the game seemed to use systems that simply didn't work. The marvellous thing for him was that they really didn't appear to care if they won or lost.

I am going to become the world's greatest gambler, he thought. I shall dedicate my life to understanding systems and probabilities and will find someone to back me. It may take time, but I am patient, applied and extremely numerate. There are too many fortunes being squandered in the gambling establishments of Europe without any of it coming my way. That situation needs to be rectified.

It was a night that would change his life forever.

Chapter 7

1915–16 ENGLAND

With the outbreak of the First World War in 1914, the immediate reaction amongst the younger generation in the Coats household was to want to sign up to fight. Jack's older brother Tom decided on the infantry and with his education, age and background he naturally went in as an officer. He moved to Stobs Camp, outside Hawick in the Scottish Borders, where he completed his training in early 1915. He made an imposing figure astride his chestnut brown mount, his uniform being embellished by a beautiful sword, which dangled from his left-hand side.

His younger brother was still finishing up his university education and the call to arms was therefore less immediate. A year went by and, once Jack graduated, his father assumed he would follow Tom into the army. But Jack had other ideas.

"I fancy this flying lark," he informed his father. "It is more glamorous and exciting than getting bogged down in the trenches. And I hate the idea of taking horses into battle – it seems too cruel, so forget the cavalry. I like my odds of doing well up in the air."

"That's all very well, but it seems a rather unnecessary complication." Willie Coats looked vaguely annoyed at his son, but to Jack's mind this was a lot better than indifference. He continued, "I don't understand why you can't just follow Tom. How would you even go about volunteering to fly?"

But Jack wasn't to be dissuaded. "I've heard that an excellent and fairly safe way to get started is at the Royal Aero Club at Lake Windermere, where I can pay for private tuition. If I like it, I can go on to apply for the RFC; and if not, then the army or navy is available."

His father frowned. He looked genuinely worried. "Sounds fine on the surface, but from what I understand there are very few men in the Royal Flying Corps and the chances of survival are so terrible that it is nigh-on committing suicide. They lose over a hundred pilots a month in training alone."

"Don't worry, Father. I'm naturally coordinated and very lucky. I'll be fine!" He was mildly surprised at his father's concern for his safety, but he decided not to comment further. He reckoned that he was only raising a token objection, and if previous experience told him anything, it was that his old man didn't really care. His lack of interest in his children was still a source of irritation to Jack, but in this particular case, it was a positive help.

The truth was that Willie Coats was really concerned about Jack's developing taste for gambling. Up till now, it had been manageable – if wildly extravagant, by most people's standards – but he had had to pay the debts from one French casino and the fateful cruise, so it was a trend he wanted to discourage. His protestations that it was ruinous had fallen on deaf ears, so maybe this "flying lark", as Jack called it, was the sort of distraction he needed. He decided to capitulate.

"Fair enough. If you complete the training and it gives you the option of entering any of the services, then I can hardly stand in your way. Just make sure you don't get side-tracked." Willie could see little danger of that. Windermere was a long way from any big city and that would limit Jack's opportunities to party and gamble. It actually might turn out to be a good thing. He smiled quietly to himself.

So, Jack got into his spanking new 38/90 Metallurgique, gunned the motor and set out for Cockshott on Lake Windermere.

It was September 1915 and he felt a thrill of excitement, partly because he just knew that he would love flying and partly because he was away from home and parental supervision. Despite his new-found freedom, he doubted he'd be able to gamble much in this remote part of the country, but he suspected that the sheer exhilaration of soaring above the clouds would surpass any buzz he got from winning at cards.

The journey took over six hours, despite his scarily fast car, which could theoretically do seventy miles per hour, but never got anywhere close to that due to winding roads, horses, carts and other obstacles. As he drove, he reflected on how strange it was that his father had given him and his brother both one of these and a Rolls Royce. It was most unlike him, but Jack reckoned that it was one of the few cases where Willie reasoned that: if you have money you might as well spend it, otherwise what is it for? Jack smiled ruefully as he thought that his dad normally reserved this attitude exclusively for his art collection and his yachts.

The headquarters of the RAC were rather basic, consisting of a hangar and some offices. Jack parked his car in front of the buildings and entered the administration area, where a pretty young woman greeted him from behind her desk.

"Good afternoon. How can I help you?"

He grinned. "I can think of several ways, but we can discuss that later." She smiled demurely, blushing slightly, and waited for him to continue, which he did. "My name is Jack Coats and I am here to get myself an aviator's certificate. I wrote to you earlier and had a reply confirming that I should appear today."

"Ah yes, Mr Coats. I have your paperwork here. Before we deal with that, you should meet the trainer and at least get introduced to the others. They're in the classroom, which is at the back of the hangar. Please follow me."

They walked across a courtyard and into the hangar, where Jack got his first look at the plane he would be flying, the Waterhen. It seemed terribly flimsy to his eyes. Just a thing like a large, partially covered bathtub, supported by a series of horizontal and vertical struts with two enormous wings across the top and underneath it, held together by more struts. He could swear the wings were made of paper. The front end had a smaller piece of fabric across it. The whole thing looked as if it might collapse under its own weight.

"Doesn't look very safe," he said as he stared up at it.

"Don't worry. Mr Parker's a very accomplished instructor and he's managed to train lots of pilots without any major mishaps. You're in safe hands." She smiled at him and led the way to a door at the side, through which he could hear the sound of voices. She opened the door and he was presented with a strikingly young-looking man at the front of a class of ten pupils, all apparently about the same age as their teacher. Jack was beginning to feel old.

The class stopped and everyone looked up. The receptionist introduced him and then left.

"Come in, Jack. I'm John Parker. As I'm about to finish up for the day, could you sit at the back for a couple of minutes and then we'll get you introduced to everyone?"

After the class had finished and the introductions were made, John took Jack back to the office and they did all the paperwork. He explained that he had learnt to fly at Brooklands and got his certificate there back in June 1914, after which he had rapidly been made an instructor. He indicated that Jack would be staying with the other trainee pilots at the Beech Hill Hotel, where the school had an arrangement for them to get room and board for thirty shillings a week.

"The hotel is about three miles south of here, but we can arrange transport for you."

"It's okay, I have my own car. In fact, there's room for three or four others, if you want. After all, we're all going to the same place!"

"That's kind. We may take you up on that."

After settling into the hotel, which turned out to be simple but comfortable and with a beautiful view over the lake, Jack was up for breakfast the next morning, where he came upon Davey Robertson and Horace Benson, both recent arrivals at the school.

"So, what's it like?" asked Jack.

Davey replied, "John's a good teacher, even though he's younger than just about all of us."

"How old?"

"Nineteen. I'm twenty-two, and Horace here is a year younger." He sipped his tea. "But don't let John's relative youth fool you – what he doesn't know about flying could be written on a postage stamp. He appears to be a natural flyer. When you go up for the first time it's quite nerve-wracking, but he's cool as a cucumber and that helps put you at your ease."

"What's it like up there?"

"Bloody cold!"

"Really?"

"Oh wow yes. Wear plenty of gear. Have you got a silk scarf?"

"Yes, several."

"Good. You'll need 'em. They're not for glamour, even if it looks like it. They keep the oil and bugs out of your mouth and are handy to wipe down your goggles."

Horace intervened. "You asked what it's like to fly. If you can forget the discomfort, seeing everything from the air is indescribable and I'm willing to bet you'll love it. At various stages in the training you have to learn to fly the plane with the engine off, and the sensation of soaring through the air in silence is almost mystical. You'll see."

Davey got up from the table. "Time to go."

"I'll give you both a lift, if you like," Jack suggested.

"Sure," they said in unison.

When they got out to the car, Davey whistled and asked how Jack had got such a sophisticated automobile.

"My family is quite wealthy," he said. "You, being a Scot, Davey, may have heard of them. I am one of the Coatses, of sewing thread fame."

"I wondered about that when you were introduced. You must be loaded."

"You could say I'm well off, but it doesn't help me fly any better than the rest of you. And that's what we're here for. I'm as keen as anyone to get qualified and then go after the Hun. Off we go."

When they got to the Aero Club, John was setting up the day's classes in the room at the back of the hangar.

"Good to see you, Jack. I always like to start with a bang, so I'll take you up for your first flight today. Hope you brought your kit?"

"I have it all here."

"Good. After the flight you can store it in a locker for future use. Be ready to take off at fourteen hundred hours."

Jack was there at one-thirty, wrapped in sweater and leather flying jacket with his white silk scarf jauntily tied around his neck. He thought he looked rather dashing. He scanned the skeletal frame of the hydro-aeroplane, as John called it, and felt decidedly uneasy. Jack had heard that Winston Churchill had coined the term Seaplane, which seemed less of a mouthful, but even with the catchier name it still seemed awfully rickety.

There was a ramp from the hangar down to the water and the plane was being winched down to the lake in preparation for their flight. John was helping get the plane in the water. "Come on,

Jack, time to climb aboard."Jack hopped onto the left float and hoisted himself into the cockpit. There were two seats, one behind the other, and John indicated that he should take the one at the back, and then slid into the front seat and had the engine fired up. This was behind Jack, as the plane was of the "push" type, where the propellers drove the plane forwards rather than pulling it from the nose.

Once the engine started, the noise was deafening and it only increased as they taxied out to the middle of the water. Once John increased the power to take off, the plane shook, the sound from the motor was overpowering and Jack wasn't sure he would survive the buffeting as they surged through the water. However, once they parted ways with the lake, things calmed down and he found he could take in the countryside on either side and the shimmering water below. Horace had been right: it was positively exhilarating.

They turned back and levelled up for landing. It had only been a few minutes, but despite the odd bump, which had scared him at first, he was hooked. Jack knew this was what he wanted to do.

The next few months were filled with endless, rather tedious classes on flight theory, meteorology, navigation, wireless telegraphy and engine mechanics. Jack absorbed these with moderate ease and concentrated on the actual business of flying. Progress was painfully slow as he had to go through several stages: flying as a passenger, as he had already done; handling the control lever under John's hands; then alone; and finally holding control lever and rudder with supervision. The next stage was taxiing solo, take-off and straight flight: this was then followed by full practice. By February 1916 Jack was ready for his certification flight.

This involved three tests. Two were figure-of-eight flights round specific markers 500 yards apart, lasting at least three miles and cutting the motor at the point of, or just before, landing, coming to rest fifty yards from a pre-designated point. These two went without a hitch.

The third test was an altitude flight, where the plane had to ascend to at least 300 feet above the lake and then he had to cut the motor and glide in to land in front of the examiners, without restarting the motor. Unfortunately for Jack, the weather closed in for this final run and when he cut the motor, a gust of wind, combined with an updraft, hit the plane and brought it almost to a complete standstill, with the left wing banking sharply. For a moment he lost control and started to spin at a dangerously low level, but finally, by putting the plane into a dive, which seemed suicidal to the spectators, he managed to pull the nose up and re-establish level flight not twenty feet above the water. He thought he would be penalised and had failed the test, but the examiners were very impressed with the unflappable way he had tackled the situation and by his daring in trying such a hazardous manoeuvre. They duly awarded him his certificate, number 2404.

It was February 4th 1916 and he was ready for war. However, unless the enemy decided to attack very close to water, he could not take part, as he had never put a plane down on dry land. In order to qualify for the Royal Flying Corps and engage the Germans, he would need to acquire that skill, so he set about finding a way in. Enlisting would not necessarily get him to where he wanted to be, which was within striking distance of London and the nightlife. Training would be tedious, but that didn't mean he had to be bored in his spare time.

As he was scheming to secure a suitable place to train, he reflected on how his desire to gamble had completely evaporated. It was as if the thrill of flying had replaced the buzz he felt when holding what he considered a winning hand, anticipating the pleasure of collecting his winnings whilst admiring eyes looked on. As a pilot, the adulation he received was different, but no less satisfying. He was now happy to go dancing, sip cocktails and tell exaggerated tales of derring-do to his female companions for the night.

He set his sights on Northolt, which had opened less than a year before as the RFC Military School, Ruislip. Not only was it new, it was well equipped and under fifteen miles from central London and the nightlife. The best and easiest way to get enrolled there was through contacts, and the best of these were to be found in the city, so he established a base at the Ritz and went out dining and dancing every evening in the hope of meeting someone who could fast-track him into his chosen training programme.

One of his early sorties proved to be fruitful. He went to the Gaiety Theatre to see Theodore & Co. and sat next to Ruby Miller, an ex-Gaiety girl and aspiring actress. They got talking during the interval and after the show he invited her to go dancing at the Embassy Club in Old Bond Street. They agreed to meet there the next night.

When Jack got there, slightly late, he found no sign of her, but after he had nursed a cocktail for a few minutes, she breezed in, dragging a veritable entourage behind her. This turned out to consist of Ivor Novello ("He wrote the music for the piece we saw at the Gaiety, along with Jerome Kern – I *had* to invite him") and Lily Elsie, one of the most beautiful women Jack had ever seen, who was Novello's partner for the evening. The other couple were Ethel Levey, an American actress, and Claude Graham-White. They were engaged to be married and obviously besotted with each other, but what piqued Jack's interest was not their relationship, nor her obvious talent as a dancer, but rather Claudie (as he liked to be known). He was probably the most famous aviator of the day, being the winner of various trophies and the first man to complete a flight at night, and that in a monoplane.

Drinks were procured and they settled around their table. The girls all went to powder their noses and Novello wandered off to talk to the bandleader, so Jack took the opportunity to see what Claudie could do for him.

"I wondered if I could bend your ear for a second. I've heard of your exploits in the air." He paused for a moment, trying to gauge how best to get what he wanted from the flying ace. He decided on a direct, comradely approach. "I'm also a flyer, just qualified at Windermere and keen to get to war. Do you have any contacts in the RFC?"

Claudie took a sip of his drink and put it down. He looked up at Jack with a frown on his face, but he answered in a friendly enough manner, "I do have a lot of contact with the government air programme as I'm overseeing the airplane construction effort. However, my role, as you can imagine, is involved with the actual planes, rather than the people who fly them. I resigned my commission for precisely that reason, to concentrate on infrastructure."

"But you must have friends in high places."

"I know a lot of people in the air industry and the RFC, naturally. What are you after, specifically?"

"I really want to do my air training at Northolt, but if I simply turn up and apply, they will assign me to whichever airfield takes their fancy. I wondered if you could put in a word for me? If you could, I would certainly stand you and Ethel a magnificent dinner at, say, Simpson's."

"Now that is tempting." Claudie thought for a moment and then beamed. "I have it. D'you know who's in charge at Northolt?"

"I heard from a contact that there's to be a change of command there and that Sholto Douglas will take over with a new squadron, number 43. The idea is for them to fly over the front in France, mapping out the German positions and giving the enemy a hard time. It seems like exactly what I want to do."

"I don't know Douglas, but I have heard of him. Very young – only twenty-two or twenty-three – but a promising flyer." He picked up his cocktail and took a sip. "Ice water in his veins. I think he's just been awarded the Military Cross. Give me a few days and I'll find a way to contact him and put in a word for you. You seem keen, and we need to have more like you to take on the Hun."

"Thanks so much. I'm extremely grateful and I really mean it about that dinner. I love eating there and it would be my pleasure to host you."

"And where would that be?" asked Ethel, who had returned with the other two girls.

"Simpson's, my dear," said Claudie. "We're going to be treated to a slap-up dinner there."

"Count me in as well." Ruby looked enthusiastically at them and Jack beamed.

"Why, of course, you're all invited!" He looked towards the dance floor. "But I think it's now time for a dance – shall we step out and light up the joint?"

◆

Two weeks later, Jack walked onto the airfield at Northolt and introduced himself. The group of trainees facing him was a motley crew of every kind, from fresh-faced lads who looked as if they should still be in school, to blasé know-it-alls who would be fazed by nothing. A search for a friendly face revealed someone he thought he recognised but could not place. When the introductions were made, he realised why the man looked familiar. This was none other than Vernon Castle, partner to spouse Irene and half of one of the most famous dancing couples in the world.

Jack recalled that Vernon had made a name for himself as a dancer with his American wife in and around the New York area in the years before the war. They taught ballroom dancing and gave exhibitions, converting themselves into the darlings of American society and eventually appearing in some early movies. She became a fashion icon – the bob haircut originated with her – and they opened clubs and appeared on Broadway. They also popularised ragtime and jazz music for dancing and managed to remove some of the stigma from close dancing, which became *very* popular with wealthy socialites, who were charged exorbitant amounts for dance lessons from the couple.

As soon as there was a break, Jack made a beeline for Vernon and introduced himself. "Jack Coats. You must be the famous dancer. How did you manage to get into the RFC? You surely arrived not long ago from the US."

Vernon grinned broadly and shook Jack's proffered hand firmly. His chiselled features and slicked back blond hair gave him the aspect of a minor film star and his slim athletic posture made it look as if he were ready for anything. He was immediately likeable.

"I did my flying training with the Canadians and got a flying certificate from the Aero Club of America. I then pulled a few strings once I reached London. I met Robert Loraine at a luncheon at the Royal Navy Yacht Club and persuaded him to vouch for me.

"I've heard of him – isn't he an actor?"

"Yes. Robert is famous for being a stage actor, but what you probably don't know about is his prowess as an airman as well. He's becoming quite senior in the RFC and his word was enough to get me in here as a second lieutenant."

"What a coincidence. I also used a connection: Claude Graham-White put in a good word for me, but I met him at the Embassy Club. His flying exploits are legendary, though he is not an actor like your man. But he is engaged to be married to an actress." Jack chuckled. "Talking of the club, I am sure you'll want to keep your hand in – or should I say feet – on the dance floor. So how would you feel about accompanying me up to London for a little night-time entertainment? My treat!"

Vernon was cautiously enthusiastic. "Delighted, old chap. I admit that I find the dancing styles here about five years behind what we have been doing in the States, but I couldn't face being stuck in the airfield all the time and was hoping for an escape. There is one snag. As I am just over from the US, I have no wheels. Can you oblige?"

"Absolutely. I not only have transport, but also a spectacular set of female friends who will accompany us. I have been in the city a couple of weeks and have spent the time well. We shall not be short of entertainment."

"Well, that makes two of us. I have been staying at the Savoy and although chic girls have been hard to come by, I have collected a few beauties who are also competent dancers."

"Me too, but I went for the Ritz."

"Nice place, but not as handy for the theatres."

"Agreed, but I prefer it and I have a car. Also, it's better situated for the nightclubs and hotels where I like to go dancing. Do you enjoy the theatre?"

"I do. And I specifically wanted to be near the Gaiety, where my sister's husband, Lawrence Grossmith, is performing. He has amazing contacts, but he didn't come up trumps in this particular case. My meeting Robert Loraine was pure luck."

"As was my connecting with Graham-White. We really do seem to be remarkably alike!" Jack smiled broadly and slapped Vernon on the back. "So, what about that excursion to the old smoke?"

"I'm game, but will we be allowed out?"

"I managed to lay the groundwork for that prior to arriving here. As long as we are on parade at 06:00 hours, bright-eyed and bushy-tailed, nobody minds what we do. Most days, we should be able to get away by 7:30 p.m. and can be on the dance floor by nine – a little early, but acceptable. Two or three hours of entertainment and we can be home and tucked up in time to get four or five hours' kip, which will do me. We'll get longer at the weekends, with any luck."

"Sounds good to me."

In the weeks that followed, they became inseparable. To Jack, Vernon was a kindred spirit. He loved fast cars and women, was a fearless – some would say reckless – but gifted flyer, and he spent money with gay abandon, although he was also a kind and caring man. They soon discovered that they had both lost their mothers at a very early age, though Vernon's father appeared to be as affectionate as Jack's was cold. They began to spend several evenings a week in central London at Ciro's, the Embassy Club or one of the big hotels. The tango was the latest dance craze and Vernon was naturally brilliant at it, though Jack proved to be no slouch.

The training regime required, as Jack had indicated to Vernon, that they be up before 6 a.m. for an hour's flying, followed by breakfast. Practical mechanics, lectures on aeronautics theory, more flying and lessons in wireless telegraphy and signalling would follow, the long day ending with dinner at 7:30 p.m., which they skipped in order to get into London. They would return to base well after midnight, but they managed to survive on remarkably little sleep.

Given their hectic social timetable, it was just as well that neither was required to do much flying when they started off. Vernon was made responsible for keeping the various bonfires lit overnight, luring the German zeppelins away from London. Jack, although he was a lowly subaltern, was put through a rigorous series of landing exercises. As their skill level and experience improved, they were given more onerous tasks, such as delivering mail to the troops in France.

Eventually, however, their lack of sleep was bound to catch up with the pair, and it was no surprise when one of them came a cropper during a flight. The unlucky one was Jack. He had set out for an early morning sortie over the countryside, with the intention of doing a series of landings to solidify his already considerable ability at putting his plane down on dry land. Unfortunately, either due to fatigue or plain bad luck, his left wing tip just touched the ground on his second approach and the aircraft cartwheeled and broke into several pieces. Jack hit his head and lost consciousness, but was amazingly found by the hospital staff to be otherwise unhurt.

Vernon visited him the next day. "How are you, J? I heard that the tumble you took looked pretty nasty."

"It was idiotic – a lapse of concentration on my part, but it looked worse than it actually was, so no real harm done. I want to get out of here so we can go dancing again, but they insist on keeping me in 'under observation', as they say, though I don't see too many people observing. The one compensation is that there are some jolly pretty nurses here. I have invited a couple of them out on the town once I am released."

"If one of them is meant for me then just remember that I am a married man and that Irene is coming to visit next month."

"All the more for me, in that case. I had no intention of sharing!" Jack laughed and punched Vernon on the shoulder. He smiled and feigned intense pain by grabbing his arm and grimacing.

"That hurt." He looked at his watch and stood up. "I'll leave you in peace with your nurses. I need to go and get a typhoid jab, which they're now recommending for anyone deploying to France, would you believe? I don't really want it – I gather it can make you feel pretty rotten – but I don't want anything to stop me getting involved in the fighting."

"Well, best of luck – you're pretty fit, so I'm sure you'll be fine. I intend to be out of here tomorrow, come hell or high water. We have some partying to do."

But Jack's carousing would have to wait. When he did get out of hospital the next day he almost passed Vernon who was on the way in. He did have a bad reaction to his inoculation and needed several days to recover. By the time he was better, Irene's arrival was imminent, so Jack found he did several trips to London on his own, though the company of his favourite nurse sometimes made the journey less lonesome.

With their training nearly over and the serious business of war looming, Vernon began to become more introspective. Irene's arrival lifted his spirits, but only briefly, and although he had three wonderful days with her, by the time she left for New York he was unsure if he would ever see her again. He went back to his flying.

Jack had no such despondency leading up to his deployment. He continued to sneak up to London, now without his comrade, and seemed to positively relish the prospect of the dangers that lay ahead. Both men were given their assignments at the same time, not far from each other in France, and Jack persuaded Vernon that they should throw a joint party before they set off.

"Let's invite everyone we've met and partied with over the last months. We should make it a real blow-out. Things are so depressing at the moment and nobody knows when the war will end, so a bit of extravagance is just what the doctor ordered."

Jack's enthusiasm raised Vernon's spirits and his mood brightened at the prospect. "Great idea, J. Tell you what – I'll leave the catering to you; you're good at that stuff. I'll start to get the word out and see if I can scrape up a decent band."

"Excellent. No expense spared, mind. We have a reputation to protect."

"Absolutely. I'll invite all our theatre friends and I'm going to see if the Prince of Wales'll come. He's usually up for a party, particularly if the dancing's gay and the female company congenial."

The night of the party duly arrived. Oysters, caviar and champagne were plentiful despite the war, and the band was, as Vernon had promised, one of the best around. He had managed to engage the Stroud Haxton Band, which had become available with the closure of the 400 Club.

The guest list was as illustrious as they had anticipated and even the Prince put in an appearance. The combination of Jack's wealth and Vernon's celebrity was an enormous draw and both men were handsome and flamboyant, which did them no harm either. The night was a supreme success.

As the party was wrapping up, they found themselves together at the bar.

Vernon was about to speak when Robbie Guinness, an old Etonian contemporary of Jack's came rushing up to them. "I say you chaps, what a splendid party. Haven't enjoyed myself so much in years. Just wanted to say good bye and thank you."

Jack smiled and shook his old friend by the hand. "Lovely to see you, Robbie. Very glad you had a good time."

"Indeed – great company, fabulous food and copious booze. The perfect formula for success." He put his arms around both of them in a rather drunken embrace and drew them towards him. He then almost whispered, "But do tell. Where on earth did you manage to get oysters, caviar and all those goodies? For Christ's sake, there's a war on!"

With this he released his grip on them both and looked from one to the other with a quizzical expression on his face. They, in turn, looked at each other, raised a finger to touch the side of their noses and winked, intoning simultaneously, "You'll never know."

They all laughed heartily and Robbie turned to leave, shaking his head.

With Robbie's departure, Vernon was the first to speak. "Well, J, I think we can both be extremely satisfied with the way the party's gone. It's a long time since I've seen so many smiling faces."

"Agreed, V, and just as well, as who knows when, or indeed if, we'll next get the chance."

"I know. With us both leaving soon to fight, it'll be hard to keep in touch, but we should try: we've had some really great times together and I value our friendship more than you could know. The last three months have been a blast. Let's hope we get the chance to do it again, but in more agreeable circumstances."

Jack raised his glass in a toast to his friend. "I'll drink to that, and now that we have our full flying credentials, courtesy of the Fédération Aéronautique Internationale, it would seem appropriate to say, as they would, "A ta sante!" He put his glass down, looked his friend straight in the eye and added, *"Je ne vais pas dire 'adieu', mais plutôt 'au revoir'."*

"I won't say *adieu* either, but rather *au revoir,* my true friend," and both men embraced with tears in their eyes.

Chapter 8

1916–17 FRANCE & SCOTLAND

"Jesus, where on earth did they come from?" Jack was sitting in the cockpit of his Airco DH2, high above the battlefield of the Somme, as two German planes passed directly over him in quick succession having just released bursts of gunfire. He knew he was in trouble: although he was a match for a single enemy plane, two of them would probably be too much, and he still had to protect the reconnaissance plane that he was escorting over the front.

His training in Northolt kicked in. His flying style had developed to the point where he was considered reckless – he would have said daring – but at the same time a sound pilot with good technique. He was going to need it now.

He pushed the plane earthwards and increased speed, but when he looked over his shoulder he could see the two Huns coming after him. At least he was drawing them away from the observer plane, which had turned and headed home. He kept losing altitude, but would have to pull up soon if he wasn't going to break the plane apart. It also dawned on him that he was now well beyond the German trenches and even if he could get down in one piece, that would be the end of his war. Moreover, he was getting so low that they were starting to take pot shots at him from the ground. He levelled off, banked left and turned back towards the Allied lines.

The two enemy planes were after him in no time. He climbed

towards some clouds he could see to his left, in the hope that he might shake his pursuers by disappearing into them. It would be bumpy in there and he might get disoriented, but that was a better risk than being shot at by two Fokkers. He continued to climb, but could see that he probably wasn't going to make it. He decided to go with a really dicey move. He waited till they fired at him and dropped the nose, putting the plane into a spin.

It struck him as ironic, as six months previously this model had been dubbed the "Spinning Incinerator", due to the ease with which it would spiral out of control; this had caused several fatalities, but squadron commander Major Hawker had taught him and the rest of the squadron how to get out of a corkscrew descent, and it had become a legitimate way of confusing their adversaries.

He calculated correctly that this would leave the Germans unsure for a few seconds and that might buy him some time. His plane was more nimble than the Fokker Eindeckers and his top speed was a few miles per hour faster than theirs (he seemed to recall that they top out at about eighty-five, whereas he could get more than ninety from his kite), but that would only help him if he could get beyond their firing range.

Their hesitation only lasted a few seconds and then they were diving after him. As he levelled out, he felt the impact of several bullets behind him and he knew his engine had been hit. His first thought was, better the engine than me, and he thanked his lucky stars that his plane was a "pusher". He immediately started to lose power and knew that it was only a matter of time before he had to ditch. He cut the fuel supply to the motor and started to glide.

Now he had to find a good spot to land. He was over the German trenches and going towards the British side, crossing no-man's land, so at least he would be safe once he was on the ground. He could see a field ahead, well behind the Allied lines, and he strained both physically and mentally to will his aircraft over the last mile. Then he saw there was a wood in his way, but he still thought he could clear the trees even though the crate was becoming more leaden with every second.

The fuselage made it, but the wheels did not, and they were ripped away just before he hit the ground. He kept the nose up and scraped along the grass with his feet raised, coming to a halt a hundred yards beyond the copse that had separated him from his undercarriage. The plane collapsed in a heap of twisted pieces and he covered his head with his arms to prevent any sharp protuberances penetrating his skull. He was in luck: he emerged in one piece and unscathed.

He breathed a sigh of relief, jumped down from the plane and started back towards where he reckoned the army were embedded, somewhere beyond the woods he had almost cleared. The two German planes had lost interest and gone after other prey, so he seemed to be home free.

As he walked on, he became aware of a vague aroma not unlike newly mown hay. This was strange as it was June and the grass was green. Then it dawned on him with horror that what he smelt was probably phosgene gas. He held his breath and wondered what to do. He knew that the gas was heavier than air and tended to hug the ground, so his best bet was to climb a tree and hope that would reduce the potency of whatever he was ingesting. The problem was that he didn't know where it was coming from or how long it would linger. He felt all right for the moment, but that didn't mean the damage was not already done.

He then looked down at his right hand and noticed that there was blood dripping from his fingers. He guessed he had either been hit when the bullets had got his engine, or maybe he had been cut by a loose piece of fuselage during his crash landing, but what with one thing and another, he simply hadn't noticed. He still didn't think it would stop him climbing, and he was reluctant to investigate further in case the wound was serious. What the eye doesn't see, the heart doesn't grieve, as his governess used to say.

He had reached the woods by now and he found an oak tree that would be fairly unchallenging to climb, and he managed to scale it despite his wounded arm. He looked around him and could see activity in the middle distance and assumed that this was where the Allied troops were based. Now what? He could no longer smell anything, but was not sure when it would be safe to descend. There was a slight breeze blowing, so he hoped that if what he had smelled was gas, then it would have dispersed fairly quickly. He reasoned that he couldn't stay up there forever, for if he had been exposed to gas, he needed to get to a field hospital as soon as possible. He also had the as yet unseen wound in his arm to worry about.

He jumped down and started to walk as quickly as he could to where he thought the British line was. Coming over the brow of a small rise, he saw what was definitely army activity a couple of hundred yards ahead. He increased his pace.

An army lorry was stopped in the mud well short of the main concentration of troops and he shouted at the driver.

"I say, excuse me, but is there a field hospital nearby? I just got shot down and I think I may've been gassed as well. Oh, and my left arm is beginning to hurt, and by the look of the blood I must have gashed it."

"If you go over to your left about 500 yards, you'll find it. They're going to be busy, as the Jerries just lobbed a barrage of gas shells at us. Most people have masks, but they don't all get them on in time."

"Any chance of a lift?"

"Sorry, mate, but we're completely bogged down in this stuff. I've been trying to move this damn thing for half an hour, but it just sinks in deeper."

Jack glanced at the rear wheels of the vehicle, which were nearly buried up to the axle. "Okay, thanks, and good luck. I'd help you, but given my predicament I think I'm better to soldier on, if you'll pardon the pun."

The lorry driver laughed. "Ha, ha! Nice one! Best of luck to you too, chum."

Jack turned and strode off in the direction that his newfound friend had indicated. He still felt remarkably okay, although he had noticed a slight difficulty drawing a deep breath. He couldn't be sure if this was an indication of worse to come or simply the power of suggestion.

He soon reached a large tent with a Red Cross sign on the top and went inside. People were running all over the place and it was difficult to find someone to talk to. He eventually stood in the way of a nurse who was striding from the bedside of a lifeless soldier towards a stretchered patient.

"I hate to bother you, but I've just been shot down, wounded and gassed. Can you help?"

"Not at the moment. As you are still walking and conscious, you're unfortunately not high on the priority list. Sit down over there and someone'll get to you."

He went to where she indicated and sat on the ground, gingerly removing his flying jacket and sweater, to expose the injury in his left arm. It had bled quite a lot, but it was obviously not serious, or at least not to his unprofessional eye. The bad news was that his breathing was now becoming laboured and he was coughing. He was beginning to feel fatigued, as if his heart were not working properly. He tried to cry out, but had suddenly become too weak. He passed out.

◆

When Jack came to, he had no idea where he was, though it appeared to be a hospital. He lay there trying to recollect what had happened, but nothing came to him. His chest hurt like blazes and he had an oxygen mask (he supposed that was what it was) over his mouth. Breathing was quite difficult.

"Ah, Mr Coats, welcome back to the land of the living." It appeared that the person speaking was a nurse, but he couldn't be sure. He still felt groggy. He tried to say thanks, but he found speaking too hard.

"Don't try to talk, sir. You just rest and I'll get the doctor to come and have a look at you." She bustled away and left him with his thoughts.

How long had he been here, what had happened and would he be all right? Many things flashed through his mind, but it was still a bit of a muddle. He was just drifting off to sleep again when a smart fellow in a white coat appeared and greeted him. He then went to the end of Jack's bed and picked up a clipboard.

"My name is Dr Ferguson. You're probably wondering what's going on, hmm? Let me explain what you've been through, which is quite a lot. Frankly, you're damned fortunate to be alive, but I'll get to that." He looked down at chart he was holding and cleared his throat.

"You're in a clinic in England. You probably won't remember much of the last few weeks, but you got a fair dose of phosgene gas just after you pancaked your plane. It was really touch-and-go for several days. You might be surprised to hear that the fact you had a wound in your arm probably saved your life. One thing we do to recently gassed patients is draw blood from them, as it seems to help, though we don't understand exactly why. Your wound did it for us."

He paused for breath and continued. "So, we gave you oxygen and morphine to try and improve your breathing. You were having heart problems, so we drained your lungs, which helped for a time, but eventually you developed pulmonary gangrene in one lung and we had to remove most of it. The other lung was not as bad and has now recovered almost completely." Dr Ferguson smiled for the first time. "We never know how each case of gas poisoning will develop; everyone is different. As I already said, you were lucky to survive, but you were unlucky in the sense that you were hit particularly hard. It's a shame you didn't have a gas mask, but how were you to know where you would end up? You were just in the wrong place at the wrong time."

Jack was only taking in about half of what the doctor was

saying, but this last statement helped lift the fog. He had reckoned he was doubly blessed when his plane not only cleared those trees but landed in one piece behind the Allied lines. He now appreciated that he had, with hindsight, been incredibly *un*fortunate. Odd really, considering that he still considered himself as having a lucky streak. Perhaps he would have to stop testing this assertion so often. He started to drift back to sleep.

"Your recovery will be slow," Dr Ferguson continued. "Months rather than weeks, and then I'm afraid you'll no longer be fit for active service. This type of injury's too hard on the heart and your one remaining lung for you to be pirouetting about the sky trying to shoot down the enemy. For the moment you need to concentrate on getting better and then I'm sure there'll be something you can do to help, unless the war is over by then."

Jack spent most of the next two months either prone in his bed or sitting quietly on the sofa at Skelmorlie, staring at his father's collection of paintings and wishing he could be out partying and dancing. He had lost a lot of weight at the beginning, when he was too weak and apathetic to eat. He had obviously given up smoking, and he was getting used to breathing with only one lung, but he found almost anything he tried to do required a huge effort and left him breathless. He started to notice how much more energy was required when the weather was cold and he ventured outside. This he did sporadically for short periods and even shorter distances.

He saw little of his father, who was away sailing or visiting art dealers in Glasgow or Edinburgh, but as he gained both his strength and his appetite, they started to eat dinner together, seated at the enormous mahogany dining table, surrounded by Willie's favourite pieces of art and often in silence.

On one such occasion, when he was well on his way to recovery, his father was in a convivial mood and started to tackle Jack about money.

"You should take the time, with this enforced inactivity, to learn something about investing," Willie said. "You'll one day be fairly wealthy – if you can stay away from the gambling halls – and it'll be important that you understand the workings of the stock market, business and even art, if you want to preserve your capital."

"How did you learn about it all?" Jack asked.

"From my brothers and my father, but I also read a few books and talked with knowledgeable friends. I keep my ear to the ground and read the *Financial Times* most days. It's also true to say that once you've got investments to look after, you're naturally forced to learn how to manage them. There are professionals who do the analysis and recommendations, but it's up to me to make the decisions."

"The *Financial Times* . . . That's the pink newspaper I've seen around the house, isn't it? I've tried reading it, but it's exceedingly technical and rather dry."

"That's partly true, but if you have investments you are monitoring, then you'll soon see the value in it. I promise you it's both educational and interesting once you are an investor." His eyes narrowed and he leant much closer to Jack. "I tell you what, I will call my broker tomorrow, and then he can come and visit you and begin your education. I'll then pass you a portfolio of stocks, which you can keep an eye on, discuss with him and buy and sell as you and he see fit. That'd be a useful way for you to spend your time."

Willie leant back and looked rather pleased with himself, but after a moment's pause he continued, "Now art investment is another thing . . ." At which point Jack switched off; he found his father's expositions regarding the world of paintings to be incredibly dull and unexciting.

♦

A week later, a Mr McGregor appeared at Skelmorlie, looking for Jack. He was shown into the library, where Jack was practising dealing and shuffling cards.

"Mr Coats, I am Hamish McGregor. I work for Mr Hector Morison, who is from Glasgow, but now works in London as a stockbroker, both for the Coats company and, more importantly, for your father. He has asked me to travel here to talk to you about investing."

"Are you going to show me my father's portfolio?"

"Er, no. That is not what I have been asked to do. I intend to go through the fundamentals of sound investing, what to avoid and how to create a balanced selection of stocks. I will also attempt to teach you some of the language of stockbroking, so that by the end of a few sessions, you will be able to discuss your holdings with a professional and can ask pertinent questions."

Jack did not feel very enthused, but settled down to listen and at least try to learn. The day dragged on and he was having trouble absorbing it all until McGregor came onto a subject that got his full attention. This was the question of risky investments.

"Given your level of assets, you will perhaps want to make the occasional speculative investment. This could be, for example, a company that is starting up and you feel has huge potential, or it could be in an area of the world where the political situation is unstable – basically anything that causes the chances of a big win or a huge loss to be significant. In this case, you need to make sure that a total loss would not cause you any hardship; in other words, it can be easily absorbed."

"Sounds like my sort of thing. How do I find these opportunities?"

"It requires a lot of reading, a good deal of lateral thinking and a modicum of luck."

"That'll suit me! Can you give me an example?"

McGregor thought for a moment and looked at his shoes. "I don't think I would be talking out of turn if I mention one of your father's failures."

"Now you're talking. Go on."

"Well, as you know, your father was very keen on coal mining as a young man and apart from working in a coal pit for a year before he started with the family company, he invested in, and was a director of, the Cardiff Steam Coal Collieries. The company also invested in coal to keep the family mill at Ferguslie running, and he was involved in that area as well."

"I'm aware of all that, but that doesn't sound very speculative."

"Well, it isn't as it stands, but you perhaps were unaware of your great uncle George, who was a managing partner of one of the collieries that supplied Ferguslie."

"I don't remember him being mentioned."

"Hardly surprising, as he never worked for Coats and wasn't close to your grandfather or any of his brothers. Anyway, there was a massive explosion at the Victoria pit, which was one of George's, and sixty-one people were killed. It was the largest mining disaster in Scotland at the time and reflected badly on the Coats company, even though they had nothing to do with it. George's name led everyone to assume it belonged to Coats."

"I still don't see what this has to do with speculative investing."

"I am coming to that. Your father discovered a small colliery in Germany, where the industry is largely in the hands of massive cartels. They mostly mine lignite, or surface coal, which is very dirty. He decided that it was sufficiently specialised – it mined underground, which yields a much cleaner product – and well enough managed to outperform the larger rivals. He took a substantial share in the company and for many years was very content with the deal. However, some time later they had a similar explosion and loss of life, confidence collapsed and your father, well aware of how things had gone in the earlier incident with great uncle George, withdrew what he could, at a substantial loss. As a result, the company went bankrupt shortly afterwards."

"That seems like plain bad luck."

"It is, but the fact that the company was small and only had one pit made them vulnerable to this type of thing. That's what makes it a speculative investment."

"So, big is beautiful is what you are saying?"

"Well, yes and no. If you invest in something big, there is little chance of making a killing, but you are unlikely to lose your shirt either. It is a question of your tolerance for risk and how important it is to make a mint from a particular investment. That is what you need to think about."

"Well, I guess I'd enjoy the thrill."

The lesson continued into the late afternoon and Jack had plenty to read by the end of it. He thanked Mr McGregor and saw him out, but threw his "homework" in a pile and decided he would examine it another day. In the meantime, he wanted to get back to his playing cards.

♦

Jack's enforced immobility had given him plenty of time to think, and he had started to reassess his life and what he wanted to get out of it. He was wealthier than he had any right to be and that brought some responsibility. His father's chat about investing was not the first time he had thought of such matters and he was well aware of the need to preserve and grow capital, though he had blandly assumed that someone else would handle that for him.

He was aware of the philanthropy of his ancestors, though his father didn't seem particularly strong in that department and Jack's view was that he should distribute his fortune in a way that was enjoyable to him. What he really adored was fast cars, parties, dancing and gambling, not necessarily in that order, and although he was more than competent at the first three, his forays into the world of gaming had been fraught with setbacks, largely due to his lack of experience and his sheer exuberance.

He decided that *practice makes perfect* would be his new motto.

His health improved steadily to the point where he could venture out to the occasional house party. And although he wasn't ready to ride to hounds in his relatively delicate state, he was able to join in the card games that were part of the after-dinner ritual at such affairs, and he persuaded many fellow guests to abandon the bridge table in favour of more chancy pastimes, baccarat amongst them.

But as he got back into playing, it dawned on him that his enthusiasm for betting was not what it was. He yearned to be back in the cockpit and found that the thrill of the wager, which had previously produced a feeling of euphoria, now seemed rather anaemic compared to the thrill of flying and especially aerial combat. He needed to get back to battle.

Once well enough to take long walks and occasionally ride a horse, he informed his doctor that he was ready to make some contribution to the war effort again. There was some reluctance to allow him unlimited freedom, but it seemed likely that he would take matters into his own hands if not allowed to at least contact the War Office. So, on a clear cool day in late October, Jack phoned through to Whitehall and, although he could not get a satisfactory answer to his enquiry, he was eventually rewarded with a call from an official who sounded as if he knew what he was doing.

Jack picked up the phone and the operator informed him that the War Office was on the line.

"Hello, this is Captain Jack Coats speaking."

"Good morning, sir. Captain Arkwright here from Whitehall. I am calling about your query as to how you can help with the war effort."

"Capital. I trust you have good news for me."

"Yes and no. The good news is that we have a vital job that you can do. The bad news is that it will have to wait. Let me explain."

Jack sighed. "Please do. I don't much fancy waiting around."

"Although your fighting days are over, your flying days are far from done. As an experienced and skilful pilot, you are an important resource for us. You will never be cleared for combat, but we feel you will make an exceptional trainer and it's in that capacity that we want to use you – not here, but in Canada. We cannot recruit enough pilots in England, but the Canadian Air Force has plenty of young men available, so we are sending a few experienced airmen over there to bring them on as fast as possible."

Jack was slightly deflated by this news but gave no hint of his disappointment. "Sounds great. When can I start?"

"Well, that's where there's a snag. It is called winter. In Canada it is not the best time to be taking off and landing, extreme cold not being a friend of either pilot or airplane, so from around now till at least March the weather is too cold for flying up there. There'd be no point in sending you over to sit around twiddling your thumbs. Much better to remain in Scotland so you can complete your convalescence and then you'll be perfectly fit to start in March."

"Seems a bloody shame. Couldn't I do some of the same down in England?"

"A nice idea, but we are more than covered here, and we like to keep the same trainers as long as we can. It makes for more consistency, which we find is best for survival rates – which, let's face it, are not that good."

"Well, I accept under protest. But I'd like to be considered for anything that comes up in the meantime. And I mean absolutely anything."

"We'll bear that in mind. If nothing is forthcoming, we will contact you in early March to arrange for your move to the airfield over there. It's just outside Toronto."

This was a disappointment for Jack, but in the light of subsequent events, it turned out to be useful. He had slightly exaggerated how well he was feeling and had a couple of relapses in the following months. By the time his deployment was due, his health was as good as it was going to be and, as he had continued to play cards, albeit rather half-heartedly, by the time he set sail for New York the following March, he was an accomplished player.

However, now he was going to be able to fly again, so any thoughts of gambling and casinos were shelved. The thrill of the cockpit would be all the stimulation he'd need. Teaching novices would not be quite the same as engaging the Germans in aerial combat, but there would be plenty of excitement if what he had heard was even half true, and that was all he craved.

Chapter 9

1914–19 GREECE

After returning to Athens from France, Nico decided to devote himself to becoming a serious professional gambler. To do so, it was not sufficient to simply gamble. Unlike Jack Coats, he decided he had to study.

Although most of his time and energy had been dedicated to playing poker, he had got a sniff of the rarefied air offered to those who played baccarat at the highest level. This was the territory of royalty and the ultra rich. His limited examination of the game to date indicated that the tiny edge he was trying to acquire meant that an astronomical amount of money had to pass through his hands if he was to make an acceptable living. Developing that edge was the first stage in his plan.

Before getting to that level of expertise and exposure, he would have to improve his skills. He started with card counting. He noticed that most casinos operated with shoes containing six to eight decks of cards. He practised shuffling six decks of cards together and improving his card counting technique. He also played eight-pack bezique, training himself to remember every card.

He was still not sure how much help this would be. Objectively, knowing what cards were left near the end of a shoe did not tell him whether they would be dealt to the players or the banker, and the chances for each were the same, but he still reasoned that knowledge was better than ignorance. After all,

Francis Bacon was surely correct when he said that "Knowledge is power'.

Another thing he had come to appreciate was that many players unconsciously change their behaviour according to the cards they hold and don't even realise they are doing it. In the modern world this is called a "tell" but when it dawned on him, no such thing had been identified or given a name. He added this to his card counting skills to give him a further edge.

He dedicated weeks and months to practising hypothetical scenarios and continued playing games with anyone who would take him on. It was through one of these games that he first encountered Eli Eliopulo.

Eli was born in Missolonghi, a small town on the Gulf of Patras, which is famous for being the site of various sieges and heroic resistance during the Greek War of Independence, as well as the place where Lord Byron died in 1824. Eli was elegant, charming, wildly successful with women and renowned for wearing a monocle and bowler hat.

They began to play against each other regularly and became firm friends. They discussed strategy and tactics and, being much older than Nico, Eli took the younger player under his wing and helped him develop his skills, without either of them having to risk a single drachma.

Eli's knowledge of baccarat was far greater than Nico's, so one thing he could impart was wisdom. He helped him understand the systems people use to try and win, none of which were, in his opinion, any good. He went through the main ones used by so-called professional players quickly and concisely.

"First and most famous there is the Martingale. This requires little understanding. The player quite simply doubles his bet every time he loses, until he (hopefully) eventually wins."

Nico looked at him and nodded grimly. "I know it already. I used it with spectacular lack of success when I was in Monte Carlo."

"Well, there's no substitute for trying a system to understand its shortcomings." Eli paused, as if expecting a response, but getting none he added, "Also, it's not very lucrative and if you get on a bad run, the geometric progression of bets gets you out of your depth in a hurry. *And*" – he emphasised the word – "it fails if the table has a maximum."

"I see that." Nico was alert and attentive. "If you lose six times in a row, having started with a minimum bet of 100 francs, your stake will be" – he did a quick calculation – "6,400 francs. If you then win, your net gain is only 100 francs. If the table maximum is 5,000, your seventh win will leave you 1,300 francs out of pocket."

"It is over a hundred years old."

"It may be old, but it is for fools."

"So you won't be interested in the Grand Martingale, which simply does the same thing more aggressively?"

Nico shook his head. "No. That's for bigger fools."

They went over several other similar systems. Eli highlighted the Anti Martingale. "This is the exact opposite. You double your bet when you win and revert to the original bet if you lose. It gives you a good chance of a small loss and a small chance of a big win, the reverse of the Martingale."

"Not very interesting. I am beginning to see a pattern and it is not one I find very attractive."

Eli shrugged his shoulders. "Okay. So I won't bore you with the others, though you should know of them: Jean d'Alembert used an additive version of the Martingale for playing private roulette games in eighteenth-century France. The 'Labby', invented by Henry Labouchere, an English editor and wit, was more sophisticated, but had the same problems as the others, and the Paroli was favoured by the top gamblers and usually applied to large stakes, say 100,000 francs; if you win, you leave the total for the next bet, and if you win a third time you withdraw

200,000 and start again."

After this discussion, Nico developed systems of his own to test. All failed. But his study gave him clear insight into how and why they didn't work and also allowed him to understand the game more clearly. He studied the law of averages and the way that affected the run of play. He could now appreciate that varying one's bets according to the situation was an essential skill in baccarat and he developed strategies for given positions as much as he could. He recalled that somebody once said, "It is not the way you play the cards, but how well you handle the money." How true, he thought.

As their relationship developed, Nico would visit Eli's house and gradually got to know his family. At one such get-together, Nico was introduced to the beautiful Yola Apostolides, Eli's niece. It was love at first sight, but although this seemed like a match made in heaven, there was one major problem: she was already married.

Nico continued to woo her by stealth and it was evident that she was equally smitten with him, but her husband was the jealous type and arranging a separation was never going to be easy. In fact, Nico decided it was impossible, so he resolved to persuade her to run away with him.

Months went by, and although they had discussed various elopement plans, nothing came of any of them. Yola's marriage was disintegrating and she moved back with her parents. Then the perfect opportunity presented itself, courtesy of Eli.

He had been sizing up what he liked to think of as his protégé, although there was no doubt that Nico had become more his partner at the baccarat table. It was evident that the younger man's skill level was such that his ability had long surpassed that of his older colleague and had in fact reached a point where he could compete at any level. It was time to put all that training to good use. Eli decided to explore the possibility, as he felt that the timing was right.

The First World War had ended and Europe wanted to

celebrate. The stress of having imminent death hanging over people's heads had been removed and it was like a cork coming out of a bottle of champagne: they were going mad. Nobody wanted to work and everyone who could wanted to party; the post-war boom was starting, there was money splashing around, and how better to spend it than by gambling? Clubs and bookmakers sprung up all over the place, especially in France, and the casinos were bursting at the seams. Separating clients from their cash was easy. Roulette was still taboo and boule was shunned by the wealthy due to the excessive house margin; the main games enjoyed by the elite players were chemin-de-fer and baccarat. Eli felt that the two of them had this pot of gold within their grasp. He decided to tackle his friend.

"Nico, you are wasting your time and talent here in Athens. What we are making is chicken feed compared to places like Paris. The war is over and there are a lot of people with lots of money just waiting to hand it over to a bright young man like you. I know the city well and have plenty of connections there who can get us into the important clubs and games. My building contract business has been going well, so I will stake you, at least at the start. What do you say? Should we give it a shot?"

Nico beamed and said, "I've been thinking about it as well, and you're right – I have been doing all this training for a reason, and it is not to continue with our friendly games here. I said I wanted to become the greatest gambler in the world and to do that I need to be on the biggest stage, which is definitely in France."

"Then what are we waiting for?"

Nico expression quickly changed to a frown. "One thing. I will only go if I can persuade Yola to come with me. I want to marry her and get her away from her awful husband, and I am not entirely sure how to go about it. However, this may be the opportunity I was looking for. I will talk to her and see what can be arranged."

The couple met the next day. He got straight to the point. "I want to make a proposal to you."

"But you know I am married," she replied. "We can do nothing until that changes, and I still can't see how it will."

"Not that sort of proposal, though in a funny way it is. You see I'm going to Paris to make my fortune as a professional gambler. Nothing would make me happier than to take you with me as my wife, but only if you can extricate yourself from your marriage. If you can't, then I am sorry, but I will have to go alone. I know that this puts unfair pressure on you, but I have no alternative. Is there nothing you can do?"

Yola was sorely tempted by the offer. She adored Nico and wanted to spend the rest of her life with him, but she didn't want to seem too keen given that she could see no way, short of murder, of escaping from the clutches of her husband, so she didn't want to get his hopes up. She decided to play it cool by pressing him for more detail.

"Before I even think about going to Paris with you, I want to understand what you will be doing and how we will survive. Is this a real plan or is it just a pipe dream?"

"Your Uncle Eli thinks it is workable – really, it's on his initiative that we would be going. He's going to finance us until we are established; and I have gained a reputation and some wealth."

"Well, that's comforting, I suppose, and is fine as far as it goes. But I am more interested in our longer-term prospects. How do you intend to get established, as you call it?"

"We will live off my winnings from gambling and I don't mean just at the start. We will be able to have a comfortable life – you can expect us to become significantly wealthy."

She appeared unconvinced, to put it mildly. "That sounds extremely risky and wildly uncertain."

"It's not really. You know how they say that 'a fool and his money are soon parted'? Well, I'm no fool, but I can easily take advantage of others who are. Gambling's a mug's game, but I will not be playing the way that others do. I have a method which gives me a statistical certainty of winning in the long run."

She looked at him with a mixture of scepticism and incredulity. She knew him to be logical and methodical, but this sounded crazy. "I'm sorry, but in the end you'll also be gambling so surely just as much a 'mug' as everyone else. You'll have to explain – it just sounds too fanciful to be true."

"Fair enough. You understand the basics of baccarat, don't you? You've seen your uncle and me play often enough."

"Yes. I know the basics."

"Good. Then you know that each player and the banker receive two cards and can ask for a third one. The object is to score as near to nine points as possible. All tens and court cards count as zero."

"That's clear."

"Okay. When all of the cards have been played and revealed, the winners and losers are declared and the relevant amounts paid to the winners and collected from the losers. I'll get to betting in a moment. If, for example, player one scores eight and player two seven and the bank has seven, then the bank pays player one and nobody wins between the bank and player two."

"It seems to me that being the bank is pretty dangerous."

"On the contrary. If I take the bank, I will have a small but significant edge. *That* is how I will win."

"Why do you have an edge? It would seem to be quite the opposite. The bank has two opportunities to lose but will seldom win against both opponents."

"Because the banker is the last to draw a third card, if it gets to that."

She looked unconvinced. "That sounds pretty marginal, at best. And certainly not enough to make a living, let alone a fortune."

"That's what most people think, particularly as the casino only pays out ninety-five per cent on a bank win, but in fact that minimal benefit is more than sufficient, provided we play often enough for a lot of money. It's a mathematical certainty, brought about by that last card I just mentioned. Also, I have a couple of other things that help improve my odds of winning." He paused and looked at her. "You know, you are so beautiful. I just want to kiss you, not explain cards to you."

"There'll be plenty of time for that in Paris. Go on."

"Okay. At the baccarat table there are usually twelve to fourteen people actually betting – six or seven on one side (or tableau) - of the banker and the same number on the other side. The banker plays against all of them, even though he is only playing against two hands of cards. The people can either bet for their side or for the other side, but not for the bank. Spaces are laid out on the table for them to place their bets."

She looked a little uncertain, but said, "I think I understand that. How do they sort out the bets?"

"The bank pays all the winning bets and collects the money from all the losers. The right to be banker, assuming it is not the casino, is auctioned off and the highest bidder wins, but the amount of his winning bid is the maximum amount he can lose. When play starts, the banker puts down his bet and if one of the players says 'Banco,' then he plays the banker alone. If not, each player places bets in turn, but once the amount put down by the bank is reached, nobody else can bet. Play continues till one of three things happens: the shoe is empty, the banker has lost the maximum amount or he retires voluntarily."

"Still sounds scary, particularly for the bank, even with that limit. What makes you so special?"

"I have played a lot and am very good at reading people when they have cards in their hands. I can just about guarantee to distinguish between a player with a good or bad hand, just by the way he or she behaves."

"That must help, but is it enough?"

"Well, I can also memorise up to six decks of cards, so that when play reaches the end of the shoe, I know what cards are left. That is a significant help. Combined with the ability to tell what type of hand my opponent has, I can win more often than I lose. That is how I will make a fortune in Paris."

"I'm not sure I understood all that completely." She thought for a moment and Nico remained silent. He felt she was reaching a decision. Finally she spoke, with an encouraging smile. "You know, in a funny way that doesn't really matter. I believe in you, Nico my love, and I trust my Uncle Eli, so I'd love to come to Paris."

Nico put his arms around her and kissed her. "That's wonderful! When can we leave?"

"Hold your horses – it's far from a done deal just yet. There's still a major snag: if my husband gets the idea that I am going, he will be even more stubborn about the divorce. His refusal's more to do with making me unhappy than anything else. But we've been apart for so long now that I suspect he's found another woman and will be more amenable."

"Isn't that just wishful thinking? He struck me as being fairly determined to make life as hard as possible for you."

"I know, and of course you're right, my angel, but I think I may be able to either persuade or bully him into signing the papers. Given the right incentive, he should be willing. And if not, I have another plot that I've been hatching for a time: I'm going to hire a private detective, and if I can prove that he does indeed have a new lover, I can use that fact to either convince him or a judge to agree to a separation. Let's plan to get married just before we leave, and we can flee the country as soon as we are wed."

Yola's plan worked and the detective came up with the

requisite proof. Although her husband refused to cooperate voluntarily, she found a judge who was willing, given the existence of the new girlfriend combined with a substantial bribe, to allow the divorce without spousal consent. So Nico and Yola got married, with just her uncle attending the simple ceremony, and they set out for Paris as a couple.

Chapter 10

1917–19 CANADA

Once winter was over, Jack found himself in Canada as planned, in April 1917. As he approached the airbase in Desoronto in his Marmon 41 Speedster, he was unsure what to expect. He had bought this outrageously expensive American-made, six-cylinder car from the manufacturer in Indiana and had it shipped to Toronto by rail. He hoped it would impress the locals, the girls especially, and he was not disappointed, for as he entered the village – he had to admit it was no more than that – people began to point and stare. Once he had parked, they gathered round to admire it, as this sort of vehicle was uncommon in that part of the world. Amongst them was a rather dashing fellow who approached him with his hand extended.

"Nice wheels," said this individual with a broad grin as Jack jumped down from the driving seat. "Eardley Wilmot at your service. I've been asked to fill in for the CO, who's off base marrying his brother's widow, of all the crazy things. You'll get to meet him in due course – Lord George Wellesley, no less – he'll be back in a couple of days."

Jack took Eardley's outstretched hand in a firm grip. "Captain Jack Coats, but then you know that."

He looked Eardley up and down and immediately knew he would like him. He had a relaxed demeanour and was devilishly handsome, reminiscent of Douglas Fairbanks, who Jack had seen in a Nickelodeon when he was dragged there recently by a prospective girlfriend. He had not enjoyed the experience, but Fairbanks had impressed him.

Eardley grabbed him by the arm. "So, it's my job to show you around and help you settle in."

"First class. I assume I will be living on the base?"

"Yes. I'll take you to your quarters in a moment, but first let's get the lie of the land, as it were."

"Where do you billet?"

"I actually commute from Belleville, which is nearby. I only arrived a couple of weeks ago, just after they opened the place, which is now known as Camp Mohawk. You will see that it is all brand new and although that has its benefits, it means that not everything works perfectly. You will need a little patience."

As they got to know each other, Jack discovered that Eardley was an accomplished flier and stunt pilot who had earned his wings and been sent there as a trainer. His good looks made him a big hit with the ladies, particularly as he was an avid partygoer. They were like two peas in a pod and soon became good friends.

Jack learned that Eardley had two younger sisters. Audrey and Gwen Wilmot were more handsome than pretty, with bob haircuts, narrow, vibrant eyes and very firm jawlines, a fair physical reflection of forceful personalities. They were vivacious, accomplished dancers and excellent horsewomen, something that he particularly admired. When shown photographs by Eardley, he immediately demanded to meet them.

However, he was not content to simply have his friend introduce him to the sisters. He wanted to make the encounter as memorable as possible and set about devising a plan. A couple of weeks later he discovered that they were both staying with the Burrows family at Glanmore, a mansion on a huge and more importantly flat estate about twenty miles from the base on the same stretch of water. This was his chance to engineer an unforgettable introduction.

The next day, he took off from the base with almost no fuel and, when he was near the house, flew in circles until his supply was depleted. He then glided in and landed on the grounds of the estate, coasting to a stop near the building. The girls and their host came out to see what was happening and were met by his dapper figure, leaping out of the plane and removing his flying helmet.

"Frightfully sorry to drop in like this, but I found I was out of fuel and had to put the kite down somewhere. This seemed like as good a spot as any, so here I am. I'm Jack Coats, by the way. Very nice to meet you."

The girls stood there with mouths agape, unsure how to handle the situation, so he continued, "I know this may seem rather forward of me, but could I trouble you to get one of your lackeys to find me some juice for the plane? And if it were at all possible, while we are waiting, I would love a cup of tea and you can tell me your life stories, which I am sure are fascinating."

The girls – and Audrey, in particular – were thrilled and rather awestruck by Jack's nonchalant manner and easy-going charm. She sat and talked with him well into the afternoon and by the time he took off to return to Camp Mohawk, she was well and truly smitten.

He also found her fascinating. She was so much more forthright than most of the girls he normally met, so he found they could get into quite heated discussions on everything from politics to foxhunting, which both of them loved. Her enthusiasm for partying was almost legendary and he found that dancing with her was both a joy and an education. They seemed to be made for each other, so it was not long before they were "stepping out" as a couple.

On an evening out together, which her mother had encouraged as she viewed Jack as quite a catch, they were sitting in a restaurant in Belleville sipping champagne and listening to the band play a Scott Joplin rag. He had still not asked her about her absent father, who he knew to be dead, but had heard little more as the family never mentioned him. He decided a direct approach would be best.

"What happened to your father?"

She looked slightly sheepish, but didn't try to evade the question. "Nobody is a hundred per cent sure, but he perished in a hotel fire in Toronto. The origin of the blaze was never discovered and we don't really know what he was doing there, but it was definitely him."

"I'm so sorry. Do you miss him?"

"I've got used to him not being around. It's been several years and time is a great healer. The thing that affects me and the whole family most is that our only source of income has effectively dried up. My mother gives piano and singing lessons – you may've seen her – to make ends meet, and Eardley is very good to us and sends whatever he can." She paused as though she was unsure whether to divulge more information, but decided to soldier on. "I've never told anyone this before, but we sometimes borrow a little from the bank. My mother likes to put on a brave face and keep our relative poverty hidden, so we can 'hold our heads high in polite society', as she puts it."

Jack looked horrified and took her hand across the table. He was mildly embarrassed that he had not picked up on this before, but guessed it showed how well Audrey's mother had disguised their impecuniousness. "Why didn't you tell me before? You know only too well that I come from an extremely affluent family and could easily help. You silly girl."

"Oh, Jack. Of course I'm aware of your family's wealth, but I didn't want to be seen as a gold digger. I love you too much to have you think that of me and was afraid I might lose you."

"Don't be a chump. I'd know if you were after me for my money. What we have together is way above such mundane considerations. Don't give it another thought. I will sort it out tomorrow."

A deep frown furrowed her brow. "Please don't mention this to my mother; she would never forgive me if she finds out I told you."

Jack chuckled wryly. "It's going to be dashed hard to help you without her knowing. I think she knows that we are serious about one another and that gives me the chance to tackle her directly about the family's finances, without you even being involved. Leave it with me."

A few days later, he found himself alone with Audrey's mother and decided that the moment was right. He started gently with a speech he had been mulling over in his mind. "Mrs Wilmot, I can't help noticing after a couple of months with Audrey that you must be suffering financially from – and please don't take this the wrong way – the lack of a man about the house. Eardley is away and I am probably the male who spends most time with the family. I feel it only right that I make a small contribution to help you – to coin a phrase – keep Audrey in the manner to which she is accustomed."

"That will not be necessary." Audrey's mother thrust her chin out and both her tone and her expression became obstinate. "We are fine as we are and would never dream of seeking charity from others."

Jack looked hurt. "I hardly feel I could be classed as 'others'. I am almost one of the family and, as such, should be allowed to pull my weight. Nobody but us need know about it and I am sure it would be a help. I can keep it discreet." He was almost willing her to say yes, but she still looked adamant. He continued, "It need not be a large amount – just enough to take some of the strain off."

He was pleased to note that a crack was appearing in her dogged resistance. She was slightly hesitant when she spoke. "It would be nice to have less to worry about moneywise, and you are right – you're really one of the family now. I will have a think about it and let you know." She smiled. "Thank you for thinking of us. You are really a sweet boy."

At this point, Jack knew he had won and, sure enough, a week later she agreed to accept a minimal amount of support. With a little subtle adjustment this quickly became substantial, but he never heard a word of complaint. On the contrary: it bolstered the family's standing and further enhanced his position with her.

Meanwhile, another arrival at the base came as a delightful surprise for Jack. After Vernon Castle had completed his military training, he became a highly successful and well-respected pilot, carrying out daring and dangerous raids over the German lines in northern France. However, on March 17th 1917, he was shot down for a second time and it was decided that his fame and expertise would be better used to attract and train pilots in Canada.

If Jack's arrival had caused a stir, Vernon's was frankly sensational. He rolled up in a bright yellow Stutz Bearcat, with two German shepherds and a monkey called Jeffrey in tow. When the townsfolk of Deseronto – along with Jack – became aware of his presence, they were thrilled. A man this famous was bound to be a boon for the town, and Jack was looking forward to the opportunities for merriment that Vernon's presence would bring.

Eardley, Vernon and Jack soon became inseparable, often seen around town in the Marmot or the Bearcat, becoming known as the "Three Musketeers". When they weren't buzzing the local populace in their planes, they were attending parties at the finest homes in Belleville and wowing all the ladies, though Jack only had eyes for Audrey.

It was at one such party, not long after Vernon's arrival, that the two old friends rolled in to be greeted by Eardley and his two sisters. Jack gave Gwen a peck on the cheek and Audrey a chaste kiss, as required by society etiquette. He then hugged Eardley and turned to Vernon who was already eyeing Gwen with obvious admiration. Jack spoke. "V, old chap, this is my beloved Audrey." Vernon tore his eyes away from Gwen for a moment and shook Audrey's hand. "And this is her younger sister, Gwen."

Vernon adopted his most seductive manner. He took Gwen's

hand in his and stooped to kiss it. He then moved even closer to her without letting it go and half-whispered, "What an absolute delight to meet you at last. I have heard so much about you."

Gwen took this all in her stride. "As have I of you. They tell me you're a brilliant dancer – you'll have to show me."

With this he led her off, ignoring the other three, who stood there in stunned silence, until Audrey piped up. "Well, that was unexpected – and him a married man!"

After that night, Gwen and Vernon were an "item". They went everywhere together. The attraction was magnetic and immediate, which really should have been a surprise to nobody. Jack and Vernon were so similar, as were Audrey and Gwen, so the same things that united Jack and Audrey applied to the other couple. Irene, who was still very married to Vernon, was quickly forgotten and the two great friends and the two sisters rapidly became a fixture amongst the cream of local society.

Both Vernon and Jack were fine instructors and although they had to occasionally fish downed flyers out of Mohawk Bay with Jack's motor launch – another "toy" he had bought for his own and others' amusement – the training went well. Jack had a knack for encouraging the more nervous pilots, who quite regularly would take fright whilst trying to complete their initial hours aloft.

One such pupil, Vivian Voss, approached him to ask for a few days' leave, as he had become terrified by the prospect of flying and the likelihood that he would be killed. This was after only two and a half hours aloft.

Jack recognised the symptoms, which he had seen many times before. He explained, "I'm afraid it is currently impossible, old bean. You need to complete your five hours in the air so you can be transferred to Camp Borden for further training. But, tell you what, I promise to write to the CO there to see if you can be given time off." He knew this was unlikely, but it seemed to soothe the jittery flyer's anxiety and he went off looking marginally less panicky. Jack understood that he needed to do something further to try and restore the lad's confidence. He decided on a technique he had used a couple of times before.

Later that same day, when the ashen-faced student was standing nervously by his plane, Jack approached him with a small puppy in his arms. "I say Voss! Look at this jolly little chap!" He handed it over and continued, "Why don't you take him up with you and do a run of eight landings, just to see how it goes."

The reluctant flyer got into his plane and did just that. Exactly as Jack had planned, his concern for the puppy took his mind off his nerves and by the time he had finished, he found his confidence had returned and that he actually loved flying. He rushed off to find Captain Coats.

"Excuse me, sir, but I don't think you will need to write that letter, after all."

"You sure, Voss? All right." And Jack walked away with a twinkle in his eye and a knowing smile on his lips at a job well done.

Inevitably there were tragedies, and one such befell Vernon when he was on a training flight with a cadet called Fraser.

He talked to Jack about it afterwards. "We were executing a turn at about 200 feet and the trainee panicked and pulled the nose of the plane up, causing a stall. The plane plummeted earthward and I couldn't avoid the crash in the short time I had to wrest the controls from the petrified pupil."

"How ghastly, V." Jack looked his friend up and down. "You seem remarkably unhurt. What happened to the trainee?"

"I was sitting in the rear cockpit, so although the impact was severe, I only suffered a couple of bumps. He was in the front and took the brunt of the collision. He was killed outright." He looked to be on the verge of bursting into tears, but remained stoic. "I feel so terrible for the poor boy."

"It is not your fault and there was nothing you could do. Don't beat yourself up."

"Maybe I couldn't then, but I can now. I am going to visit his parents to express my condolences, which I feel is the least I can do."

"Fair enough. Do they live nearby?"

"No. I'll have to take a train to the other side of Toronto."

Jack looked surprised. "Wow! That's a trek."

"I don't care. I feel an obligation to see them face-to-face and tell them about their son."

"You have always had such compassion, V. It is one of the many things I like about you."

Vernon put on a wry grin, but Jack could see the sadness behind the smile. After they had sat together for a while, silently contemplating the tragedy, Vernon looked up and said, "There is one other thing I can do. It is unfair that these novices take the front cockpit in our training planes. They are put there so we can see what they're up to, but the truth is that there is almost no view of their movements from the back. I can react more quickly to odd manoeuvres if I am up front, and it puts them at less risk if they are behind. I'm going to swap places with them from now on."

"Awfully dangerous, but I know you: once your mind's made up, I won't be able to change it. I guess if it makes you feel better then fine, but don't say I haven't warned you."

As summer transitioned into autumn and the weather turned colder, Jack and Audrey became engaged. Vernon and Gwen were also keen to wed, so a plan was developed whereby Vernon would arrange for a divorce from Irene so that there could be a double wedding. As they calculated that it would take the best part of a year to achieve all this, a date in September 1918 was set for the epic event.

But almost as soon as this plot had been hatched, fate intervened: both men and most of their Canadian trainees were transferred to Texas. Here the instructors could teach both Canadian and US pilots, as America had now entered the war, and training up north in winter was viewed as a very hit-and-miss affair, given the vagaries of the weather.

They arrived in mid-November and were airborne immediately, but a snowstorm three days later triggered major disruption, even while making the Canadians feel right at home. Although flying was immediately suspended, the subsequent tacky mud caused by the melting snow produced a large number of nose-over landings and the fracturing of forty propellers in only one morning after training resumed.

Despite these setbacks, aerial instruction went on and although the weather made in-flight conditions excessively bumpy and the lack of discipline led to some truly hair-raising stunts, the level of training gradually improved, thanks in no small measure to the skill and discipline of the two friends. Conditions were rather Spartan to begin with, but again improvements were made, even while an unusually wet winter played havoc with both the living quarters and the flying schedules.

Social life, on the other hand, was hardly affected at all, and frequent groundings due to inclement weather just added to the opportunities for entertainment. Vernon was very popular and, despite doing little dancing, was often seen to join the band of the evening, usually playing the drums. He and Jack were incorrigible ladies' men, despite being mindful, most of the time, of their fiancées waiting anxiously for them back in Belleville.

Three months after their arrival, Vernon received a letter from HQ. He rushed into the mess, where Jack was sitting having a coffee.

"J, look what just came from the command centre."

He handed the piece of paper to Jack, who quickly scanned it, a broad grin spreading across his face as he read. "So, you're to be promoted to commanding officer of a new camp being built at Beamsville for" – he glanced down – "advanced training in gunnery and aerial combat. Congratulations! Thoroughly deserved, even if I say so myself."

"Rather exciting, and it will take me much nearer Gwen again. I hope they'll transfer you north too."

"I am ever hopeful. The war is surely going to be over soon and I'll be able to return to Canada as well, though not to as prestigious a position as yours."

Vernon smiled and shook his head once. "Well, I can't be dwelling on it too much as there are still the 'greenhorns', as they call them here, to train. See you." And he wheeled around and set off for his plane.

This turned out to be their last ever conversation. Only two days later, on February 15th 1918, Vernon was coming in to land with a cadet from the American Signals Corps when a plane started to take off underneath them. Had Vernon been in the rear seat, he would have seen it, but his view was blocked in his newly adopted position up front. By the time he realised what was happening, all he could do was attempt an Immelmann turn, which is basically a climb-and-yaw movement designed to allow the plane to increase altitude and then dive and gain speed, thus avoiding a stall. It is a difficult manoeuvre at the best of times, but so close to the ground it proved impossible: even a hundred feet higher in the air, they would have had a fighting chance. The plane dived head-on into the ground. The engine ended up pinning Vernon to the rear compartment.

Jack was at the airfield when it happened and ran to the plane to try and help get him out of the cockpit, but the engine had squashed Vernon so badly that it proved impossible, even though Jack skinned his knuckles and cut both arms in the attempt. By the time they got Vernon out and transferred him to hospital, it was too late. He never regained consciousness.

His funeral procession brought Fort Worth to a standstill as his body was borne on a gun carriage to the station and the citizens lined the streets to pay their respects. Jack walked beside the coffin, completely distraught, unable to acknowledge that he would never see his friend again. They had known each other for a little over a year, but had formed a bond that would stay with him for the rest of his life.

Gwen was sewing a pair of socks for Vernon when she heard the news. She retreated into the bosom of her family to grieve and was not seen for over six months.

Jack went through the motions of training the many recruits who passed through his hands, but his heart was not in it anymore. He missed his friend dreadfully, to the point that he even gave up partying and would sit for long periods alone in his billet, staring at the walls. At long last he was transferred back to Canada in the summer and on September 25th 1918, he married Audrey at St. Thomas' Church in Belleville. The double wedding had become a single one, but the bride of the "second" marriage emerged from her grief to attend the ceremony as the maid of honour, all dressed in black satin. Gwen was still far from over her enthralment with Vernon.

When the end of the war came less than two months later, Jack and Audrey started on a hectic social round, caught up in the post-war euphoria. They rented a house in the fashionable Rosedale district of Toronto and became firm fixtures in a lively group of officers and débutantes, partying almost every night and spending lavishly on entertainment. Gwen would appear occasionally, but firmly rebuffed the advances of any prospective suitor.

Despite all the nightlife, Jack was yearning to return to his homeland. At the end of January the young couple set sail for England, with Audrey already expecting their firstborn, who was inevitably to be named Vernon. Gwen was to follow a few months later.

Jack had briefly found a substitute for gambling, having spent the war risking his life in the air. The dangers of flying had given him an adrenaline rush different from, but a more than acceptable substitute to, what he had experienced at the tables.

His time as a trainer had been less intense, but sufficiently hazardous to be a decent alternative. His relationship with Vernon had also been enormously fulfilling. Now he found that the end of hostilities and the absence of his friend had created a vacuum, which he needed to fill.

For him, there was only one way of doing this. He must return to the real love of his life, which was not a woman. He had to revive his affair with the less dangerous but nonetheless exciting game of baccarat.

Chapter 11

1919–21 FRANCE

Nico and Eli, along with Yola, reached Paris with a little money accumulated from their gambling exploits in Athens, but not enough for a lavish lifestyle. They decided to stay in an inexpensive hotel and start to trawl around to find out where the most lucrative games of baccarat were to be found. They soon discovered the Cercle de L'Industrie, a small gentleman's club where the stakes were high, the bankrolls fat and the gamblers as vulnerable as any they had met.

The two men decided they should take turns playing either chemin-de-fer or baccarat, which they preferred as they could take and retain the bank more easily. Through endless practice and extensive study, they had confirmed Nico's notion that the bank has a half per cent advantage over the punters so if they played enough, it would allow them to gradually build up capital. The Cercle was amenable to their wishes, as most gamblers were reluctant to take the bank, which they deemed too risky. They soon became fixtures at the club and were well liked, as they were quiet, respectful and polite.

Nico was not, however, very patient. He had come to Paris to earn his fortune and the slow and erratic way their wealth was building up did not satisfy his lust for prosperity. He started to look for other opportunities. He quickly found one and decided to float his idea with Eli.

"It has become apparent to me that many of the gamblers we meet are not content to risk their money solely on games of cards. They want other outlets for their chosen form of entertainment, and the one they mention most frequently is horse racing." Nico waited to see Eli's reaction and was encouraged when his partner confirmed this view.

"I'd noted the same," Eli agreed. "In fact, there are several who actually prefer the race track to the casino and only play cards as a secondary interest."

"Okay. So I'm thinking that we should exploit the fact that we already know and interact with many of them. The sport requires a bookmaker to take their bets, but being illegal in France means it has to be operated in such a way as to avoid the attention of the police. The mere fact that it is banned makes it very lucrative."

Eli was rather sceptical. "Do you honestly reckon that a couple of novices in this field, like ourselves, can make a go of it?"

"Nothing ventured, nothing gained, as they say! Also, I've done a little digging; it's led me to the amazing but heartening conclusion that, conducted in an efficient and trustworthy manner, it will yield a guaranteed twelve per cent profit. That's a number we'd be fools to ignore."

"But what can we bring to the table to make us the bookmaker of choice for all these rich gamblers?"

"We know a lot of them, can offer our services from within one of the casinos, and I think that our reputation for open honesty and sincerity will be a winning formula."

"We're going to need capital to get going."

"I had thought of that, but I have a little put aside and if you can chip in as well and we start on a modest scale, I believe we can make a go of it."

"Seems reasonable. When do we start?"

"No time like the present. Let's make a plan."

So they set out just as they had figured and, by pooling their resources, they built up a reputation for paying on time, collecting with patience and tact, and managing the process with discretion. Being methodical, Nico kept perfect records and always knew who needed to be paid and who had debts to be collected. Within a few short months, he had become the fashionable bookie amongst the wealthier betting fraternity. If you wanted to back a horse, Nico Zographos was the best game in town.

As he had expressed to Eli, to improve his customer base and expand turnover, he required a safe place to conduct his business, where the gendarmes would not interfere. The Cercle de L'Industrie fitted the bill perfectly and with an increase in the number of people wanting his services, the owners of the club were delighted to turn a blind eye. He was soon attracting some of the richest gamblers in Paris and many stayed to play cards, which was an unforeseen bonus.

He continued to play baccarat, but not with the same fervour as Eli, who was at the tables as often as he could be. With the bookmaking business flourishing and their circle of contacts growing quickly, they were beginning to find that life was quite comfortable.

One of these contacts was an Armenian they had met over the card table in Athens a couple of years before. He had recounted his fascinating story during a game back then and Nico had never forgotten it. His name was Zaret Couyoumdjian. They had been playing for several hours when Nico had asked him how he could afford to play for so much money, so often.

"I inherited a fortune, via a rather exceptional set of circumstances. My father set up a chain of department stores in Smyrna and became a multimillionaire. Then the whole family – everyone, mark you – contracted typhoid and my seven brothers and three sisters all succumbed to the disease."

"What a tragedy," said Nico. "How on earth did *you* survive?"

"I almost didn't – it was really touch and go. At one point, my life hung in the balance and my father spent a night in a last-ditch prayer vigil with the monks at our local monastery. The prayers obviously worked, as I had apparently turned the corner when dawn broke. I gradually got better from then on."

"It seems that God smiled upon you."

"Indeed he did. Once I got better, I became the light of my father's life and could do no wrong. I left for Constantinople, where I could gamble and party with no parental interference. It was wonderful." He fell into a slight reverie as he thought back on his life then, but he soon returned to the present. "When my father died, I inherited the entire family fortune."

"Now I see why you can gamble so freely." Nico sounded impressed.

"Yes, but not for the reason you think. Unfortunately this story is far from over. With the outbreak of the war, I had to flee to Athens with as much cash as I could carry in my pockets and nothing else." He frowned at the memory. "By this time I was suffering from spondylitis – a form of arthritis of the spine – leaving my back very rigid and giving me a good deal of pain. I went to Mytilene with the hope that the climate on Lesbos would help alleviate my symptoms, but instead I was seduced by a beguiling and beautiful widow, Madame Karadakis, and ended up eloping to Athens with her and her young son in tow."

"Presumably with none of your fortune?"

Zaret sighed. "Exactly. I can no longer access my money in Smyrna, so I have taken up professional gambling. And I do interpreting for the British Navy, just on a freelance basis."

"In other words, you are not as rich as you appear." Nico looked sympathetic. "I cannot but help feel sorry for you. You are an accidental victim of war."

"I am really quite poor, though I have hopes of one day recovering what I have left back home."

He had subsequently moved to Paris, just as Nico and Eli had, and played cards in a variety of clubs in Paris. It was almost inevitable that he would run across the others again, which he did in the Cercle de L'Industrie.

Now, two years later, he was standing rather stiffly, as was his wont, watching a game of baccarat unfolding, with Nico and Eli holding the bank. "I imagine you two don't remember me," said Zaret.

It was Nico who responded. "I not only remember your face, but also your amazing story and your unforgettable name, which is a real struggle to spell. Welcome to the Cercle de L'Industrie, Monsieur Couyoumdjian, although for the sake of brevity, please allow me to address you more informally, as Zaret."

"That would be fine." He was about to continue the conversation, but the play had reached a critical phase, so he watched in silence until he could safely interject. "How long have you been in the city?"

Nico replied, "We arrived a few months ago, but we haven't seen you around. What brings you to Paris?"

"After my experiences in Athens I left for here after the war, by which time the conflict between Greece and Turkey meant that I had unfortunately lost my entire fortune back in Smyrna. I have decided to dedicate myself full time to gambling – and there is absolutely nowhere in the world more appropriate to pursue that particular profession."

"Yes." This time it was Eli who spoke. "We came to the same conclusion. So, what brings you to this particular club?"

"I heard on the grapevine that this is where the high-rollers hang out, so I thought I would check it out. You know what they say – follow the money! I also heard that you two are running a bookmaking business on the side and have gained quite a reputation. Our meeting is therefore not entirely a coincidence."

"Are you interested in backing a horse?" asked Nico.

"Oh no. My expertise is with the cards and I would never bet on anything else. I'd rather trust my hard-earned money to a game of baccarat. I was just curious as to how you were doing. And I hoped to have the pleasure of playing against some familiar faces. Better the devil you know. . ."

"Unfortunately your timing is not the best," Nico replied. "We're about done for this evening. I have some debts to settle, and I don't think Eli wants to prolong the session. However, we are nearly always here, so I'm sure you'll get the chance in the not too distant future. I look forward to it." With that, Nico stood and indicated that they would be leaving the table.

"If you are about to give up the bank, I think that may be my opportunity to take over. Very nice to see you again." And Zaret moved in to take Nico's seat and bid for the bank.

After this initial meeting, their paths crossed frequently and a mutual admiration grew between the two old friends and the newcomer. Nico, in particular, could appreciate the skills shown by Zaret, and Eli was impressed by his coolness under pressure, whilst correctly assessing his talent as remarkable, though not at the level of Nico's. What both annoyed and intrigued them all was that they found themselves constantly competing to take the bank. The eventual result was, with hindsight, inevitable, though it was Nico who first raised the idea late one night.

"Tell me, Zaret, why are you so determined to take the bank when you play? Most people are scared of the risks involved and shy away from it."

"I have studied the game, as I know you have, and I suspect that we may have reached very similar conclusions."

"Which are?"

"After playing literally thousands of hands on my own, I started to notice a pattern which gives an edge to the bank. It is small – maybe no more than a half per cent – but over time it improves my chances of winning, as long as I keep my head and neither take nor make any silly bets. I infer from your play that you have made the same calculation."

Nico was impressed. "You're right. It hinges on the bank's selection of the third card last, when there is a third card."

"I had pretty much gathered that, but it is nice to have someone else confirm it. I confess that it is by no means obvious."

"Absolutely, but all the same we are amazed that it has not dawned on any of the others. My assumption is that almost everyone who plays with us uses emotion rather than logic to form their strategy, if you can call it that: the fear of significant losses when one holds the bank far outweighs any potential gains. It is almost as if the act of bidding for the bank actually vocalises the maximum loss the bidder can make – and that scares them. Our view is that if you play enough, and all other things are equal, over the long term the bank will yield a better return than that of an ordinary punter."

"That makes a lot of sense." Zaret thought for a moment. "The one slight glitch in a strategy of always taking the bank is that you do need a huge amount of capital, as there will be individual instances where your losses are significant, even if your long-term winnings are secure."

Nico grinned broadly, a thing he seldom did. "I am glad you brought that up . . . We have a proposition for you, and it hinges on that very point." He lit a cigarette and leant forward to get closer to Zaret and spoke softly so no one else could hear. "It seems like lunacy to continue our constant rivalry over taking the bank. There is no doubt that we are kindred spirits. Wouldn't it be in all our interests to pool our resources and play as a team? A syndicate, if you like. This would allow us as a group to play for longer, as we could take turns at the table, and it would give us more wealth to play with. Deeper pockets will allow us to take more calculated risks and hopefully make more money."

They continued to discuss how they might work and play together and a deal was struck, with an embryonic form of what would become the Greek Syndicate emerging.

Over the next two years their strategy met with mixed success, but the flourishing bookmaking business kept them afloat. Nico was not entirely happy with the limitations of the three-man syndicate arrangement. He still felt that they were being constrained by limitations of cash flow, and he longed to break free and offer really large bets to the assorted millionaires who were just itching to gamble for what they considered to be serious money. He decided that what he needed was someone exceedingly rich to become part of the syndicate and bankroll the whole operation. He wanted the sort of person who could lose a fortune and not care about it. After careful consideration, he decided on a fellow Greek, who was not only a shipping magnate and a member of the second richest family in Europe after the Rothschilds, but was also a card enthusiast. This man was Athanase Vagliano.

Vagliano was an imposing figure and towered over the miniscule Nico. He had broad shoulders, bright blue eyes, an enormous appetite and a fiery personality, which proved troublesome in the years that followed.

Nico had done his research thoroughly and had discovered a good deal about him. He met with Eli to explain why he wanted this particular multi-millionaire.

"His family made their fortune mostly in shipping and moneylending in the Crimea; in fact they were largely responsible for the legitimisation of Greek shipping. One of the three pioneering brothers died rich but without children, so he split his 200 million-franc fortune between eight heirs, one of whom was Athanase. He in turn quadrupled his inheritance during the Balkans conflict and then made a series of outrageous ship rental deals throughout the First World War – they were so lucrative that he had become what could only be described as insanely rich by 1919."

Eli interrupted him. "Fair enough, but why him, apart from the fact that he is ultra rich?"

"Because he is a very keen card player and gambler, to the

extent that he has invested in the Société des Bains de Mer, which, as you know, basically controls the Monte Carlo Casino."

"Wow! I see what you mean – quite a find."

"Yes. So far so good, but – and there always is one – there are several negatives that have to be considered before approaching the man. He is a frankly indifferent baccarat player, has a foul temper and a reputation for bad behaviour, so his visits to the tables will have to be limited, which may be hard to achieve. We all make a point of being exceptionally polite – our motto could almost be 'Manners maketh man' – but he will be a very different animal. I think a meeting should be arranged so we can all assess the situation."

"I agree. I'll tell Zaret."

They met in the Cercle de L'Industrie and, after making the introductions, Nico laid out his proposal. "Athanase, we have been playing baccarat as a group of three for a time now and we have had mixed success. One of the things holding us back is lack of funds. If you were interested in joining us, you could bolster our capital and give us the opportunity to try something truly original."

"I am interesting, but how you say, what my offer except money?" Athanase's way of expressing himself was a mélange of Greek, English, Russian and French and was sometimes completely indecipherable.

"You love to play and we want that passion. A cold, calculating financier would not be interested in my proposal and would probably run a mile. It is not without its risks."

"So, what you want try?"

"It's complex, so I've written it out for you."

"I leave my *lunettes* behind. No can read it. Tell me what says." One of the other drawbacks with Athanase as a partner was that he was illiterate. Nico would only discover this later.

"Okay. So the current system is that when we play baccarat, we bid for the bank and, assuming our bid is successful, our losses are limited to that amount. The casino takes only five per cent, and the resulting low margin that it enjoys is one of the reasons why the richest gamblers like to play. This is fine, but given that we are not super-wealthy, there is a finite amount we can make."

Nico sipped his orange juice and looked round the group.

"What I propose is a game with no limits. We take the bank, agree to cover all our losses and share the winnings with the casino. With the bank's margin, we will win in the long run, as long as our pockets are sufficiently deep, we do nothing rash, and our resolve holds. In a sense, we are duplicating what the casinos do, but without their infrastructure. They depend on small margins on huge sums of money, though they take somewhat more than our meagre half per cent."

Zaret interjected. "So, what is my liability in the case that we lose everything? It sounds slightly scary."

"You're covered by whatever you put in to start with. I am counting on Athanase to contribute the lion's share and the amount I am proposing will mean we are very unlikely to go bankrupt. I will agree with him and you how we share the winnings."

"So, I do big risk and less profit?" Athanase frowned. "Don't seem like good deal to me."

"If you study the full proposal, you'll see it is fair. We each have a part to play. Zaret and I are the best players, so we'll be at the tables. Athanase has the cash, and Eli will run the bookmaking business and fill in from time to time."

"I want play, *aussi*," interjected Athanase.

"Well, that can perhaps be accommodated once we see how we get on. Given that possibility, would you be interested?"

"How much you want?" His tone was brusque, which had as much to do with his language skills as anything else. He had never learnt to express himself elegantly and didn't see any need to do so now.

Nico was becoming annoyed, but he bit his tongue and continued to explain in a measured tone, "I was thinking that 50 million francs would allow us to do what I am proposing. We would hopefully never need all of it, but to have it there would be sufficient. I know you can afford it and the chances of a significant return will make this a very sound but exciting investment."

Athanase raised his eyebrows. He had not anticipated being asked for such a sum. "I need think about that much. I see you week coming and talk again."

"Okay, but I am going to talk to Eugène Cornuché and François André about setting this up in Deauville. Cornuché is the owner of the casino there, and André runs it and will probably take it over shortly. We will need a base and that looks to be the best one, with the racetrack nearby and the cachet that the place has acquired in the last few years."

The group split up, but Eli stayed back to talk to Nico. He frowned deeply. "Do you trust Vagliano?"

"I think we can get him to invest and we'll get a lawyer to draw up an agreement which will hold him. My main worry is that he will want to play too often. I have watched him in action and, unlike Zaret and myself, he is impetuous at the card table and, frankly, not very good. He can also be incredibly rude, as you have seen, which will not go down well with the type of players we are going to attract. We will have to see how it goes and try and limit his participation as much as we can. We can't do without him; the money he is hopefully contributing will be the difference between success and failure. I just don't see any others who fit the bill."

"I hope you're right, but I think we need to be prepared to pull the plug if we run into problems."

"Agreed."

As the meeting appeared to be over, Nico stood up ready to leave, but then turned to Eli as if he had just remembered something important.

"I never asked you before, but are you okay with taking on a larger role in the bookmaking? That'll be an important side-line and is vital for the syndicate: it gives us a lot of information on the financial positions of the customers who'll no doubt also want to take us on at the tables."

"Hmm...I'd already thought of that. It is certainly helpful to know as much as possible about a man's resources when you face him across the baize. It definitely affects the way he's likely to play." He paused for a moment and drained what remained of his drink. "In answer to your question, I will miss the tables, but I know that I'm not in the same league as you and Zaret, and we must give ourselves the best chance of winning, which precludes me playing except on odd occasions."

He rose from his chair, as if about to leave, but then sat down again and leant across to place his hand on Nico's arm. "I've always enjoyed the undercover nature of our bookmaking operations and now that I'm getting to know the clientele, there is even a rather agreeable social aspect to the role. So, yes, I am more than happy to become the front man for that part of our enterprise."

"Glad you agree. Now I have to tackle Eugène Cornuché, but I'm going to get at him through François André, who I think could be a useful ally going forward. Eugène is getting old and will not necessarily embrace our vision with the required enthusiasm. François is young and eager."

Nico strode towards the exit. "This is going to be exciting," he cried over his shoulder, "but I have a good feeling about our idea."

"So do I," was the enthusiastic response.

◆

The next morning Nico set out early for the Cercle Haussmann.

He knew that François André would be there, as it was his fledgling club and needed his full attention whilst establishing itself.

He had had previous negotiations with François, who had heard about the activities of the newly formed Greek Syndicate and wanted a piece of the action. François had successfully persuaded them to transfer some of their gambling activities to the Haussmann and was already therefore an associate supporter of their cause. Nico hoped that this morning's meeting would cement their relationship and bring the club owner closer to being a full member of their group.

"Good morning, François. I trust you are well."

"I'm fine, but busy. How can I help you, Nico?"

"I have a proposal for you. As you well know, I play baccarat with Eliopulo and Couyoumdjian against all-comers, and we run a bookmaking business on the side, which has brought a lot of extra business to the Cercle de L'Industrie and more recently to this club."

"I'm only all too aware of this. And?"

"I know that you and Eugène have been wanting to attract more high-spending customers to your casinos. The stunt you pulled at Cannes last year with the girls from Maxim's was genius. Nobody knew that they were merely showgirls dressed up to look like rich young heiresses. I'm sure the cost of setting all that up in secret must have paid off handsomely."

"It did, though it wasn't cheap. It was one of Eugène's shrewdest ideas. There's nothing like a pretty girl to pull in the millionaires!"

"Well, what I have for you is at least as good – I would argue even better – but won't cost you anything."

"Tell me more." He seemed interested rather than enthused and there was a subtle nervous tension in his posture.

"We have added a fourth member to our syndicate, Athanase Vagliano, who you will be well aware is extraordinarily rich. He has agreed to bankroll us and we would therefore like to start a game of baccarat en banque, where we always take the bank, but where there is absolutely no limit on the highest bid." Nico carefully ignored the fact that Vagliano was still yet to accept the offer of joining their group – he did not want there to be any doubt in André's mind as to the potential success of the venture.

André shook his head almost imperceptibly and frowned. The uneasiness he had shown earlier was now obvious. "That is incredibly brave, some would say foolhardy. There are some very rich gamblers who will want into that game, and the amounts they will be prepared to risk are astronomical."

"Exactly. I think that anyone who is a serious player will want to bring us down and they will beat down the doors of any casino offering such a game. That is where you come in: we'd like to start in Deauville."

"When?"

"In a few weeks' time at the Grande Semaine. Most of the wealthier patrons will be there for the racing, and the casino will be well attended in the evenings. This offers you an extra attraction, which should guarantee record attendance, with the associated revenue increase."

"Sounds interesting. But what exactly is in it for us? I will have to sell the idea to Eugène if I think it worthwhile."

Nico took his cigarette case from his jacket pocket, extracted one and lit it. He inhaled deeply before replying. "It's a great deal for you. We take the bank, absorb any losses and share the winnings with you. The final details can be sorted out in the next week or two, but I wanted to float the idea, as it does require a commitment from you."

André's body relaxed visibly, the earlier strain gone. "On the face of it, provided our cut is fair, I can't see too much downside. What would you want from us?"

"A special table reserved for us; that is all. You can put it in a private room, charge spectators to watch the games and there will probably be additional income generated by these onlookers gambling on the regular tables. I have thought this through carefully. The notion is so sensational that it will mean that none of the rich gamblers will want to play chemin-de-fer anymore. They will all be hell-bent on ruining us at our game."

André's reserve about the venture had disappeared completely. He spread his arms wide and smiled. "As far as the table is concerned, you know we already have our table four, which is reserved for what we call our 'wealthier clients'. It'll be easy to assign it to you and the syndicate. I will talk to Eugène, but I am pretty sure he'll go for it. We should all meet to work out the final numbers. I'll contact you to set that up."

"Excellent. Without wishing to get ahead of ourselves, if this is as successful as I think it will be, we'll take the show on the road and run the same games in Cannes, Monte Carlo and anywhere else we can generate interest. I'm sure we can even set up a game here from time to time."

"Sounds good, but we need to prove the concept works in Deauville first. Then I can sell the rollout to other casinos without too much trouble."

The two men shook hands and Nico went back to his apartment to share the news with Yola. The Greek Syndicate had taken its first steps to fame and fortune.

Chapter 12

1919–22 SCOTLAND & FRANCE

When Jack and Audrey first reached Britain, they had to contend with the imminent arrival of their firstborn. They opted for Scotland, as Jack had family there, and rented Auchans House, a 100-year-old mansion in Ayrshire. Their son Vernon duly appeared, but interfered little with their social life, as the availability of nannies and assorted servants meant that they could get on with introducing themselves to British society. The social scene locally was much more low-key than what they had encountered in Toronto, but Jack liked being near the family, even if his favourite Uncle George had perished not two months earlier, just after the end of the war.

Gwen arrived, which was much appreciated by Audrey, even if Jack found her presence rather intrusive. Although the two sisters were close and loved each other, they bickered constantly and could come to blows when tempers flared, as they often did.

Jack had been promoted to the rank of major whilst he and Audrey were still in Toronto, but had left the Air Corps just after that. He had employed a series of valets before the war and had an adequate batman whilst in Canada, but he had only ever been comfortable with one of them, a man named Jim Taggart who had served him admirably in early 1914. 'Tag', as Jack liked to call him, had managed to come through the conflict unscathed, at least physically, and when he enquired as to his availability, Jack was pleasantly surprised to find that the man was unattached, so he was invited to join the household.

Taggart was in his early forties by this time and was slightly rotund, with an air of authority that belied his age. People who met him guessed that he was north of fifty years old, and found him to be polite, charming, reserved and above all reliable. He was fond of Jack and made it his mission to shield him from anything that might disrupt his life, so he soon became much more than a simple valet. His only fault as far as Jack was concerned was that he disapproved of his master's gambling. As a result, he had seldom accompanied Jack to France.

Jack was now at a loose end, but found solace in visits to the Western Club in Glasgow, where he was able to satisfy his newly revived infatuation with betting. Although theoretically illegal, card games held in private clubs between gentlemen were common and there was little that could be done to regulate them.

He also took his first trip back to France since the war. This time, his interest was in the gaming clubs of Paris and in particular the Cercle de L'Industrie, which he had heard was the place for high stakes gambling. This club was frequented by many of the famous gamesters of the immediate post-war era, including Harry Selfridge, André Citroën and even Winston Churchill. The chance to pit his wits against such famous people added a frisson to the already considerable adrenalin rush he got from risking his wealth at the tables.

Another of the players in this group was none other than Nico Zographos – far less famous at this time than the others, but nonetheless already a force to be reckoned with.

Jack came across Nico on only his second night there. The tiny Greek was holding the bank as usual when Jack joined the group after a particularly delicious dinner, which had included one of his favourite dishes – foie gras. He always sought it out when in France, as it was never the same on the rare occasions when he could find it in Scotland.

He hardly noticed Nico on that first occasion and it wasn't

until he returned on the following evening that it dawned on him that this olive skinned little man had been monopolising the bank over both sessions. He asked his neighbour at the table if this was usually the case.

"Yes, he and his partner usually end up holding the bank by outbidding us all. It is rare that they allow anyone else in."

Jack was sceptical. "Why do they do it? The risk is enormous."

"They seem to think it worth their while. I would go so far as to say that they relish the opportunity."

"What is the man's name? I'd be interested in talking to him about why he does it."

"He's Nicolas Zographos – Greek chap who has been here only a few months. He and his partner are really making a name for themselves. He has gained quite a reputation for coolness under pressure and a knack for making the right plays at the right time."

Jack looked across the table at the little man and frowned. "So he is successful with this strategy? Probably won't last, not with so many millionaires to contend with."

"They also run a small bookmaking business on the side. You can lay bets on the horses right here if you're interested."

"I'm not one for the gee-gees - don't know enough about them, but thanks for the info."

Jack decided he would seek out this rather interesting character after the session was over. However, he never got the chance as one of his fellow challengers thwarted his plan by being accused of cheating.

They were well into the third shoe and the cards were being collected as a hand had concluded with a win for the opposite side of the table. A player on Jack's side had bet 8 plaques of 100,000 francs and his pile of tiles was sitting in the winning space. Before the croupier could pay out, a large gentleman had emerged from the shadows, placed a hand on his shoulder and murmured, "Monsieur, you have committed a *poussette*."

Amid sharp intakes of breath from the other participants, Jack's neighbour leant over and asked, " Pardon, Monsieur, but what is a poussette?"

"It's when a player nudges his pile of plaques to the winning side. When he originally placed the bet, he probably left his pile close to the line, so the movement would be minimal: the idiot hoped that no one would notice. Fat chance! The high stakes area has observers everywhere – it'd be easier to rob the Louvre."

The subsequent disruption caused by the perpetrator's vehement protestations of innocence followed by the arrival of the police and his abrupt removal from the club meant that the game disintegrated, with many wandering off. Nico decided that it was best to call it a night and he then disappeared to talk with the law, as he was the aggrieved party along with the club.

Jack therefore lost his opportunity and when he returned the next night the Greek was nowhere to be found. He returned to Scotland the next day.

Despite this, the short stay had revived his interest and expertise to the point where he could be called, for want of a better word, competent. The concomitant perks of being a serious player, the chance to rub shoulders with the rich and famous and the envious stares from the onlookers, continued to appeal to his need for validation: it was the nearest thing he could find that compared to his flying exploits in the war, but considerably less dangerous.

He began to make the pilgrimage to the gaming tables on the continent with greater frequency, but despite gambling in several of the Greeks' favourite venues, always managed to arrive too late or leave too early, thus avoiding a renewed encounter with Nico for the next few years.

◆

Back in Scotland, one of the things that drove him across the Channel was the presence of Gwen in the family unit. This had become more disruptive and rumblings of discontent began to surface within the household. She was forthright with her opinion.

"It is all very well taking bracing walks and going riding and hunting here in the backwoods of Scotland, but the parties are tedious, the company boring and you can forget about me finding a husband. I need to be down south where the action is."

Audrey was having none of that. "Good grief, Gwen, you live in the lap of luxury here, all thanks to us. Jack has family here and there is talk of him joining the firm. We can't arrange our lives to suit you."

"I'm not asking you to do that. You hate it up here just as much as I do, but you just won't admit it. You'd far rather be in London. It's not as if Jack can't work in Glasgow while we live there. We hardly ever see him now, as he spends so much time in France. And if he were working, it wouldn't be much different. I can't see the point of hanging around here getting bored."

"I may not find this ideal, but I have to think of Vernon as well. The countryside is good for a little boy. He would hate a big city."

"That's silly. He has a nanny who could take him to the parks and you'd spend time with him every day. It would make almost no difference to him; he's too small to notice yet. Once he gets a little older, you can spend more time in Scotland and teach him to ride and so on. I don't see why we should all suffer in the meantime."

"Well, we don't see it as suffering – far from it, in fact." And Audrey turned on her heel and left to go and walk in the garden.

What her sister had said was at least partially true, she thought. It would be fun to live in London, and she knew Jack would enjoy it. She would have to broach the subject, but preferred to think it over for the moment, giving herself time to decide how best to approach him.

As luck would have it, the opportunity arose a few nights later, when they were having a cocktail before dinner. As he savoured his second French 75, Jack was holding forth about the origins of his drink. "Did you know that his little concoction is named after the 75-millimetre field gun used by the French back in the war? It was fast and accurate and had a kick not unlike this little beauty."

"I admit it seems quite powerful." Audrey was on her third one and feeling quite tipsy. She had started to imbibe rather more liberally of late – a reflection of the strain of dealing with a small boy, a constantly absent husband and a recalcitrant sister whilst cloistered in the wilds of Ayrshire.

Jack had moved on to another of his favourite topics: why the Scots are superior to, and friendlier than, the English. "No question that we are more hospitable and fun than the southerners, though I suspect that one of the reasons is that we do not have an equivalent to the gay life of London, more's the pity. We are forced to make our own entertainment, which makes us necessarily more gregarious."

Audrey saw her opening. "So, why don't we go to London more often? We should get ourselves a place and then we could spend more time there, going to the theatre, visiting nightclubs and calling on all the friends you have from school, who we never see."

Jack now saw that his wife was well on the way to getting plastered and that meant he would have to tread carefully, as her temper when inebriated was legend. He moved towards the cocktail cabinet and took on a cautious tone. "I admit it would be fun, but I'm not sure how keen I am to run two households. I'd have to talk to Father about it, as I couldn't afford it as things stand. Also, I am not sure how often I could get away and it'd be hard to make much use of it. I could only get south once in a blue moon."

"But it wouldn't stop *me*." She almost spat out the last word. "You could scale back this house as you'd be using it alone most of the time, and we could have a larger staff in London. That might persuade you to spend more time with me. You could also cut back on the gambling, which would give you more time for both travelling south and your family."

Audrey could not resist this last dig and looked stubborn and defiant, which was always a prelude to some sort of outburst, particularly if she had been drinking. Jack wanted to avoid this, so he meekly succumbed and mumbled, "Let me have a think about it," before moving on to the subject of the hunt, which was guaranteed to distract her.

♦

Nothing further happened with regard to a move south, apart from the occasional mutter from Audrey, but it was becoming more and more appealing to Jack.

He was dressing one evening some months later and as usual Taggart was in attendance. "Will you be wanting to go into Glasgow this evening, sir?" he asked with a slight note of disapproval in his voice.

"You know Tag, I'm frankly getting a little bored with the Western Club; it's just too austere. The clubs down south are much more interesting and glamorous." He paused as Taggart helped him with his cufflinks. "I'm toying with the idea of getting a place in London. What d'you think?"

"It is hardly my place to opine, sir."

"Poppycock! Indulge me. You're usually very good at it and I always respect your judgment even if I don't agree with it."

Taggart thought for a moment and then said, "Well, it would certainly be agreeable to Mrs Coats and Miss Gwen, which would help. I can also assume that being based in the capital would give you much easier access to France and those dreadful casinos." He paused for a moment and cleared his throat as if what he was about to say might be indiscreet. "It is hardly my place to ask, but will running two households not put a strain on you and your resources, sir?"

"You've hit the nail on the head, Tag, as usual. As a family we can easily afford to have two places, but I'll need help from my father if we're to acquire a house in the capital. The money exists, but the old man's very mean about distributing it to his offspring, particularly me. It annoys me intensely that I have to go cap-in-hand to him any time I want something and you know how cantankerous he can be."

"I am sure you can use your considerable powers of persuasion with him."

"I hope you're right, Tag, I hope you're right." After a moment's reflection he turned to Taggart with a determined look in his eye. "Prepare me a bag. I shall go and visit him this weekend."

"Should I accompany you?"

"No – no need. I'll just stay the one night."

"Very good, sir."

So Jack invited himself to Dalskairth, his father's new house near Dumfries, where he lived a reclusive existence with his art collection. Now sixty-nine, he was beginning to have mobility issues similar to those of his father, who had been confined to a wheelchair at that age, so he had largely stopped entertaining. He took an interest in the company, as his wealth was dependent on its prosperity, but his contact with the family members was largely when he invited them on board one of his luxurious steam yachts.

Jack arrived on the Saturday evening and was shown to one of the multiple spare rooms by the butler. "Cocktails at seven and dinner at eight, Master Jack. If you need anything, you know where the bell is."

Jack dressed himself for dinner and made his way downstairs to the library, which was where his father liked to greet his guests.

He was very nervous, as he never felt comfortable around his father. He had the distinct feeling that he still did not rate much in the way of paternal approval, despite a distinguished war record. He wished it were otherwise.

He entered the room and found his father seated in his favourite chair. He shook him by the hand and said, "Hello, Father. I see you are in fine fettle. Audrey sends her love and Vernon asks after you."

"You do not visit me very often, so I don't know how Vernon can even remember me."

"You'd be surprised," he lied. "It is amazing what these little ones register and retain."

"Yes, well, I am sure you are not here just to be sociable. It is my experience that whenever you visit me it is for some specific reason and not just for the fun of it. So, fix me a cocktail and tell me what is on your mind."

"What would you like? I make an excellent Dubonnet and Gin."

"Fine. Make me one of those."

He took a deep breath and swallowed. This was the moment of truth and he would have to tread carefully if he was to get what he wanted. He moved to the drinks cabinet and started to make the cocktails, but did not look at his father as he spoke.

"Of course, you are right. Wonderful though it is to see you, I do have a purpose. I think it would be sensible if we discussed Tom's and my financial situation and our inheritance. You are not as young as you once were and although I'm sure you will continue for many years to come, it is always healthy to clarify one's intentions going forward."

His father remained silent and looked rather grumpy, so Jack made himself busy mixing the cocktails whilst deciding which tack to take. "I am aware that Tom has already got company stock, whereas I have nothing. You give me a very generous allowance and I cannot complain, but I would like to start building some capital and managing my own finances, now that I am over thirty. The small portfolio you gave me when I was incapacitated during the war has grown nicely and Mr McGregor has been very helpful, but the amount involved is pretty small. I am hoping for something more substantial." He omitted to mention that he had spent most of it to finance his gambling losses.

"That would be fine, but I have two problems with you, Jack. The first is your total lack of concern for the family business. By this stage in your life, you should be establishing a profession and, with the education you have had, you could easily make a significant contribution to J&P Coats. You appear to have a gift with numbers and your propensity for taking risks might actually inject some energy into some of our less adventurous relations."

Jack brought his cocktail over and placed it on the table beside Willie, who frowned and looked Jack straight in the eye. "But your only interest appears to be having a good time. You have absolutely no self-discipline and even less application."

"That's a bit harsh."

"Not particularly. It has been suggested several times that you join the company, but you seem hell-bent on avoiding it. The only thing that seems to warrant your commitment is gambling, something I disapprove of wholeheartedly."

"But, Father . . ."

"No buts. I had guessed that this'd be the reason for your visit, so I've actually given it some thought and I have a proposal for you. Firstly, you join the company as a director. I've spoken to the other family board members and they're looking to fill the vacancies left by my brother Thomas Glen and my cousin Daniel, who, in case you hadn't noticed, both passed on last year. This'll give you the right to a percentage of the company stock in a similar way to your brother and will allow you to establish some capital. Does that seem fair?"

"Absolutely. Will I need to be there full time?"

"I'd imagine so. You should get to Glasgow as soon as you can to discuss your role with my namesake, the new chairman. He'll fill you in on the details."

Willie took a sip of his cocktail and raised an eyebrow – whether in approval or distaste, Jack couldn't tell.

"Which brings me on to my – or rather, your – other problem. You're gambling way too much and it has got to stop. Your receipt of company stock is going to be contingent on you curtailing your visits to all gambling establishments, especially in France. If I don't see you making an effort to rein it in, we'll have to look at your allowance as well. Why don't you take up bridge or something less costly?"

Jack had not anticipated this turn of events and he was left almost speechless. He gathered himself and decided that his best option was acquiescence.

"All right, Father. I'll get to Glasgow as soon as I'm home and I promise to limit my gaming to the club in Glasgow, where the bets are never that big. I do enjoy it so much that I'm not sure I can stop completely. Will that be okay?"

"We'll see how it goes, but that seems workable for the time being."

At that precise moment the gong sounded to announce that dinner was ready and they repaired to the dining room, Jack helping his father into his wheelchair and guiding him to his place at the table. Once they started eating, the conversation inevitably turned to art and Jack steeled himself to listen patiently and ask the occasional appropriate question, all the while wondering how he would handle the restrictions his father was placing on him.

What was abundantly clear was that any move south would have to wait.

When he got home, he broke the news to Audrey, who was

furious. "And that's the end of it, is it? Here we are, one of the wealthiest families in the country and we can't live where we want to. Well, I am going to start going to London and will stay where I want, and Gwen will no doubt come with me. I'll be back for the hunt and the family's shooting get-together in the autumn as well as the occasional social event, but otherwise I am no longer prepared to go on living this rural existence. When you get it sorted out, you can join me."

Audrey stormed out of the room and slammed the door. Jack had a sinking feeling that this could be the beginning of the end for their marriage. He desperately wanted to try and save their relationship for Vernon's sake and also because he still loved her, not least because he found her spirited nature incredibly stimulating and attractive. On the other hand, her absence would clear the way for more frequent trips to France even though his father's restrictions made such sorties nigh-on impossible. He found himself in a bit of a quandary.

His visit to Glasgow was more harmonious. The new chairman, William Hodge Coats, greeted him with open arms and invited the other directors, amongst them his brother Tom and his cousin, another Tom, his Uncle George's son who he had shepherded through his early days at Eton, for lunch in the boardroom. His main role was to sort out the company's ever more complicated tax position, and once it was explained to him, he became sufficiently interested to make him think that his enforced employment might not be too bad.

The position with regard to betting was another thing altogether. He would have to see what could be done without his father, and therefore everyone else, finding out. He would need to find somewhere in France that flew under the radar, and that would not be easy. Come what may, it would need to be sorted if he was to keep his sanity.

Chapter 13

1922–26 FRANCE

For the first time ever, the Grande Semaine of 1922 in Deauville was preceded by a preliminary June season, which was inaugurated that year to try to prolong the relatively short period of extravagance that accompanied the influx of tourists, previously limited to a few weeks in August. The early days of the celebrations were more subdued than the hectic time when Nico wanted to put his plan into action, but that suited him fine.

For the opening day of the official festivities, anyone who wanted a room in any of the hotels, villas or pensions of Deauville – or even Trouville, across the other side of the River Touques – had to book it weeks and even months in advance. People were so eager to be seen there that they would share a bathroom with a complete stranger, one on a mattress on the floor and one in the actual bath. Sofas were occupied and people would sleep on anything in order to participate. New gowns, hats and silk scarves – the rage that year – were purchased in Paris. Cornuché and André had been extraordinarily successful in promoting the event, by hinting that the Kings of Belgium and Spain would be attending, as well as the Prince of Wales.

The typical participant in all the excess would arrive on the express train from Paris and then head for the Potinière, a place "to be seen" at midday, and where there was a good chance of running into somebody famous. Nico had arrived early to get the lie of the land and see who might be there to challenge the syndicate and was pleased to run across the King of Spain as well as the wife of William Wrigley Junior, the founder of the chewing gum empire, together with her daughter. These three would not be gambling, but lent the occasion a certain celebrity. More importantly, he also saw three others who definitely *would* be at the table. André Citroën, James Hennessey and Harry Selfridge – who had made fortunes on the back of motor cars, brandy and a department store, respectively – were inveterate gamblers and essential to making a success of his venture. There were many less well-known people as well, all trying to sell something, find a husband or wife, or con somebody out of a portion of their wealth.

By 1922, the resort had lost some of its cachet and had become a magnet for the nouveaux riches from Paris and the rest of Europe, as well as numerous Americans over in France to escape the strictures of prohibition. It was exactly for this reason that Nico had chosen this place and moment to set the Greek Syndicate loose – plenty of money and not too much class suited his style of gambling perfectly.

Two principal attractions brought people to Deauville: the racecourse and the casino. Both involved betting, but the latter was where the main event, baccarat, took place. The afternoon was when everyone went to the races; the ladies dressed in their finest millinery and the gentlemen in suits and Panama hats. Eli was there to be available to many of his clients who wanted a wager on the horses before taking on the Greeks in the evening. Some played or watched polo or tennis, but these attractions were over long before twilight, allowing the revellers time to relax and prepare for the night's entertainment.

This started at about half past nine, with a sumptuous dinner, exquisite wines and further carousing. The women donned the latest gowns, far too much jewellery and had their hair coiffured to perfection: the men were in smoking jackets with bulging wallets, ready for the long night ahead. Fireworks were let off on the terrace in front of the diners, which just heightened the excitement for things to come. Dancing followed, first by the professionals, and then the diners had a chance to trip the light fantastic in preparation for the main event.

People finally began to filter into the baccarat room. The attendance there was always a function of what was being said on the grapevine. If there were rumours that there were a lot of heavy gamblers going, then people would flock to either get a look or a piece of the action. This year, speculation was rife of something big happening, so the crowds were larger than ever. This was hardly surprising as, after agreeing to Nico's deal, both Eugène Cornuché and François André had been dropping hints in the clubs of Paris, and this had set the rumour mill going. The Greeks had also been indicating that something was up, so expectations were high.

People started to gamble in the main rooms, but the action at table four, the high-rollers' domain that had been set aside by André, was still non-existent. Then Nico, who had dined quietly on his own, away from the throng, entered the cordoned-off area and sat down at the table. Several others soon joined him, and within fifteen minutes the chairs were all filled and the croupiers were in position. A sizeable crowd of spectators also gathered behind the brass rail surrounding the playing area, despite the exorbitant fee of 500 francs, merely to watch. Amongst them were the King of Spain and Nico's three accomplices.

The main croupier then asked for bids to determine who would have the right to hold the bank. Several takers offered substantial sums and there appeared to be a winning bid, when Nico, making use of a moment of relative silence, quietly intoned, "*Tout va.*"

Everyone, spectators included, turned to look at the tiny man sitting in the middle of this group of excessively wealthy individuals. The croupier asked Nico to clarify what he meant.

"It is quite simple," he replied in a measured tone, "I, in representation of my associates, will accept any bid for any amount from any legitimate player. To put it in crude terms, the sky's the limit."

A gasp ran around the onlookers, apart from Eli, Zaret and Athanase, who looked at each other and smirked.

An American sitting several seats away from Nico stammered, "D'you mean that if I bet a million francs and several others do, you will accept all the bets? How can you manage to do that? If you lose a couple of times, you'll be bankrupt. This seems mad."

"It may seem mad to you, but I have rich associates with deep pockets. If you want an idea of how much we can accept, just take it from me that we are good for 50 million francs, which is beyond the reach of most, if not all, gamblers. If someone manages to break us, then they will have become extraordinarily rich. I wish you all *bonne chance*."

The evening thus got under way with Nico holding the bank. The white 100,000-franc plaques piled up all over the baize and although there were some of the red and blue tiles worth 10,000 and transparent 1,000-tiles, they were conspicuous by their absence. The players around this table had come to play for serious money and 10,000 francs was loose change.

The night progressed and fortunes ebbed and flowed, but as dawn was breaking it was apparent that the Greek Syndicate's first night had been a moderate success. They were slightly behind in terms of absolute winnings, mainly due to a rather unpleasant American going on a tear and taking nearly a million francs in a two-hour period. The rest had been well controlled by Nico.

Though financially unprofitable, it was commercially successful, in that the publicity generated for the casino and this particular game was almost incalculable. Word reached Paris, Cannes and Monte Carlo overnight, and people who had never even considered Deauville as a venue were now scrambling for tickets to get there and play. Accommodation in the area, which was already scarce, became inaccessible, even to the super-rich, and many sailed there, anchoring their yachts in the river and living on them, just to get a shot at the big game.

By the end of the season, the Greek Syndicate was marginally in the black, but their reputation had been cemented as the only gambling option for the prosperous and fearless.

Back in Paris after the frenzied weeks of gambling, there was much discussion amongst the members of the syndicate as to how to proceed. Nico was clearly the inspiration and leader of the group and he called them all to meet at the Cercle Haussmann, as he wanted François André involved as well, for he could open doors for them as they expanded their operation.

"The short time we had in Deauville accomplished what we hoped for," said Nico, "but there are several things that are going to need to happen if we're to get this to work."

The others listened out of respect for Nico's obvious talent, despite him being the youngest by ten years.

"The first thing is that we'll need to split the time spent at the tables, so those of us who are playing can remain fresh. I'm happy to take the evening sessions and I know that Zaret likes to do afternoons. As I've said before, I reckon we're the best players and with Eli running the bookmaking, we can get Athanase to fill in for us from time to time.

"Next, we need to decide where we go and when. A certain amount of dedication will be needed to make this a success and I need everyone's commitment to ensure that we're where we need to be at the appropriate time. This is no longer a game. It is a business and needs to be run that way."

"Finally, I need François to help me set up games in the casinos in and around Cannes. And you, Athanase, should be able to help us with Monte Carlo through your contacts in the Société des Bains de Mer."

Nico looked round the group to see if all of his partners had understood their role and were committed to his vision. He was pleased to note that even Athanase seemed happy with the way he was running things. He decided he had achieved what he wanted and could wrap up.

"Everyone who is anyone in the high-stakes gambling world is going to be coming after us. We are going to lose badly sometimes and it may get frightening at times, particularly if we get near to bankruptcy, but with skill, time and perseverance, we will end up ahead. Most of these rich gamblers do it for fun and don't bet either systematically or sensibly. We are totally different and that is why we cannot fail to win in the long run."

After this meeting the syndicate set out to fleece the richest people in Europe and America.

◆

Things did not go entirely as planned. The deluge of rich gamblers did indeed emerge and there were very lucrative days, followed by less profitable evenings. Slowly but surely their capital increased, though not significantly.

Many of the gamblers who played against Nico were famous, and the depth of the syndicate's pockets was tested on numerous occasions.

Early on in its existence, the Chilean finance minister, a Señor Ross, won 17 million francs from Nico – and then wanted to play double or quits. Nico declined, saying he had gone as far as he was prepared to go. Ross taunted him: "Is this bank open or closed? This was supposed to be a game with no limits." Nico, not for the first or last time, showed a level-headed nerve and repeated that he was done. Mercifully, those who witnessed the game viewed this positively, and this helped enhance his reputation for honesty and integrity.

André Citroën, who developed and became rich on the back of his eponymous motorcar, regularly lost a million francs in an evening, but was delighted to do so. He said that big losses brought him abundant publicity, which was what he sought, nay craved. He won from time to time, as the law of averages dictated, but that really didn't interest him. Nor did the glamorous *cocottes* seduce him, and he was almost completely teetotal. He lusted after power and publicity and was, unfortunately for him, a compulsive gambler. Nico viewed him as one of the syndicate's favourite customers.

He finally met his day of reckoning playing against Nico at

Deauville, losing 13 million francs in a single session. It would have been more, but his wife was playing chemin-de-fer in the casino and heard what had happened; she burst into the private room where the high-stakes game was being played – the first time a woman had ever entered the inner sanctum – and pleaded with the Greek to stop the game, saying, "My husband is crazy."

"Madame," Nico replied, "this is highly irregular. You ask me to persuade your husband to play for smaller amounts. I have done just that, but all he said was that an aviator ought to die flying, otherwise what's the point of being an aviator? Despite that, I will suspend the session immediately."

He turned to the remaining players and said, "I apologise, but I think it is better like this." He left the room, thus automatically ending the game.

He was very unhappy with both these incidents, as they reflected badly on the syndicate, which tried never to finish a game early. He was so concerned that he called a meeting of the group a few days later.

"I am sure you're all by now aware that I pulled the plug on two games in the recent past, one against the Chilean minister of finance, who wanted a frankly silly bet, and the other with Monsieur Citroën a few nights ago. I don't do such a thing lightly and I want to make sure that all of you are clear that we only cut a session short in extreme circumstances. It is bad for our reputation and that is bad for business. If any of you need to do so, please try and contact me beforehand if possible."

There were nods of assent all round. Nobody spoke.

"In this latter case, Citroën's wife was hysterical and I really had no alternative."

"I heard it was pretty unusual, particularly with her being a woman." Zaret was trying to be supportive.

"It was. I'd honestly never seen anything like it at the tables before. And yet, not everything about it was so awful – I can now see that it has presented us with an opportunity." Nico looked at the expressions of mild surprise on their faces. "Bear with me and I'll explain."

He paused for effect and then continued. "First, the bad news. Monsieur Citroën's loss has forced him to call in Lazard to help finance his huge car factory. He is one of our regulars, but even *he*" – Nico emphasised the word – "realises that he's gone a bridge too far in seeking publicity from his losses. It means he'll be doing less gambling and losing – for the moment."

His expression, which had been rather sombre, took on the suggestion of a smile. "But the good news is that now that a female has penetrated the high stakes area as Madame Citroën did, women are being permitted access to both the private baccarat room and, more importantly, the table: this introduces a new and lucrative group of players for us to exploit. Some of them, like the Dolly Sisters, will be playing with other people's money, something we should encourage, as they don't care if they lose something that isn't even theirs in the first place."

"Ah yes, the Dollies are cleaning out Harry Selfridge, who I'm sure you all know." Eli glanced at the others, who all nodded – except for Athanase, who spoke for the first time.

"I no know this man who sell fridges. Who is it?"

It was Nico who replied. "He's the founder of the famous London store that bears his name."

"Must be rich," muttered Athanase, sounding vaguely jealous.

Nico's assessment of the importance of Citroën to the syndicate was absolutely correct. His losses over the years to the members of the Greek Syndicate were estimated at 30 million francs.

One of Nico's favourite sayings was, "You win some, you lose some," and over the following year the balance worked in the Greeks' favour. They were able to extract some of their winnings and finance a more elegant lifestyle. Nico even bought himself a yacht, which he would have considered a wild extravagance some years before, but which he now viewed as a just reward for hard work.

But there was one very serious fly in the ointment, which became a major difficulty from several angles. Their problem was Athanase. He was not content to be a sleeping partner and insisted on playing rather too often. Nico tried to keep his participation to an absolute minimum, but he became belligerent and would either play against his own team, by financing and guiding a stooge to actually sit at the table, or would go and play chemin-de-fer in the outside rooms and lose large amounts there.

When he did represent the syndicate at the tables, he was very much a second-rate player, particularly compared to the brilliant Nico and the highly rated Zaret, and whilst these two were both renowned for their politeness and honesty, Athanase's strange way of speaking, and his habit of throwing his cards across the table when he lost, meant that he was viewed with suspicion and mistrust, and his temper tantrums scared some of the rich patrons away. He once spat at an American who had taken a lot of money off him.

Nico decided that, despite the capital infusion that Athanase had put into the partnership, they would have to find a way of extricating the syndicate from their agreement with him. He therefore approached François André with a view to him taking a twenty per cent stake, in exchange for which he would facilitate and promote games in the various casinos where he had influence or ownership, including the Cercle Haussmann in Paris. François readily accepted.

Fate intervened, however. Not long afterwards, in 1926, Athanase lost a great deal of money supporting the former Greek prime minister Eleftherios Venizelos, who had gone into exile. He asked Nico if their arrangement could be reviewed. Despite the risk involved in leaving themselves with a lower capital base, and with François securely on board, Nico leapt at the chance and they parted ways. From this point, the syndicate was always looking for financial backers to re-establish their safety net, though most declined.

At around the time the deal was struck with François, Sidney Beer, a young and wealthy amateur orchestra conductor, had a run against Nico where he won seven and a half million francs, in what he described as "one of those extraordinary streaks of fortune which come to some people once in a lifetime and to others not at all".

When everything was going well, Sidney decided to go to the bar for a drink, but was called back almost immediately by the little Greek, who was keen to get some of his money back. Alas, it was not to be. In the last five coups, Sidney won one and a half million francs more, by betting 100,000 on the first coup and raising it by that amount for each hand, with half a million going on the last one. He won them all, at which point Nico suddenly stood up, bowed to everyone and announced, "That is enough for this evening."

The next day, Nico approached Sidney in his hotel and offered him a stake in the syndicate. He refused but regretted it later on. In the very next season at Deauville, he lost his million and a half, and by the end of the following year had given back all he had won and more.

Sidney's losses were partly from betting on the racecourse, where he was allowed a 2 million-franc floating credit line. This was something that Eli, who ran that side of the business, had started to offer to many of his high-worth clients, as he found it very useful in both facilitating big ticket betting and, almost more importantly, to get a feel for exactly how much each of his customers was worth in both liquid and other assets. This information was shared with Nico, whose encyclopaedic memory allowed him to use his knowledge of a particular player's finances to judge how he would bet.

In the course of the first few years of the syndicate's existence, Nico came close to bankruptcy on numerous occasions, but the large capital base they enjoyed, courtesy of

Athanase, had saved him. Even so, it was not unknown for him to interrupt a session halfway through a shoe, even more abruptly than in the incident with Sidney Beer. He had done this several times when playing against Citroën and another of his frequent adversaries, James Hennessy, of cognac fame. Although Nico disliked these sudden exits from the game and had warned the other members against them, they gave the syndicate a vulnerability that emboldened the other gamblers and helped to increase the number of challengers. Everyone thought they could get the better of them, and that played to the syndicate's strength: the more money they churned, the greater their chances of coming out ahead.

But with Athanase's exit and their lower capital base, they were exposed as never before. A clearly less financially secure Greek Syndicate was about to enter the most vulnerable chapter of its existence. Nerves of steel would be required.

Chapter 14

1926 FRANCE

With Athanase now a memory, the syndicate moved south to the French Riviera and the area around Cannes. The high-stakes gamblers went with them and activity on the main table at Cannes was particularly frenetic that year. Although the syndicate had built their reserve back up to 30 million francs, each member started to withdraw money to support a more lavish lifestyle, so that Nico soon found that what he had feared all along was happening: their lower capital was a little too small for comfort, and they could easily find themselves on the verge of insolvency if the cards ran against them for too long. One such streak occurred in 1926.

The collected gamblers could scent blood and knew that the syndicate was close to breaking; so betting had been particularly heavy. Nico was literally down to his last million: his partners could not help and François André, their newest recruit, did not dare, given his position at the casino.

The play had reached the stage where there was a million francs riding on the latest coup. Nico dealt the cards and turned to look at the player on his right, who waved his hand over the top of the cards he had been dealt, indicating he did not want a third card. That meant he had either six or seven. Nico turned his attention to the man on his left. He shook his head and turned his cards over, showing the jack of spades and the eight of hearts – a "natural". Nico felt a gnawing sensation in the pit of his stomach, but maintained an implacable expression.

He stubbed his cigarette out, turned his cards face up and looked down at them. The king of hearts and the queen of spades, which is known as a bouche or baccarat – the worst hand possible. His heart sank.

The spectators started to murmur amongst themselves. They all knew from the way things had been going over the previous nights, and the evidence of the ever shrinking pile of chips in front of the banker, that the situation were pretty dire. It appeared that they could be witnessing the end of the Greek Syndicate.

Now Nico's only salvation would be to pull a nine, and he knew that nineteen of the twenty-four nines in the shoe had gone, with a little less than half of the 312 cards to go. For once he wished that he didn't have the ability to count the cards and calculate the probabilities. That way he would be able to draw the next card with blind ignorance like everyone else, rather than with the sure knowledge that his chances of getting one of the remaining nines was about one in twenty-nine, or just over three per cent. He grabbed another cigarette and lit it. Anything to postpone the moment of truth.

He extracted the next card from the shoe and held it face down on the table for a moment, trying to control the trembling of his right hand. He was normally icy cool when playing cards, but the stress of the moment was almost unbearable and he could feel the sweat breaking out down his back and on his brow. The next ten seconds would shape the rest of his life. He felt quite faint, but could put it off no longer. He turned the card over.

It was the nine of diamonds.

He had won the coup, doubled his money and averted the crisis. There was a ripple of uncharacteristic applause from the throng of onlookers and he let out a deep sigh of relief. He was safe!

"I am sorry, ladies and gentlemen," he said, "but the emotion of this last coup was such that I am forced to take a break to recover. I will be back in due course. Please excuse my abrupt exit, but I hope you will understand."

He arose from the table, moved hastily to the bar and broke with a lifelong tradition by ordering a glass of champagne.

He had been right about this game shaping the rest of his life. He was so enamoured of the nine of diamonds that he had a tie-pin made with nine diamonds, cufflinks with the card on them, and used it for the personal pennant of his yacht. His treasured cigarette case was engraved with the card and he even had his glassware and china decorated with the same emblem.

As this crisis passed, the number of investors grew and the various members of the group were able to continue withdrawing cash from their accumulated winnings. Long streaks of bad luck mercifully disappeared and the syndicate was finally well established, so Nico could turn his attention in part to other things.

One of these was his family back in Greece, with which he had had little communication. His relationship with his father had been strained after his abrupt removal from university, and even his mother had found him distant during the years he spent in Athens after his return from Germany. Since leaving Greece, he had had little to no contact with his parents or indeed any other family members. He still resented the fact that he had been forced into his current precarious career, but as things got easier and his plan seemed finally to be working, his animosity towards them lessened. He began to feel sorry for his behaviour and wanted to make amends. He also became more interested in the reason for his father's impoverishment.

He started to ask around amongst the Greek community both as to how his parents might be faring as well as the cause of the fateful bankruptcy. The last he had heard was that his father was poorly and that they were struggling to make ends meet, despite some support from his siblings. He began to send money to them anonymously, which helped to assuage his guilt, but he made no attempt to communicate with them directly.

Then he received a message from a total stranger that read as follows:

M. Zographos,

I would like to introduce myself. My name is Dmitri and my surname is unimportant. I am a Greek national and, having lived all over Europe, I have finally settled in France, which I find is the most agreeable country in the region, despite the damage inflicted on its infrastructure during the war and the rather tedious language.

The reason for contacting you is simple. I became aware of your father's unfortunate situation while I was still in Greece, and my subsequent travels through Germany and the United Kingdom brought me into contact with both the fallout from the mine disaster that would prove so devastating for your family and also with the person in the UK who was indirectly the cause of your misfortune.

I know you are a man of means and wonder if you would be willing to negotiate a fair price for me to disclose to you the name of this person and where he is located. My absolute discretion is guaranteed and I assure you that the information I have is reliable.

I look forward to hearing from you.

Dmitri K.

Obviously his curiosity about his father's ruin had brought someone out of the woodwork. His interest piqued, Nico arranged for a meeting at a café he often frequented. The whole thing struck him as being ridiculously cloak-and-dagger, as his informant said he would carry a copy of *Le Monde* under his left arm, whilst he asked Nico to wear a red carnation in his buttonhole.

He arrived at the appointed hour and sat at a table outside the café. It was a beautiful morning and he liked to sit and study the people going by. It amused him to try to guess what each of them did, how wealthy they were and how they lived. He viewed it as an extension of what he did with his rivals when playing cards.

He ordered an orange juice and waited patiently. After about twenty minutes he was about to leave when a tall, olive-skinned gentleman with a neat moustache and a copy of *Le Monde* under his arm approached the table.

"I assume you are Monsieur Zographos? I am Dmitri. May I sit down?"

"Please do."

"Thank you. Let me order a coffee and then we can talk."

He called the waiter and ordered his coffee and a croissant. He then leant over and almost whispered to Nico. "I think you will be interested in what I have to tell you. It will give you some background on what actually happened in the coalmine and, in part, it exonerates your father, as he could not have foreseen what happened. He was a victim of extremely bad luck."

"That is definitely not my view," Nico replied, "but I can tell you that I am willing to compensate you if the intelligence you have is what I'd classify as useful and trustworthy. I will have to be the judge of that."

"This leaves me in a bit of a quandary. How do I know you will pay me once I have divulged my information?"

"You don't, but as I am sure you have already learned from your no-doubt extensive research of my well-known exploits in the casinos of France, I am renowned for my honesty in all things, and particularly when it relates to payments and debts. You'll have to trust me." He took a sip of his almost depleted drink, whilst the waiter appeared with Dmitri's order. "But before we even get to that, what sort of sum had you in mind?"

"I know that the syndicate is doing well, so you can afford to be generous. I was thinking in terms of half a million francs."

Nico raised his eyebrows and shook his head. "I am afraid that we will be unable to do business at that level, but I would like to thank you for your time. I will bid you farewell." He made to get up and leave.

"Wait a minute, Monsieur Zographos. I have given you a quantity that I believe is fair, but I expected you to at least make a counter-proposal."

"It is difficult to counter an offer that is so far from reality, but if you want a number, I would be prepared to go as high as 25,000 francs. That is a number where we could do business."

"We are a long way apart from each other indeed. I am not sure that will be enough."

"Then, as I already said, we should part company." He regarded his companion with interest. This man was obviously out for whatever he could get and would certainly take that amount of money, so he continued, "Look, your knowledge of events is of interest to me, but is not vital for me to continue with my life. You, on the other hand, are in a weak position, as the only person for whom your information is significant, and has the resources to pay you, is sitting across the table. If I walk away, what you have ceases to have any value at all. It is therefore better for you to take what I am offering, as you have no alternative."

Dmitri looked dispirited. "Could you not make it a little bit more?" He was obviously not above grovelling.

"No. This is a 'take it or leave it' situation. I am taking the risk that the name you give me is useless, but I am prepared to do so at this level of financial commitment. You must understand that money doesn't grow on trees. It is a fair offer and I will pay you right now, before we leave this table." Nico extracted an envelope from his pocket and put it on the table. "Here is the money. Tell me your story."

"All right, I can see your point." Dmitri looked longingly at the envelope and licked his lips as he prepared to reveal his secrets. "As I said before, the failure of the mining company was not really your father's fault."

"I am sorry," said Nico, "but the fact that he made such a speculative investment means that he has to take at least some level of blame. I accept that the failure of his other asset at the same time was unfortunate, but mathematically probable, at quite a significant level."

Dmitri regarded Nico for a moment before continuing. "Well, when I was in Germany, I stumbled, quite by accident, on the story of the German mine. It was situated in the Ruhr valley and was not an open-cast lignite mine like most in that area, but rather an underground pit. During the early shift on that fateful day, there were about 200 miners working down below. At around 7:45 a.m., an explosion occurred in one of the shafts at a depth of more than 1,500 feet. The explosion was strong enough to lift the manhole cover off the shaft and fourteen miners were killed outright, while another twenty-two were injured. Some of those who died underground were burned beyond recognition."

"That sounds horrible."

"It was, but the investigation into what happened exonerated the management. The guilty party seems to have been one of the miners who was smoking, in direct contravention of the company rules. The company went under, not because of the accident or any mismanagement, but simply because one large investor got cold feet after what was an admittedly bad, but not disastrous, explosion. It never got into the press and didn't seriously threaten the solvency of the company involved. Other mines have survived worse and come back to prosper."

"Okay, but I find it hard to accuse one single person of engineering our family tragedy. It's a naïve way of absolving my father of all guilt and it doesn't sit well with me. It strikes me as an easy way out."

"I'm just telling you what happened and not passing judgment, but for what it's worth, I don't think your father was that gullible. The investment was sound and the sudden withdrawal of funds was the straw that broke the camel's back."

"But you now know who the 'guilty party' was? That is the information for which I am willing to pay."

"I spent time in the UK subsequent to this and was sufficiently intrigued to follow up, as the records in Germany didn't name him. After asking around, I was reliably informed that it was a Scottish investor from the family that runs the very successful textile business called J&P Coats: his name is William Coats and he is one of the family."

Nico frowned. The name rang a bell, but he couldn't think why. Perhaps one of his gambling cronies had mentioned it at some point. "I have never heard of him, but that is interesting and I will store the name away for the future." Nico placed his hand on the envelope in front of him, tapping it with his fingers. "You have obviously spent a good deal of time on this, so you will be pleased to discover that when you open the envelope in front of you, it contains not 25,000, but 30,000 francs."

"That is most kind. Does that mean you had intended to pay me that all along?"

"Yes, but there is a small caveat with the extra cash. I have good contacts with some people who are less agreeable than myself, and if I find out that you have cheated me in any way, I will send them to find you."

"I'm not concerned. The information you have is rock solid and, as a show of good faith, I have a sheet of paper where I have noted the names of all the people I contacted and a synopsis of what I have divulged today. You can check it for yourself." He handed Nico a piece of paper, scooped up the envelope, bowed slightly and hurried away.

So now Nico had the name of the man who had changed his destiny. He was not sure whether to curse him or thank him, but at least he could now weigh his options.

Chapter 15

1926 SCOTLAND & ENGLAND

While Nico Zographos was discovering who had changed his life and the Greek Syndicate was restructuring its finances, Jack Coats had already spent several years at the family firm, something he endured rather than enjoyed. He found tax matters intellectually challenging, but the mundane nature of most of the problems and the frustration of dealing with the UK tax authorities did not stimulate him in the same way as the cut and thrust of high-stakes gambling. He also found that, although he now had a share of the company, the fight over minimising their tax liability did not give him the same buzz as risking large amounts of his own money. He missed the people too.

But his father's control of his behaviour did not slacken and he was conscious of Willie's constant interest in where Jack had been and what he was up to. The occasional trip to London was accepted, as Willie understood that Audrey was spending less and less time in Scotland and something had to be done to preserve their marriage. In truth, most of these "conjugal visits" degenerated rather quickly into shouting matches, interspersed with the very occasional tender moment, one of which resulted in the birth of their daughter April in that very month of 1926.

But most of his time in London was taken up with finding clandestine gambling establishments, and it was during one such visit that he stumbled across Club 43, a place Kate Meyrick, the nightclub queen, had opened at 43 Gerrard Street in Soho in November 1920. Although there was little gambling to be had there, he liked the atmosphere and the sheer thrill of being involved in something at the margin of the law, for although serving alcohol was not illegal as such, the new licensing laws prohibited it after ten at night – and as the club stayed open till six in the morning, they frequently ran afoul of the London constabulary.

The basement was used as a dance hall and the ground floor housed a large lounge. The bar was located in a small room accessed via a locked door, with the manager holding the key at all times. The 43 Club offered dinners, suppers and breakfasts alongside the illicit alcohol. It cost ten shillings to get in, collected at the door, and customers paid to dance to jazz bands and artists, with "Meyrick's Merry Maids" encouraging them to spend even more. The club was popular with royalty – notably the Prince of Wales, who Jack knew from both his time in London during the war as well as in post-war Paris – and luminaries, including actors Rudolph Valentino and Tallulah Bankhead, jazz musician Harry Gold, and authors J.B. Priestley, Evelyn Waugh and Joseph Conrad. Jack enjoyed this celebrity aspect of the place.

For gambling, hopefully away from the prying eye of his father, Jack relied on his friends who were members of clubs such as White's and Brook's, where he could be invited as a guest and would have to content himself with whatever games were available, even settling for bridge, which at least allowed him to practise card playing. But it certainly was nothing like baccarat.

Most of his time, however, was spent in Scotland, riding with the Eglinton Hunt when the opportunity arose, and commuting from Ayrshire to Glasgow to wrestle with the company's taxes, which had become more complex and draconian, as the government was trying to pay for the First World War. In particular, they had introduced a new tariff in 1915 called Excess Profit Duty, and Coats contested the government's interpretation of EPD, the matter dragging on till 1926, by which time the Inland Revenue's demands had been whittled down to one and a half million pounds. A meeting was set up to see if an agreement could be reached, with government representatives on one side, and the company lawyer, their accountant and Jack Coats on the other. It had been going for hours and they had been round the houses several times, but had reached an impasse with a difference of 100,000 pounds between the parties.

"I don't see any alternative but to go to court." The company lawyer sighed. "We really didn't want to get to this, but we will not cede this last 100,000. No way."

The exhausted and frustrated Inland Revenue team looked at each other, not quite sure what to try next.

Jack piped up. "Why don't we get your boss over to see if he can help break this deadlock? I know that nobody wants to fight this in court, where we'll get an arbitrary decision that's unsatisfactory for both parties and expensive."

A secretary was dispatched to call Mr Benstead, the Glasgow area head of the tax office, and everyone broke for a cup of tea. Twenty minutes later he appeared and agreed to sit and listen to the two sides' points of view. He then requested a few minutes with his team, after which he promised he would have a compromise of some sort for the Coats trio.

When they returned to the meeting room, he stood in front of the whole group and summarised. "We have beat this thing to death and I can see that nobody is going to budge. I have suggested to my team that splitting the difference might work, but they are not keen, and it seems that you three from Coats will be even less so. Nobody wants recourse to the law, so I therefore have a rather unusual suggestion." He swallowed, adjusted his tie, rooted around in his pocket for some loose change and extracted a two-shilling piece from his pocket. "We should toss a coin for it."

You could have heard a pin drop. The Coats team sat there open-mouthed at such an outrageous idea. When they had collected themselves, Jack asked for a moment to consider the proposal. The tax team filed out.

"We should go for this," he said, his instinct as a gambler immediately coming to the fore. "Win or lose, we will incur no legal fees and we know that a court decision will be just about as capricious as a coin toss but will be costly and take a lot longer. At least this way we will have a quick result and the whole thing will be behind us."

Given that he was a director of the company, the other two were in a relatively weak position to argue and after some nominal objections, they agreed.

For the first time since joining the company, Jack actually felt a buzz as he re-entered the meeting room. "You're on," he said and prepared to call.

"Okay," said Benstead, "I'll flip the coin and you choose heads or tails." He sent the florin spinning high in the air with his right thumb. As it rose, the electrified audience heard the flying ace call heads. The coin duly fell to earth and, after wobbling on the ground for a few seemingly interminable seconds, the result was revealed. He had called correctly, saving the company a small fortune in less than a minute.

But that was not the end of the story. Two weeks later, Jack was sitting in his office when he received a call out of the blue from Benstead, who politely but firmly requested his immediate presence at the Glasgow office of the Inland Revenue.

Jack called the company lawyer. "David, can you think of any reason that the tax people would want to see me? Have we done anything unusual that I don't know about?"

"Not that I'm aware of," was the reply. "Best to go along and see what he wants, but say as little as you can."

Unsure what to expect, he set out.

When he was shown into Benstead's office, the taxman greeted him warmly and handed him a small presentation box. "I wanted you to have this as a memento of our negotiations. It is certainly one of the most long-drawn-out discussions I have ever been involved in and I think it merits a souvenir of some sort." Inside was a silver florin on a piece of purple velvet and the inscription *To the only man who tossed the Inland Revenue for £100,000 and won.* Jack would treasure it more than his many casino successes.

This turned out to be one of the last important jobs Jack did for the company, for not long afterwards Willie Coats died. Jack was not in Scotland when it happened, so he never had the chance to say goodbye, but Audrey and he attended the funeral. The father-son relationship had never been warm and Willie's natural antipathy towards his offspring, combined with his rather unemotional demeanour, had always got in the way of any chance they had at intimacy. Jack had a grudging respect for his dad, though he never really loved him.

His demise released the purse strings for Jack, who inherited the rather magnificent sum of 2 million pounds. Unfortunately, not all this wealth came in liquid assets, and the scale of inheritance tax, which had been introduced in 1894 at eight per cent, but which had reached much higher levels after the war – a sliding scale up to forty per cent – gave Jack and his brother Tom a real headache. As their father had died intestate, they ended up with a colossal tax bill, and this time Jack had no way of negotiating his way out of it. They ended up selling many of Willie's paintings to help settle the debt.

But what was left was still a fortune and, given Jack's profligate nature, he started to spend it immediately.

He acquired a number of horses, both for recreation and racing, and he began to maintain several stables and a trainer. This, as with many of his disbursements, was partly to appease Audrey, whose temper was as fiery as ever, which could and did make things most uncomfortable for him. He preferred a quiet domestic life, which allowed him to pursue his other interests, so anything he could do to keep her happy was worth any effort and expense.

Both he and Audrey had always enjoyed entertaining, but now they began to do so on a grand scale, initially in Ayrshire. They had held many lavish dinner parties at Auchans when they first arrived there, but now they raised their game, flying in oysters from the south, champagne from France and all manner of exotic dishes to delight the palates of their guests. They took over Turnberry Hotel, which had been refurbished after the war, to hold one of the most elaborate fancy dress balls ever seen in Scotland.

They were at their best when partying: he was the gracious host and she was the life and soul, bolstered up by ever increasing amounts of alcohol. At these affairs, they scarcely had to converse with each other and were a paragon of politeness when chatting to guests together, so a form of armistice existed within the family. Jack even came to tolerate Gwen.

But his extravagance did not stop there. He bought one of the most luxurious houses in the world, in Gloucester House on the corner of Piccadilly and Old Park Lane, and they spent 60,000 pounds refurbishing it, 10,000 of it on marble bathrooms. It had twenty-two rooms, eleven servants and a view out across Green Park, towards Buckingham Palace. A delighted Audrey installed herself there along with sister Gwen. Their visits to Scotland were reduced to the occasional sortie either for sumptuous festivities, or to ride with the hounds, where both sisters were expert horsewomen and genuinely enjoyed the thrill of the hunt.

Any restrictions on Jack's gambling were now lifted, as no other family member could wield the financial power over him that his father had exerted. With Audrey appeased, he set his sights on the casinos of France and an inevitable encounter with Nico Zographos and the Greek Syndicate.

Chapter 16

1927 FRANCE

Once they had the place in London, Jack's interest in all things to do with the company waned rapidly and his trips to France resumed. He found that getting to Paris from London was quick and relatively painless, and it was pretty simple to get to the south of France from Paris. The train was an option and although flying was still quite primitive and dangerous, the risks involved were as nothing compared to his exploits as a member of the RFC.

His first sortie after his windfall inheritance was to the Cercle Haussmann in Paris. He set out to find a high-stakes game, but there was none to be found as it was still early in the year and the Greeks were in the south of France. As usual, most of the heavy-hitters had followed them there.

He played a shoe at the highest stakes table he could find, but despite taking the bank, he found the action bland and uninteresting. Even the people playing seemed grey and lifeless. He quickly became bored, so he ceded the bank to another player and went to the bar to speak to the barman. "Where can a fellow find a serious game of baccarat? I've looked around and there is no sign of any action at all at the main table. Where is everyone?"

"Monsieur, this is always a quiet time of year for the big games. We sometimes get a little action, but those nights are few and far between until the Greeks return. If you want to get better information, I can find the boss for you."

"And who is in charge here? Is it still François André?"

"Indeed, sir. I'll go and get him for you."

Jack sipped his gin-and-French and waited for François to appear. After a few minutes a tall, good-looking and incredibly suave Frenchman in his late forties appeared and greeted Jack like a long-lost friend, with a firm handshake and an overzealous hug. "Monsieur Coats, it seems ages since we last saw you here in Paris. What has kept you away?"

Jack was slightly taken aback by this display of Gallic affection, but he responded in kind. "It's not for want of trying to get here, but circumstances have conspired against me and it's been frankly difficult to get away. However, that's about to change, and I'll be back far more often from now on."

"Delighted to hear that. What can we do for you?"

"I am looking for some *divertissement* on the baccarat table, but have been sorely disappointed so far. What has happened to the famous Cercle Haussmann? The last time I was here, the joint was jumping, and all the usual suspects were here – Citroën, Selfridge, Hennessy and various royals. I hear they're in the south; chasing the sun, no doubt."

"Chasing the Greeks is more like it."

"Ah, yes, I have heard a little bit about them. So, what's the story? I know bits and pieces, but I am sure you can fill me in."

"They're a small group of gamblers who have substantial financial backing and play cards more as a business than a game. They will take absolutely any bet, no limits. All your wealthy friends are trying to break them, with little success so far."

"Interesting. I look forward to meeting them. Can you keep me informed as to where they will be playing? I will give you my contact details."

"Certainly. It would be my pleasure, as I am now a sleeping partner with them and we are always looking for new competition."

"Who are the main players? Would I know them?"

"A gentleman called Nico Zographos is their front man. You must have heard his name."

"It is familiar, though I'm not sure if I've met him."

"You'd remember him. He's a very gifted gambler and is really dark-skinned and tiny. He stands out in a crowd precisely due to his stature, or rather lack of it. But make no mistake – he is a formidable opponent."

"I seem to remember coming across him just after the war, but in those days he was just another player, albeit a highly skilled one. Always took the bank, if my memory serves me well. I can't wait to cross swords with him once again. Truly good baccarat players are uncommon, even if I can't say I necessarily approve of his current methods. Card games should be fun, and gentlemen should treat them as such. That is my philosophy."

"You two are going to be an interesting contrast." François frowned and then his expression changed as if he had just thought of something amusing. He chuckled. "It just occurred to me – you are Scottish, no?"

"Yes, though it doesn't affect my prowess with playing cards." He laughed at what he thought was a clever remark.

François ignored him. "It's just that Monsieur Zographos has become obsessed with the nine of diamonds after winning an unlikely and lucrative hand because of it. I am sure you know what they call that card?"

"No."

"It is known as the 'Curse of the Scots', which I find rather amusing."

"I have honestly never come across that term. Where does the expression come from?"

"That's a good question and one that I can answer, as I've

done a little research on the subject. Like all good legends, there are several theories as to its origin." François looked rather pleased with himself and waited.

Jack, who had been toying with his drink, looked up and, sensing a void in the conversation, made an encouraging grunt. This seemed to satisfy the Frenchman, who continued.

"One is that James IV, King of Scots, wasted time searching for that very card before the Battle of Flodden in 1513 against England, instead of preparing for the conflict, which Scotland lost. Another was that a thief tried to steal the jewels from the crown of Mary, Queen of Scots, and got away with nine diamonds. As a result, all Scotland had to pay tax for the theft."

François was warming to his subject and leant forward so close to Jack that he recoiled slightly. His voice dropped to a whisper and his tone became almost conspiratorial.

"But the most cogent has to do with the card game Pope Joan, popular in the last century. In this game, the nine of diamonds is the most powerful card, and it is called the Pope, who the Scots detested. Hence, the curse of Scotland."

"I'm amazed never to have encountered it before." Jack leant back and picked up his cocktail and was about to take a sip when he put the glass back down and asked, "What is our Monsieur Zographos like?"

"He is cool and calculating, has a phenomenal memory and an amazing knack for knowing when to bet heavily and when to abstain. Nobody quite understands how he does it."

"Well, you've certainly managed to whet my appetite for a game with this gentleman. You are a highly effective salesman."

François smiled warmly. "Just part of my job. I look forward to introducing you to each other."

"Excellent, but that doesn't solve my current problem. What do I need to do to get some decent action this evening?"

"It's hard to pull people in at this time of year. They want to see more heavy gamblers before they are prepared to venture out. I can call around and see if your name might not bring in a few of the regular plungers, but I'm not hopeful."

"Tell you what, François. I'll go back to the table, take the bank and promise to pay anyone who wins against me twice the normal pay-out. They make the same wager with the same losses as ever – I will assume all the additional risk. Tell them that and prepare for a stampede."

With that, Jack turned and headed back to the table, drink in hand. He waited while the current crop of players finished the last few coups of the session. He made good use of the time, watching the participants to see who were the more gifted, and how they reacted to wins and losses. When the break came, he repeated his offer and was immediately given a seat at the table. By this time, François had got word around and several of the wealthy locals had turned up, hoping to make a killing.

The first coup was typical of the rest of the evening. The cards were dealt and whilst one opponent declined a third card, the other asked for one and was shown a king of clubs. Jack turned over his cards and had a jack and a four. Not great. He pulled a third card and was rewarded with a second four. The player who had not drawn showed he had an ace and a six, so Jack had won both sides.

Play continued for several hours and although the bank lost the occasional hand, these setbacks were very occasional. By six in the morning, everyone but Jack was exhausted and significantly poorer. François André, who had been keeping an eye on proceedings, was impressed.

◆

The next day, François called Nico to fill him in on what had happened at the club.

"Nico, I am sure you have heard of Major Jack Coats. They sometimes refer to him as Dashing Jack. He has not been over in

France for some time, but I think he has been honing his skills. He did something I have honestly never seen done in any of the casinos that I run. It was extraordinary."

Nico's ears pricked up at the name – Coats – but he retained a nonchalant tone. "So, what exactly did this gentleman do to impress you so much?"

"He wanted to get a high-stakes game going on a quiet night here, so came right out and offered to take the bank and pay anyone who played against him double their winnings. Extremely foolhardy, in my view, but it had the desired effect. People flocked in once they heard about it."

"Sounds slightly desperate. The man obviously doesn't care what he loses."

"That's what caught my attention. He has an attitude to playing that is unusual and I think it makes him dangerous. He has very deep pockets and a devil-may-care attitude to the game. He was a pilot in the war and was apparently fearless and unflappable."

"There are many like him. I have beaten them all."

"He appears to be a cut above the average millionaire with a gambling urge. His play was first-rate, despite the pressure. He almost seemed to thrive on it."

"So, how did he fare? The odds would have been heavily against him."

"He cleaned them all out. He played for six or seven hours and whilst his opponents all looked exhausted, he appeared to go from strength to strength. You will have to be careful with this one."

"François, my good friend, as my fellow Greek Aristotle once said, 'One swallow does not a summer make.' Anyone can be lucky once or twice, but in the long run they will lose, unless they adopt my methods. I am sure that Coats is an audacious player, but only time will tell if he can really match us. If he keeps making rash bets like the one you describe, his fortune will not last long."

"Well, don't say I didn't warn you."

"Thank you, François. I will bear it in mind, but I am not too worried. I look forward to doing battle with him, but you can be sure that I will prevail."

"Okay, goodbye, Nico. I'll see you in a couple of weeks."

Nico replaced the receiver and sat staring at the view from his hotel suite. The beach looked lovely and the sun was shining. He hoped that this was not the beginning of a problem. He looked forward to meeting this Coats fellow and getting the measure of the man in person. And it was not only his gambling that was of interest; his name was only too familiar and Nico wondered whether he was in any way related to the William Coats that his informant had mentioned. He got up and set out for the golf course.

Chapter 17

1927 ENGLAND & FRANCE

Jack was oblivious to the conversation that had taken place between Nico and François, but he was now keenly aware of the Greek Syndicate and their methodology. He had been out of the loop during his enforced ban from the French casinos over the last few years, and he had just missed the sensational period of *tout va*, though he had heard rumours of what was happening. He started to ask around to find out where and when they operated and was rewarded by a phone call from Harry Selfridge, who he had met at the tables on several occasions while he still travelled to France prior to his father's embargo.

"Hi, Jack. It seems ages since we last ran into each other. What've you been doing all this time?"

"Confined to barracks, or at least I had to spend a few years helping run the family business, but I have largely given that up now. What about you?"

"Well, the store is going great and we are busy expanding. The Charleston craze has created a huge demand for silk chemises, headbands, those outrageously provocative directoire knickers and feather fans, without even mentioning the flappers' shoes with a powder compact under the buckle. It's supposed to be for touching up their faces, but many of them keep a different product in there, for shoving up their noses!"

Jack chuckled. "Must be keeping you busy and away from the

tables."

"Well, I don't get too involved in the day-to-day organisation. I find it rather dull, so I just push them along and try and get newer and better promotions going. I just got a crazy Scotch inventor called John Logie Baird to show his new Televisor in the store. That brought a lot of people in."

"What the devil is a Televisor?"

"It's a real neat box that can show moving images transmitted from elsewhere. It's pretty primitive, but if they ever get it right, it'll be phenomenal. It won't be long before everyone is talking about television."

"Sounds crazy. I can't say I have much time for all these new-fangled gadgets, although I do enjoy the radio occasionally. It makes a change from listening to a bickering wife and small children."

Selfridge decided he had had enough small-talk and wanted to get to the real reason for his call. "Hell, talking about getting away from the stresses of family life, I was calling because I heard you are interested in playing baccarat against the Greeks."

"Yes. I'm told that this chap Zographos is quite a player and that they play with absolutely no limits. I wouldn't mind a shot at that."

"Well, we're not too far short of the Grande Semaine at Deauville and I know they'll be there. That's where they first introduced the no-limit game five years ago and it's a very popular venue. You can take in the racing in the afternoon and then the Salle Privée is usually open sometime before midnight. The food is superb and I know you love dancing – they usually have a very good band. There's also the golf course."

"It is odd, you know, but I've never been there. I've spent very little time in the north of France and whenever I am there, I always gravitate towards Paris."

"Well, Deauville is great fun. I can highly recommend it. And I never miss it."

"Any chance of seeing you before then? I was thinking of having a small dinner party in a few weeks' time and it would be an absolute pleasure if you could come. You can tell me more about these Greek fellows. I just bought Gloucester House, which is a fabulous abode that I think you'd enjoy – it's only ten minutes' walk from your place at Lansdowne House."

"Send me an invite and I'll almost certainly be there. Or, even better, call me. The number for the department store is Gerrard 1 – nice and easy to remember. They will find me, even if I am not in the store."

"I'll do just that. Hope to see you soon. Good to speak to you, Harry. Goodbye."

Jack hung up and sat back to think about his next trip to France. Deauville. He would reserve a suite at the Normandy Hotel, which he had heard was excellent. Then he'd talk to Audrey, as she might enjoy the trip. She would love the hobnobbing and relish the dancing. The beach would be absolutely made for the children, particularly Vernon, about to be eight years old. Little April was just walking, but the nanny could look after her, and what small child doesn't enjoy the sand and sea?

The weeks leading up to August dragged by. Audrey declined the offer of a holiday in France, as she said he would just spend the time gambling and never pay any attention to the children. She preferred to take the opportunity to visit her mother in Canada with Gwen and the children, as the weather was at least tolerable at that time of year. He therefore saw her off from Liverpool and returned to the house in London, determined to get in a few nights of cards so he would be in good form for his trip across the Channel. He also decided that he would take Taggart with him to minimize any distractions from the gambling.

The dinner party with Harry Selfridge proved to be great fun and he managed to corner the store magnate later in the evening over a glass of brandy to bend his ear about the Greeks.

"Nico Zographos is a phenomenon." Harry took a sip of cognac. "He can retain every play throughout a six-deck shoe. He seems to know everything about everyone and has an uncanny knack of guessing when to take or leave a large bet. I don't quite understand how he does it."

"François André said the same thing, but I find it hard to believe. It must be just luck, surely."

"I don't think so. I'll give you an example of this knack he has. Some years ago, one of my fellow Americans, an annoyingly brash guy, challenged him to play one hand for a million francs. After sizing up his rival for a minute, Zographos agreed to the wager, but said it would have to be the best of three hands. The American agreed, won the first hand and promptly lost the other two. It was as if our Greek friend knew this would happen."

"Sounds like he has made himself into some sort of legend. Doesn't he have any weaknesses?" Jack leant forward conspiratorially. "There must be something, no?"

"As far as baccarat is concerned, I don't know of any. He is cool under pressure, doesn't seem to be fazed by even the largest of bets and is polite and even-tempered, no matter what happens. His partner at the tables, Zaret Couyoumdjian, is almost as good. They never do anything rash and their play is basically flawless. They sometimes lose, but that is the luck of the cards and it never seems to unnerve them. The Greek Syndicate make for formidable opposition – the combination of skill, determination and a lot of money seems to be a winning formula."

"You say 'as far as baccarat is concerned'. What about elsewhere?"

"The syndicate also operates a bookmaking business through a third partner, Zographos's uncle, whose name is Eli Eliopulo, and that's also well run and highly successful, so nothing there. But there's one place where Monsieur Zographos is less sure of himself: the golf course."

"How so?"

"I don't play so I can only report what I've heard, but they say that although he'll take a bet for millions in the casino, he will not even play for fifty francs on the golf course. He's a fairly decent player, but his nerves get the better of him when he plays for money on the links. Strange but apparently true."

"Well, that is interesting – and may be useful. I do play, but I'm not sure how I can use the information. All the same, thanks very much."

"My pleasure."

At this point Jack rose from his seat and nodded politely to his companion. "Now I'm afraid you'll have to excuse me, but I should circulate. I can't be seen to be hogging one guest!"

He then made a beeline for one of his Old Etonian pals who he had not had a chance to chat to at dinner.

♦

Finally the Grande Semaine was upon him and Jack set off to France with a spring in his step and a mild case of butterflies. He decided to fly over on the new Silver Wing service, which had been inaugurated by Imperial Airways at the beginning of May. Sailing from Southampton directly to Deauville was an option, but he did not share his father's enthusiasm for the open seas, and a night or two in Paris held many attractions.

He left Croydon at midday and after two and a half hours, cocktails and a four-course lunch, he and his nineteen fellow passengers alighted in Le Bourget. He decided that he would not gamble in Paris this time and therefore avoided the Cercle Haussmann, preferring to stay in the Hotel Westminster and walk to the Casino de Paris – paradoxically, a music hall and not a betting establishment – where he was intrigued to catch a performance by the Dolly Sisters, who he had heard about from

Harry Selfridge.

After an early night and a refreshing sleep, he caught the express train from nearby Saint-Lazaré station to Deauville, the very same train that Nico had taken fourteen years earlier. However, unlike Nico, who was jammed into a carriage with the rest of the general public, Jack had a first-class compartment to himself. Taggart, who had come over to Paris ahead of Jack in order to prepare things for Deauville, travelled in the back.

He had decided against a suite at the Normandy, as he wanted more space and privacy, so had opted for renting a villa, which Taggart had arranged. This was situated not far from the racecourse and the casino. Deauville is a small place, making it practical to walk almost everywhere and he was keen to take the air, so he changed into a double-breasted blazer and white slacks and took a stroll along the promenade to get a first look at the throngs of people and soak up the atmosphere. The crowds were impressive and the swimming looked quite dangerous, given the strength of the waves and the crush of the bathers. He did not spot anyone he knew, but the opportunity to stretch his legs after three hours on the train was extremely welcome. Duly invigorated, he wandered back towards the hippodrome to catch up with the racing.

When he got there, he went straight to the paddock to size up the runners and riders for the next race. He reckoned he had a pretty keen eye for a promising racehorse and after ten minutes of perusing the field, he strode over to where the bookmakers plied their illegal trade, clearly exempt from scrutiny by the local gendarmes, and placed a bet with one of them. Because of the size of his wager, not all of them would accept it and when he found a taker, he didn't appreciate that this was none other than Eli Eliopulo. Jack was taking on the syndicate before he even knew it!

Eli, however, knew exactly who Jack was, as they kept tabs on all the potential high-stakes gamblers likely to appear in France, in order to be sure that they were good for the bet. As no money changed hands, he took Jack's local address, so he could pay out winnings or collect any losses the next morning.

Jack retreated to the stands to watch the race and see if he could spot the diminutive Greek that he was anxious to meet and, more importantly, play against. He reflected that it was strange he could only recall facing Zographos once before, as they had played in different places on his visits to France immediately after the war. He was also rather annoyed that he didn't have a clearer memory of the little man.

Whilst lost in all these thoughts, he ran into Bert Ambrose, the violin-wielding bandleader from the Embassy Club in London.

"Hello, Ambrose. What brings you to Deauville? Don't tell me you and your band are playing at the casino tonight. That would be just too much good news."

"Oh, hello, Major Coats. No. I'm actually between jobs. I have left the Embassy Club and am about to start at the Mayfair Hotel."

"Why are you leaving us? We all love you and need you at the Embassy."

"I can't broadcast from there and I have to make more money from recordings, which I'll be able to do at the Mayfair. It's not that I dislike the club. It's purely for commercial reasons."

"That's terrible news. I'm sure the Prince of Wales will be very unhappy when he finds out. Have you told him?"

"Yes, and you're right, he seemed rather distressed by the news. But my mind's made up and nothing'll sway me to reconsider. I have my future career to protect, not to mention my finances."

"I'll have to see what I can do. Maybe if I hold a big party there, you can be persuaded to play one last time, and if it is a success, we might convince the club to consent to broadcasting and that would allow you to stay."

"Sorry, but I'm afraid the deed is done."

"Nonsense. Any arrangement can be undone if there is enough resolve to do so. I shall take it up with the club when I return to London."

Jack took out his wallet and wrote a quick note in it. When he had put it back in his pocket, he asked, "So, what *are* you doing here? You never answered my original question."

"I'm here to play against the Greeks."

"Snap! So am I. I've always just missed them before now, but I hope to take them on and clean them out."

"I'm just looking for revenge for what happened to me last year."

"And what was that exactly?" Jack looked genuinely interested.

"It actually started when I was watching you losing to André Citroën a couple of months ago. He had taken over the bank and took a lot of money – over 15 million francs – off you, James Hennessy, Jean Patou and Leon Blum, the banker."

"I remember it well. André had a very lucky streak that night. He doesn't usually do so well."

"So, as I had already been losing quite badly too, I decided to drive down to Biarritz with a couple of friends in my Hispano-Suiza."

"A beautiful car."

"On that particular night it was not so beautiful. I was going fast through some godforsaken village on the way there and I hit a drain that was rather deeper than I anticipated. That damaged the rear axle and nearly crippled the car. I managed to coax it the rest of the way to Biarritz and found a local garage to fix it. With the problem solved, I started to play baccarat, which had been my original intention."

Ambrose's eyes shone as he recalled the events that

followed. "I had the most incredible run. All I could draw were eights and nines. People were coming up to me to touch my jacket in the hope that some of my good fortune would rub off on them. I had made 10 million francs within a week, an absolute fortune. At that point I decided to call it a day and go home – something I had never done before."

"Hmm." Jack furrowed his brow. "I can't see where revenge comes into this story."

"You will – it unfortunately doesn't end there. When I went to pick up the car, it wasn't ready, so I went back to the casino with the intention of watching the big game, as I have always admired the Greeks, particularly Zographos, for their sheer gaming skills. This was where things started to go wrong. I let myself be persuaded that my winning streak could continue and started to play them once again."

"Probably not a brilliant idea."

"No. Within four days I'd lost the lot and an additional 200,000 francs. I had the humiliation of being forced to telephone the Embassy Club to borrow a hundred pounds to pay for the car and my hotel bill."

"And you think you will be able to beat them this time?"

"If I don't try, I certainly won't." He looked up at the racetrack. "Hey, the race has started. What have you backed?"

"A rather fine-looking pony called Le Polisson. It looked good in the paddock and I liked the name, which translates to 'prank' or 'scamp' in English. I can identify with that."

"I'm on Mon Brave. No analysis of form for me. I just stick a finger on the list of runners and wherever it comes to rest, that's where I place my money. Are we going to watch from here, or do you want to get down nearer the action?"

"I'm fine up here. By the time we get down there it'll be over and I'd rather not get my trousers dirty in all the mud."

"Here they come. I can't see who's winning. I didn't bring binoculars."

"Nor I. But I can just make out the colours and I think, unless my eyesight is going, that my horse is in the lead. The jockey should be wearing blue and white. Can you see?"

"Yes, the horse in front is definitely in blue and white. I can't find my selection anywhere. He's all in red."

Two minutes later, Jack's horse had crossed the line, a clear winner, and Bert Ambrose's choice was in the pack at the back of the field.

"Off to get my ill-gotten gains," said Jack, smiling. "Hope to see you this evening."

"Sure. See you."

They parted company and Jack made his way back to the bookies to claim his winnings.

"I'm afraid, sir, that we don't operate that way." Eli was most apologetic, but firm. "You'll have to wait till tomorrow to receive your money. I always collect and/or deliver the day after. You will appreciate that what we do here is not completely above board and a certain degree of discretion is required."

"Quite understood, old chap. I don't need it anyway. Just like to be sure that it will appear."

"If you recollect, I took your details when you made the original bet and you can be sure that I will be at your villa with the correct amount tomorrow."

"Not too early, I trust. I have a long night at the tables ahead of me. If I'm not awake or available, you can leave an envelope with my man, Taggart."

"I will be sure that I do not disturb you too early, and now that I have your permission, the settlement will be given to Monsieur Taggart. Thank you."

Jack then returned to the stands to watch a bit more racing, chat to the occasional acquaintance and search, in vain, for the tiny Greek.

◆

The reason that Nico was nowhere to be seen at the Hippodrome was that he had been resting at his villa, preparing for the evening ahead. He did not enjoy horse racing anymore, a hangover from when he was a bookmaker in the early days in France. Now that Eli had taken charge of that part of the syndicate's activities, he felt no urge to participate, especially as his partner handled it so well.

By seven in the evening the racing was over and people were dressing for dinner, preparing for a night of carefree extravagance, profligacy and downright fun. Nico, on the other hand, was sharpening his skills, with the intention of relieving the ultra-wealthy of a portion of their fortunes. This was a serious business for him, but he would do it as politely and light-heartedly as possible. He recognised that one of his great gifts was his ability to take huge amounts off the rich and famous of Europe and yet cause little resentment. This always brought them back for more and his plan depended on them doing just that.

Eli had phoned him to let him know of the bet that Jack Coats had lodged with him. It was a significant amount, but this never worried them, as there were always others with large wagers on horses that weren't so fortunate. He looked forward to meeting this fellow who François André had warned him about. He was evidently one of the richer men in Britain and a dedicated, devil-may-care gambler. Precisely the type of individual he was keen to cultivate. The surname also had him intrigued. He must find out if he had anything to do with the man who caused Nico's father's downfall.

He finished dressing, donning his favourite white dinner jacket and straightening his bowtie. He fully appreciated that white was not really the thing to wear, as they weren't in the tropics, but it helped him stand out, and anything he could do to remind his opponents that they were up against the Greek Syndicate gave him a psychological advantage.

He strolled along the boardwalk in the direction of the casino, knowing he would be in plenty of time for dinner. These elaborate meals were a necessary part of the ritual leading up to the baccarat table, but he found them rather distracting and he had to be careful about what and how much he ate, as it could affect his concentration.

Once in the casino, he was greeted by several of the attendees, many of whom had played against him either in Deauville or further south. He nodded to André Citroën and James Hennessy as he passed them, and saw Baron Henri de Rothschild in the distance, but eventually found François André and Zaret Couyoumdjian.

"Good turnout tonight, Nico," said Zaret. "I saw King Alfonso of Spain earlier and I am sure that Harry Selfridge and the Dolly Sisters are here. There are also several Americans looking for action and, of course, alcohol. Prohibition has driven them over to civilisation here in Europe."

"Good," replied Nico. "A drunken gambler is usually a poor gambler, though they sometimes scare me. Most sober people start to restrict their bets when they are winning, trying to protect what they have, whereas when they are losing, they do the opposite. Too much drink can make them overconfident and that, paradoxically, makes them bet more when they are ahead, which my calculations and experience tell me is the way to win big. With luck, they will just play foolishly."

He looked around to find a waiter and ordered an orange juice.

"Has either of you come across this Scotsman, Jack Coats?" asked Nico. "You told me, François, that he wants to meet me and I would quite like to size him up before we get started."

"I have not seen him, but I can't imagine it will be long before he appears. I know he is here."

"Oh, so do I. He took over 100,000 francs from us at the Hippodrome this afternoon. I just had a call from Eli."

"That's not necessarily all bad. It may loosen his purse strings tonight," commented Zaret.

"From what I have seen, his purse strings don't need loosening – quite the contrary." François had seen Jack play and had his own opinions on the man. "He has an impulsive attitude to card games, as if he doesn't care whether he wins or loses, and that seems to me to be fraught with dangers for us. We had one too many close calls last year and the last thing we need is a seriously rich card player with a foolhardy attitude to risk and a certain skill level. Our capital is still not that substantial."

"You say he is seriously rich. Do we know how wealthy he is and where his money comes from?" asked Nico.

"He is one of the Coats family, who own an incredibly successful thread business, though I am reliably informed that he no longer works for them. His father died last year and left him about 200 million francs, so his pockets are even deeper than ours."

"What was his father's name?" Nico was thinking of the conversation he had with the mysterious Greek informant and wondered if he could possibly be the man responsible for his father's misfortune.

"I believe his name is William, but was known by his initials W.A., or affectionately as Willie."

"Now that is very interesting," said Nico, without elaborating or explaining why.

At this point François glanced over Nico's shoulder and a look of recognition crossed his face. "Aha! Unless I am very much mistaken, here he comes now."

Jack came striding towards the three of them and extended his hand for François to shake. "Delighted to see you once again,

François." He turned to look at Nico. "And you are the famous Monsieur Zographos. My name is Coats, Jack Coats. We have actually met once before but were never formally introduced. I played against you for two evenings and was going to seek you out, but a *poussette* got in the way."

Nico put his cigarette down and shook Jack's proffered hand. "I remember the occasion well. The crook tried to take me for almost a million francs, not something I forget easily. A pleasure to see you once again, Monsieur Coats. Your reputation precedes you: I have heard stories of your extraordinary double pay-out game in the Cercle Haussmann."

"I had a bit of luck that evening, but it was the only way I could get a decent game. I could think of no better way to attract the sort of opponents I needed. "

"Nothing ventured, nothing gained, I suppose," said Nico, holding Jack's gaze. "I am afraid, Monsieur Coats, that I do not see it the same way as you. There is no such thing as luck, only mathematics. It takes a modicum of skill, and a great deal of recklessness to pull off what you did. I am not sure whether I should be horrified or impressed."

"I hope the latter."

"Maybe." Nico took a sip of his orange juice and noticed that Zaret was looking slightly annoyed. He realised that he had failed to introduce the Armenian. He put his hand on Zaret's arm. "This is Zaret Couyoumdjian, who is a member of my little group and an extremely able baccarat player."

"How do you do." Zaret shook Jack by the hand.

"Can I offer you gentlemen a cocktail or a glass of champagne?" Jack looked around the trio with an inquiring expression. He did not think it likely that they would accept.

"I do not take alcohol, Monsieur Coats," replied Nico. The other two shook their heads and raised their glasses to show that they were already full.

"Well, I do," said Jack. He looked over his shoulder and beckoned to a passing waiter. "Garçon, a bottle of your finest champagne and a glass, please."

The waiter hurried off, and Nico said, "I understand that I, or rather my group, owe you money from the Hippodrome this afternoon."

Jack looked surprised. "So that bookie was an employee of yours? I had heard that you run a bookmaking enterprise on the side, but I hadn't appreciated that I had laid that bet with you. I will not apologise for winning. It could so easily have fallen the other way."

"It is of no concern to us. Eli, who you met, is not an employee, but is rather the fourth member of our syndicate and also my wife's uncle. He will be round to bring you your winnings tomorrow."

"I will put it together with my profit from this evening's game."

Nico smiled. "You are very confident, Monsieur Coats. As I believe you English say, do not be too hasty in counting your chickens before they are hatched. Tonight's game could have many outcomes, so I hope you will play prudently."

Jack ignored Nico's mistake with his nationality; he was only too used to being called English by most foreigners. "My confidence is born of a lack of concern as to whether I win or lose. I am only here for the sport and the joy of sharing the cards with like-minded parties. I do it for thrills – nothing more. I am also one of the luckiest fellows I know, so you will have your work cut out this evening."

"So you do not believe that baccarat is a game of skill?"

"I have spent long enough playing it to know that the level of ability of any one player has almost no effect on how much they win or lose. I have heard you are a good player and that probably helps a bit, but not enough to beat the lucky man."

Nico drew deeply on his cigarette. "Not my view, I'm afraid, monsieur. I have found from experience that there is a lot of truth in the proverb 'I find the harder I work, the more luck I seem to have'."

"But that does not negate my proposition that luck overrides skill at the table. Even the law backs my view." Jack drew himself up to his full height and stared down at Nico, who remained defiant.

"The difference," he replied, "between a good baccarat player and a poor one is the same as the difference between a scratch golfer and a man with an eighteen handicap. However, in the card game the scratch man is not required to give the duffer any shots."

"That is an interesting analogy." Jack laughed and added, "I think we will just have to agree to disagree."

At this point his champagne arrived and an attractive, rather petite young woman came up behind Jack and whispered something in his ear.

"If you'll excuse me, gentlemen, the rest of my dinner guests are here, and I need to attend to them. I will see you later, no doubt."

"I look forward to it," Nico replied. "If you wish, I'll keep you a seat at our game."

"That would be very kind. Thank you." Jack turned and took his young companion by the arm.

Nico bowed slightly and a polite, thin smile crossed his lips. "Enjoy your dinner."

"I shall." Jack turned and left arm-in-arm with his escort and disappeared into the throng.

"He might give us a few problems." Nico looked pensive and a slight frown creased his brow.

"Why so?" asked Zaret.

"People who don't care about losing do not behave rationally, and we don't have the capital we once had to fend off crazy betting. I will have to watch this one."

But that was far from being his only concern. If this were indeed the son of the man who, albeit unknowingly, caused his father's downfall, then playing against him would not be business as usual – it would be personal. This was something he had never experienced before and he was unsure how to tackle it.

Chapter 18

1927 FRANCE

With dinner over, people were beginning to drift into the casino. The usual assortment of tables offering chemin-de-fer and boule were already busy, but the private room with the brass railings around it was deserted. The serious players had yet to put in an appearance.

Gradually the first of these wandered in. There were a couple of Americans with high hopes of success and, inevitably, André Citroën and James Hennessy showed up. Over the next twenty minutes the places on both sides of the table filled up, and the spectators who had paid the requisite amount to be allowed to watch this flagrant display of wealth were lined up behind the rails, craning their necks to get a glimpse of the plaques in front of the players, one of which would be enough to buy a small house and would certainly exceed the annual salary of most of those present.

Nico arrived and took his place in the banker's chair, sitting slightly higher up than the other participants, despite his lack of stature. Only one seat was empty, the one to the immediate right of the banker. Several hopefuls tried to occupy it, but were tactfully turned away, leaving with a rather puzzled look on their faces. After everyone had been waiting for over five minutes, Jack ambled in and took this place, a large brandy balloon in his hand and a broad grin on his face.

"Excellent dinner, I think you will all agree," he said. "I feel quite relaxed and ready for a sporting game of cards. It will be an enormous pleasure to finally be able to challenge the great Nicolas Zographos, face to face. Could someone pass me fifty plaques of 100,000 francs? I am sure that the casino will accept that my credit is good, no?"

François André was watching from the sidelines and nodded almost imperceptibly in assent. "We know you and your reputation for honesty and will, of course, extend you whatever credit you need."

"Thank you, François. Before we begin, I would like to go on record as saying that I will play tonight until I either double my money or lose it all. I don't care how long it takes. I hope that Monsieur Zographos can agree to such an arrangement?"

Nico looked at him with a neutral expression on his face. "That's fine with me. We'll wait till you've lost it all and then you will go. It needs to be clear that once you have no money left in front of you, there will be no chance of going to the bank for more. That'll be the end."

"I agree and, by equal measure, when I've accumulated an additional 5 million francs, I will cash it in and go home. Shall we begin?"

"*Messieurs, faites vos jeux, s'il vous plaît.*" The quiet voice of the croupier easily penetrated the hubbub of small talk, and plaques and chips were placed in front of each player. Jack started with ten of his.

Nico dealt the cards.

As the first player on the right-hand side of the dealer, Jack had the privilege of playing the hand and was delighted when he turned over an eight of hearts and ace of clubs. He threw the cards face up on the table. "Well, what a stroke of luck – a 'natural' to start the evening. I can feel it is going to be my night."

The player on the left side asked for another card, which was a jack of diamonds. He looked slightly downcast, as did the others on his side of the table.

Nico turned over his cards to show that he had a total of seven. He looked slightly bored as money was handed out to those who had bet successfully, which included Jack, who won a million francs.

"So, Monsieur Zographos, I am well on my way to my goal, but the night is young and I am sure you will have your moments as we progress."

Jack grinned in a rather self-satisfied way, but the Greek continued to smoke and said nothing. Although his expression remained impassive, he was wrestling between the needs of the syndicate and the desire for revenge for his father – if Jack really was the son of the man who had brought about the downfall of his family. He decided to put the latter to one side until he could hatch a sensible plan.

The second hand also went Jack's way, but for the third one he was dealt a six of spades and the king of clubs and had to stand on what was a fairly poor hand. Predictably he lost and the next hand was dealt to the player on his right. He began to bet more cautiously this time and won.

The evening progressed and the fortunes of the various players rose and fell, but Jack began to accumulate a tidy stack of plaques in front of him, whilst two or three others had to ask for more chips as they had burned through their initial pile.

The group went through five shoes, by which time some had decided to call it a night, so that several of the seats became vacant, with no more takers. There were no clocks in the casino, but James Hennessy, who had been losing steadily, suddenly announced that it was 4:30 a.m. and time to be thinking about calling it a night.

Jack looked down at his chips and reckoned he had gained about 3 million francs.

Nico knew exactly how much he had, as he did for every other player at the table. Jack was up by more than anyone else and, apart from a couple of small slip-ups of practically no consequence, he had been playing well. The Greek banker was impressed; he could see that Jack was gifted at noting which were the good players on both sides of the table and was betting accordingly. His only flaw appeared to be that he was emotional rather than logical, and he would sometimes make a large bet where he really should be showing more restraint. He also was wont to take a few more cognacs than would be deemed appropriate. Apart from these foibles, his overall game was sound. It would be up to Nico to make sure that the bank made the most of any lapses.

Additionally, Nico had noted that the same emotion that Jack exhibited came through when he was playing the cards on his side of the table. He would view his hand and if he drew, there was an almost imperceptible movement of the eyebrows that showed his level of satisfaction with the result. This made the Greek's decision as to whether to draw or not much easier.

The play was coming back to Jack more frequently as several places on his side of the table had emptied and there were no takers to fill them. Everyone was beginning to tire, though it was indiscernible in the case of the banker. As dawn was approaching, the cards were once again dealt to Jack and he declared, "This cognac" – he raised his brandy balloon and drained the contents – "will be my last for the night. It is time to put an end to this session. The truth is, I could retire now, as I am handily placed, but I will honour what I said when we started and will take my 10 million francs away from the table. This winning bet will be enough to double my original stake." He then placed twenty plaques of 100,000 francs in front of him and looked at his cards. "*Carte*," he exclaimed and Nico passed him a two of hearts. He seemed unmoved by this and said nothing.

From his calculations of what was left in the shoe at this point, Nico reckoned that the two was an exception and that there were more higher value cards available than lower ones. He had an ace and a king, so drew another card, which turned out to be a seven.

"*Huit à la banque*," declared the croupier and Jack turned over a king and a five, which gave him a losing hand. His stash of 8 million had reduced to six.

He then had to pass the privilege of playing to his next-door neighbour and he sat out the next two hands, played modestly for the remainder, betting occasionally, but losing almost every hand.

"My luck seems to have deserted me," Jack said. "I am pretty much back to where I started. It is time to end this."

By this time, the cards had come to him once more. He took the tiles in front of him and pushed them forwards. "I feel fortune smiling on me and that this will be the moment of truth. The law of averages must soon work in my favour – and I just know that this is the moment."

He turned his cards over and eyed them: the jack of diamonds and the seven of spades. A good hand but not great. The bank would need eight or nine to win. He knew that the chances of this were a little more than one in six with the first two cards, but as the banker had not declared a "natural", he could assume that this had not happened. He was a little hazy on the probabilities beyond that, but he knew that he was definitively the favourite. He indicated that he did not want a third card.

Nico looked down and then returned his gaze to the other side of the table. The American who was playing there asked for a card and was shown the king of spades. That would not improve his situation and as the amount of money wagered on that side was way less than Jack's bet alone, Nico's whole focus was now on Jack's hand.

He turned over his cards to reveal a five of clubs and a queen of hearts. This was certainly not enough to beat Jack, but might tie him, though he doubted it. The look on the Scotsman's face when he viewed his cards was not one of doubt, and his lack of hesitation in waving his hand horizontally indicated with some certainty that he held six or more likely seven. Nico would have to draw.

As they were nearing the end of the shoe, he knew that the proportion of low-value cards remaining was slightly higher than it had been at the beginning, so his chance of turning over a two, three or four was better than the twenty-three per cent it would be in a brand new deck, but only by a couple of percentage points, so still highly improbable. This had been calculated in the blink of an eye, so his decision to draw appeared to be arbitrary, which it certainly was not.

He pulled the next card for the shoe and held it face down on the table for a moment. There were few spectators left at this late stage in the proceedings, but he was conscious that a little suspense added to the drama.

He turned the card over. The four of hearts. The assembled players and onlookers stared in amazement. The syndicate had triumphed once more and the Scots millionaire had lost.

Jack shrugged his shoulders and stood up. "You win some, you lose some. I promised I would stop when one of us was up 5 million and this time it was you." He leant over and proffered his hand, which Nico took and shook. "Well played, sir. We will compete again and I will have my revenge. But for now, please let me buy you breakfast, unless you wish to continue playing?"

The banker looked at the rather bedraggled group around the table and said, "I think this would be an appropriate moment to wrap things up, unless there are any violent objections?"

There was a collective shaking of heads, so he asked for his pile to be collected and cashed and indicated to Jack that he would be delighted to have a quick breakfast with him.

Once they were seated in the restaurant, Jack asked Nico how much time he dedicated to practice and play during the season.

"I like to practise for an hour or so, no more," replied Nico. "And I usually play eight to ten hours a day when there is the demand. I share playing time with Zaret Couyoumdjian, so we tend to split it, with Zaret taking the afternoons and I the evenings."

"Don't you get tired of playing night after night? It is quite demanding."

"Not really. I treat it as a job, so I do not expect to enjoy myself, though I confess that a big win does give me some pleasure and the success of our strategy is satisfying, in that it proves that my initial premise – if you play often and well, you will make money – has been vindicated."

"I've been told that you are enormously successful, but I feel that your domination takes some of the joy out of it all, which to my mind should be left to us sportsmen who simply play for the love of the game."

"We do not stop you playing – in fact, I would argue that we create an environment in which you have more opportunities to indulge at the highest level."

"That is perhaps true, but I used to enjoy the chance of bidding for the bank and playing as banker – not always, but at least from time to time. That joy has been eliminated."

Nico took a mouthful of croissant and a sip of coffee before concurring. "Agreed, but we have opened up a world where you can gamble for the sort of stakes that make the game exciting for wealthy men like yourself. Previously, the amounts of money you could risk or win were inconsequential and therefore uninteresting. You can now experience a tangible thrill, which is, I understand, what you really play for."

"I will reluctantly agree with that. It just comes at a hefty price, and I don't mean in money." Jack took a gulp of his coffee and looked round the deserted restaurant. "Anyway, let's change the subject. It is a strange life you lead, so what do you do for entertainment? You don't strike me as being much of a beachgoer, and I assume you don't go to the races after having spent years as a bookmaker. Are you an avid reader, or do you have some other secret passion?"

"I have taken to collecting luxury motors and am fond of the speedier varieties as well, but my real passion is golf."

"Splendid. Do you play a lot?"

"I find that my lifestyle limits my opportunities, but with more courses opening up in places like Deauville and Cannes, I am gradually getting to play rather more. I have a new set of clubs and am working at reducing my handicap to single figures, though I am not there yet. Do you play?"

"As it happens I used to, though not with your enthusiasm or dedication. Like all Scotsmen, no sooner was I able to walk than a golf club was thrust into my tiny hands. I then hit the links as soon as I could. As a young boy, I played on a local nine-hole course a mile from our house south-west of Glasgow."

"You're lucky to have started so young and in a country where golf is so popular – it is a huge benefit compared to us late beginners. I always reflect on how unfortunate I was to be born in Greece, where the game is unheard of. I would also have liked to play with my father and brothers."

As he spoke these final words, Nico saw that he had created an opening to delve into Jack's past and discover if his father was indeed the William Coats who had ruined the lives of the Zographos family through the German mine closure. He decided to take the opportunity.

"Talking of family, I know nothing of yours. I know that you inherited your fortune from the thread business, which must have been started by your great grandfather, if I have done my maths correctly. So, who was your father and what did he have to do with the business, if it is not an impertinent question?"

"Not at all. My father's name was William." The piercing Zographos eyes narrowed at this disclosure. "As a young man, he was passionate about coal mining, but was obligated to join the family business. He was a director for a time, but his heart was never really in it, particularly after my mother died when I was not even two years old. That loss crushed him and not long afterwards he resigned and dedicated himself to collecting paintings. He sailed a bit, but was largely reclusive. Rather sad when you think about it. He died last year."

These revelations were a real eye-opener for Nico, who was now 100 per cent sure that he was facing the son of the man who inadvertently destroyed his father and his family's life. He was not quite sure how to deal with this, for although he was enraged by what had happened to his father, he found it hard to discharge this feeling onto Jack, who he found to be charming, affable and eminently likeable.

"So, I assume he didn't play golf?" Nico asked.

"My father had no interest in golf and I only have one brother, who never showed much talent or desire for the game, although he did play occasionally with me."

"We should have a game."

"I have hardly picked up a club since before the war, but I admit that I would enjoy the chance." Jack thought for a moment and then his expression brightened. "I have an idea. I am a founder investor in the new Cannes Country Club. Why don't we have a game there? I will be down south at the beginning of next year and I am sure you will be there. We can fix a date nearer the time."

"That'd be magnificent. I accept your offer."

"Splendid. I look forward to it. And if I haven't managed to recoup my losses from tonight in the meantime, it may give me an opportunity to do so."

Nico looked cagey. "I'm afraid that there I'm going to have to disappoint you, Monsieur Coats. I never play golf for real money. It is my recreation and, as such, I don't like to bet large amounts on it, as that only makes it stressful and more like my business. You know what they say – never mix business with pleasure!"

"No matter. We can work out the details in the next few

weeks."

With that, Jack rose from the table, stooped to shake the hand of the little Greek, who had also stood up. "It has been an absolute pleasure losing money to you – but I'll be back and next time you may not be so lucky. The odds were heavily against you on that last card. The outcome may well be quite different when we cross paths again. I am looking forward to it."

"As am I," said Nico, who really meant it. He had warmed to this devil-may-care Scotsman, despite his almost polar opposite attitude to the game they both loved and the fact that it would appear certain that Jack's father had caused the ruin of Nico's. He felt he should do something about this, but he wasn't sure what – or even whether he wanted to.

Jack returned to his villa to snatch a few hours sleep and awoke relatively refreshed when Taggart brought in a tray with coffee, croissants and English marmalade which he had smuggled over in his luggage, as he knew that his master was most partial to it with toast or French pastries. He drew back the curtains.

"Good afternoon sir. I hope you slept well after a satisfactory night at the tables."

Jack yawned, stretched and looked at his valet through puffy eyelids. "Slept like a log, but my night was less successful than I'd hoped, thank you Tag. Did you collect my winnings from the racecourse?"

"Yes sir. A Mr Eliopulo was here first thing and left a rather bulky envelope, which he explained contained money from the bet you won yesterday afternoon."

"Good, that is at least some consolation for my losses at the tables."

"Will you be playing again tonight, sir?"

Jack pondered for a moment before replying. "Yes, Tag. I

must try and recover some of what I lost."

Taggart shook his head almost imperceptibly, but refrained from comment. Jack caught the gesture. "I know you disapprove, but I love my gambling and will only give it up the day I stop enjoying it or feel that I can no longer sustain it. In the interim I shall continue."

"Very good, sir." Taggart withdrew to the adjoining room to prepare his master's bath. Jack threw back the covers and looked out the window. It was going to be another lovely day.

Chapter 19

1928 FRANCE

Jack and Nico skirmished numerous times over the next six months, with nobody coming out a clear winner. Nico's thoughts of vengeance had been forgotten as the syndicate continued to consolidate its position, accumulating a tidy fortune, slowly but surely.

However, there were nights when they had to dip into their pool of capital. Nico usually started the day's play with around 5 million francs, but an evening of losses could quite quickly dissipate this amount. Jack cleaned him out on two or three occasions after their first ill-fated encounter, sending one of the syndicate scurrying off to reinforce their pile of chips. In equal measure, the Scotsman was sent off to the bank to replenish his "pot" more than once.

The exit of Athanase Vagliano from the syndicate had only caused them one major crisis since then – and Nico had rescued them from that situation in the now famous game where he drew the nine of diamonds. They were gradually beginning to feel invulnerable, though they remained far more exposed than they had been prior to 1926.

Their weakness was once again laid bare two years later. Nico had a series of evenings when the cards ran against him, with several of the wealthier gamblers, principally Jack Coats, betting heavily and winning consistently. By the fourth night, Nico was getting nervous and was not looking forward to the final session, as he was all too aware that they were hours away from being bankrupt. Despite this, he put on a brave face and was waiting in his usual spot as the players filed in, Jack Coats leading the way.

"So, Monsieur Zographos. It would seem that the bank is finally vulnerable. Perhaps we can have our revenge for the many times you have cleaned us out."

"I assure you, Monsieur Coats, that we are good for any bets you care to lay down. We have a reputation for honesty and integrity and, to paraphrase Mark Twain, rumours of our impending demise are, as usual, wildly exaggerated."

"Good, because I feel that I am in for an outstanding night's sport and it would be a shame to have it cut short."

"Unless something exceptional happens, that is very unlikely. The law of averages would indicate that the run of play against the bank will soon come to an end, so I would measure your wagers with that in mind."

"Rubbish. I am on a winning streak and want to take full advantage!"

"Don't say you haven't been warned. Ladies and gentlemen, shall we get started?" Nico indicated that everyone should take their seats and within a few short minutes play had begun.

The run of bad cards against the bank resumed, much to Nico's dismay. He had soon consumed his opening stash of 5 million and called in François to get him more. This was brought to him, but the quantity was less than he expected. He whispered to his partner, "Isn't there any more than this?" to which the reply was, "That's the lot and we have no reserve. You'll have to find an excuse to leave early. Could I suggest some sort of illness?"

"The way things are going I won't have to invent anything. I am about to have a nervous breakdown." He looked around at the eager faces at the table. "They know we're in trouble, but will not deny me if I feign some exotic malady. Leave it with me. I'll do it soon, as it shouldn't coincide with the total depletion of our funds."

He continued to play and lose, but on a more modest scale. However, he could see the end was in sight if the cards didn't turn, so he decided the moment was right for a strategic withdrawal.

"Gentlemen, you'll have to excuse me, but I'm not feeling a hundred per cent and find it hard to concentrate. I will therefore be terminating tonight's session, but will make it up to you by returning stronger and sharper tomorrow. I would ask Zaret Couyoumdjian to replace me, but he is unfortunately nowhere to be found, so I must reluctantly withdraw and bid you all goodnight." He rose and quickly left the room, amidst howls of protest.

Those who remained were not taken in by his feigned illness and word spread quickly that the Greeks were in trouble. Jack had already taken a substantial amount off them over the four days and sat there disconsolate and frustrated. "I thought I might become famous as the man who finally broke the Greek Syndicate," he intoned to nobody in particular. "But what I do not achieve today can easily be accomplished tomorrow. I shall be ready to finish them off when we return to the table – and then baccarat can resume being a sport for gentlemen and not a business for Greek rogues." He pushed back his chair, got up with an indignant air and rushed off to see if the band were still playing.

Nico, meanwhile, had made his way to the bar and found one of his old friends from Athens, Yiorgos Papatonis.

"Yiorgos, buy me an orange juice, please. I'm having a terrible week."

"Certainly, Nico. I hear things've been going badly. Anything I can do to help?"

"As a matter of fact, there is. We've had an incredibly poor run over the last few days. Jack Coats, in particular, has been winning almost continuously. For the first time in six years, we have run out of money. We are broke."

"And you want to borrow from me?"

"No. I would propose that you finance us and take a share in the enterprise. I won't need much, as it is a mathematical certainty that I will start winning tomorrow evening. Sequences of luck always come to an end and this one has run its course. I won't need more than a couple of million francs, and I know you are good for much more than that."

"Nico, we've known each other for years and you appreciate how I feel about gambling and the dangers involved. I do it for fun, but the risk profile of your operation would make me feel too nervous. I am sorry, but I am just not your man."

Nico's hands were shaking. His normally cool veneer was cracking under the weight of the situation. He reluctantly had to admit to himself that it would take more than the nine of diamonds to rescue him this time. His voice took on a tone of mild desperation.

"I really don't know where else to turn. The position is critical, but I know I have it under control if I can just lay my hands on some cash. Forget about investing . . . Would you *lend* me some, Yiorgos?"

"I'm sorry once again, but if I won't invest, I certainly will not lend you that amount of money. It could damage our friendship and, as I have said before, much as I like you, I am not a fan of high-stakes gambling. I'm afraid you must look elsewhere."

Nico downed his orange juice in one, grunted in disapproval, nodded a perfunctory goodbye and set out at a fast clip across the casino. He exited the main door and almost ran to the Hotel Royal, where he and his wife were staying. He went up to his room and flung the door open, awakening his wife from a deep sleep.

"Why are you back so early? What's the matter?" she asked.

"I need to go to Paris, now. We are in serious trouble, but I have no time to explain. Trust me; I will be back tomorrow."

He gave her a kiss, grabbed his keys and a coat and rushed out, banging the door behind him. Once out of the hotel, he found his car and set out for Paris. His thoughts raced as he drove through the night. What if he couldn't get the money? What if he did, but then lost anyway? This would be the end of his dream and his purpose in life. Then he remembered that he had a revolver in the car, which he carried in case of accidents, and that gave him some reassurance. He could not take the humiliation of total defeat, but was calmed by the thought that he always had a way out. He had not yet reached the level of despair he had felt as he made his way towards the bridge in Munich, but if he couldn't raise enough money and ended up bankrupt, he felt pretty sure he would be close. He tried to stay positive.

He reached Paris as the sun rose and, after a futile attempt to find people with money to lend at that time of day, he decided to try his brother Spiro, who he had not seen for a long time but lived in the city. He knocked on the door and waited. After what seemed like an eternity, a bleary-eyed figure appeared on the doorstep. "Nico! What on earth are you doing in Paris? And why are you visiting me at this ungodly hour?"

"Spiro, I need a favour. Can you lend me some money?"

"You'd better come in and have a coffee. You look awful."

"Okay, but let's make it quick."

They both went through to the kitchen and Spiro prepared the paraphernalia for two cups of coffee. As he did so, he asked if Nico had communicated with their father recently.

"No. I don't have much to talk to him about. Ever since the debacle with my degree in Munich, we have grown apart."

"He asks after you. We have told him you are a banker, which is not a lie – technically – and seems to keep him happy."

"His happiness is not my particular concern. He ruined my life at a critical stage and almost drove me to suicide."

"But surely you appreciate that was not really his fault?"

Nico took the coffee cup which his brother had offered him and lit a cigarette. "I met with a strange gentleman in this very city who told me the same thing. He fed me a story about a Scottish millionaire who sold off his share of the mining company where Dad had his money. He gave me the gentleman's name – William Coats."

"That's what I've been told as well. Your contact obviously had good information."

"Well, it turns out that William Coats is the father of one of my main rivals at the tables, which is an amazing coincidence. I would've liked to get my own back on this William Coats personally, but he died a couple of years ago, so it is tempting to seek some form of reparation through the son. The trouble is, I am sure that he has no inkling of what happened, so even if I try and exact revenge he won't understand, and we can hardly hold him responsible, even if, to quote Shakespeare, 'the sins of the fathers are to be laid upon the children'. I am unsure what to do."

"I think you should just leave it. As you say, the son is really not to blame for what the father did."

Nico seemed to be thinking aloud when he said, "Maybe I should try and relieve him of a substantial amount of money, to the point that it completely changes his life. Then he can experience some of what I felt. Our family could benefit from whatever I win and that way justice would be done, at least in part."

"I think you could usefully stop obsessing about what is now ancient history. Is the son such a hateful person?"

"No. He is actually rather charming, but I still feel a need to do something, given this opportunity, and the best way to do it is through the gaming tables." He looked pensive for a moment but then seemed to pull himself round. He stubbed out his cigarette, which was down to his fingertips, and grimaced as it burnt him. "Talking of the tables, I will not be able to manage any of that if I don't solve my current problem, so let's get back to the matter at hand – can you lend me 5 million francs?"

A look of shock crossed Spiro's face and he shook his head. "You're joking! I can probably scrape together a million, but I'm afraid that's your lot. Take it or leave it."

Nico looked deflated. "It is not enough, but it will have to do."

"Let me go to the safe and I'll get it for you. I assume you will pay it back?"

"Within the week, you have my word as a Zographos."

"Not sure whether that makes me feel very confident, but, as you say, it will have to do." Spiro laughed and gave Nico a hug. He then went off to the safe and came back with a bundle of notes that he handed to his older brother. "Spend it wisely."

"I will make it count, you can be sure of that. Thanks."

As Nico made his way back through the French countryside, he tried to think of ways to limit the amount that his rivals would bet. They had certainly scented his fear last night and would be baying for blood. He had to find a way to stop them making large bets and then hope that the amount he had with him would be enough and that the cards would finally begin to run his way. As he approached Deauville, an idea came to him.

Before the evening session, he asked François André to get the casino to remove all the 100,000-franc tokens from the cashier, leaving 10,000 as the largest denomination available. This did not affect the normal gamblers, as they did not bet the heady amounts that the high-stakes table was used to, but it meant that someone wanting to bet a million francs (his total capital) would have to shovel out a hundred plaques and the sheer amount of plastic involved would be psychologically daunting.

When the game started that night, the players were surprised to find no 100,000-franc plaques on the table. Jack Coats sent for François and asked what was going on.

"We have had a counterfeit problem and have had to withdraw them all until we get to the bottom of it. It should only be a matter of days, but you must understand that we cannot risk such large sums if there is any danger at all of there being fakes mixed in with the real ones."

"Seems damned irregular to me," was Jack's retort, but he knew there was nothing to be done, so they started the game.

Nico's strategy had the desired effect, in that the betting was more modest, and he won several of the early coups, so that by the end of the evening he had gained back enough to be able to carry on. Additional capital was also forthcoming as a result of some unexpected good fortune from Eliopulo's bookmaking operation, with a few results going their way, against the odds. Nico's revolver remained untouched in his car.

♦

The circus that was the group of high-rollers reached Cannes in the spring of 1928, and the day finally dawned for the much anticipated golf match between Nico and Jack.

Nico was up early and practising putting on his hotel room carpet. He knew little of Jack Coats's abilities on the links and was slightly annoyed that he had been talked into playing at the Cannes Country Club, which had opened only a couple of years previously and was therefore an unknown quantity. Nevertheless the chance to play such a fine golf course had outweighed his conviction that he would be at a disadvantage because of Jack being a member of the club. In truth, Nico suspected that his rival had never actually played the course, so his knowledge of the layout would probably have little effect.

The game was scheduled for nine o'clock in the morning, so Nico made his way over there in one of his cherished motor cars. He wanted to continue his putting practice, but on a properly cut green. He also wanted to loosen up with his recently acquired clubs. He had jumped on the bandwagon of steel shafts as soon as he could; they were ridiculously expensive, but nothing should be allowed to get in the way of making improvements to his beloved sport, and the increase in power and accuracy over the older hickory shafted clubs was significant.

He was so engrossed in trying to judge the distances on his long putts, that he did not notice Jack's arrival, despite the deep growl from his latest automotive acquisition. He gave a start when Jack addressed him from just off the practice green.

"How's your game, Monsieur Zographos?" Jack's French was, as usual, almost flawless.

"I am continuing to improve, thank you. I find that practice makes perfect, much as it does on the baccarat table, though I confess that the physical aspects of golf make it less amenable to well-organised drills and dedicated practice. It is rather annoying."

"Well, as I told you, I only play from time to time, but as I was introduced to the game at a very young age, it seems to come fairly naturally and I do not need to beat lots of golf balls to keep my swing in shape."

"You are indeed fortunate. Being tall helps as well. I assume you have a handicap. We never really discussed it when we set up this game."

"I play so seldom that I do not have an official handicap, but I am probably the equivalent of about thirteen, or at least that's what I am told."

"Then we should be able to play off level, as I am also a thirteen, and that is official. As you intimated, we should have a small wager on the result – I would suggest ten francs."

Jack looked aghast. "Nobody gets me out of bed at this ungodly hour for less than 10,000. I am sure that you can afford to wager such a modest amount, given the success of the syndicate. You lay out millions on the gaming tables, so I do not see any reason why you wouldn't want the same sort of excitement on the links."

"As I already told you, I do not believe in extravagant wagers when playing golf. It is not a question of affording it, but when I play baccarat, I have much more information both before and during the game, so I am largely in control of my destiny. Out here, the weather, the grass and above all my opponent are largely unknowns, so I would be foolish to risk more than a token amount."

The truth was that although Nico was cold and calculating in the casino, he knew that he became a nervous wreck when playing golf for money. He couldn't understand or explain it, but heavy betting in this environment had a frightful effect on his game. An accomplished player when in a friendly match, he could make the most appalling blunders when there was significant cash on the line. However, he disliked admitting to this weakness and was also keen to win the match, as a matter of honour. He was not sure how to extricate himself from the situation.

Jack knew of this foible and was using a form of gamesmanship. He looked upon it as fair game and an equivalent to the psychological edge the syndicate held in the casino. But he could see the discomfort of the normally poker-faced Greek and admitted to himself that he was rather enjoying it. However, he didn't want his opponent's nerves to get in the way of a decent match, so he relented.

"Perhaps we could find another way of making the game interesting," said Jack. "Instead of playing for money, we could have the loser buy dinner for the winner, and I will give you a shot a side to further entice you. Would that be agreeable to you?"

Nico considered this for a moment. He still felt uncomfortable, but was unwilling to be seen as overly mean, particularly given his reputation in the gaming world, and he rationalised that this could be viewed as a business expense if he lost, as he would be able to discover more about his gambling opponent over a meal – that would further enhance his superiority where it really mattered, at the high-rollers' table. Moreover, with his rival spotting him two shots, he fancied his chances. He reluctantly agreed. "It would amount to more than I normally stake on a game of golf, but in the interests of good will, I will make an exception on this occasion."

Having decided on the stakes, they set off for the first tee, their caddies trailing behind them with the bags of clubs over their shoulders. Nico had chosen a caddy from the pool at the club, but Jack had travelled over with Taggart, who he felt would be a useful asset, as he had played as a young man. The two competitors made a rather comical duo, with the tall, rangy figure of Jack Coats ambling along rather nonchalantly and the pint-sized Greek hurrying along beside him as quickly as his short legs would carry him. To any outsider it looked like a one-horse race, even more so after Jack's opening drive split the fairway, whilst Nico's hardly left the ground, ending up in the left-hand rough, some sixty yards behind.

But golf is a strange game and things did not all go Jack's way. After predictably winning the first hole, his mashie to the short second ended up on the green, but on the lower tier and after three putting, he found himself back at all square.

They halved the next four and it was evident that the tension Nico had felt on the first tee was gradually easing. It was almost as if he was beginning to enjoy himself, though this never manifested itself in the form of an actual smile. There was even some conversation between the two men, which had not been the case over the first few holes, despite several fruitless attempts by Jack.

On the seventh hole, a par five of some length, the fairway sloped from right to left for much of its length, so many players found themselves in the left rough off the tee: Jack and Nico were no exception, but whereas Nico's ball was sitting up, the Scotsman's ball had found a particularly gnarly lie.

"Bad luck," said the Greek, though he was having trouble

hiding his satisfaction with his opponent's misfortune. He was being given a shot at this hole so his chance of winning it had just been significantly enhanced.

Nico hit a good second up the middle, but Jack's shot, which was going like an arrow towards the green, just caught a branch of the tree on the front left and bounced into thick woodland. A search proved fruitless and the hole went to Nico.

This piece of bad luck shook the former pilot and he lost the next two holes, even though the Greek did not play them well. They had reached the turn and Nico was three up.

Unlike a lot of golf courses, the Cannes Country Club did not return to the clubhouse after nine holes and so there was no opportunity for a brief respite and a small libation in order to fortify the spirit and recover from a poor front nine. Jack, desirous of a cocktail and never one to be thwarted by such a minor inconvenience, asked Taggart to extract a flask from his golf bag and proceeded to take a swig of the rather fine whisky that had been decanted into it earlier. He watched as his rival hit a wonderful drive right down the middle, into what seemed like a fine position, even though the landing area was over a mound and therefore blind. Jack stepped up to the tee, duly fortified, and, after a couple of waggles, topped his drive. It bounced along the ground and disappeared over the brow of the hill. But instead of cursing or looking annoyed, he announced that he would like to increase the wager, given his distinctly unfavourable position.

Taggart looked at him as though he had taken leave of his senses. He whispered in Jack's ear, "Are you sure about this, sir?"

"Of course", Jack replied, sotto voce, "I know what I'm doing. Just watch what happens." Taggart fell silent.

Nico raised an eyebrow and looked concerned for a moment. He was counting the odds, calculating what the chances were of him losing four of the next nine holes, with a shot to come and his opponent obviously in trouble at the tenth. He reasoned that he would likely win the current hole and would have a better than even chance of winning the thirteenth, where he had his other shot. That put him five up, effectively. He was playing well enough and was enjoying the round and the beautiful golf course. He felt confident and relaxed, and whilst the Scottish millionaire showed occasional moments of brilliance, his golf was certainly no better than his own. Although he hated betting when playing golf, this seemed like an exception, so he didn't turn down the offer out of hand.

"What did you have in mind?" he asked, rather cautiously.

"I thought that a single plaque from the baccarat table would be appropriate – but the largest one, of course."

Nico was incredulous. "You mean 100,000 francs? You only mentioned a tenth of that when we started."

"Well, I feel that I need an incentive to start playing better, and this is one way I think I might find some inspiration. Ten thousand francs will not get my juices flowing, but the larger amount will have my full attention. You can hardly say that the odds are in my favour, but I am willing to take the risk, even though I accept that my chances of winning are slim. I am three down, you have a shot to come, and I can tell you that this hole turns sharp left at the bottom of the hill and my drive will not be long enough to reach the apex. It puts it out of reach for me but not for you, so I am basically giving you another shot. You must be the heavy favourite!"

Nico had already done this calculation and more. He knew that, on one hand, it would be foolish to take the bet, for he was well aware of the nervous tension caused by any wager on the golf course. On the other hand, the odds were outstanding. He also persuaded himself that it was only one plaque – and he handled, lost and won many of these plaques every night, so surely it was reasonable? He decided to take the bet, but with one proviso.

"Fine, but I want two shots and not one on the back nine."

Jack raised his eyebrows, asked Taggart for the card and looked at it. "So you will get a shot on both thirteen and seventeen? Makes it pretty hard for me."

"I fully understand that, but if I am to play for what is a significant amount of money, I need to have the odds stacked in my favour. Take it or leave it."

Jack extended his hand to his opponent, who took it in a firm handshake. "May the best man win."

They strode off the tee and down the hill. Taggart looked agitated. "You'll never win the match, not from this position with those shots to give."

Jack looked confident. "You watch, Tag. This chap will be a bag of nerves if he loses a couple of holes. He's famous for it when he plays for cash, particularly large amounts. And if I lose, it's not the end of the world – it's only money!"

When they reached their drives, Jack was pleasantly surprised. Not only had his ball just made it to the corner, but his opponent's had obviously hit something and had careened through the fairway into the far rough, which looked particularly lush. A glimmer of hope had appeared and when Nico found a bunker and failed to get out with his next, Jack had won the hole. Two down.

He also won the short eleventh where Nico's putt for a half came up short, and a half at the twelfth in sixes brought them to the thirteenth tee with Nico one up and Jack giving him a shot.

After good drives Jack was away and topped his second, which ended up thirty yards short. The Greek, sensing blood, hit a good shot towards the green, but it bounced hard on the left side and kicked left into a creek. He had to take a drop and when they both chipped on and missed, the hole was a tie. He had failed to make use of one of his shots and was now only one up with five to play. He began to feel nervous.

Despite this, his play continued to be solid if unspectacular, and they halved fourteen and fifteen. One up with three to play and a shot to come at seventeen was a fairly healthy position to be in.

At the long sixteenth Jack had some bad luck and after three shots ended up well short, with Nico on the green some six feet from the hole.

Jack had about forty yards to the pin, so Taggart handed him his jigger so he could play a Scottish-style pitch and run. "Don't see much evidence of these nerves you were talking about, Sir."

"No", replied Jack. "He does seem to be holding up well under pressure. Let's see if we can rattle him." He hit his shot and the ball set off too fast, but luck was on his side and it hit the pin, hovered on the edge of the hole and fell in. That meant that the unhappy Nico needed to hole his six-footer, which he duly missed. Incredibly, they were back to all square. Jack looked at Taggart, grinned and winked.

Seventeen was a fiendish par four, with a pond in the middle. Both played conservatively short of the water and could not reach the green in two. Jack's third shot came to rest about ten feet beyond the pin and Nico played a similar shot, with a similar result, but unluckily for Jack the ball came to rest about a yard closer than Jack's, right between his ball and the cup. The Scotsman was stymied.

"Well, that's a blow," exclaimed Jack. "To have any chance of winning, I need to hole this and now you've blocked me. I hope that was not on purpose!"

"Much as I would love to be that good, I am afraid I have neither the ability nor the desire to try to win in such an underhand way. However, the rules are the rules, and you will have to find a way of playing it."

Jack asked Taggart for his pitching niblick and set up to try and get the ball to jump over Nico's on its way to the hole. When he hit it, it looked to be too short, but it landed on the far side of the other ball and kicked forwards into the hole. As a result, Nico's ball was actually knocked further away from the target. The Greek still had a chance to win the hole, but his putt needed to go in. He hit it too softly, so it rolled up a few inches short. He had taken five to Jack's four and they were still all square, shots gone.

As they walked to the eighteenth tee, Jack whispered to Taggart, "What a fluke! I always tell you how lucky I am."

"Let's not count our chickens just yet, sir", was the sombre reply.

Eighteen was a short par four, fairly straightforward, apart from the lake on the right side. Both men managed to avoid this, though Nico had a nervous moment when his drive seemed to go in that direction. He gave a sort of strangled cry as he watched it, but it turned out fine and he ended up with a clear shot to the green, as did his opponent. Jack's second was a little long, but gave him a fairly straight putt of some twenty feet. His opponent hit the shot of the day and the ball ran up to the hole, hit the stick and bounced away to two feet.

"Great shot," shouted Jack. "That looks like a match winner, but you still have to hole it!"

"Thank you. I was very pleased with both the execution and the result. You can still hole yours, so this is not over yet."

Jack got to the green and lined his putt up. It rolled nicely towards the hole, but just turned left as it slowed, ending up six inches away. He tapped it in.

"Over to you, my friend," he said.

Nico was only now starting to appreciate how nervous he was. The putt was one of those which would turn a little, and it needed to be struck with authority. However, he could not stop his hands from shaking and he felt far from confident. He stood over the putt, took his putter back and struck the ball. The moment he hit it, he knew it would miss, as he had jerked at it rather than hit it smoothly. It missed the hole and ended up further away than he had started. Now he was in a panic. If he missed this one, he would lose. He walked over behind his ball and looked the putt over. Fairly straight, he decided. He took a practice stroke and as he stepped forward to address the ball, a hand reached down and picked it up.

"I think that one is good," said Jack. "An honourable half and an exciting and well-fought match. And as neither of us won, I will buy us the dinner we were originally playing for, as a gesture of goodwill – but let's make it in Paris, when we are next in town together."

All the stunned Greek could stammer was, "Agreed." He shook hands, hurried to his car and sat shaking in the driver's seat for a full ten minutes. He made it a rule that he never smoked on the golf course, but now he lit a cigarette – no mean feat with your hands shaking as much as his were – and drew hungrily on it, hoping that the drug would help to calm him. He then gunned the motor and set out for Cannes and the safety of the casino.

Jack and Taggart made their way back to the car and as the valet packed the clubs in the boot, he turned to Jack and asked, "Why did you not make him putt that last one, sir?"

"Seemed like the sportsmanlike thing to do. I could see he was quaking in his boots and honestly felt sorry for him. I also think it gives me a small psychological advantage over him when we play cards, though only time will tell."

"I hope you're right, but one thing's for sure: sometimes, sir, you are just too – excuse me for swearing – bloody nice."

Out on the road home, Nico reflected on what had taken place. He would never have conceded that putt the way Jack did, and the nonchalance with which it was done was astounding and admirable, but at the same time arrogant and, as far as Nico was concerned, rather demeaning.

The thorny issue of revenge was beginning to crystallise. He had no doubt that Monsieur Coats really was utterly charming and had a good word to say about everyone. He was generous, warm-hearted and compassionate, which made it really hard to hate him.

But the air of superiority that he had shown when he picked up Nico's ball at the end of their game was something that the Greek now realised had been annoying him for some time. This latest incident had only helped to highlight it. The Scotsman really needed taking down a peg or two!

But, above all, he was Willie Coats's son, and somebody should suffer for what had happened to Nico's father.

For the last few months, Nico's conservative nature meant he had resisted taking action against Jack Coats – he had been determined not to do anything rash that could have unforeseen consequences for the syndicate. But now his resolve was weakening.

Chapter 20

1930 FRANCE

Given the wealth required to play cards for such breath-taking sums of money, not many people could afford to compete with the Greeks by the end of the 1920s.

The main protagonists in the effort to beat the syndicate were André Citroën, James Hennessy, Sidney Beer, the Aga Khan, Harry Selfridge and Fritz Mandel, husband of Hedy Lamarr and the richest man in Austria. There were also assorted European royals, including the Prince of Wales. Winston Churchill played, gambling at four tables simultaneously, but never for more than 400 francs. And there was, of course, Jack Coats, who now had the reputation for being one of the finer players in Europe.

However, none of them could get the better of the Greeks, whose wealth continued to grow. They took on additional investors to allow themselves a more substantial capital base in all the centres where they operated; and they expanded their business – from the main hubs in Deauville in summer, and Cannes and Monte Carlo in winter – into a pattern of playing year round, adding Le Touquet and La Baule in the north, Juan-les-Pins in the south, and supplementing these with Biarritz and Aix-les-Bains when others were less busy. They also played occasionally at both the Capucines and Haussmann clubs in Paris.

This obviously meant that Nico, even with the help of Zaret, could not cover everywhere, so he trained up an Englishman, Reggie Simmons, to cover Biarritz and La Baule for him. His brother Spiro also played at the former. Reggie had married Yola's cousin, so as one of the family, he was viewed as eminently trustworthy. He also spoke English, a huge benefit when they were trying to fleece the wealthy Americans who were coming across to France in ever-greater numbers to escape prohibition.

Other syndicates sprung up: the Battisti brothers operated in Le Touquet, but had nowhere near the success of the Greeks. They even made an attempt to break Nico by bringing nearly 20 million francs to the table, but were sent packing in less than a week.

Jack now did a lot of his gambling in Juan-les-Pins, in the casino that was owned by the American Frank Gould. Jack would also go out of his way to try to play against the Greek maestro, though that was not always possible. And, however good he was, it was inevitable that he would lose money – and this he did gradually over the period after his game of golf with Nico. Added to his lavish lifestyle, the expense of keeping up his houses in London and Scotland meant that Jack soon started to burn through his wealth.

He also took to financing expeditions to Africa to catalogue and photograph big game and rare species, and that also added to the strain on his purse strings. His love of foxhunting meant that he essentially financed the Eglinton Hunt, where he and Audrey were duly made joint masters. His generosity was legend, though usually for the purpose of entertaining, rather than doing "good works". He would fly his friends over to France for dinner and kept several London restaurants going by ordering caviar or oysters by the hundreds, often for shipment to Scotland or across the Channel. He did not inherit the philanthropic instincts of his grandfather, who would have called him extravagant.

But Jack largely ignored any financial problems and continued to play often and aggressively.

In the casinos at the top tables, it was quite common for large amounts of money to be won and lost in an evening and sums of 10 million francs were hardly the exception. The French government was conscious of the accomplishments of the Greeks and the huge amounts of money that were flowing through the casinos as a result of baccarat, dwarfing the takings from lesser games such as chemin-de-fer, boule and vingt-et-un. No taxes had been levied on their winnings and, as is the way with administrations the world over, the French authorities could not resist the temptation to take their pound of flesh from the syndicate's success. A new levy of twenty-five per cent was introduced, effectively rendering the business of professional gambling at baccarat non-viable.

The members of the syndicate were dismayed at this turn of events and they met to discuss their tactics. Nico opened the proceedings.

"Our margin from the high-stakes tables is tiny, so we can no longer make any money with this new tax. There is not enough revenue from the bookmaking business to sustain us, so we must either bleed cash or cease operations. My vote is for the latter. How do you see the situation, François?"

François stood up and addressed the group. "Our position is far worse. They have also introduced a series of luxury taxes on deluxe hotels and, by extension, on casinos. We are beginning to feel the pinch as a result of the situation on Wall Street and I have been draining my reserves for the past six months, hoping for better times ahead. I have to pay sixty per cent on my profits to the government and another eighteen per cent to the local authorities. As the season in each place is short and the cost of upkeep is a year-round extravagance, I have little to play with at the end of the day. Without the additional revenue from the syndicate, all my places will be in serious trouble."

"So, gentlemen, what do we do?" Nico looked around the group. The answer came from Eli.

"We should stop playing – go on strike, if you want to put it that way. That will mean that the authorities will have no revenue and what they take from the casinos will be much reduced, as we know that our games attract a lot of additional traffic. François can confirm that."

François nodded. "That is true, but it will hit me and the other casino owners and managers hard. I don't know how long we can live with this situation. If the government doesn't weaken and rescind the tax, there will be closures."

"I think we should try to make some sort of demonstration," Eli suggested. "The Grand Semaine in Deauville is coming up shortly. I propose that we appear as usual, but instead of offering the usual *tout va* game, we will play for matchsticks. That will get people talking – and there is nothing like negative public opinion to make a government change its mind. What do you think, Nico?"

"I agree. Just stopping is not enough. We need to be seen to be poking fun at the authorities and what an excellent way to do it. As Molière said, 'The most effective way of attacking vice is to expose it to public ridicule. People can put up with rebukes but they cannot bear being laughed at: they are prepared to be wicked but they dislike appearing ridiculous.' I am sure the French government is the same."

His colleagues looked both impressed and puzzled by this quotation, but said nothing.

Nico continued, "Do we have time to get the word out?"

"Yes, I will make sure that everyone knows." But François looked worried. "Of course, we will no longer be able to charge for spectators if we are only playing for matches. That means a further loss of revenue. I really hope this gets sorted out quickly."

The Grand Semaine at Deauville rolled round and word had indeed spread of the syndicate's protest and their intention to play with matches. Many of their traditional opponents – the Aga Khan and James Hennessy amongst them – duly turned out in their finest evening dress and sat down to play with nothing more than matchsticks. The curious onlookers, now allowed in for free, crowded around the table but soon drifted away, as a cluster of Swan Vestas exchanging hands across the baize doesn't have anything like the cachet of 100,000-franc plaques.

With waning interest, the "match" games became pointless and after a week the group decided to sit out the rest of the season. Other lesser syndicates, notably the Battisti brothers, followed suit. What happened next had not been anticipated, but Nico said later that it was inevitable.

The void created by the syndicate strike became a source of temptation to the more adventurous millionaires who spotted that there was money to be made by taking over the banks, now left vacant for the first time in the nearly ten years of operation by the Greeks. A few of the more adventurous and wealthy patrons were prepared to confront the considerable risks involved: the first of these was John Factor, a swindler who grabbed the bank in Deauville after the match games evaporated.

Prior to this, he had lost 8 million francs to Nico in an evening and had sworn he would get his revenge. When the bank became available, he saw his opportunity and took it over, but had to retire, financially battered, after losing about seven and a half million francs in only four hours. Even for a man who had skipped England with 160 million francs in his pocket, this was not a rate of loss he could sustain. The damage was inflicted by the syndicate, or rather their surrogates, who started the session by betting a million francs at one end of the table and a half million at the other and cleaning up on both. It was really surprising, given their concerted efforts, that he lasted as long as he did.

However, this was not the only challenge to the Greeks' exalted position as bankers in the French casinos. In Juan-les-Pins, Jack decided that he would have a shot at it and announced that he would hold it all summer "to break the Greek Syndicate and put baccarat in the hands of sportsmen who play for the love of the game."

"Sportsmen," he poignantly observed, "do not necessarily play for profit." How right that proved to be. In what was described as an orgy of baccarat, Jack held the bank for a solid four days. He had previously had a successful night playing against the syndicate in the days leading up to the match games and had pocketed a million francs in an evening. It was just as well, for over the period when he held the bank, he lost that and 9 million more.

Part of the reason for his heavy losses was that when the word spread that "Dashing" Jack had sat down in the banker's chair and taken hold of the shoe, people came from all around to get a shot. This influx consisted partly of the high-rollers who had thought that their traditional game was a thing of the past with the exit of the Greeks and welcomed the chance at a substantial gamble. Their numbers were swelled by the more adventurous who would not dare have a flutter when confronted with the syndicate machine, but fancied their chances against a lesser opponent such as Jack Coats.

They flocked into Frank Gould's casino on the south coast, often dressed as they were: dinner jackets, morning coats, knickers, casual dresses, evening dress, beach robes and even bathing suits, though these last were politely turned away. In a major faux pas, the doorman excluded Prince Habib Lotfallah of Saudi Arabia, a big game regular, as he turned up in his pyjamas.

Jack finally decided that he was bleeding cash faster than even he could sustain and reluctantly withdrew, but with his head held high. As he left the table he was heard to say, rather despondently, "My only consolation is that it is my friends who are winning my money."

What neither Jack nor Factor ever discovered was why they lost so much so remarkably quickly – for it was not bad play that caused their demise, but rather skulduggery.

Factor was not a bad player, but Nico had delved into his history when he heard that he planned to take on the bank in Deauville, and used what he discovered to beat the gambler.

Nico found out that whilst his elder brother Max went on to legitimate fame and fortune in the make-up business in California, John Factor took the low road to success. He left Poland for the USA and committed both stock and land fraud in Chicago and then in Florida. Indicted several times, he moved to

England and, backed by 50,000 pounds from Arnold "the Brain" Rothstein, perpetrated one of the greatest stock swindles in European history. Handsome and debonair, he was the perfect conman and found it easy to sell worthless penny stocks in a Ponzi scheme that hooked the victims with promises of guaranteed returns of between seven and twelve per cent, unheard of at the time. He then disappeared, secure in the knowledge that his victims, allegedly including members of the royal family, would be too embarrassed to report him. He was right.

A second fraud involving worthless plots of land in Africa was equally successful and he then left for Monaco as the USA was attempting to extradite him for his earlier crimes. Whilst there, he rigged the tables at Monte Carlo and managed to break the bank. It was during his time there that he ran into the Greeks, which led to him taking over their game in Deauville.

All this information convinced Nico that Factor was so concentrated on trying to cheat other people that he would not be too fastidious about observing his opponents' behaviour. He was correct. Sleight of hand went totally unnoticed over the entire four hours he held the bank, and he was completely unaware of two gentlemen on either side of the table using every trick in the book to fool him and take his money.

It was probably naïve of anyone to think they could replace the syndicate without some reaction. Although Nico had insisted on a reputation for scrupulous honesty, he now decided to abandon that principle, rationalizing his decision by arguing that they weren't actually cheating to win, but rather for others to lose. In any case he felt that their very livelihood was at stake, so it was a case of 'desperate times mean desperate measures'.

When he discovered that someone was usurping his position as banker in Deauville, he immediately hatched a plot to make this as difficult as possible. For years, he had had an excellent relationship with the croupier at the high-stakes table and he had ensured that the man was well tipped, in return for which he would keep an eagle eye on the play and suppress any attempts at cheating, always a temptation and threat when such large amounts of money were involved. He had already caught a number of people using counterfeit plaques, marked cards and the famous *poussette,* which had foiled Jack's first attempt to meet Nico just after the war.

Nico arranged for the croupier to conveniently turn a blind eye to anything he noticed during the session with Factor. He then contacted two of his friends who were part-time magicians and whose special skill was sleight-of-hand. When Nico first set up the syndicate, he had been concerned about cardsharps cheating him and he reasoned that the best people to teach him how to detect such systems were those who practised the art themselves. They had helped him over the years and were good friends. They willingly accepted disguising themselves as high-rollers and, financed by Nico, took their place at the table. Using a combination of card manipulation with a spare deck and the boosting of their stakes on winning hands, they systematically fleeced Factor, without him even knowing it.

In the case of Jack, Nico knew that he needed something different, as Jack was too sharp and too experienced to let a similar scheme go unnoticed. It would also be difficult to sustain for a longer period of time, and he was pretty certain that Jack would not relinquish the shoe with the same alacrity shown by his namesake.

He therefore plumped for a different technique, whereby the croupier would do a faux shuffle and introduce a slug of cards into the six-deck pile in a predetermined order. Nico then had stooges playing for him, who would receive a signal when the predetermined set of cards turned up and they would know exactly how to bet to maximise their winnings. This only needed to be done a few times a day to make a lot of money, and this was precisely what happened. Jack just thought he was having a run of incredibly bad luck. He had no inkling that he was playing against the Greeks, but with two distinct handicaps – he didn't know it, and they were cheating.

These two incidents had a dampening effect on others'

enthusiasm for taking over the bank and so high-stakes baccarat became a thing of the past – for the moment, at least.

Jack's decision to take the bank also sealed his fate with Nico, who was so annoyed at the audacity of his rival that he put aside any last vestiges of rapport he felt for him and finally stopped vacillating on the question of revenge for his father's financial ruin – he took a solemn vow that, come hell or high water, he would destroy Jack and avenge his father's misfortune.

Chapter 21

1930–31 FRANCE & ENGLAND

The first year of the new decade proved to be a difficult one for French casinos. The knock-on effects of the Wall Street Crash were beginning to be felt. Although prohibition was still in force, there were fewer Americans visiting France to have a good time. The disappearance of the high-stakes baccarat games, even though it only affected fewer than a thousand millionaires, made the gambling establishments which had housed those games less attractive to the ordinary punter and slowed traffic through the other games. The newly introduced taxes just exacerbated the situation. François André, who had casinos at Deauville, Cannes, La Baule and Pau, was suffering badly, and dismal results for 1930 confirmed that the situation was serious.

It was at this unlikely moment that Nico offered to buy out François's share in the syndicate. Ever since the exit of Athanase Vagliano, François had been a partner in the enterprise, facilitating big tables in all his casinos for the group to use and publicising their existence, whilst steering the very rich in their direction. But now he sorely needed the capital he had invested in the syndicate back in the heyday of the mid-twenties, to help shore up his own deteriorating financial position. The proposal was like manna from heaven for him.

Nico's timing seemed insane: with no heavy gambling going on and an uncertain future with the French government, it was a real possibility that the syndicate would fold, in which case he was simply spending money to take a larger slice of a pie that was destined for the rubbish bin; but he calculated that there was a good chance of the government folding quickly and that real, hard-core gambling would resume at an even more frenetic pace, given the enforced layoff. The risk was colossal, but his total faith in the laws of probability led him to the inevitable conclusion that it was the right thing to do, even if it gave him moments of unease. The contract was signed, François breathed a sigh of relief and Nico went back to polishing his cars and trying to reduce his golf handicap. He was also mulling over the plan to ruin Jack.

This was not going to be easy, particularly as there were no baccarat being played. Moreover Jack was stubbornly refusing to come to France; if the rumours Nico had heard were to be believed, he had given up gambling completely. Even if he could get Jack back and the high-stakes tables were revived, he still had to devise a scheme without endangering the livelihood of the syndicate and without the knowledge of his other partners.

He had never contemplated anything like this before and it made him feel decidedly uncomfortable, not only because he would be deceiving his partners but also because of his dicey financial situation on the back of the deal with François.

♦

Another person who was experiencing troubles of his own was Jack. His relationship with Audrey, which was always tempestuous and depended heavily on good times and much partying, had become strained. Her drinking, which was always heavy, became excessive and her temper deteriorated with it. They spent more and more time apart and although he could see that there was a need for some restraint in their outrageous spending, she would have none of it.

He had been hit by the secondary consequences of the catastrophe in the US stock market. He also had to pay some unexpected tax bills in the wake of his father's death and his sale of a part of his holdings in Coats in order to pay for his house in London and his gambling debts had just made things worse. A visit to the family lawyer, who had ostensibly asked to discuss some tax problems, confirmed that the financial picture was far from rosy.

"Good morning, Jack." Mr Murray shook him by the hand. "Please, take a seat. Good of you to come in to see me. I hope this won't take too long."

"Thanks. I have plenty of time this morning, so please tell me what is afoot."

"Let's wait for your brother Tom, who is also affected by the same tax issues. He should be here any minute." He looked down at his desk and shuffled some papers. "Actually, while I have you here, there is another matter we should discuss."

"Fire away," said Jack. "As I said, I have plenty of time."

Hamish Murray drew a deep breath and exhaled gently, but completely. He knew he was on very thin ice with what he was about to say, but others from the Coats family had spoken to him over the past months and persuaded him that he would be the best person to tackle the issue. He had reluctantly agreed.

"It concerns your wealth – or rather, the gradual lack of it."

"What on earth are you talking about? This has never been mentioned before. The last time we spoke, everything was fine. I can understand that the crash on Wall Street has had an effect, but that will surely be temporary. For you to bring it up, the situation must be serious." Jack was guilty of being rather deceitful by saying this. He was more aware of his position than he was letting on, but he wanted to push the blame onto the lawyer rather than accept it himself.

"Well, yes and no. It is not critical, but a series of factors have led to what could be described as a perfect storm. Permit me to explain."

"Yes, I think you had better!"

"The situation on Wall Street is serious, as you know, and does not appear to be likely to improve for some time to come. I would therefore be reluctant to call it – as you do – temporary. It is having a huge effect elsewhere, so commerce and business are suffering badly. This immediately affects your capital. This would not be a concern under normal circumstances, but your gambling expenses, the costs associated with both buying and redecorating the house in London, a flurry of acquisitions by your dear wife, and the costs associated with your expeditions to Africa – these have put a severe strain on dwindling resources."

"Are you saying I am insolvent?"

"Oh no, far from that!" Mr Murray smiled. "You are still okay, but . . ." He thought for a moment, measuring his words with care. "If you maintain your current lifestyle and the market continues to fall as it has been doing, you will soon be in some trouble; and I mean within the year. You should make judicious choices as to where and how you rein things in, at least until we see a bottom to the market, and ideally for a time after that, which will allow your capital base to recover."

Jack looked shocked at first, but then regained his composure. "I assume you mean my gambling?"

"Well, that is the single largest drain on your resources. I don't say you should give it up, but maybe play less time at the private tables. You could go back to chemin-de-fer or something which is less profligate."

"I get no fun from playing for peanuts, so I either have to give it up or face the consequences. If you really believe it is that serious, I'll have a look at what else I can do, but I take the matter under advisement. I have no immediate plans to be in France, so I needn't decide for the moment. I only gamble for enjoyment and I can give it up any time."

At that point Tom made an entrance and they greeted each other rather stiffly. Then they sat down with the lawyer and got stuck into the tax problem, which was a hangover from their father's lack of a will. Once they had concluded their business, they went their separate ways.

♦

Several months went by and Jack made an effort to spend more time with his children. Vernon was now eleven and at boarding school, but when home for the holidays Jack took him to the theatre in London and foxhunting in Scotland. Little April was only four years old, so spent most of her time with her mother or nanny, but he did at least see her in the evenings. He even made an attempt to reconnect with Audrey, but they were coldly friendly at best and usually ended up quarrelling.

His one consolation was his faithful valet Taggart. He found he turned to him more and more for both advice and encouragement. When the next opportunity to travel to France came up, he sought his counsel. "What do you think Tag? Should I go?"

"I assume you hope to be gambling, in which case I will always advise against it, sir."

"Your assumption is correct."

"But isn't the strike still on, sir? You couldn't get a game there even if you wanted one."

"Good point. I suppose the question is therefore moot." Jack's expression darkened. "I'm getting so bored; the only activity I do still love is riding with the Eglinton Hunt. Being joint masters gives Mrs Coats and I something to do together, and God knows it's the only time we're ever civil to each other. But it's hardly sufficient. I crave excitement. I never thought I'd say this, but I honestly wish the war were still going. "

Taggart looked troubled. "That seems somewhat extreme, sir."

"I'm sorry, that was insensitive." Jack put a hand on Taggart's shoulder. "I know you suffered in the trenches and hate to be reminded of it."

"I'm afraid so, sir. I still have nightmares, but I know you had it just as bad, so I can't see why you would want to revisit such dark times."

"I don't really." Jack's expression took on a glazed look "And yet I do – it's hard to explain. I've tried everything I can think of to keep myself entertained; fine dining, fast cars, racehorses, bobsledding, cavorting with celebrities, even jungle exploring in Africa, but none of them do the trick. I need real stimulation and that seems to come from either combat flying or gambling. Nothing else works."

"Well, you can't do the former, so you'll have to wait for the French government to give in to the Greeks before you can consider the latter, I'm afraid."

"Yes, Tag, I guess you're right, as usual."

♦

But all things must pass and, eventually, the French government recanted and amended the gambling tax. A well-rested and hungry Greek Syndicate started up again, after nearly a year's hiatus. The usual suspects and many other rich gamblers breathed a sigh of relief and flocked to the tables to try to win the bankers' money.

Jack, however, was still not amongst them. His brother, cousins, friends and even Taggart persuaded him to hold off, and it became a point of pride that he continue to abstain. They all insinuated that he had a gambling problem, but he knew better. He could control it and his current abstention just helped to prove that.

But every man has his breaking point, and Jack's came on the back of a furious argument with Audrey. They were at home in London, with Vernon away at school and April in Scotland with the governess. They had been getting dressed for a night out – at different venues – and were having a cocktail together before departing when the conversation drifted to finances.

"Tag couldn't find my collar studs or cufflinks this evening. You keep moving things around, as if it were just to annoy me, though it is probably because the furniture keeps changing. Can you not stop redecorating the damn house, Audrey? Apart from the disruption it causes, I have already explained our financial situation, so you are well aware that we can ill afford it."

"I did not marry you to just sit around doing nothing. I have standards to keep up within polite society and part of that means keeping the house modern and contemporary. That costs money."

Jack raised his voice now, his frustration beginning to show. "Well, I've given up the tables in France, so I would have thought it would be reasonable to ask you to refrain from *buying* tables in London, at least for a time."

Audrey herself was almost shouting now. "You have no right to take a holier-than-thou attitude to my lifestyle, just because you are behaving like a saint. I will do as I please, and that's an end to it. Don't even think of trying to stop me."

She got up and walked towards the door. "And, by the way, I have decided to go to Canada with Gwen to see our mother. I will be taking April with me – you can do what the hell you like."

Later that night, Jack had returned home for an early night after drowning his sorrows in the wake of Audrey's outburst. Taggart helped him up to his room and was undressing him for bed, but his master had managed to pour himself a large Remy Martin before attempting to negotiate the stairs and that was not making the job any easier.

"Be careful, Tag, you don't want me to spill this excellent brandy" he slurred.

Taggart continued to struggle with his the collar of Jack's shirt and then moved to the cufflinks, whilst maintaining a tactful silence. But Jack was having none of that.

"You know, Tag, I despair of my wife," he exclaimed and then added, "I depend on you to keep me straight. She can't do it, and in any case she's usually too whiffled to care."

"I am sure it is not as bad as all that, sir."

"It bloody well is." He took a gulp of his brandy and resumed, "And she won't stop spending. I sometimes wish that I didn't have and had never had any money. Then she wouldn't have the option and life would be so much simpler." He gave Taggart a defiant look and paused, as if expecting a rebuttal.

"I don't know what it is like to be wealthy", said the valet, "but it must bring its complications almost as much as its compensations."

"You're telling me." He fell silent, but then perked up. "You know what I decided this evening? I need to go back to France to see all my chums over there. Mrs Coats is off to Canada and I'll be on my own. London's a shadow of its former self; the 43 is long gone and the dancing clubs that are still open are not much fun anymore. It's as if the joy's gone out of it all. I need to savour the nightlife across the Channel – they know how to enjoy themselves, unlike the bloody British."

"Are you sure that's a good idea, sir? We've discussed this before. The bad luck you had when you took the bank last year in Juan-les-Pins seemed to hit you really hard. Are you prepared to go back to all that?"

Jack dismissed this with a wave of his hand. "That was an aberration. It was almost as if there were a curse on the cards – I am still at a bit of a loss to explain it." He took Taggart's arm and leaned in close to him, whispering conspiratorially. "In any case, who says I need to play cards? It's not obligatory!"

"That is very true, sir, but it *will* be a temptation."

Jack sprang back and looked annoyed. "Nonsense. I can control myself. And in any case I'm getting so stale over here that a change of scenery is vital if I'm not to go stark raving mad. The games have started up again so everyone'll be there and, to tell the truth, the enforced layoff's done little for my wealth and a lot less for my mood."

"In that case, would you like me to accompany you to help you remain abstinent?"

Jack's mind had drifted over to France so he didn't appear to hear this and continued. "And whether I decide to play or not, I can always go to the races, play a little golf and see my friends. Yes! *That* is what I'm going to do. I trust you approve."

Taggart now understood that what Jack was really looking for was what amounted to permission for a trip back to France and that his protestations about not visiting the high-rollers' table were at best half hearted. Jack knew this deep down as well, but would never admit it out loud. Taggart decided it would be churlish to protest, so he simply said, "Indeed, sir." He hoped that his inebriated master would have forgotten the conversation by the next day.

His mood buoyed, Jack downed the last of his brandy and leapt onto the bed. "Thanks, Tag. That'll be just the ticket. Please arrange travel and a hotel so I can take a swing over there in the next couple of weeks. No need for you to come too. You should take the chance to visit your family."

"Thank you, sir. That would be most agreeable. I shall get everything arranged and your packing done. Then, with your permission I will take a few days in Edinburgh."

"Absolutely. Good job, old chap." With this he collapsed onto his pillow and was asleep within seconds. He started to snore.

♦

Over in France, the Greek Syndicate was back in business, but Nico still had plenty to worry about. Since he had bought out François, the cash running through the hands of the syndicate had been significantly less than he had expected. Several of the more adventurous players had found other ways to amuse themselves, and the Wall Street Crash had had a more substantial effect than he anticipated. If things didn't take an uptick and soon, they would once again be in serious trouble. He had already looked at selling the yacht, but if he did that he was afraid that word would get around – and part of his tactics for success meant projecting confidence. Offloading assets did none of that.

He was in a no-win situation. They could end up cash poor, despite owning several luxuries, and if they ran out of cash they might as well shut up shop. After all, the syndicate not only took on the role of the bank at all their games – they also faced the same problems as a real bank: if customers lost confidence in their ability to pay and there was a "run", they could end up losing everything.

Although he projected ice cool calm whenever playing, Nico started to have trouble sleeping. Their vulnerability was playing on his mind to the point where he started to dread going to the casino. But a business is a business and the show must go on, so he steeled himself to his task – although he had almost taken to crossing his fingers every time he sat at the table, even though he knew it would do no good.

Added to this, he still had to deal with Jack, and he was coming to the painful conclusion that any plan to bring him down must inevitably involve a huge element of risk, unless he were to cheat. This he refused to do, for fear of tarnishing the syndicate's reputation. He had done it during the strike, as he could justify it in his mind as being necessary to defend their territory. Moreover, they had got away with it. But it was a different story if they were playing baccarat under normal circumstances. Discovery would be death.

Chapter 22

1932 FRANCE

It turned out that Audrey's trip to Canada could not be arranged as quickly as she had hoped. April was ill for a time, which caused them to postpone, and then Gwen decided that she wanted to wait till the weather improved, so it was late May by the time they set sail. Although Jack was champing at the bit to get over to France, he also decided to wait, in part with the hope that he and Audrey might become a little more civil to each other, but also as an act of pure self-discipline.

By the time he was ready to leave, it was early June and the south of France was already predictably warm. When he reached Monte Carlo, the beaches were teeming with tourists anxious to take the sun; and the casino was full of punters itching to try their luck on the tables, but conspicuously devoid of rich gamblers willing to risk a small fortune at the big game. The syndicate had moved north and dragged their usual entourage with them. This included all of Jack's acquaintances, so he was unable to find anyone for dinner, dancing or just a chat.

Even the golf course held no joy. He swung by there for lunch, but knew none of the members who were there to play golf or bridge, so he abandoned that idea and returned to his hotel to decide on his next move. The thought of traipsing all the way to Deauville was not appealing, and in any case it was too early in the season for the real action. He reckoned that Paris would be his best bet and a couple of phone calls confirmed that the big gamblers were in the city, awaiting the summer season. He resolved to fly up there and stay near the Haussmann, where he would surely find company. However, a plane proved more difficult to find than he anticipated and in the end he plumped for the train.

He was not disappointed. He boarded the Méditerrannée Express in Monte Carlo and over dinner ran into an American gambler who was heading for the same part of Paris, also chasing the syndicate. Jack discovered this when his fellow passenger sat down at his table and produced a deck of cards that he placed to one side.

"I see you are a man after my own heart." Jack's eyes sparkled as he viewed his companion with interest.

"How so?"

"You obviously play cards and . . . perhaps you are familiar with the best gambling game known to man."

"I assume you're talking of baccarat? That is indeed my favourite game."

Jack picked up a bread roll and applied some butter to it. He then asked, "Are you in France to compete with the Greeks?"

"Absolutely. I have heard that they are open to any bet you can imagine and I would love to get a bit of that action. Do you play?"

"Well, I have actually given up at present. I enjoyed the game too much and gradually realised that you cannot sustain the sort of 'action', as you call it, for long periods of time, unless you are backed by substantial funds. I was, but the combination of high living, heavy betting and an unreliable stock market have made a considerable dent in my resources. I would love to play, but will have to bide my time until there are some signs of a recovery."

At this point a waiter appeared and took their order. Once they had made their choices and agreed to share a bottle of wine, the American asked, "So, why are you across the Channel?"

"Most of my good friends are of the same persuasion as you – they want to bankrupt the Greeks – and the easiest way to find them together is when they are trying to do just that. I shall just be socialising and will not venture onto the baccarat tables, but they are all good company and the food is always superb. I may even get to take some exercise on the dance floor."

The American looked mildly deflated, but at the same time was eager to quiz Jack about the syndicate, as he obviously had plenty of useful information. "I am sorry we won't get to face each other across the baize. You see, I've got a system that cannot be beaten – those Greeks won't know what hit 'em!"

"If I had a pound for every time I had heard that, I wouldn't be in the pickle I find myself in."

"Well this is different. It's based on the Golden Ratio or Fibonacci sequence, which we use in engineering. You basically add the last two numbers in a sequence together to give the next number."

"Ah yes, I remember it. One, two, three, five, eight, thirteen, twenty-one and so on."

"Exactly. So I bet starting with 1,000 Francs, using that sequence until I win. Then I revert to the beginning."

"Sounds like a Martingale, but I'm afraid you're missing the point and underestimating the amounts involved in challenging the Greeks. They'll not entertain anyone betting less than 10,000 francs and even that is considered a paltry sum. I've seen many people lose fifteen hands in a row, in which case your last bet would be," – he thought for a moment, took out his wallet and wrote a few figures on a small piece of paper – "er, nearly 16 million francs. By that time, you will have paid out 42 million. And if you win that hand, you only break even. Seems like a lot of effort for very little result."

"But foolproof, in the long run."

"Agreed, if you have the resources. I am a rich man, or at least

I was, but could never have taken that sort of risk. One bad run will easily wipe you out."

The American's disappointment showed immediately on his face, but he was an eternal optimist and not one to be easily discouraged. "Well, I may not use it, but I'll have it in my back pocket. I want to approach these professionals with something more than a positive attitude. I don't fancy just leaving my chances in the lap of the gods."

"I wish you luck. My view of baccarat is that it should be played for the sheer fun of it and if you can't afford it then you shouldn't be playing. A system takes the thrill out of it – and that's why I play, not just to win."

When dinner was over, they said their goodbyes and made their way along to their sleeping quarters with promises of getting together in the future.

After passing a rather fitful night, due largely to the shortness of the bed and the incessant movement of the train, Jack took a taxi to the Hôtel Ritz and established himself in his suite. It was rather an extravagance, but his accountant had said that as long as he kept away from the tables he could treat himself to the usual luxuries. He had not gambled for over a year and although the market continued to be dismal, he was managing. He had a firm belief that everyone has a certain amount of luck and as things had gone so badly for him just before he gave up, he must be due a really profitable streak. He also was convinced that when God (or whoever decides one's fate) had divided things out, Jack had been permitted rather more than anyone else. He could therefore afford to splash out.

He ordered a bottle of champagne and started to make enquiries as to whether the syndicate or any of the high-rollers were in town. He quickly discovered that there was a game planned for that night in the Cercle Haussmann. He sipped his drink, letting the bubbles tingle the roof of his mouth and lift his spirits. An afternoon nap was his next priority, in preparation for the evening's entertainment. He would invite a few of his friends to dine and then watch the game, but not participate. He closed his eyes and drifted off into a dreamless sleep.

♦

As Jack slept, Nico was planning. He'd had word that Jack was in town and Nico's intention was to persuade him back to the tables and then all but bankrupt him. The problem was how. His resources were at the lowest they had been for several years, and his partners would be unlikely to endorse any dicey scheme designed to bring the Scotsman down. He would have to persuade his rival to embark on a betting spree, which he knew was extremely unlikely given his recent history. Or he might be able to goad him into one huge bet, but that had a substantial downside.

What worried him most was that he would be exposing the syndicate to significant danger, in that this plan deviated from their normal playing practice. He had decided it was better not to tell them anything about his scheme as he was sure they would stop him, so he had to continue to shoulder this burden alone; he longed to talk it out with somebody, but couldn't.

He would take things one step at a time. First he needed Jack back at the tables, then he could decide how to deliver his comeuppance. Now that the Scotsman was here in France, he could at least put the first part of this plan into action. He sat down to write.

♦

Jack was awoken by a knock at the door. He looked at his watch and was surprised to find that it was already eight o'clock in the evening.

He threw on a robe and went to answer the door. A bellboy handed him a message on a silver tray. To his great surprise it was from Nico Zographos.

Monsieur Coats – I heard from one of my colleagues that you are in Paris. I am sure I will see you this evening, but as I shall be very busy, I will have little time for socialising. It would therefore be a huge pleasure if you would stop by for afternoon tea in my suite at the Hôtel de Vendôme, which is just round the corner from the Ritz. Could I suggest tomorrow afternoon around 4:00 p.m.?

I have something I need to discuss with you.

Nico Zographos

Jack asked the messenger to wait and rapidly scribbled a reply in the affirmative. An invitation like this from the great man was too intriguing to miss. Having tipped the boy and dispatched him to get his note back to the Greek maestro, he put on his dinner suit and set out towards the Haussmann.

It was a pleasant evening and as it was less than ten minutes' walk to the club, he decided to take a stroll along the tree-lined streets. The sun was setting, so he ambled down to the Place de la Concorde to watch it disappear beyond the Arc de Triomphe. He then turned and walked back past the Opera, arriving at his destination in time for a late dinner. Several of his sparring partners from the old days were there and readily accepted an invitation to dine.

Once seated, they ordered escargots and a bottle of Sancerre and settled in to reminisce. He had forgotten what good company they could be, even without a pack of cards in their hands, and soon settled back into the familiar ambiance that kept bringing him back to France. He even reflected that perhaps it wasn't so much the gambling that captivated him, though he had to admit to himself that, nice though they all were, he did miss the excitement of turning over a winning hand with a pile of plaques in front of him on the table.

They wandered into the casino and, amid protestations from everyone, he duly took his place amongst the spectators. He was very pleased with his self-discipline and his ability to resist the pleading from friends and acquaintances that he should take a place at the table.

Nico was in his traditional seat as banker and nodded to Jack amidst a haze of cigarette smoke. The game commenced and seemed to be going the banker's way until one lucky punter turned up a couple of unlikely nines with big money on the table. After that, the play fluctuated with no one showing any clear lead.

Jack felt impotent as a spectator. He could see mistakes being made by several players and that was exasperating as there was absolutely nothing he could do about it. He wanted to get in there and take control and longed for that feeling of exhilaration that accompanied a winning hand. As the evening dragged on, his frustration gradually became what felt like a form of torture and he could take no more; he would either have to meet his friends elsewhere or start playing again.

He wandered over to the bar and ordered a large brandy. As he turned around, he found he was facing his fellow passenger from the train.

"Hi, Jack. How's it going?"

"Fine, old chap. Have you had a chance to test your system yet?" He chuckled light-heartedly.

"No. I couldn't get a seat at the table tonight, but I am hopeful that a place will open up later on. How about you?"

"I had a pleasant dinner with friends, but to tell the truth I am finding my pledge to keep away from baccarat rather hard to fulfil. I am absolutely itching to play."

"Surely you can find some other way of satisfying your craving. What about games of chance away from the casino? Do you like the horses?"

"I don't know enough about horseracing to risk large amounts, and it doesn't interest me anyway. No thrills."

At this point, a waitress appeared and beckoned to the American. "I was sent to tell you that there is a seat available at the baccarat table, monsieur."

"Thanks. I'll be right there." He turned to Jack. "Looks like it's my lucky night. Are you coming to watch?"

"No, the temptation is too great. I'm going back to my hotel."

♦

A good night's sleep does wonders for a man and Jack awoke the next morning late, refreshed and ready to face the new day. A leisurely lunch was followed by a brisk walk over to the Eiffel Tower, during which he mulled over his upcoming meeting with Nico Zographos. What on earth could he want with him? It would be unlikely that this was a social occasion: the man was not given to the niceties of entertaining, although he was never less than polite, but he would have a very specific objective in mind. It was so long since Jack had last gambled that it could surely have nothing to do with any previous encounter, but then Nico was such a meticulous individual that it could be some long-forgotten incident. He was truly puzzled.

By the time he turned back towards the Ritz it was nearly four o'clock, so he decided to go directly to the teatime meeting. He entered the Hôtel de Vendôme and announced to the gentleman at the reception desk that he was there to visit Monsieur Zographos. After being given a suite number, he took the elevator and then made his way along an ornate corridor towards the double doors at the end.

The little Greek opened the door and greeted him. "Hello, Monsieur Coats. How delightful to see you, and thank you very much for accepting my invitation." He smiled, but the emotion never got anywhere near his eyes, and he came across as aloof.

"I could hardly refuse," Jack said. "I am so intrigued as to why you would want to talk to me in private."

"Curiosity killed the cat, as they say. However, in this

254

instance, my motives are partly selfish." He paused and gestured that Jack should move through to his sitting room. "But let us have a cup of tea before I explain what is on my mind."

They sat opposite each other in the beautifully embroidered Louis XVI armchairs, and the maid poured them tea. The bone china cups clinked as they sipped. Finally, the Greek broke the silence.

"As you know, we have been shut down for about a year and there has been no action on the high tables in any of the casinos where we operate. Since we have started back, business – for that is how I think of what we do – has been a lot slower than we had hoped. There are two main reasons of this. Firstly, the Wall Street Crash has had a sobering effect on some of the players; and secondly, people have fallen out of the habit of gambling and have found other ways to amuse themselves. Realistically, there are only a few hundred people in the world who want to and can afford to gamble at our level, so it doesn't need many to drop out to have a significant dampening effect."

"So, you're going round all those who no longer play, to try to persuade them to restart. Is that why I am here?"

"In part, yes. A player of your calibre and resources is obviously vital to us, but it goes further than that. We have, I think, formed a mutual respect for one another and I honestly miss our tussles over the table. It would give me great personal pleasure if you would return."

"I am afraid you're going to be disappointed. I have pledged to leave the baccarat tables for the foreseeable future and it will take more than a little flattery to persuade me to resume."

Nico was prepared for just this response. "I was afraid of that. I admire your self-discipline and I know that you are a man of principle, so I knew it would be hard to convince you. Could I therefore suggest a rather unusual way of resolving our little impasse?"

"I am listening."

"I would like to offer you a small financial incentive to return, and a game of chance to help you make a decision. We will draw cards from a deck and the high card wins. If I win, you will return to the game; if you win, I will never bother you again."

Jack paused for a moment to consider his proposal. "That hardly seems very fair to me. I can just walk away without drawing a card, so there is nothing in it for me. But unless I am mistaken, you did mention an incentive. What do you have in mind?"

"If I win, I will give you a million francs with which to start playing again and, as a small private inducement, I will pay you double anything you win off us for the first two nights. That will not be publicised and cannot be mentioned to anyone."

Jack could not believe his luck. He had already decided that he would begin playing again, so this just made his decision that much easier. He would play the first two nights and then stop. It would be a chance at absolutely free money. He now hoped he would lose the card draw.

"All right. I can agree to that."

"I have the cards here, so shall we just do it now? If you would do me the honour of shuffling, I will allow you to draw first."

Nico reached behind him and opened a small drawer from which he extracted a brand new deck of cards. He removed the cellophane, took the cards out of the box, skilfully separated the jokers from the rest and handed the deck to Jack. Jack shuffled and cut, placing the stack of cards on the table between them. He then lifted a few from the top and revealed the jack of hearts. He was crestfallen. This was far too high a card if he hoped to lose, but he hid his disappointment and smiled as he said, "How appropriate. You could almost say it is my card."

"Then I hope I don't draw mine, which would naturally be the nine of diamonds, of course, although in this case it would not be the curse of the Scots."

Nico reached for the deck and cut a much larger pile of cards.

He turned over his choice, revealing the king of diamonds. Jack suppressed a shriek of delight and smiled enigmatically. His luck had held once more.

"It would appear that you have won," Jack said. "So I will see you tonight. I assume my credit will be good?"

"Absolutely. Would you care for some more tea?"

"Thank you, but on this occasion I will decline your offer. I wish to return to my room and prepare myself for tonight. It is a long time since I last played."

Jack stood and extended his hand to the Greek, who shook it. "In that case, goodbye, Monsieur Coats," he said.

"I prefer *au revoir*, as we will be seeing each other again this evening," was Jack's reply. He then turned and silently left the room.

Nico leaned forward and proceeded to cut the cards several times in quick succession, always turning up a king. "These doctored cards make life so much easier," he mused, as he put them back in their box.

Chapter 23

1932 FRANCE

Both his friends and rivals welcomed Jack's return to the Cercle Haussmann. An almost party atmosphere prevailed as they all dined and discussed the upcoming game. Nobody was aware of the deal he had made with the syndicate leader and when they all eventually sat down to play, the mood was conducive to heavy gambling. There were a lot of 100,000-franc plaques on the table.

By the end of the first night, Jack had lost all of his "free" million, despite betting in a modest fashion compared to many of his rivals. There was little doubt that he had lost some of his edge through lack of practice and he made several mistakes with his betting, getting caught up in the moment.

The second night was no better and he found that his initial stash had disappeared, along with a couple of million more. His plan to leave after two nights fell by the wayside. He resolved to return for at least a third night, with a plan to bet aggressively and give the syndicate a real shock. He was absolutely convinced that his luck would turn.

Nico, on the other hand was cautiously optimistic. His risk at paying out all that money to Jack had paid off and his rival certainly seemed to be hooked on the game once again. The only fly in the ointment was that his betting style and strategy were too conservative for what Nico had in mind.

He had decided that the only way he could inflict the sort of damage he wanted on Jack was to goad him into an enormous bet. Anything else would take too long and Jack would be bound to stop before things got truly out of hand. He had concluded this whilst watching him on his first evening back.

This tactic was tremendously risky and so far from the normal way he played that it made him feel quite light-headed even considering it. The syndicate had always said that *anything goes,* but in practice few people, even the ultra rich, would risk more than a million in one go. It was part of what made the syndicate's scheme workable. Nico had calculated that somewhere around ten times this level of bet was what was required to effectively wipe Jack out – the only snag with this was that it would also wipe out the syndicate if he lost.

Despite this, his determination to avenge his father's downfall was such that he convinced himself that he didn't care. If it worked out then fine, he had achieved his goal; and if it didn't, he had done his best and would probably have to take what he euphemistically thought of as the "other way out". He would die a proud man.

At the end of Jack's second day back at the tables, Nico received a call from his accountant, Louis Fournier.

"Nico – how are you?" Louis was always upbeat whenever he called, so it was hard for Nico to tell if the call was good or bad news.

"Fine, Louis, but busy. What can I do for you?"

"We have a small problem which needs your attention. I have been monitoring your portfolio and although your liquid assets are fine, as usual, the capital reserve has taken a particularly hard hit in the last couple of weeks. It will recover – don't worry about that – but as a precaution I would recommend keeping things low-key for a while."

"Easier said than done." Nico sounded mildly peeved.

"I know. I'm not suggesting stopping, but you could perhaps

reduce the number of evenings you play and keep the actual playing time short. Anything to minimise the likelihood of a run on your resources."

"Hmm . . . not impossible, but difficult. We must never show too much vulnerability to our clients. It could have the exact reverse effect to what you are wanting." Nico was wondering how they could achieve this in practice, but he was also worrying about how to deal with Jack in these circumstances.

Pierre decided to be direct, as he knew it was what Nico would best understand. "To put it bluntly, if you have a bad run against you over several days, you will be in real trouble. This deal with Monsieur André has left you significantly exposed and it will take time to re-establish the sort of security you had back when Monsieur Vagliano was funding you. It is not a crisis, just a question of time. You should be fine in a couple of months if everything evolves as I expect."

This was not what Nico wanted to hear at this moment in time, and he hastened to end the conversation quickly. "Okay, Louis. Thanks for letting me know, but I'm afraid I must ring off now as I have a meeting coming up."

"Goodbye, Nico. Please take this seriously."

"I will. Goodbye."

Nico hung up the receiver and sat to think. It was frustrating, but he recognised the wisdom underpinning the accountant's advice. The syndicate could simply spend more time travelling between games, and he had other psychological techniques they had used over the years to limit the amount the punters bet. In combination with subtly shortened sessions, they could certainly get through a couple of months.

Of course, this would mean that he had to postpone his revenge against Jack Coats, but that could wait. He didn't imagine that his victim would be going anywhere fast, now that he had the gambling bug once again. Nico knew his type only too well and was confident that Jack's nature would keep him coming back for more.

When they sat down for the third night, Jack pointedly asked Nico once again if his credit was good and was assured that there would be no problems on that score. He settled in to play and was slightly up when they came towards the end of the third shoe. He thought he had a pretty good idea of the cards remaining, as he had devised a method to allow him to duplicate what the Greek maestro did when counting cards. It was not as perfect, but better than nothing. He liked his chances of winning and decided it was time to do or die.

He put out ninety plaques.

Even Nico, normally implacable, was taken aback. "Monsieur Coats, you do appreciate that that is a bet of" – he counted the tiles on the table – "9 million francs?" He looked up at Jack with a quizzical expression and inhaled deeply from his cigarette.

"Yes. I have decided that there has been enough prevaricating on my part and it is time that I started betting seriously."

"I appreciate that, but even by our standards, that is a colossal bet. You could buy several mansions for less."

Jack shrugged his shoulders. "I've been losing too much and it's time I won it all back. I have every confidence that this hand will be the start of a winning streak."

"Be it on your own head, but I will tell you that this is the biggest bet I have ever taken on one hand."

"Then I shall be famous, win or lose. Deal the cards."

Nico could not believe it. Jack was attempting to ruin himself and Nico had had absolutely nothing to do with it apart from luring him to the table. Despite his earlier resolution, Nico had still been contemplating how to convince Jack to make a huge bet – and now he had done it himself without the slightest persuasion. Amazing.

But the timing could not be worse. Nico was barely off the phone with his accountant and had not even had time to implement the strategy he had decided on, including the delayed showdown with Jack. Now it was out of his hands. Momentarily immobilised by the impotence brought on by a situation beyond his control, he steadied his nerves by telling himself to weigh up the position dispassionately.

If Jack lost this bet, Nico was sure that even he would be in trouble. He kept close tabs on the net worth of all his main opponents and estimated that Jack had spent at least eighty per cent of his fortune, so at best he would have 30 million francs left, probably somewhat less. Moreover, much of it would be wrapped up in property, so he would be very cash poor indeed, effectively bankrupt, which meant that Nico would have achieved his objective.

The wrinkle in this universe was what Nico would do if the cards fell the other way. As Louis had stressed, the syndicate could not afford a – what had he called it? – "bad run", and a loss of this magnitude constituted the equivalent of exactly that, but all in one minute. It would cripple them to the point where they would probably never recover.

He suddenly felt unnaturally warm and could sense the sweat forming on his back, even if his expression did not change. He reflected that it was as well that he had transferred his revolver from the glove compartment of his car to his hotel suite, which was nearby.

He slowly and reluctantly pulled the cards from the shoe and three hands of two each appeared. He continued to appear unruffled, even if his stomach was in a knot.

Jack was the first player to declare. "No *carte*."

The other Jack – Hennessy, that is – said, "*Carte*." A king of spades was produced, which meant that his participation in the hand was at an end. His hand would be worth five, at best.

The banker turned over his cards. A nine of diamonds – how

ironic, he thought – and four of clubs. He would have to draw, but any card other than a four, five or six would be no use. He knew from counting that there was only one of these left, a five, so his chances of winning were less than five per cent.

Despite his almost hopeless position and the amount of money involved, Nico remained steely-eyed and suppressed his nerves by telling himself that although he and the syndicate could never recover from such a loss, he had decided what he would do in that scenario. His mind drifted back to the gun.

Jack, on the other hand, was metaphorically licking his chops. He had a king and seven and had done roughly the same calculation as Nico, so he knew that the 9 million was as good as his, as the Greek was over ninety per cent sure to lose. A couple more hands like this and he would be in excellent shape. He felt an enormous sense of relief.

Nico reached for the shoe and withdrew one of the few cards remaining as if it were a viper and held it face down on the baize. He normally did this for effect, but this time the delay was caused by sheer terror. He had never been so nervous in his entire life and had enormous difficulty stopping his hand from shaking. He could hardly bear to look, but after what seemed an eternity he turned it over.

It was the five of hearts. His total was eight.

"*Huit à la banque*," said the croupier and collected all the plaques, including the huge pile in front of Jack, who was frozen in place with his mouth slightly agape, in a total state of shock. He couldn't understand how he had lost. Although theoretically possible, it was too unlikely.

He quickly recovered and smiled ruefully. "You win some, you lose some. That's just the way it goes. There is no doubt about it, Monsieur Zographos: you are a lucky son of a devil. There must have been between twenty and twenty-five cards left in the shoe and you picked the only one that could win you that hand."

Nico remained outwardly unmoved, but the inner jubilation

he felt was huge, the feeling of immense relief combining with the satisfaction of having brought down his adversary.

He finally shrugged his shoulders and spread his hands in a gesture of regret. "There were twenty-three cards and you're right – this was my only winner. As I've always said, there is no such thing as luck, just probability and mathematics. I admit that my drawing that card appears lucky, but there'll be others that fall the other way. In the long run what you call luck will even out due to the laws of chance. We cannot change that."

He glanced down at the shoe and motioned to the croupier that it was finished and that the remaining cards should be discarded in preparation for the next game.

Play resumed after the shoe had been replenished, but Jack's heart was no longer in it and he continued to lose. At just after four in the morning, he sat back in his chair and addressed the room.

"I am thinking of calling it a night. Could somebody kindly tell me know much I owe?" he asked.

An individual who was lurking behind the dealer emerged from the shadows and walked up behind Jack. He leaned forward and placed a slip of paper discreetly in his hand. Jack opened it and read, *Your current bill is for 10 million, 800,000 francs.*

Jack leant back and quietly whispered to him, "I haven't seen the exchange rate recently. How much is that in good old pounds sterling?"

The mysterious figure did a quick calculation on a piece of paper and leant forwards. He whispered, "That makes 111,340 pounds."

Jack stood up abruptly and gave a slight bow to the table in general. "Thank you all for a very interesting night's play. I shall need to arrange for my debt to be paid – it will take a couple of days, as the sum involved is considerable."

Nico looked up from the table and took a drag on his cigarette. "That is quite in order. We know each other of old and I accept that you are good for the sum in question. Good night."

Jack made his way out of the casino and stopped on the pavement in a daze. Then he turned and strode towards his hotel, as if he had made up his mind about something.

He entered the hotel lobby and went to reception to collect his key. The receptionist stirred from his stool and looked at his watch. It was 4:45 a.m. He greeted his guest. "Good evening, monsieur. Did you have a prosperous night at the casino?"

"Yes, thank you, Pierre. You know I am always successful, and tonight was no exception."

"How gratifying." He paused. "There is a message for you which I can give you now or you can collect it tomorrow morning. Sorry, I mean later today."

"Just hand it to me and I will read it when I get to my room."

He grabbed the piece of paper and made his way towards the elevator. The liftboy stirred and greeted him. "Good evening, monsieur. Fourth floor, isn't it?"

"You have a good memory. Yes, please."

The lad closed the gates and engaged the mechanism and the lift ascended slowly. He looked at his companion dressed in his dinner jacket and thought, not for the first time, how wonderful it must be to be rich, without a care in the world beyond how best to enjoy yourself. However, he said nothing until he had stopped the cage and opened the doors.

"Good night, monsieur."

"Good night, and thank you."

The liftboy went back to his stool, where he had been dozing gently. It occurred to him that it was odd that he had not received a tip from this particular guest. It had been his custom to slip him a few hundred francs after a night's gambling, but maybe he was distracted. No matter.

Jack went along the passageway to his suite. He entered and went to the bedroom, where he sat on the bed, undid his bowtie and loosened his stiff collar. He removed his jacket and went over to the drinks tray to get a brandy. He sat at the table and downed it in one. He then remembered the note and extracted it from his jacket pocket. He read it quickly and then arose and made his way back to the living room.

It was only now that he began to fully consider his plight. The note was from his accountant and asked for Jack to call him as a matter of urgency. That could not be good news. As far as he could tell, doing a rough calculation, he was down to his last thousands. Another ruinous evening at the tables had included the loss to his arch-rival with the stupidest of bets on a single hand of baccarat. But it was too late to do anything about it now. To think he could have bought a yacht or two and a mansion in Paris with what that wager cost him . . . And whilst he could still afford his suite, he was no longer wealthy; and with the stock market continuing to plummet, a life of gambling and entertaining was over. He was ruined.

He wasn't sure if he could face Audrey, who was mercifully still in Canada visiting her family. But she was, in an odd way, the least of his worries, as she might vaguely understand what he had done, even if she could never forgive him. He was also grateful that his father was no longer alive, as the shame would have been too much for him.

The main problem was that he still had to face his creditors. They would be merciless and although he still had assets, they were not necessarily that easy to liquidate, so generating the sort of cash he needed to pay them off would take time and be expensive. He had not moderated his spending enough and now his betting had got completely out of hand with this last sortie, despite advice to the contrary. He had believed in his ability and his luck. What arrogance!

With hindsight he now realised what a huge mistake he had made leaving Taggart behind. He would have counselled him well and have kept him from doing anything stupid – Jack could imagine him saying, "Are you sure that's a good idea, sir?" That would have made him at least stop and think. Perhaps even now, he might be a voice of calm in a world gone mad.

Jack went back to the bedroom and crossed over to the desk. He picked up the phone and when connected to the switchboard, asked for his London number. The phone rang and rang and it was only then that it dawned on him that he had closed up the house and told Taggart to go and visit his family in Edinburgh. He quietly hung the receiver back on its hook. There would be no conversation with Tag, no reassuring voice in his ear. The Taggart family did not have a phone in their house, so there was no way of contacting his faithful valet. So be it.

He stared blankly into space for a moment and then turned his attention to opening the drawer of his desk, only to find that it was locked. He fumbled for the keys in his pocket and then spent a full minute trying to put the correct key in the lock. His hand was trembling so much he could hardly control it. Eventually the drawer yielded and he found his service revolver in the back, along with a box of bullets. He opened the gun and with the same trembling hands made several attempts to load it, ending up with a number of bullets on the floor and only one in the chamber.

He placed it on the desk and stared into space. Even if he managed to extricate himself from his current situation, he would never be able to go on gambling and he just could not imagine his life without the thrill at the tables. It would be unbearable.

But, despite evidence to the contrary, he still held an unfaltering belief in his innate good fortune. Had he not been born with the largest of silver spoons in his mouth, survived the rigours of the Royal Flying Corps whilst most of his colleagues were killed, and lived a charmed existence full of party-going and general frivolity? It had deserted him temporarily at the tables these last few evenings and he was staring at a very different future as a result, but perhaps that was just a setback designed to test him. He was not a religious man, but if there was a higher power, then this must be part of his plan for Jack. He decided that he needed to test his luck one more time in a truly meaningful way.

He looked down at the weapon. Perhaps the fact that his shaking hands would only allow him to load one bullet was part of that same plan. It was destiny. He was being tried with the ultimate test of fortune, with the biggest stake imaginable – his life.

He took the revolver in his hand and spun the chamber hard. It made a whirring, clicking sound and then stopped. His fate had been decided. He raised the barrel to his temple, grasped the trigger firmly with the index finger of his right hand, drew a deep breath and fired.

The noise was deafening, and the effect of the bullet immediate and devastating. A small dark red hole appeared in his temple and, as the gun fell to the floor, his body crumpled and slid to the ground.

He had paid for his final wager with everything he had.

Epilogue

That would appear to be the end of the story, but not quite.

The stock market reached its low point almost exactly on the day Jack Coats died. It recovered steadily after that and although he had managed to squander a lot of money over his lifetime, by the time his will was published several months later, he had left 700,000 pounds – the equivalent of 70 million francs – much of it wrapped up in non-liquid assets, but part of his wealth nonetheless. Nico's calculation had been rather pessimistic, and even Jack's assessment of what he had left was extremely low.

He was only forty when he died and although the newspapers reported it as heart failure, his daughter April intimated that it was suicide, not uncommon among young men surviving the horrors of war. The version of his heart giving out is also believable, as with only one lung it would have been under tremendous stress. His lifestyle probably didn't help either.

Two of the three Musketeers from Jack's time in Canada had already died prematurely. Eardley Wilmot survived until the Second World War, when he was promoted to squadron leader at the age of forty-nine, but was tragically killed when he walked into the propellers of a taxi-ing aircraft in October 1941.

Audrey Coats was remarried in the late 1930s to an American, Don Haldeman. They moved to Nassau, where her drinking spiralled completely out of control. She was said to mix gin with her milk in the morning, switching to Martinis after lunch and Scotch in the evenings. Despite this, she survived another twenty-odd years, dying when she fell down a flight of stairs at home in 1957.

Gwen Wilmot married Captain D'Arcy Rutherford in 1930. He was a handsome, debonair playboy, who was credited with inventing the sport of water skiing. They had a daughter and apparently lived happily ever after.

The subterfuge surrounding Jack Coats's losses when he took the bank in Juan-les-Pins only came to light many years later when investigations were being made into the Stavisky scandal. This villain's supposed suicide exposed multiple swindles with connections to famous politicians and financiers. One of the related enquiries turned up a signed confession by a croupier in Frank Gould's casino that he had rigged the cards when Jack took over the bank, and although the matter was dropped, the local newspapers published the full story. The casino owner, who was famous for his litigious nature, never sued them for libel, so it can be assumed that there was more than a grain of truth in the discovery. No link to the Greeks was ever alleged or established.

Jack owed money to the syndicate when he died. It was certainly not as much as the amount he lost on the last fateful evening – a function of chronology and the credit lines extended by the Greeks - and there is no indication as to whether it was ever paid back.

Nico Zographos went on to become one of the most successful gamblers of all time, accumulating a fortune of some 50 million francs (5 million pounds) by the time of his death in Lausanne in 1953. Adjusted for inflation, this is the equivalent of over 150 million pounds today, and only a handful of gamblers before or since have been able to match this. He was sixty-seven, and years of smoking in the casinos of France had caught up with him in the form of throat cancer.

By that time, he had retired to Switzerland, where he continued to pursue his ultimately unsuccessful bid to reach a single-figure golf handicap.

Printed in Great Britain
by Amazon

34993109R00155